X

Bokuto Uno

ILLUSTRATION BY
Ruria Miyuki

Reign
of the
SEVEN
SPELLBLADES

"......"

Oliver Horn

"I'm walking my own path. Like you are. I've made my choice."

Yuri Leik

Demitrio Aristides

"Chloe Halford's people?"

"...In 1525—"

"This one's winding weed. And that's chuckleshroom. And...stained lantern."

Chloe Halford

CONTENTS

Reign of the Seven Spellblades
Bokuto Uno

Reign of the SEVEN SPELLBLADES

X

Bokuto Uno

ILLUSTRATION BY
Ruria Miyuki

YEN ON
New York

Reign of the Seven Spellblades, Vol. 10
Bokuto Uno

Translation by Andrew Cunningham
Cover art by Ruria Miyuki

NANATSU NO MAKEN GA SHIHAISURU Vol. 10
©Bokuto Uno 2022
Edited by Dengeki Bunko
First published in Japan in 2022 by KADOKAWA CORPORATION, Tokyo.
English translation rights arranged with KADOKAWA CORPORATION, Tokyo
through TUTTLE-MORI AGENCY, INC., Tokyo.

English translation © 2024 by Yen Press, LLC

Yen On
150 West 30th Street, 19th Floor
New York, NY 10001

Visit us at yenpress.com
facebook.com/yenpress
twitter.com/yenpress
yenpress.tumblr.com
instagram.com/yenpress

First Yen On Edition: January 2024
Edited by Yen On Editorial: Rachel Mimms
Designed by Yen Press Design: Jane Sohn, Andy Swist

Yen On is an imprint of Yen Press, LLC.
The Yen On name and logo are trademarks of Yen Press, LLC.

Library of Congress Cataloging-in-Publication Data
Names: Uno, Bokuto, author. | Miyuki, Ruria, illustrator. | Keller-Nelson, Alexander, translator. | Cunningham, Andrew, translator.
Title: Reign of the seven spellblades / Bokuto Uno ; illustration by Ruria Miyuki;
v. 1–3: translation by Alex Keller-Nelson ; v. 4–10: translation by Andrew Cunningham.
Other titles: Nanatsu no maken ga shihai suru. English
Description: First Yen On edition. | New York, NY : Yen On, 2020–
Identifiers: LCCN 2020041085 | ISBN 9781975317195 (v. 1 ; trade paperback) |
ISBN 9781975317201 (v. 2 ; trade paperback) | ISBN 9781975317225
(v. 3 ; trade paperback) | ISBN 9781975317249 (v. 4 ; trade paperback) |
ISBN 9781975339692 (v. 5 ; trade paperback) | ISBN 9781975339715
(v. 6 ; trade paperback) | ISBN 9781975343446 (v. 7 ; trade paperback) |
ISBN 9781975352240 (v. 8 ; trade paperback) | ISBN 9781975369545
(v. 9 ; trade paperback) | ISBN 9781975369569 (v. 10 ; trade paperback)
Subjects: CYAC: Fantasy. | Magic—Fiction. | Schools—Fiction.
Classification: LCC PZ7.1.U56 Re 2020 | DDC [Fic]—dc23
LC record available at https://lccn.loc.gov/2020041085

ISBNs: 978-1-9753-6956-9 (paperback)
978-1-9753-6957-6 (ebook)

10 9 8 7 6 5 4 3 2 1

LBK

Printed in the United States of America

Characters

Third-Years

The story's protagonist. Jack-of-all-trades, master of none. Swore revenge on the seven instructors who killed his mother.

Oliver Horn

A samurai girl from Azia. Believes that Oliver is her destined sword partner.

Nanao Hibiya

A girl from Farnland, a nation belonging to the Union. Has a soft spot for the civil rights of demi-humans.

Katie Aalto

A boy from a family of magical farmers. Honest and friendly. Has a knack for magical flora.

Guy Greenwood

A studious boy born to nonmagicals. Capable of switching between male and female bodies.

Pete Reston

Eldest daughter of the prolific McFarlane family. A master of the pen and sword, she looks out for her friends.

Michela McFarlane

A lone wolf who taught himself the sword by ignoring the fundamentals. Determined to beat Oliver in a rematch.

Tullio Rossi

A transfer student. What he lacks in sense, he makes up for in boundless curiosity. Chummy with everyone.

Yuri Leik

Oliver's Family

Oliver's mother. An unparalleled talent who held the Two-Blade epithet.

Chloe Halford

Oliver's father. A mage driven by logic—the polar opposite of Chloe.

Edgar Groves

Seventh-Years

Watch member known and feared as the Toxic Gasser. Wears women's clothes as the whim strikes him.

Tim Linton

A gentle girl and Oliver's cousin. Supports Oliver's secret activities as his vassal.

Shannon Sherwood

Shannon's older brother and Oliver's cousin. Supports Oliver's secret activities as his vassal.

Gwyn Sherwood

A hedonistic, degenerate elf. Her immoral nature and appetites resulted in her being driven from her homeland.

Khiirgi Albschuch

Keeps a tight rein on Kimberly's student body as the Watch's overseer. Harsh on herself and others.

Lesedi Ingwe

An alchemist specializing in liquors. Treats friend and foe alike as customers and serves as their bartender.

Gino Beltrami

Student council president. Nicknamed Purgatory by his peers. Boasts incredible firepower.

Alvin Godfrey

Leader of the previous student council's faction. Once battled Godfrey for the presidency and received burns to the right side of his face, which he refuses to heal.

Leoncio Echevalria

Instructors

Astronomy instructor. Driven to protect the world from tír incursions.

Demitrio Aristides

A sword arts practitioner renowned as the Blade Master. Friends and rivals with Darius since their student days.

Luther Garland

Kimberly's headmistress. Proudly stands at the apex of magical society.

Esmeralda

Magical biology instructor. Feared by her students for her wild personality.

Vanessa Aldiss

Magical engineering instructor. Prone to outrageous lessons designed to maim students.

DECEASED **Enrico Forghieri**

Chela's father and the man who sent Nanao to Kimberly.

Theodore McFarlane

~ **Frances Gilchrist**   ~ **Darius Grenville** DECEASED

~ **Dustin Hedges**

Prologue

There'd been a single loose thread on the garment he'd prepared, so small you had to be searching for it to notice.

On the morning five days after learning this fact, the tailor was found hanging from a tree in his backyard. He'd spent those five days ensuring his successor was ready to take over. He left not a spot on the grass beneath his feet. Arguably a flawless approach to suicide.

No one had specifically ordered this, yet even the most minor Echevalria servant shared this same mindset. Carrying out their duties with the utmost craft, and taking their own lives the moment they realized their skills were deteriorating. As if the concept of perfection was a curse upon them.

"One error leads to the next. Such is the nature of man."

These were the words of the elderly servant charged with dressing the young master. Watching the wrinkled hands close the buttons on his shirt, the boy listened in silence. His features were as even and beautiful as any statue, yet his visage was devoid of expression.

"The loose thread was likely not his sole motivation. He was sixty-two. One can assume he sensed the focus necessary to perform his role deteriorating. Thus, he chose to retire early. Before the unsightly imperfections could sully your eyes, Master," the servant explained. "Your father is well aware. He allows nothing to enter this manor that is anything but perfect. All to ensure you grow up to be a flawless mage."

The boy nodded.

Even at his tender age, he knew the nature of his house. Roses with the faintest of dimples in their petals were swiftly removed from their vases. Spot a single scale astray on any ornamental fish, and the next time he passed that aquarium, that fish would be gone. Humans were no exception. This place had run on those rules since before he was born.

"Polish yourself to perfection, Master Leoncio. Every life here exists only for that purpose."

Hardly the first time he had heard this plea. Two months later, this man—who'd served him longer than anyone else—drank poison in the same spot as the tailor. According to the note found in his chambers, the reason: His back no longer allowed him to stand up straight.

These memories crossed Leoncio's mind as flames scorched the right side of his face.

"...Ha-ha..."

He attempted a smile, but his cheeks objected. He could feel the asymmetry, and that struck him as hilarious, his twisted smirk growing all the more pronounced.

He knew then—he was no longer perfect. These burns made him unfit for that manor. Like the dimpled roses, the scaleless fish, the clumsy tailor, and the bent-backed valet. He had become a blot, defiling that perfection with his flaws.

"Heal that up, Leoncio. I'll wait."

The man responsible was speaking, wand held in a hand burned by his own fires, standing before the one he'd foolishly stepped in to protect. Eyes glaring his way, unwavering.

Nothing about him was perfect. Not his features, his fashion, his manner of speech—all lacking in polish. All aspects of the man were rough-hewn, devoid of grace. One glance, and you knew he was a stray dog. From the moment of his birth, this man had no place in the Echevalria manor.

So why could he not tear his eyes away?

"...No need," Leoncio said through that rictus grin. His visage likely bore no trace of his former features. He didn't care. That veneer of perfection had already peeled away, burned off along with any reason to cling to it.

Now he was free. Free to face what lay *within*.

"Did you fall asleep, Leo?"

An amused female voice. This dragged Leoncio from his nap on the couch in their base. He opened his eyes.

"...Merely reflecting. On the day I received these burns."

"Ah! That explains your *arousal*," Khiirgi purred, her eyes sliding down his length. He'd been born with a massive trouser snake, and it now stood at full salute, as if straining to reach the ceiling. The elf stroked the tip with one finger, whispering, "You are too devoted for your own good. Taking a rod this large would pose no real challenge to any mage. Surrounding yourself with five or six lovers dedicated to delighting it... That would be more productive than throbbing in isolation for a man who will not yield."

Paying no heed to her admonitions, Leoncio swatted her away. Khiirgi fanned her stinging hand, sighing.

"It is a sweet nectar—embracing another while your mind is on the one who got away..."

"You are a paragon of bad taste, Khiirgi," came a quiet voice from the corner: the Barman, Gino Beltrami, polishing glasses behind the counter. He glanced at the clock on the wall. "Time we left. We don't want to leave Percy hanging."

He put down the glass and stepped out from behind the counter. Leoncio snorted and rose from the couch.

"Our presence will make no difference. Percy will win. I have ordered him to do so."

CHAPTER 1

Laws of Nature

A day since the migration and their brush with the tír threat. The night before the senior league finals, upon which hung the future of Kimberly.

No one had suggested it, but they all felt the need—the Sword Roses were assembled in the living room of their secret base.

"…We're all here," Oliver said, breaking the silence.

There was a cup of tea placed before each of them, and three pots with more placed evenly on the table. A clear sign all thought this could take a while, yet there were no cakes to accompany the tea. This was not a topic one should address with sweetened lips. No matter how bitter the words that emerged, they were *necessary*.

"Take your time. But share with us, Katie: What drove you toward the tamper pillar? And what did you hope to gain through contact with it?"

"…Okay."

Katie nodded gravely and took a deep breath. She scanned the faces there in turn. Once she'd looked each in the eye, her gaze dropped to her hands.

"First—I apologize for scaring you all. I know it's not something I can just say sorry for, but let me start there."

Her tone conveyed the weight of this apology. They felt the sincerity of it, yet remained silent. How easy it would have been to take her at this word, give her a hug, and call an end to this intervention.

"Katie, no one here is still angry with you," Chela prodded gently. "We wish to discuss what lies ahead. How can we keep you safe in the future? In hopes of finding an answer, we first wish to get an accurate measure of your state of mind."

Katie nodded, then began to speak, picking over her words.

"…I've always been prone to these…compulsions."

Mages, as a general rule, require far more food than ordinaries. This is a simple biological need; producing mana internally requires a great deal of fuel.

The more mana one possesses, the stronger this tendency. And then, there are phases where mages' bodies simply require more nutrition. Adolescence, for instance. The child's capacity as a future mage is taking form, a process that cannot be done without sufficient nourishment. Those in the lower forms at Kimberly were still within that bracket, so the cafeteria's nigh-endless supply of provisions was designed to meet that urgent demand.

The same principles apply during early childhood. Children beginning to learn magic generally have healthy appetites, and if they don't—well, some would go so far as to advise getting a funnel and force-feeding them. It is vital to focus on nutritional quality, not merely quantity; and the importance of meat is widely established. There are a few exceptions—elves, for instance—but by and large, you cannot raise a superlative mage on vegetables, beans, and water.

Yet at the same time, within the civil rights faction, there is strong support for vegetarianism. This is not unrelated to a love of animals, but more fundamentally it is the antithesis of the core mage belief that pursuit of sorcery must come at the expense of other lives. This movement seeks to correct attitudes not only toward humans and demis, but to the exploitation of *all* forms of life.

Naturally, those espousing this philosophy are both dedicated and desperate—but by the same logic, no mages attempt to force vegetarianism on their own children. As vital as it is to change minds, they cannot well afford to ruin their children's futures. A mage who grows up weak has little potential, and their words will reach few ears.

"Ooh! Lihapulla! Yummy!"

Katie Aalto's parents were no exception. When it came to raising a child of their own, they followed the same path.

They had spent their days and nights buried in research and activism in pursuit of the No Life Eaten ideal to a downright dangerous degree, yet it took no time at all for them to conclude they could not inflict that on their daughter. Not only for the nutritional deficiencies, but because the echoes of their own failures and broken dreams were still sounding deep within. Yet more than anything else, they respected the rights of each individual to make their own choices, as civil rights proponents should.

Setbacks in one mage's life may ironically lead to greater freedom for those who come after. That was the case for Katie. The Aaltos' sorcery had come to an abrupt end in her parents' time, which meant Katie herself had far fewer pursuits to inherit from them. They certainly had thoughts on that subject, but they chose to view it as a good thing. They hoped that freeing her of their burdens would allow their daughter to find her own way, at her leisure.

They were good parents. As mages go, nigh ideal.

It was their daughter who went wrong.

"Daddy! Mommy! Fix this!"

Katie had turned five not long before. Accompanied by her best friend, the troll Patro, she came running up with her hands covered in blood. The sight certainly got her parents on their feet.

"Wh-what happened, Katie?"

"How'd you hurt yourself?!"

Katie was fighting back tears, so they hastened to heal her. Wanting an explanation, their eyes turned to Patro, but he could not speak. Instead, the girl herself launched into an inarticulate attempt.

"They were picking on Teppo. I stopped it! But Hely got mad."

That clued her parents in. Teppo and Hely were wargs the Aaltos kept on their expansive property. Mages' breeding processes regularly produced wargs not worth selling, and the Aaltos made a habit of acquiring and protecting these creatures.

Normally, the wargs got along great with Katie, but by their nature, they had a hierarchy within the pack. Those deemed at the bottom of the stack were often not treated well. Unable to watch, Katie had interfered—and paid the price.

Simple bites were easily healed. Katie looked over the results of her parents' administrations, smiled, and turned to go.

"Thanks, Mommy! I gotta go!"

"Huh?"

"Wait, Katie, where—?"

"To see Hely! We gotta make nice again!"

Katie was gone before they could stop her. Her parents and Patro raced after her. The girl had already completely forgotten the biting and the bloodshed.

Similar events occurred too often to count. Sometimes these left their talons deep in her heart, where magic could not help.

"Daddy! Mommy! Look!"

Her parents were writing letters in the living room when Katie burst in, holding something in her tiny hands. Her curly hair was covered in feathers, and she had countless scratches on her face and shoulders, inflicted by tiny claws. Her parents shot to their feet, drawing their wands.

"What happened, Katie?"

"Settle down; we'll get you—"

"Not me! This birdie!" she said over their fussing. "It fell out of a coated dove nest! It wasn't moving, and a snake almost ate it!"

But the moment her parents saw the listless baby bird in her hands, they both furrowed their brows.

"...A con bird's mimic chick," her father muttered.

Katie's mother knelt down to meet her daughter's eye. She chose her words carefully.

"Katie, I'm afraid we can't heal this birdie. We must watch it pass together."

"?! Why?! It's just a baby!"

"Listen close, Katie. You didn't find this in our yard, but under a coated dove's nest *outside*. But this wasn't the coated dove's fledgling. Con birds use a technique called brood parasitism to trick other animals into raising their children. This birdie's not a dove at all."

"...Parasit...ism?"

"They hide their eggs in another bird's nest, and when the egg hatches, it pretends to be that bird's baby," her father said, taking over. "If it works, they grow up, but sometimes the mommy bird figures it out. That's what happened here."

That much was plain as day. The coated dove realized the mimic chick wasn't its own and kicked it out of the nest. If it didn't, this chick would kick the real fledglings out—so that it could get more food itself.

"We could give it some food and help it survive. But that's not the natural order of things and shouldn't be done lightly. It's hard to explain why... For example, if this bird grows up, then it'll lay eggs in some other bird's nest. And that chick will kick the real fledglings out of the nest."

Katie listened to her mother's words in shock. In her short life, she'd yet to face this fact—that all living things survived at the expense of others.

She couldn't bring herself to agree. They were saying she should just let the little life quivering in her hands die. That letting it live was a

mistake. The logic wasn't sinking in, so she shook her head. She racked her little mind for a solution and voiced it.

"I-I'll make it listen! Tell it to stop acting like that. Help it learn to raise its own!"

"That's not possible, Katie. The con bird isn't making a mistake. This is how that species does things, how they learned to survive in the world," her father explained. "That's the same for the snake that tried to eat this bird. Because you took its prey away, the snake didn't get to eat. Maybe it was really hungry! Because you saved the bird, maybe now the snake will starve."

The girl's shoulders shook. She'd tried to save a life—only to harm another. Now that she knew that was possible, she couldn't look away. Katie loved all creatures. She liked snakes just as much as birds.

"And…it's already…"

Having said his piece, her father let his eyes drop to the girl's hands. Katie gasped. The bird no longer drew breath. She couldn't feel the faint pulse of life on her palms.

"…Wait… No… Don't…," she spluttered, tears welling up. Her parents put their arms around her shoulders, pulling her close, unable to do anything else but be there for her.

"…You…aren't eating again, Katie?" her father asked.

Fresh-baked bread and hot soup on the table. His daughter frozen before it, spoon in one hand. She'd been eating less and less every day since the mimic chick incident, and yesterday she only drank water.

"…I understand," her mother said. "You've worked it out. This food, too, was a life."

She knew firsthand how that felt. Katie was going through the same thing both parents had. Eating—and by extension, living—were only possible by taking lives. A brutal realization.

"But you can't do this. You can close your eyes and push the problem away, but you *have* to eat. Your body is growing. If you don't get enough nutrition, you can't grow up right. If you keep refusing food… you might even die."

Because she knew how big a struggle it was, she was being extra firm. Fret all you like, but you can only do that alive. Put aside the unanswerable questions and focus on what you need now. Conveying that was her parental responsibility.

She took the spoon, scooped up some soup, and held it to her daughter's lips.

"Eat, Katie. You love lihakeitto. Doesn't it smell good?"

A hint of fear flickered in the girl's eyes. Her mother had made one of her favorites, a meal that always brought joy. And a day without food left her starving—she didn't want to worry her parents. She knew she *should* eat. She had every reason to.

Making up her mind, she let the spoon in her mouth. The rich flavor, the sweetness, the warmth on her tongue—and visions of all the dead animals flooded her mind. Animals that died so she might live. Countless lives that would be lost for her sake. She could feel their gazes out there in the darkness.

"…Urk…!"

Her throat refused to swallow. Hand on her mouth, she doubled over, spitting it out. Her mother moved around the table, rubbing her back, and her father grabbed a napkin to wipe her lips. Katie apologized profusely, saying "I'm sorry" over and over. She was no longer even sure who—or what—she was apologizing to.

When dire circumstances leave a child unable to eat, there are several treatments. An IV, for instance. Significantly less abusive than the funnel approach, but being forced to resort to this was not much easier on her parents.

They tried everything else first: talking it over at length, ransacking papers on the subject, switching her food to things deemed less likely to provoke a negative reaction. They bowed their heads to every magical doctor they knew—but from the start, they had a feeling this was where they'd end up. The dilemma their child faced was far worse than their own. And until the girl herself made headway, all they could do was wait.

While the IV kept her alive, it hardly left her as energetic as she had been. Coupled with the toll of her distress, young Katie was visibly wasting away. But the girl herself refused to stay cooped up in her room.

With Patro supporting her unsteady steps, she sought even more contact with other creatures, as if looking the problem in the face might unstick her thoughts. This was her struggle, her attempt to progress.

Two months into Katie's fast, the moment arrived—in a way her parents could not have possibly predicted.

First, Patro came calling for them, clearly upset. Exhausted, they'd been napping in the living room—but both mother and father quickly sensed something grave had happened and rushed out, wands in hand. They regretted assigning no protectors to Katie but Patro; they had yet to settle on just where the line between protection and surveillance lay. Patro was in the same boat—he was the girl's friend, and when she asked to be left alone, he could not refuse.

"…Daddy… Mommy…"

They reached the scene and found Katie lying limp on her back.

Her arms were missing from the elbow down.

"""_____~~~~~~~!!!"""

They had no time to scream. Ironically, they were used to this. Their home should have been safe, yet their daughter had gotten injured countless times before. That forced her parents to adapt, to act despite the shock. This was certainly her gravest injury yet, but it was technically an extension of what had come before—and thus, they handled it.

"…What happened? Tell us, Katie," her mother finally managed to ask, clearly beside herself.

They'd rushed Katie back and given her the necessary treatment. There'd been no sign of her arms anywhere. Only a few scraps of flesh were left, and from the state of them, they'd clearly been nibbled away by something very small.

That didn't clarify much. The Aalto garden was much more than a hobby. It was a biotope for magical research, and the creatures living there were strictly cordoned off according to their natures. Of course, Katie was not allowed anywhere near anything dangerous, and since she'd stopped eating, her parents wouldn't even let her in the warg pen without them along. There should not have been anything in the area that would harm people, much less eat them.

"She, um…," Katie began, her eyes on the corner of the room.

A small magical creature was resting on another operating table. An adult female egg badger, a species known for adaptively switching between pregnancy and egg laying according to their environment. Katie's parents had found it lying right next to her, equally injured and weakened, and they'd given it treatment, too. It was now asleep.

"…Not long ago, she laid eggs. She was taking very, very good care of them. And they finally hatched…"

Katie got choked up. It took her a long time to say the next part.

"…The newborns were all around the mother…eating her."

Her voice trembling, she described what she'd witnessed.

And this was enough to clue in her mother and father. The first act of a newborn—to feed upon their parent. Behavior seen mainly in spiders but found in quite a few other species. An instinctive survival strategy, allowing feeble organisms to last a little longer in a harsh world.

Though egg badgers were primarily herbivores, this behavior had been observed in the species before. Two crucial factors encouraged it—first, the birth took place in inhospitable conditions. Second, how weakened the mother was at the time. The Aalto garden was well maintained and did not meet the first condition. But while rare, this could happen with the second alone. If the mother laid eggs late in life and used up the bulk of her remaining energy birthing the children, then she might choose to feed herself to them. In a natural environment, that would likely improve her children's odds of survival.

"I tried to stop them. But they were all very hungry and wouldn't listen.

"So I thought, if I give them *something else* to eat..."

Katie trailed off. If she'd run to fetch her parents, they'd have kept eating their mother. Their survival instinct demanded nutritious meat, and there was no replacement nearby. So she'd given the only thing she had to give. Not in fit of madness, but through a clear and logical decision.

The truth before them left her parents speechless, gasping for air. The girl's eyes turned toward them.

"...Daddy...I'm hungry. Can I have something...to eat?"

"...Can you eat?"

He looked shocked. She'd refused food for so long.

Katie nodded, whispering, "I think...I've worked through things. Now that I've been eaten, too."

Once the girl's missing arms had regrown, and she could move her fingers normally again, her parents sat her down across from them in the living room. This was a parental duty they could not avoid.

"We need to talk, Katie," her mother began. "This is an important conversation about how to keep you safe."

Katie nodded, fully aware of the implications.

"Nature has its own laws. These laws don't line up with human morality, and at times they appear unfathomably cruel. You know that much already, yes?"

"I do."

She said that loud and clear. Katie didn't just grasp the logic—her eyes conveyed that she'd grasped the truth of it bodily. The conviction that lay within terrified her mother more than anything.

"But still you dive on in and try to change it. You don't care if that gets you hurt. You even gave them a part of yourself. You do these things no matter how many times we stop you. No matter how many times we cry and beg you not to go that far." Her mother then asked a question: "Why is that?"

Her voice shook. This was the crux of the matter. Katie's head went down. A long silence passed before she spoke.

"…The laws of nature."

Every meal she'd eaten crossed her mind. Piping hot food laid out on the table, a happy family gathered to eat, propped up on a foundation of innumerable lives and deaths.

"…They really can't be changed…?" she asked.

She remembered the warmth of the chick dying in her hands. Kicked from the nest, dying before it knew any other way of life, that alone encompassing its entire existence.

"…There's no stopping the pain, the suffering? They're just a part of it?"

She saw the egg badger being eaten by its own young, then remembered the strange peace she'd felt as their tiny teeth tore into her proffered arms.

"Then I—"

Katie's head came up. She wore a dazzling smile that did not belong on human lips.

"—I want to shoulder it *all*."

The look on her face made her parents finally realize—they'd lost this fight for good.

There was no more denying it. Their daughter was something entirely unlike themselves, and the lot her soul bore was beyond their capacity to handle.

*   *   *

When Katie finished speaking, a leaden silence settled over the table. These tales had given her friends a glimpse of her nature, and each needed time to reflect on it. They were processing it all, searching for the next words.

"What do you *want* to do?" Pete said, breaking the silence.

Katie put a hand to her chest, shaking her head.

"I'm still flailing around, trying to define the shape of it. I know there's a *wish* inside me that's incredibly vast. But I don't know how to express it. Perhaps we don't have a word for it in our world just yet."

"So you tried to ask a tír god? Talk about rash," Guy spat.

Sensing the kindness behind it, Katie winced and nodded.

"You're right. I'm thoughtless, reckless, driven by impulses far stronger than anyone else's... Why am I like this...?"

She let out a long sigh, looking inward.

"Do not put yourself down for it," Nanao said. "In my eyes, that is merely a glimmer of the vessel you were born with. All those with a great purpose must possess such a fire within."

"Don't build this shit up, Nanao! Sorry, but I don't see this as anything laudable." Guy's tone was severe. "We don't stop her, she's gonna run off and get her ass killed. And so much for her great purpose then."

This argument got a nod from Nanao.

"As Guy says. Yet such is the nature of any deed before it bears fruit. I dare not deem myself wise enough to draw the line between promise and madness. Perhaps no such distinction exists."

A strong purpose carries always a whiff of the deranged. That notion made Chela turn to the Azian girl.

"Nanao, are you arguing that Katie should stay the course?"

"Hardly. I merely lack the words to stop her. A samurai sworn to give their life in battle will not surrender to the views of another."

She spoke dispassionately, tapping into the distinctive resignation she alone possessed, having arrived at Kimberly after years of wars back home. Oliver longed to say something here but dared not. Her words resonated far too deep within him.

"We don't have time for this," Pete snapped, glaring into the silence. His voice was extra flinty. "I'll keep things simple. This has nothing to do with Katie's feelings. It's merely a question of: How do we stop her from being stupid? How do we keep her ass alive? If it comes to it…we chain her to the damn wall."

A shudder went through the room. The way Pete's eyes bored into Katie made it clear he was not joking at all. Oliver was on his feet immediately. He moved around behind Pete and put his arms around the boy's shoulders, cradling him tight.

"Settle down, Pete," he whispered. "We hear you. You're angrier than anyone else here."

Pete's words had gotten to everyone. They knew he was hell-bent against letting this discussion die out, even if that meant he had to play the bad guy. His chilling statement spoke to the urgency within; Pete was willing to turn his own friends against him if it kept them safe.

"…Sorry," Pete said softly, gripping Oliver's hands. "Can you…stay there for now? Otherwise…I think I'll run my mouth off again."

Oliver granted that favor without hesitation, pulling the boy closer. Watching the two of them like a hawk, Chela moved to sum up the discussion so far.

"We all have thoughts on the matter, and each view has merit. With respect to that, I'd say our consensus is thus: Katie's nature cannot easily be altered. Therefore, we must find ways to keep her safe despite that."

Katie kept her head down, but everyone else was nodding. That much, they'd known from the get-go. If this was merely a matter of making her reflect on her choices, things would never have grown this grim. That was why Pete's suggestion, while extreme, had merit. Ultimately, he meant that if she herself couldn't change, they would have to change things *for* her.

But Oliver had one other card to play before taking any such measures. Aware he was grasping at straws, he laid it on the table.

"Just one thing—it's been bothering me from the start. We're leaving someone out of this discussion."

"? Meaning?"

"We can't stop Katie from where we stand. In which case, we should ask someone who knows her from another angle. For instance... someone in the next room."

Oliver pointed at the door to the base's main chamber, reminding all six friends that they were not the only ones here capable of speech.

"Mm. What's up? Why the long faces? Did something happen?"

Marco looked up from his book, scanning their grim expressions. His low, relaxed tones made Guy blink.

"Uh, Marco...are you getting a lot more fluent?"

"Am I? Nice to hear. I've been practicing."

"...Not just conversing. You're reading a lot, too. Magical history?"

"Mm. If I don't know a word, I ask. Books are too small, and the pages are hard to turn... But I'm starting to understand what's inside."

Marco proudly showed them how he managed to turn the pages with his hefty fingers. Everyone was impressed, and Katie watched that, grinning.

"Isn't he great? But this is actually not surprising. Marco's brain—troll brains have always had this potential. Their raw intelligence is no different from a human's. They simply didn't choose to evolve the same way."

This was a fact she and Marco had worked hard to prove. And this told Oliver his idea had been right on the money. He took a step forward, addressing their oversize friend.

"In that case, we definitely need your input. What are your thoughts on Katie?"

"Hmm... How do you mean?"

"I imagine you know. When she starts running toward a goal, she forgets all about the harm it does to her. That scares us, and we were discussing what we can do about it. How do we make her look after herself?"

He was consciously choosing easier language but held nothing else back, laying the question out there. They'd all spent enough time with Marco to know he'd catch the implication. And that faith proved true—Marco closed the book and turned to face them.

"...When our villages are attacked, the first to fight are those without children."

A loaded statement. His lived experiences and values had led him to that answer. And he knew that this was what Oliver was seeking.

"Those with children take them and flee. That just makes sense. You can't raise a dead child. That goes for men and women."

Listening to Marco's straightforward explanation, Guy cocked his head.

"Um...so you don't just send the mothers?"

"We learned this in class, actually," Katie chimed in. "Male trolls produce milk, too. It varies which one takes the lead in child-rearing, with different settlements following different systems. There's variations even in the same regions—fascinating stuff!"

Katie was in her element here, excited. Then she frowned and turned to Marco.

"...But what's your point? That doesn't relate to me!"

"It does. If you had a child, Katie, I know you'd change. A child with someone you care about."

That answer froze her up completely. Guy looked equally astonished and elbowed her in the ribs.

"...Yo, that's a hell of an idea."

"...Um. I—uh..."

Her lips flapped, but no real words emerged. One eye on her, Pete thought this through, then snorted.

"Hmm, not sure I believe having kids changes anyone. Might be worth a try with Katie, though. Having something to look after—something other than a demi-human or an animal—could help save her from herself."

"Er, uh...?"

Pete's calm analysis just served to make Katie's head spin faster. Oliver and Chela each opened their mouths to try calming her down, but Pete was faster.

"...So who's it gonna be?" he asked.

"Buh?!"

"I'll help. I'm down to get knocked up or knock someone else up once or twice while I'm still in school. You may all have lineages, but mine starts with me. And there's upsides to sharing reversi blood with those I trust."

"Yo, yo, yo, yo, Pete..."

"Slow down, Pete. That's not something you just dip your toes into! You are *way* too eager today."

Oliver put his hands on his friend's shoulders, trying to cool the fire, but this time Pete brushed it off, spinning around to face them all.

"You just don't get it, do you? This is a matter of life and death! I've got no problems putting my body on the line for that. And not just for Katie! I'd do the same for Oliver, Nanao, Chela, or Guy."

He rattled this off with such ferocity that everyone fell silent again. His glare made it clear that he had no interest in being picky about the means. And that Katie's problems ran so deep no sensible measures could ever hope to solve them.

While Oliver dithered, Chela stepped forward and cupped Pete's cheeks. She wasn't reproaching his outburst; this was simply an expression of love.

"I adore you for saying so, Pete. But cooler heads must prevail. Being rash to stop Katie from being rash is hardly the answer. And—perhaps you can't imagine it just yet, but the toll is considerable whether you bear a child yourself or have someone bear it for you."

Her gentle soothing slowly drained the tension from Pete's shoulders and provided him with the leeway to reflect on his own words.

"…Yeah, fair. Even if I did have a kid, I couldn't exactly go back home for help. Which makes my proposal a careless one. Sorry."

He pushed Chela gently away, delivering this apology to everyone. But before anyone could respond, he spoke again.

"Still, the approach itself is worth considering. If not me, then maybe ask Oliver or Guy to do it. We'll all be fourth-years soon, so it's hardly too early to think about these things. At least chalk it up as one available option."

With that, he zipped his lips. The two names he'd mentioned only added to the blush on Katie's cheeks, and Guy and Nanao flanked her, settling her down. Oliver decided it was time to wrap things up.

"…Regardless of the specific approach, I sympathize with Pete's concerns, and I appreciate that his statements stem from them. But I still can't help thinking it's too big a leap. Katie's head is spinning, and I doubt we'll calm down enough to make much progress here. Let's put a pin in this for the day."

Everyone nodded. No one had expected this to get resolved tonight. That they'd managed to all get on the same page was progress enough. Before anything else happened, they'd need Katie to work through her own feelings.

"Let's go to bed early and prepare for tomorrow," Oliver offered. "Might be hard to sleep after this conversation, but do your best to rest up. It'd be rude to watch the upperclassmen's matches only half awake."

The next day, just past noon. Once again the arena was packed to the brim. Five matches had played out, and now the final battle of the combat league's fourth- and fifth-year division was in progress.

"…Haah, haah…"

"…Dammit…"

Ten minutes since the start, and everyone knew which way the wind was blowing. The aggressors in the match so far had slowed to a stand-still. They'd lost no one, nor did they show signs of running out of mana. Yet every plan of attack they'd prepared had come up empty.

"…They won't go down…!"

The Watch members gritted their teeth, thwarted by their opponents' tenacity. And seeing that, the opposition leader—and candidate for student body president, Percival Whalley—raised his athame, intoning, "Is that all you've got, Watch? It's time we crush you."

"…He's good," Oliver groaned, arms folded, watching from the stands.

By his side, Chela nodded. "An all-rounder, no exposure from any angle. Maintains a tactical advantage in spell exchanges, while simultaneously supporting his companions and drawing out their strengths. His style is rather like your own, Oliver."

"Yes, but Whalley is much more thorough. He takes every action to maximize the potential of his entire team and never puts himself first. That's likely one reason he's so careful to avoid getting in sword range. He's clearly a much more pragmatic commander than I am."

Oliver felt there was a lot he could stand to learn here.

"…But is that a good thing?" Pete wondered. "As a student, sure, that's an advantage, but he's gunning for the presidency. Relinquishing the spotlight doesn't really sell *him*. His teammates are making more of an impression."

"True, but that's actually quite rare at Kimberly," Oliver replied. "He's offering a clear departure from what President Godfrey or Echevalria brought. I think this teamwork is a mission statement, a demonstration of what type of leader he intends to be—"

"Gah…!"

A direct hit from a spell, and a fifth-year toppled over, unconscious. That put them down one teammate—and the match on a path to an end.

"President Godfrey was a singular leader," said Whalley. "Regardless of the discrepancies in our ideals, I respect his abilities and his magnetism."

Working in unison with his teammates, driving their foes into the corner, Whalley used an amplification spell to project his voice. This wasn't merely an expression of confidence, but a performance designed to highlight his victory and tie it to the election.

"But his was a one-term glimmer of light. Who can possibly follow in his footsteps? Can anyone else do what he did? Of course not. This match *proves* as much."

"——!"

"…Ngh…"

His words were like a knife to his opponents' hearts. Inches from defeat, they couldn't even argue. Whalley had timed his words to the moment when they would be most devastating. Off hand to his chest, he voiced the purpose burning within.

"I am not like him. During my term, I shall mold a successor better than myself. Just as Leoncio molded me from a mere jack-of-all-trades."

"…Save the speeches till you've won, bigmouth!"

The surviving opponents steeled themselves and came out swinging. The girl took the lead, and Team Whalley fired two bolts her way, but her companion cast a blockade spell at her feet. She kicked off the walls, evading the bolts and sailing over both foes, charging at the commander from behind. She committed to a thrust that might well lead to them both going down. Even if only to diminish the impact of his speech—they wanted to at least take Whalley out here.

"Heh."

Whalley kept his cool. Athame in mid-stance, he waited for her, deflecting every swing with orthodox consistency. No competition, no attempts at counters. He had no need to take those risks.

"Kah…!"

Bolts from behind hit the Watch girl's back, and she went down. While she'd been charging at Whalley, his companions had finished off her teammate. His role had been to weather the rush until his team could come to him.

A textbook victory—their foes never had a chance. Sheathing his athame with the satisfaction of a job well done, Whalley said one more line.

"I knew I'd won, thus I spoke. That is how I fight."

"It's all over!" Glenda, the announcer, cried. "Team Whalley with three straight victories, making them your fourth- and fifth-year division champions! We may have projected some upsets, but in hindsight, they steamrolled their way to victory! And Whalley's demonstrated he's got what it takes to be the next president!"

"Most impressive." Beside her, Garland launched into his evaluation. "I've had my eye on him since his first year here, but I couldn't have predicted he'd grow into such an accomplished commander. At no point were their opposing teams or opponents' skills in any way inferior. Their strength lay in how the team's talent was put to use—and in the depth of their pre-match planning."

Team Whalley's rock-solid teamwork had not been lost on him—an advantage no other team here shared.

"...He's likely done his homework, not just on teammates and opponents, but on the entire student body. From start to end, Team Whalley acted without hesitation. Arguably their victory was decided by the intel they'd gathered and their concealment of their own. The Watch fight daily in public view, and that may have cost them here."

"The outcome was settled before the league even began! The intense work Mr. Whalley put into planning his performance is as plain as day. This election outcome is still up in the air!"

"...Sorry, Prez!"

"We blew it..."

The bitter defeat had left the losing team on the verge of tears. They'd retired to the waiting room to report to Godfrey, who smiled and patted their backs.

"Good effort. Your loss is on us. Forcing you to maintain your Watch duties prevented you from focusing on league strategies. Sorry."

"That's not true…! We just weren't strong enough!"

Big tears spattered the floor. They'd felt pressured to win this one. They'd be the leaders at Kimberly with Godfrey gone, and yet here they were, making him clean up their mess again. To their shame.

When they were done reporting and apologizing, the Watch members left the room, heads bowed. Stone-faced seventh-year Lesedi Ingwe watched them go, arms folded, jaw grimly set.

"They've taken the middle league. That leaves the ball in our court."

"Bring it. All we gotta do is win!" Tim Linton—in drag—said, cracking his knuckles. He was clearly motivated.

The last person there groaned: Vera Miligan, a candidate coordinating the final push.

"It's a bit tougher on me, though," she said. "I suppose I'll just do what I can."

As the stage was set for the afternoon's matches, the Sword Roses were in the Fellowship, eating lunch.

Once everyone had food and tea before them, Oliver quietly asked, "Nobody's seen Yuri?"

All movement stopped. Five heads shook. Oliver sighed and set down his cup.

"Ah. I was hoping he'd be here for these matches…"

Their friend had been missing for a while, and concern was rising. Then an unexpected voice called Oliver's name.

"There you are, Mr. Horn."

Oliver turned around. Of all people, there stood Leoncio's candidate, the fifth-year, Percival Whalley. They'd just been watching him fight, and his presence here was a surprise. Oliver rose to his feet, greeting him.

"Mr. Whalley? Oh... Congratulations on your league victory."

"Spare me the platitudes. I'm aware you back the current leadership."

Whalley cut right through the formalities, getting down to brass tacks.

"I'm here to recruit you regardless. In the event I win the election, I'd like to name you a core member of the next council. That's with an eye on you potentially succeeding me—if that notion tickles your fancy."

"——!"

"Er, you mean...?"

"Oliver would be president after you?"

Guy's and Katie's jaws dropped. Students at nearby tables who'd overheard were buzzing. Well aware of the eyes upon him, Oliver carefully took measure of the offer.

"...It's an honor, to be sure. But you've caught me unprepared. Even assuming this is based on what I demonstrated in the combat league, your own camp should have more than enough candidates. Why bring me in?"

"Is that a mystery? After seeing how I fought? Really?"

Whalley looked his junior right in the eye, placing a hand upon his chest.

"As mages, we are similar types. We likely began in almost the same way. No obvious talents, derided as an all-rounder, forced to overturn that reputation by working far harder than anyone else. In my case, I swiftly abandoned the idea of fighting on their turf. Instead, I chose to treat notoriously individualistic mages as a group, maximizing their abilities—that is the strength I pursued. And the type of leadership I will bring to the presidency."

"...You are far too modest. You're strong enough as is, and you did well for yourself in the broom leagues."

"I certainly hoped to, but I've hit my limit there. As a broomrider and a swordfighter, I have no room to grow. I knew that when your

Ms. Hibiya downed me. The time when experience and tactics could make a difference has come and gone."

His eyes met Nanao's briefly, and a sigh escaped him. It must have been a major setback, but he showed no signs of regret. His tone soon righted itself.

"But I'm disinclined to bemoan my fate. I've demonstrated the strength Kimberly needs. Now I need to merely focus on the task at hand. Will you hear my slogan?"

"...By all means."

This recruitment was clearly not a whim. He could sense what drove the man and thus waited with the gravity demanded.

"'Lead mages as mages,'" Whalley intoned. "Accompanied by the conviction that all-rounders will be the key to doing so."

With that, he drew his white wand, casting a dampening spell around them so that his voice would reach Oliver alone.

"You remember how Team Valois fought? That's how wrong it can go. One individual of excessive strength, overriding those around them—even without employing mind control, low-level leadership is all too prone to falling into that trap. Perhaps the natural result of clashing egos, but the outcome is nothing more than mass reproduction of the originator, allowing no further progress."

With that, he dismissed the spell. Oliver had not quite followed the significance of that spell, but he realized this was a courtesy afforded to Team Valois. A presidential candidate publicly criticizing their approach would have significant repercussions. This surprised Oliver; his prior impressions of Whalley had not suggested he cared for such niceties.

"And yet, the lukewarm teamwork favored by the ordinaries suits us even less," Whalley continued. "Repressing the ego for the greater good merely makes mages weak. Thus, we leave the individual as themselves, finding ways to harmonize. I'm sure I need not explain that this requires skillful management. The outcome is proven, seen regularly at the highest levels—but the method of developing it eludes us. Practically speaking, it remains the domain of the exceptional."

Oliver nodded at this analysis. Mages had long wrestled with the notion of teamwork; without order, problems arose, but impose too much, and the strengths were lost. They had long vacillated between those twin horns.

"The upshot is that collectives of superior mages are inevitably loosely knit. Given a broad strokes directive, fighting as they see fit, any coordination decided in the moment. Even the most demanding divisions of the Gnostic Hunters are no exception. As it stands, only those with a natural aptitude for those conditions master them and survive. But I'm disinclined to overlook the sacrifices made along the way."

This was a concern that resonated with Oliver. Nanao and Yuri had the skills, and their mutual trust was a given—but they'd tackled the lead with directives left distinctly loose. That approach would hardly work with anyone. Sometimes people don't like each other or are teamed with someone they've barely spoken to.

"This is where the all-rounders shine. By their nature, they are invested in others; confined not by a single enthusiasm, their interest takes them in all directions. A mage like that in charge, and Kimberly—as a mage collective—can advance to a new stage. Are you with me so far? I believe *you* are capable of that."

Neither overconfident nor unnecessarily modest, he was simply describing the strength he'd found within himself. And that struck a chord with Oliver. Each word spoke to the time Whalley had spent peering inward—and many of these discoveries they had in common.

"I know you grasp the importance of this. Under your leadership, Ms. Hibiya and Mr. Leik realized their full potential. Neither constricted nor subjugated; the ideal approach to command. My desire is to see that approach become widespread. That will require adjustments to student relations, an attempt at creating a new order on campus. Imagine what Kimberly could become. That is hardly a future any of you would be unhappy with."

His words were no longer just for Oliver; they'd spread to the other five Sword Roses, to the Fellowship at large. Whalley was describing nothing less than the ideal he strove to bring to Kimberly under his leadership.

As Oliver searched for a response, Whalley shook him off.

"No haste required. Feel free to make your choice once the election itself is decided. No one at Kimberly would reproach anyone for playing hard to get. And this works in President Godfrey's favor—should his side lose, he can work his backers into the next council camp."

Providing an excuse for that nominal betrayal, Whalley turned to go. He had said his piece and was well aware belaboring the point would merely diminish it. One last parting shot.

"I like the way you fight, Mr. Horn. Whatever becomes of Kimberly, I hope we can fight alongside each other. From the bottom of my heart."

Unvarnished praise, and thus his recruitment ended. Oliver found himself choking up. He was aware this entire speech had been a calculated approach—but at the core of it lay something sincere. This exchange had made it painfully clear that his skills had been assessed and deemed desirable.

His business concluded, Whalley sailed out of the Fellowship. His shoulders looked far broader than they had a day before.

"…He's singing your praises," Guy said, his grin rising. "Makes me proud by proxy."

"An entirely accurate appraisal. And food for thought, Oliver."

Chela smiled, clearly tickled pink to hear her friend lauded. Putting his own feelings in order, Oliver managed a half smile of his own.

"Yeah… Honestly, parts of that got to me. Running packs of mages under the command of an all-rounder—never thought I'd hear the day when someone saw that as the future of Kimberly."

That concept alone was worth celebrating. Kimberly had long pursued raw talent above all; it was nice to have elders capable of evaluating people by a different yardstick. Part of him wanted to back that. Part of him was grateful for the praise and kind words. Still—

"I shouldn't think about it. I'm confident the Watch will prevail. We've done our part to back them—save perhaps the speech in their favor at the award ceremony. Now we just need to await the results."

He spoke with conviction. Long before this recruitment—Godfrey's side had had their backs, time and time again.

With the fourth- and fifth-year division settled, the afternoon matches began. Everyone sensed the end of the party approaching, yet they knew what lay ahead was the real feast. Glenda was but one of them. She'd been screaming all morning and downed a potion to heal her throat before throwing herself back into her role.

"And the combat league is in the final lap! We did the lower forms! We did the fourth- and fifth-year teams! Now it's time for the sixth- and seventh-year finale! The cream of the crop from the oldest and best-trained students here! We know for a fact they'll be demonstrating everything a Kimberly student ought to aspire to—but there's just one thing on everyone's mind: How's President Godfrey doing?!"

"Dr. Zonneveld gave her seal of approval. Don't worry; he's in peak condition."

Garland's declaration provoked a roar from the stands. As that fever raged, the first-match teams heeded Glenda's call, making their entrance. The sword arts instructor turned his attention to them.

"But first, eyes on this match, please. Team Miligan versus Team Deschamps—itself a vital contest. Team Godfrey and Team Echevalria are both in the running for victory and will be tough to beat—so both these teams *have* to win here."

"Exactly! Team Miligan's backing the Watch, and Team Deschamps supports the old council camp. Those positions both make victory a necessity! The outcome of this match may well be an oracle as to the future of both camps—and decide if Ms. Miligan herself is elected president!"

Glenda reminded everyone of the external pressures riding on this match. Garland nodded at this but turned his attention to the teams themselves.

"We discussed this during the main round, but Team Miligan is certainly a curious composition. Ms. Miligan is the leader, backed by Ms.

Lynette and Ms. Zoe. All three students who've excelled in their fields, yet not students anyone would have expected to appear in a combat league. These three were known primarily for their *research*."

"While the members of Team Deschamps are all mages you *know* can handle themselves in a fight! Curious about that myself, I asked Ms. Miligan what went into her team selection, but she said, 'Everyone knows you can make a strong team if you gather strong students. I wish to show what lies beyond that.' I took that to mean she had some deeper purpose."

Meanwhile, on Team Miligan's side of the arena, only their leader was showing any signs of enthusiasm.

"…Ugh, I hate this vibe. So loud! So hyper!"

"Can I go back to my workshop yet…?"

Lynette Cornwallis and another female student were grumbling up a storm. Not exactly the attitude you'd expect before their big match.

"Now, now," Miligan said, wincing. "It's just a few more matches. And I'm hardly asking you to puke blood through a flurry of blades."

"I couldn't even if you asked. Let me be clear, I could not last one minute in a sword fight with any of them. If they force their way close—"

"We'll get wiped out in no time," Zoe Colonna said, her pudgy frame swaying, her eyes bleary.

"I'm well aware." Miligan grinned. "But winning with this team *matters*."

Moments later, Garland began issuing instructions. Each team sent their first entrant into the ring. Miligan herself represented her team, while Team Deschamps put in a burly seventh-year: Gwenaël Deschamps, head shaved so close it may have taken off the top layer of skin. One of his year's champion fighters, he'd crossed wands with Godfrey's compatriots countless times.

"What a feeble lineup, Snake-Eye. Ceding victory already?"

"I care about *how* I win. Goes with the whole campaign thing."

"Did your enchanted eye bug out? It's showing you futures that will never come to pass."

Deschamps tapped his brow, trying to wind Miligan up; she simply deflected this with a knowing smile.

Garland's voice rang out: "Begin!"

Both wands shot to the team leaders' hands, their lips chanting spells.

"Tonitrus!"

"Tenebris!"

Two spells collided at the center, canceling each other. Miligan stepped toward them. Deschamps had been expecting to pursue a retreating foe and was caught off guard, but he was too experienced to let that expose him. His athame came up in time, matching her blow for blow.

"Coming for the infight?" he asked.

"You assumed I'd buy time with a spell exchange? I'm actually not bad at sword arts."

Sparks flew from their clashing blades. Deschamps weathered her onslaught without a single backward step, snorting.

"You certainly aren't *bad*," he said. "But your Lanoff isn't exactly a *threat*."

His blade locked with hers, batting it aside. She leaped back, righting herself, but Deschamps was lunging in, a thrust bearing down. Unable to block that momentum, Miligan moved sideways, and while her axis was still uncentered, Deschamps pressed his advantage.

"...Ngh..."

The Sword Roses were watching these two veteran fighters with bated breath.

"...He's dominating."

"Why isn't she using the snake eye?"

"She *can't*," Oliver said, answering the question on Pete's and Guy's minds.

"She has to focus her mana on the enchanted eye to activate it," Chela explained. "That diverts mana from other areas, making it tricky to use against an equal or superior foe. She'd get cut down before it took effect. If he didn't know it existed, she might catch him unawares—but even Ms. Miligan couldn't go six years here with one eye hidden."

Oliver nodded in agreement.

Especially since Deschamps was a Rizett master. Of the three core schools, Rizett boasted the swiftest forward and back motions, and it would never do to bank on a sluggish response at even moderate range. And he was a full-grown mage; his resistance to petrification would be far higher than Oliver's and Nanao's had been in their first year. All told, he was not someone her eye would likely finish off.

"Her *other* eye might've helped, but she gave that to Milihand," Guy noted. "Speaking of, where *is* Milihand?"

"Oh, um…," Katie said, squirming. "You'll find out."

Oliver frowned—but the answer soon revealed itself.

"Gah!"

Miligan threw up her left hand, going for a desperate parry. Deschamps saw it coming, and his blade flashed, raking her wrist. The severed hand fell to the floor below—and he frowned.

"? Why—?"

With a dulling spell at half strength, limbs did not simply *sever*. That oddity delayed his follow-up just long enough for the eye on the floor to open.

"!!"

Deschamps leaped back, and the hand's fingers scrabbled on the floor, climbing up Miligan. He threw a spell at them, but Miligan canceled it with fire and then pressed the heated athame against her wrist wound, staunching the bleeding. A mad grin played on the witch's lips.

"Impressive reflexes. I was hoping to pin you down there."

"…Dammit…!"

This twist slowed Deschamps's offense—but his teammates weren't about to take this lying down. Objecting to the very concept, they started yelling from the sidelines.

"Yo, admins! That's against the rules!"

"No familiars allowed!"

Naturally, Garland had spotted this before their voices even reached his ears.

"Interesting play. Contestants, stay your hands. Let us confer."

Pausing the match, he had Theodore drop down from his perch on the ceiling and discuss this turn of events. They soon reached a consensus. Theodore nodded, offered additional feedback, and Garland relayed it to the crowd.

"We have our judgment. Ms. Miligan is within the rules. The rules define familiars as 'servant beings separate from the mage themselves.' We can't very well forbid her bringing her own left hand into the match."

This call flabbergasted not only the rival team, but the entire audience. The logic was arguably prime malicious rules lawyering, and Team Deschamps wasn't ready to drop the fight yet.

"That makes no sense! If it starts moving once it's cut off, it becomes a familiar!"

"There's a precedent," Garland replied. "One student controlled locks of hair that were cut away; it was not deemed against the rules at the time. Ms. Miligan's strategy meets the same conditions, and it would be unfair to deem her alone in violation."

Garland was quite clear; this was not merely the semantics of the league rules, but a decision made in light of that prior judgment. This still wasn't enough for Team Deschamps.

"But that's a case where actual hair was converted to a familiar in the ring, right? Miligan has clearly smuggled in an existing familiar! We've all seen her using it around campus!"

"That's not true!" Miligan cried. "Prior use notwithstanding—today alone Milihand has exclusively been my left hand. It only obtained independent motion once it was cut off. I have met the 'converted in the ring' condition."

Team Deschamps scowled. They were well aware she had the advantage in this type of debate but couldn't just let it drop.

"That's bullshit, and you know it! Even if we concede that specific point, a hand can't move without prior prep!"

"Of course not. But meddling with your own body is what mages *do*. Even the hair manipulator must have treated it in advance. That's exactly why the combat league conventions do not view body parts organically attached as external tools. If they did, this enchanted eye would already be a violation."

"Gah…!"

"And let me add that there is not one non-biological part included in Milihand. I merely fiddled with the nerves, granting it brain-like functions. Enchanted eye aside, the component materials are one hundred percent taken from my own body. If you doubt my word, I'm happy to have the administrators examine it."

Miligan was acting like she had nothing to hide.

Shaking his head at her brash smile, Garland added, "If she'd hidden a magic tool inside her body or tried to attach an additional third arm, I'd have objected. But this was her real hand, attached to her until a moment ago. Given the precedent with the student-controlled locks of hair, we believe using a severed part of her own body is within the rules. That's the basis for our judgment. Teams, resume the match."

Scowling, Deschamps raised his athame. The judges had made their decision and clearly were not about to be shaken from it. As they began exchanging spells again, Glenda started to speak—it was hard to tell if she was amused or appalled.

"W-we've certainly exploited a loophole, at the least. But if that's not a familiar, what is it?! Does any other definition apply?!"

"I'm aware it sounds strained, but we're calling it 'a hand that moves independently when separated from her body.' Anyone who has complaints about that call, feel free to talk to me."

But even as he spoke, he knew the majority of students would go along with it. This was how Kimberly worked—the teachers made rules with loopholes in them, and the students figured out how to exploit them.

"Hard to attack? So sorry. My hand is just that much more *agile*."

As the battle resumed, Miligan piled on the sass.

"Big talk for a failed trick," Deschamps growled back. "Even you can't make your hand autonomous. How well does that eye function once it's detached? Even with an isolated mana reserve, it's good for two attempts at best."

"Correct! But that's more than enough."

The witch's lips curled. Trying to bust her bluff, Deschamps recited an incantation and stepped in as the spells clashed. However—as they neared blade range, Milihand peeked out from the collar of its master's robe.

"...Tch...!"

Deschamps was forced to jump back. On its own, this familiar was no threat to him. But combined with Miligan's own maneuvers, it was a highly effective dissuader. Loath as he was to admit that, he would need a better plan.

"The plan was always to *let him* cut it off...!" Oliver muttered, rubbing his temples. The more he thought about it, the more his head hurt.

For one thing, in order to reattach Milihand, she'd had to cut off her hand again. Pre-match surgery got her to that stage, but then, mid-match, she had to get her opponent to cut it off for her. All this to slip through a crack in the rules and bring in a familiar, insisting it was just her own hand.

"Mr. Deschamps has slowed down considerably," Chela said. "Milihand is proving an effective deterrent."

"An enchanted eye that can activate independently of her own mana manipulation. That *would* be hard to fight...," Pete added.

Guy folded his arms, grunting. "I dunno if it's clever or just crafty, but…it's very *her*."

"…Oh, she's only just getting started," Katie murmured.

Oliver nodded wordlessly. It might be a cunning ploy, but Milihand alone wouldn't win this. That meant it was just a foundation—and the Snake-Eyed Witch knew how to build upon it all the way to victory.

"Phooey, she made it through."

At the three-minute mark, both teams added another fighter. Team Miligan put in Lynette, and Team Deschamps a seventh-year girl, Hildegard Krusch. Since both leaders had been trading spells at range, the switch to two on two went smoothly. Each side broke off to make adjustments.

"Please, Lynette. This next stage is all you."

"Sure, sure. I'm here; I'll do my job. **Tonitrus!**"

Back-to-back with Miligan, Lynette fired off a spell, as if trying to get a chore out of the way. Team Deschamps assumed the spell duel was back on and responded in kind, but Lynette's incantation didn't target them at all. A bunch of glowing letters assembled at the tip of her athame, forming a ball of light, which rose diagonally upward, hanging in the air behind her. Then it began revolving around the arena, maintaining a steady height.

"——?"

"What…?"

The spells they'd fired to counter it met only empty air, and they were left watching Lynette's magic at work. Unable to figure out what she was up to, the distant orb also didn't seem to pose an immediate threat. Agreeing to let it be for now, they resumed their attack.

"**Frigus!**"

"**Impetus!**"

Figuring she'd be the easier target—not Milihand—they both aimed at Lynette. Team Miligan responded with spells of their own, and for a while they went back and forth, adjusting their positions.

"Tonitrus!"

In the midst of that, Miligan chanted a spell. Deschamps assumed it was an oppositional designed to counter his own—but instead, he watched as her spell flew upward. He was wondering if she'd blown her aim when Miligan's magic flew behind him—and was absorbed into Lynette's glowing orb. It expanded, growing brighter; Deschamps swore under his breath.

"Ms. Lynette steps into the ring and puts a ball of light in orbit! And Ms. Miligan's spell made it bigger!"

"A spell satellite. One type of three-dimensional sigil, the vocalizations transformed into written symbols. And this one allows for further growth from spells applied afterward. A pretty nifty trick."

Garland looked suitably impressed as he analyzed the technique. Glenda, who had certainly caught the scent of something highly technical going on, tried to predict the caster's goal.

"Usually people leave those floating around them! What's the benefit of placing it so high up?"

"Likely several, but to name one—it's harder to shoot down. Sigils made of suspended light letters are extremely fragile and easily crumble from the shock waves of other spells. And when that happens, the spell itself can go out of control and harm the caster; you've gotta be really careful using this in any spell duel. Mindful of that, one approach is to start by positioning it remotely."

Garland was offering what little speculation they were afforded at this juncture. The majority of spells were fleeting effects, difficult to maintain for any length without employing some sort of conduit. Converting the spell to letters was a classic means of resolving this, but given the time it took to do so, the technique was not often employed in active combat. Certainly, she'd caught them off guard at the start, but Lynette had also minimized that delay through impressive manuscript speed. On top of that, successfully charging the orb with her own magic after launch was a testament to Miligan's skillful spell control. It was like dropping a cast-iron ball into a vessel made of delicate glass. Without precision control, the satellite would shatter before it could absorb anything.

"At that distance, support spells from the satellite will be delayed. But by the same logic, it'll be tough for their opponents to shoot it down. It won't be an immediate threat, but it's definitely a distraction."

"Still, a suspended 3D sigil at that range is cut off from the caster's mana supply! Isolated, it won't last long! Just hovering alone takes energy, so at this rate it'll die on its own in a few minutes! Is Team Miligan planning to maintain it by throwing spells its way?"

"That'll be tough to do while fighting Team Deschamps. Still—"

With the extra power Miligan had supplied, the spell satellite kept floating. Keeping one eye on it, Deschamps muttered, "Okay, gotta be primarily a distraction."

"Sounds like an egghead strat, yeah. They're basically admitting they can't take us in a fair fight," Hildegard said with a snort. She had the flared-out tips of her hair dyed orange—quite eye-catching.

Miligan was up close with Milihand hidden in her clothes. The satellite was circling above, at range. Both meant that Team Deschamps had to focus on stuff other than their opponents' movements. That was certainly grating, but to Deschamps's eye, it was little more than compensating for their weaknesses.

"Impetus!"

They weren't about to stand around waiting for the next surprise. Hildegard specifically chose to cast when the satellite was out of her line of sight; she predicted its path and aimed to shoot it down. Lynette saw this and took a step sideways—and the satellite shifted with her. The spell caught only air, and Hildegard clicked her tongue.

"Tch, they planned for that. It's revolving around Lynette. Gonna be pretty tough to shoot it down."

"But it's only at two spells. If we don't let them charge it further—"

Even as Deschamps spoke, lightning shot out of the spell satellite straight at Hildegard. She gulped and dodged, swearing.

"What the—?! It just shot at me!"

"How?! They can't maintain it after that output!"

That flipped his whole premise. He glared up. The initial singlecant should have run out by now. If it followed that with an attack, the satellite itself should have vanished. But it was still floating away. Clearly odd. The math didn't add up.

Seeking an explanation, Deschamps turned to the caster. Lynette snorted.

"I wouldn't use something that flimsy in a fight. How long do you think I've been studying spatial magic?"

"Wow," Pete said. "That sigil's inhaling the mana around it."

The Sword Roses had been pondering the same questions, and the bespectacled boy was the first to figure it out.

Oliver and Chela both blinked.

"…Oh," said Oliver. "It's taking advantage of the conditions? There are hundreds of mages gathered here. Naturally, the magic-particle density is off the charts. The arena itself has been adjusted to balance that—"

"—but the sigil itself is floating *above* the arena," Chela added. "The air will be much like it is in the stands. Full of magic particles to absorb."

This was the trick up Lynette's sleeve. Guy folded his arms, head tilted.

"Is that allowed? It's basically like having a familiar hang around outside the arena."

"True, but…mages don't typically perceive sigils alone as familiars," Oliver replied. "Matches before this one allowed use of the air above the ring's surroundings, and they'll have accounted for that, making sure to stay within the letter of the rules. Maintaining a 3D sigil like that without tools is too difficult—few others could imitate her."

Even as he spoke, he felt like he was seeing the basis of Team Miligan's approach. They weren't just exploiting gaps in the rules. That alone, their opponents would adapt to. These strategies were effective because they also revolved around high-level techniques the opposition had not seen before. This was likely also a factor in why Garland allowed it. Some might look at this and call it cheating, but it sure didn't mean it was *easy*.

Chela had clearly reached the same conclusion. Miligan had intentionally gathered noncombatants to tackle the combat league—and based on that, she predicted where the fight would go next.

"Since their foes are experienced upperclassmen, they can't beef up the sigil while exchanging spells. But the satellite keeps itself fueled and grows—the more time they buy, the better Team Miligan's position."

"Flamma! Augh, suck a dick!"

Hildegard narrowly dodged a bolt from above. The satellite's irregular attacks were steadily eating away at them. Keeping half their attention on it left them a beat behind on the spell exchange—every bit as frustrating as they'd feared.

Still, they weren't inclined to dance in the palm of their foe's hand. It was clear Lynette was the core of Team Miligan's strategy, which meant she was also their bottleneck; if Team Deschamps pushed hard and took her down, they could turn this around.

"Impetus!"

A powerful wind spell, well-timed. Avoiding it meant Miligan and Lynette were separated, and Lynette was closer to Hildegard. The latter darted into sword range, moving as fast as her spell, extremely confident she could take out Lynette in a sword fight.

But they'd called this attack. Milihand popped out from the pocket of Lynette's cloak.

"——?!"

"Flamma!"

As Hildegard leaped back, Lynette chased a spell after her. She managed to counter and recover but was left gnashing her teeth.

"…When did it…?!"

She'd almost gotten herself petrified. They'd just assumed that familiar was hidden in Miligan's clothes, but somewhere along the line it had switched hosts. A trap laid in full knowledge of who'd be targeted first in this stage.

"When they had their backs together?" Deschamps guessed. "Like a pair of conjurers."

"She's a creature of whimsy! Never stays in one place for long," Miligan replied, laughing.

Deschamps had been sticking close to her, matching his teammate's moves. And that pressure had allowed them to briefly split the pair. Their first stab may have come up empty, but their turn was not yet over.

"A cheap trick. Push through."

"Agreed."

The team leader's directive put a nasty smirk on Hildegard's lips. An enchanted eye in the pocket? Who cared? She'd only backed off because she'd been unprepared. Now that she knew it was there, it would not prevent her from cutting down Lynette.

Certain she could win, Hildegard darted forward. Lynette was already responding.

"*Impetus!*"

"*Prohibere!*"

Hildegard hit her wind blades with the oppositional, darting at full speed—the speed she'd held in reserve. Lynette wasn't done yet; Hildegard sensed a bolt from the spell satellite behind her, right on target—but she never even looked back.

"*Tenebris!*"

Instead, she chanted a spell at the moment of impact. Deploying a veil of darkness within her personal space to intercept the bolt from behind, she lunged at Lynette with her full strength. Electricity from the last second cancellation scorched her back, but that hardly counted as pain now.

"…Tch! You're a savage!" Lynette spat.

"That's a compliment. Time for a sword fight, milady!"

Hildegard cheerily came in swinging—this was *her* range. Milihand's presence wouldn't matter now—the discrepancy in their sword arts skills was so great Lynette would not last two ripostes.

"Sh-she weathered *that*?"

"Caught it on her back. How did she…?"

Seeing Guy and Pete baffled, Oliver explained, "Point-blank cancellation. Oppositional in your personal space at the moment of impact; not exactly advisable."

His brow was furrowed, his friends' shock only fair. This wasn't a technique you saw often even in the upper forms. With highly skilled fighters on both sides, it was actually *harder* to pull off.

Chela, similarly taken aback, supplemented Oliver's explanation.

"The timing is extremely strict, and even if successful, it usually results in injury. But it frees you of time spent aiming your wand at the incoming spell—which hastens your next attack."

"The lady Lynette likely anticipated this usage," Nanao ventured. "Thus, she attempted to coordinate attacks from the rear and the fore—and her foe's swift footwork was designed to throw off the timing of the pincher, allowing her to handle each attack in turn. An impressive display."

The admiration was evident in her tone. Oliver nodded, watching the tides turn against Team Miligan.

"At that range, the satellite can't help much. Lynette wanted to avoid a sword duel, so this is dire. Milihand might help delay the inevitable, but for how long?"

Oliver's read was on the money—once the fight was at close range, Lynette's distaste for swordplay left things entirely one-sided.

"Yep, yep, you got nothing! Where you hidin' that familiar? Up your sleeve? In your pocket? Or is it stuck to your back?"

"...Ngh...!"

The blade pounding against hers pressed Lynette steadily backward, desperately hanging on by a thread. She was past the capacity for speech. Had this been Miligan, she could have hinted at the enchanted eye, made her opponent flinch, found ways to stay in the fight—but Lynette had no such options. She'd made the call early on to jettison sword arts practice in favor of advancing her research. Hildegard was a battler through and through, always on the front lines; a borrowed enchanted eye could hardly make up that difference.

"What's wrong? Put it out there! I'll handle it! Or would you rather go down with it?"

Lynette would love to rise to that challenge but knew full well the opposite was true—if she used the eye, she would be done. The only reason Hildegard was struggling to finish her here was because she knew Milihand was hiding on her somewhere. The moment she located it, she was free—and the fight would be over in one second flat.

"Ah—!"

But holding it back wasn't about to change the final outcome. Hildegard's leg sweep struck Lynette's ankles, permanently destabilizing a stance she'd barely maintained. Now she was reeling backward, unable to feint in either direction. And the message in Hildegard's eyes was clear: *Gotcha.*

"Impetus!"

A relentless spell, sealing her opponent's doom. Struck in the chest, Lynette was thrown helplessly from the ring. Unconscious the moment her body lifted off. Hildegard need not watch the rest. *Bye-bye, Lynette,* she thought, already focusing her mind on the battle behind her. She need focus not on a fallen foe, but on the spell satellite she'd left behind. Hard to imagine it would last long with the caster unconscious, but odds were high it could manage at least one more attack—

"Huh?"

—but then she stopped. Her mind had turned to the rear, and her body started to follow it until she found herself locked up halfway. Like her limbs had turned to stone.

"Nice work, Lynette," Miligan muttered, smiling as she traded spells with Deschamps.

At the edge of her vision, a bolt fell from the sky. Designed to unleash its full reserve of power at the moment its caster blacked out, it aimed that parting gift at the spot Lynette had specified the instant before her elimination.

This was no surprise. Hildegard had expected it. That was why her focus had shifted to it the moment she took Lynette out. It was trivial to dodge an attack you knew was coming. A last desperate attack would hardly succeed at this stage of the proceedings.

Except—Milihand was buried in the soil behind her and caught her in the grasp of its enchanted eye.

"___!"

Not even able to swear, the parting gift struck Hildegard with the full might the satellite had stored up, a hit so strong she lost all sensation.

"…Gah…"

"Hilda!"

Out of the corner of his eye, Deschamps saw his teammate eliminated—and a beat later, he found Milihand half buried in the dirt. Before he could take further action, Miligan turned her athame, getting ahead of him.

"Ducere!"

"Impetus!"

The witch's pull spell yanked Milihand off the ground a moment before Deschamps's winds raked the area. Her familiar flipped itself in the air, nimbly lighting upon her shoulder—and Miligan shot her opponent a very smug smirk.

"Such a basic trap! Even in the upper years, few students rival Lynette for stealth spatial magic. You can't let your guard down just because you've eliminated *her*."

"…She was always going for mutually assured destruction? Damned con artists."

Deschamps got what had happened, and that just left him swearing. As Hildegard pushed her backward, Lynette had used spatial magic to melt a patch of floor underfoot. Milihand had run down her leg, obscured by her skirts, and hidden in the ground. Rather than try to land a gambit on her opponent's turf, Lynette laid a trap to snare Hildegard after her defeat. She cared less about her own victory than taking a tough opponent with her.

"Ugh, I've gotta go in now."

With two fighters eliminated, they reached the six-minute mark. The last member of Team Miligan—Zoe Colonna—stepped unenthusiastically into the ring.

"Both teams lost one but gained another!"

"Hat's off. Hildegard was watching for that hand the whole duel but never saw the trick coming. In hindsight, the satellite itself was just a setup to finish her opponent after her own elimination. Very clever."

Garland was being positively effusive. How could he not praise the creative thinking required to include your own elimination in a strategy?

"Given that Ms. Lynette had little shot of winning a direct fight, going for mutual elimination is likely to Team Miligan's advantage. Oh, incidentally—I'm sure Hildegard was gunning for this, too, but if that *hand* gets flung out of the ring, Miligan herself is disqualified. Good thing she recovered it in time—that was a close call."

"So Ms. Hildegard also planned to turn their scheme against them! Her point-blank cancellation was to die for, so it does feel like she didn't really get to strut her stuff here!"

"Arguably, but one can also chalk that up to the success of Team Miligan's approach. They're maximizing the potential of a team of noncombatants, while also shutting down their opponents' strengths. As a candidate for student body president, that's likely the sort of leadership Miligan wants to demonstrate."

For a long beat after the third members joined, both teams stood there staring each other down.

"Oh, not attacking? Finally worked out you can't just overpower us?" Miligan taunted, sensing her rivals' caution.

Team Deschamps had hoped for a swift resolution, but the fight so far had been jam-packed with twists that made them think twice. And with this third member's skills an unknown quantity, they didn't dare rush in.

"I'd rather you don't play it safe. The sooner we get this over with, the better."

Miligan shot Zoe a glance, and Zoe dropped to her knees, hands on the ground. She sighed heavily—then put a spell on her tongue.

"...Lutuom limus..."

"Tonitrus!"

"Impetus!"

Team Deschamps might have been in watch-and-wait mode, but they weren't about to let an opening go unpunished. Lightning and wind mingled, rushing at their foe. Making no attempt to counter this, Miligan merely stood there, right up against her teammate.

And just before the spells hit—the floor heaved upward, completely blocking their spells.

"____?!"

"What in the...?!"

Team Deschamps could not believe their eyes. The floor of the ring around Zoe had gone claylike and was roiling. The area affected was broad enough to contain both Miligan and her—and it almost seemed alive.

"No big whoop. Just playing in the dirt," Zoe intoned before her body was swallowed up by the floor, head and all. An unnerving sight even to mage eyes, and her foes looked suitably tense.

"She...melted into the floor of the ring? What's going on?!" Glenda cried.

"An application of classic golem techniques...turning herself into the core, fine-tuning the elements at a very high level. Less like she's controlling the floor and more like she's synchronized with it..."

Garland had one hand on his chin, looking less fascinated or impressed than...alarmed. It was typical for students who reached the finals to have some secrets up their sleeve, but he was an instructor—and had to draw the line somewhere.

"It's one thing with your average ground, but the arena floor is treated with a self-repairing spell. Not a feat anyone else could pull off. She's likely entered and rewritten that spell—a sight that makes me fear for Kimberly's security. No—before we even get there—"

A few seconds after Zoe melted into the floor, this became a very different match. Ripples ran across the surface of the ring, surfaces left flat now the minority. Where they'd been was now a hill that abruptly dropped into a trough. Miligan was lightly dancing across the top of this, but Team Deschamps was barely staying on their feet.

"...Would you stop scampering around? I'm so sleepy right now..."

Zoe might no longer be visible, but her voice shook the surface of the floor. She sounded like she was talking in her sleep.

"She's in a trance?" Deschamps muttered, calmly taking stock. "Don't get hung up on how freakish this looks—she can't sustain it for long."

"I can see that! Melting the floor and manipulating it is one thing, but melting herself into the floor?! That's one step shy of getting consumed by the spell!"

The third member of Team Deschamps was Kenneth Hayward, a sixth-year student with black hair in a very uptight-looking center part. What they were seeing now was no crafty scheme or trick—it was downright unnatural, absolutely not a sight they should have encountered in a combat league. This was more the kind of nightmare Godfrey regularly faced while working for the Watch.

"Don't fall asleep on me, Zoe. I don't want to lose you yet."

"…I'll do what I can… But if I stop responding…I'd appreciate a wake-up call."

Miligan kept talking to the rippling ground, and while not exactly reassuring, the ground was answering. That alone provided proof Zoe had not yet been consumed by the spell. Team Deschamps had not a shred of evidence as to how long she might toe that line.

They were trading spells with Miligan, trying to stay upright on the heaving ground—and those waves were only getting higher. Where they stood was now always at an elevation higher than where the match had begun. And that fact begged speculation. Kenneth gulped.

"…Uh, if she alters all of it—"

"She can force us to ring out. Can you stop that with spell interference?"

Deschamps put forward a specific strategy; Kenneth thought for a few seconds, then nodded. Whatever the goal here was, letting her go to town was bad for them.

"If I can focus on only that, probably…?"

"Then go for it. I'll keep Snake-Eye busy."

Their roles divided, Team Deschamps set their jaws and went to work. Deschamps fired a spell at a mound Miligan was using for cover, flushing her out.

"Aw, you spotted me?"

"I thought better of you, Miligan! Never imagined you were quite mad enough to employ something this dangerous!"

His anger was genuine, and the spells he followed it with a rebuke.

Expertly avoiding them with the aid of the shifting grounds, the Witch spoke up.

"I've earned your ire—mind if I speak seriously for a moment?"

"____?"

Deschamps wasn't quite sure how to respond. While they talked, the fight would grind to a halt, arguably buying time—but in these circumstances, which side would benefit from that the most?

"Prohibere—Prohibere—Fortis Prohibere!"

Kenneth's resistance prevented the alteration from consuming the entire ring. That balance would only last as long as his mana pool, but would it last longer than the girl buried in the floor? Unlikely. Given the scale of her spell, Zoe was clearly burning mana fast. If she shattered that ceiling, that would prove she'd been consumed by the spell, and Garland would declare Team Miligan's defeat before that happened. At the very least, Deschamps could trust the sword arts master to know when a mage was too far gone.

"…Lay it on me."

Time was on his side. Thinking it through had made him sure of that, so Deschamps let her speak. Miligan nodded.

"I found Zoe at the end of last year. In a workshop on the third layer, melted into her own creation."

"……"

"If I'd failed to notice, she'd long since have been consumed by the spell. Happens all the time. Kimberly tacitly approves of it, and once upon a time, I'd have cheerily let it happen."

"…I don't get it. Why bother bringing that to the combat league? Trying to put her to good use before the spell inevitably consumes her?"

Part of this question was stalling for time, but it was also an honest query. He could see no legitimate reason to make use of someone like this. Given how cunning Miligan's previous schemes had been, choosing a more viable strategy would have increased her odds of victory.

He couldn't figure out why she'd ignored that and gone for this long shot.

Miligan smiled, well aware of why he was so baffled.

"I knew another mage like her, who *was* consumed. We weren't exactly friends, but…the last words we exchanged stuck with me."

"That's it? Pointless sentiment? You think you could have said something to stop her?"

"Ha-ha, hardly. The fate of a mage is not so easily overcome. But… perhaps I could have staved it off for a few days. And perhaps in those extra days, we could have exchanged more words—better than the ones we did. Maybe then it would weigh less upon me. I feel like it would."

Fingers clenching her athame, she raised it to her chest. Her mind's eye was on the face of a witch who'd been perpetually alone. She was not inclined to apologize. They'd been enemies until the bitter end—and their final words had been designed to hurt. The motives for that were as sound now as they'd been at the time.

And yet—if there was a next time, she'd like to see a better ending.

"That's one reason I brought Zoe here. Most mages are all alone when they're consumed. And it occurred to me—if they *aren't*, then perhaps they can hang on awhile longer. The league is quite a party. Enough to make you forget how isolated you were."

"……And what good does that do? A momentary delay at best?"

Deschamps's brow creased. Miligan would have said the same, once, so she merely shrugged.

"Hard to say, really. I just think time spent alive has meaning. Isn't that the fundamental principle underlying the civil rights movement?"

She herself was taken aback by how easily the answer came. She didn't even have to pick her words—they just came out.

Like a label she'd applied to herself finally fit her. That thought made her blush, and she glanced at the ground.

"She's at her limit. Wake up, Zoe!"

As she spoke—there was a crack. Half the ring slid away.

"...Huh?" Kenneth gasped, looking up from his interference. Where he stood—the entire west side of the ring—had cracked diagonally and was sliding away. His feet were still in the ring, but his body had already reached the area designated "out of bounds."

"A beautiful cut," Miligan said softly. "Nice work, Zoe. You may sleep now."

Hunched up in the cross section like the stage had been her pupa, Zoe slowly closed her eyes.

"...I'll do that, then," she replied.

From there, it was only the gentle sounds of her breathing. The audience was so quiet everyone could hear them.

After a long silence, Glenda recovered enough to glance at Garland.

"Was that...a ring out...?"

"...I believe so. Portions of the ring that fall out of bounds are no longer considered part of the stage. Unrelated to the size of the fragment."

That was how the rules had it. The fight may have been chaotic to the extreme, but he'd witnessed a clear strategy behind it.

Zoe's entrance might have seemed like they'd unleashed a wild thing, but her work had been constantly under Miligan's careful control. Specifically, they'd known their enemy would fight them—and used that to break the ring itself. Merely fighting off the interference wouldn't get them to an elimination. That's why they'd pushed—and then pulled back. Zoe had put all her effort into maintaining the fluidity of the opposing surface, letting Kenneth's interference harden the rest.

And this was the outcome. The stage had cracked, part of it had slid away—and since it was the byproduct of two different spells, it was far more dramatic than what Zoe managed on her own. That sheer scale was why Kenneth had failed to register it as an attack at all. In all the years the combat league had run, this was one of few instances where someone had been forced out of bounds while standing on the ring.

*   *   *

"Now it's just the two of us. Perhaps it's time we settled things, Mr. Deschamps."

The western half of the stage was gone, and the eastern half was now extremely uneven. Not a trace of the original left behind. Miligan quietly braced for battle, while Deschamps just glared at her.

"…You roped me into that conversation…"

"To do this, of course. Always did excel at appealing to emotions. Did I bring a tear to your eye?"

Miligan looked quite proud of herself. Not a speck of guilt. Deschamps gave up thinking about it. No point speculating on how much she'd actually meant. Even less use getting mad at her. This snake would not be silenced as long as she still breathed.

"…I'll admit I underestimated you," said Deschamps. "But the outcome remains unchanged."

"Oh dear. Won't be very impressive if I lose *now*!"

No more talk. The two survivors faced each other down. Everyone knew this was the end—whatever the outcome, it would not take long to settle.

"*Impetus!*"

"*Prohibere!*"

Spells clashed, and both fighters ran toward the end of one of the oddest matches in league history.

"…My jaw may never close again," Chela whispered, dumbfounded like many students in the stands around her. She couldn't even muster praise or analysis of the cunning strategies employed. If she had to put her feelings into words, the closest phrase—she didn't even know where to begin.

Sharing that feeling, Oliver forced his mind to move on. Whatever had come before, this was still anyone's fight to win. He needed to focus on that alone; by trimming all else away, he got his mind moving again.

"...Regardless of what's transpired," he began, "now we're in a simple one-on-one. And with half the stage gone, both parties have limited maneuverability."

"...Which makes it easy to get in sword range," Pete said. "Down a hand, Miligan's at a disadvantage..."

"I dunno about that," Guy objected. "Milihand's still in the mix somewhere."

Taking both points into account, Oliver watched the fight a moment—and the smaller stage was clearly working against Miligan. In other words, she was unlikely to win unless she had something that could compensate for that.

"Katie, what's your take?" Pete asked.

The curly haired girl was watching the battle unfold, looking increasingly tense.

"She's got a plan. Will it work? That...might come down to *my* skills."

"Huh?" Behind his glasses, Pete blinked, unsure what that meant.

The phrasing bugged Oliver, too, but he chose to focus on the battle instead.

"...Gah...!"

Heat seared her skin, and Miligan stifled a shriek. She'd backed away from a disadvantageous sword duel and been chased by this spell. Unable to cancel it completely, the fires caught her robe, and she was forced to cast it off even as she backed away.

"...Hmph."

Zoe may have transformed the field completely, but Deschamps had already adapted to that. He was keeping her from using that terrain but making good use of it himself, steadily pushing her toward the far edge.

"You're tapped out. Sorry, but this is my fight now."

His conviction was unwavering, but as his opponent cast off her robe, he scanned every inch of her. Now that she was cornered, that familiar's enchanted eye was bound to make an appearance.

"Looks like it's not in your clothes. Buried somewhere on the stage? My spatial sense covers more ground than that eye's range. Try any angle. I'll spot it."

He was steadily closing the gap, eyes like daggers scanning for the disembodied hand, turning up the pressure on Miligan—then he stopped.

"…Found it. **Flamma!**"

Deschamps threw a spell to pin her down and leaped sideways. He stomped a specific section of the floor, hardening the ground with spatial magic and sealing Milihand within—and using that step to close in on his opponent.

"I've got you now, Miligan!"

"Tch…!"

With her trap foiled, Miligan spun around, revealing her back. Normally unthinkable, but Deschamp took it as a vain bluff—an attempt to make him think Milihand was on her back. He wasn't falling for it. His senses had clearly captured Milihand in the ground behind—his foe had no more tricks up her sleeve.

"——?!"

He was so certain of this that he couldn't work out why his body stiffened up.

"Thanks for setting my robe on fire. That let me make its removal look natural."

The witch still had her back to him. With the robe gone, he could see the back of her blouse—and between the shoulder blades, a bizarre gash. With an *eye* peering out. Red and green, inhuman—a gleaming eye where no eye ought to be.

"…You…put it…on your…back?"

"My left eye is a fake! Not that I'm inclined to let you see."

Miligan pulled her bangs aside. Deschamps couldn't see from behind, but like she said, in her left socket was an elaborately constructed glass eye. No hidden abilities there, not a magic tool—so not a violation of the rules. But if her foes *believed* that was where her enchanted eye lay, then they'd assume they need only track her face and her familiar.

"Your team was a good one. But mine wins at deceit. **Tonitrus.**"

Aiming over her shoulder, the witch fired a spell. In the instant of consciousness he had left, the only thought on Deschamps's mind was an invective he'd never before let cross his lips. Namely: *What a cunt.*

The last spell hit, and Deschamps toppled over. The audience was over their confusion—and on their feet with a roar.

"It's all over! Team Miligan pulled the rug out from under them at every turn, and they emerge with the victory! A real tightrope walk across the letter of the rules, and they clearly have nerves of steel. Master Garland, what's your final verdict?"

"Well, not a battle I'd want any younger students taking inspiration from. But it's also a fact that you've gotta go this far if you want to snatch a victory away from the upper form's top fighters. And I have to give credit for showcasing students whose skill sets aren't really combat focused. Play your cards right, and you can fight like this— that knowledge will broaden the range of tactics employed. Also…"

League staff had pulled Zoe from the cross section and carried her away. She was still sound asleep. Garland smiled at her, murmuring, "Ms. Miligan might insist it was all part of her scheme, but I'm grateful she pulled Ms. Zoe up here before the spell consumed her. Not as a judge, but as a teacher."

"…Katie, the eye was you?"

As the stands buzzed with the one-of-kind fight, Oliver turned to the curly haired girl. All eyes gathered wordlessly on her.

Oliver was sure of it. Miligan had secured her victory with an enchanted eye on her back—allowing her to eliminate her blind spot and surprise her foes. But given the eye's location, she couldn't have done it herself. Given what Katie had said earlier, something must have gone down before the match.

Katie nodded listlessly. That was her work, and she offered no excuses.

"I'm glad it actually functioned," she said. "Ms. Miligan asked me yesterday. She'd worked out all the steps, and I just had to follow them."

Guy and Pete were gaping at her. She'd performed a major surgery yesterday, before their big talk?

Katie avoided their gaze, babbling. "Moving the eyeball itself from the face to the back…was gross but not that hard. If you know how to handle enchanted eyes, it's not too difficult. But extending and connecting nerves? I almost burst into tears so many times! Why would you ask a third-year to do anything like that?!"

She buried her face in her hands, wailing. No one knew what to say. But the girl who'd forced this mad surgery on her called out from the stage, athame raised high, looking extremely smug.

"I won, Katie! Are you basking in the glory?!"

"I am *not*! I haaaate you!"

Katie had rarely ever screamed louder. Oliver and Chela looked at each other and sighed in sync.

CHAPTER 2

Lovers and Rivals

Team Deschamps had lost their first match. This news sent a stir through Team Leoncio's prep room.

"…An unexpected loss. That team was rock-solid," Gino said, wondering what had changed that.

"Haaa-ha." Khiirgi smirked. "Snake-Eye got 'em good. Sly as they come and getting slier."

Meanwhile, their leader remained seated on the couch in back, saying not a word. They turned their gaze to him.

"It won't matter," Khiirgi purred. "Not once Leo gets like this."

He wasn't ignoring them—their chatter hadn't reached his ears at all. Leoncio was in a state of extreme focus, his eyes fixed on the air before him. In this state, even his friends dared not approach. They might lose a limb just entering his personal space before they even managed to tap a shoulder.

"They won? With that team? Huh."

Yet in Team Godfrey's room, Tim sounded almost appalled. Team Miligan was in their camp, but somehow, they found it hard to celebrate her victory—they were more concerned with what nefarious grifts she'd pulled. If that lineup beat Team Deschamps, they'd need at least two or three tricks so dubious they'd stun the entire audience. They'd not yet been told the specifics of the match, but their assumptions were right on the money.

Still, it *was* good news. Lesedi had been doing stretches in the back, but she straightened up, clearly ready to go.

"Then we've just gotta keep it rolling. You ready, Godfrey?"

"Of course."

Godfrey finished his own warm-ups, turning his mind to the rival he was about to face. Long had they opposed each other, often they had clashed—and romantic overtures had been made.

"…It's been a while since we last committed to a duel."

He hadn't noticed the smile playing on his lips. As they rose to leadership within their factions, it had become tougher for them to square off. He got why there was a need for self-control, but acquiescing to propriety left him feeling deeply frustrated. He was done competing over ancillaries like support from the student body, acceptance of policies, or the number and quality of their followers.

"Time! Team Godfrey, head on in!"

A staff member leaned into the room, calling out—and all three teammates turned toward the door.

"Everything we are rests on this fight. Let's knock 'em dead."

""Aye, aye!""

They stepped out. To where their rivals awaited. To their final battle, the climax of their time at this academy.

As the start of the second match approached, league staff cropped up in the stands. They cleared the front row seats and began strengthening the barriers. That alone told the Sword Roses how fierce this fight would be.

"…They're really amping up those barriers. Like they're expecting a dragon rampage," Guy said.

"Entirely appropriate," Chela replied. "Given what each side is capable of…"

Most students were fully aware of the threat here and were voluntarily calling out to first- and second-year students, urging them to retreat to the back rows. Yet, despite those concerns, nobody seemed inclined to *leave*. Every soul here knew for a fact that this fight would be worth seeing—no matter the risk to life and limb.

"A fight between the strongest fighters Kimberly has to offer. I imagine I won't be saying much here," Oliver warned, adjusting his posture. They were seated toward the front, but since all present had reached the main round of the lower forms league, no one felt the need to warn them off. Rather, they were expected to be looking after the students around them—Oliver did a quick scan to ensure there was no one at risk.

"Ain't no reason for us to back off!"

"C'mon, Dean. Don't be like that."

"It's just a precaution. This way, we can focus on watching."

He saw Dean Travers passing by with Rita and Peter each pushing him toward the back row. Teresa was tagging along after them, which brought a smile to Oliver's face. Them backing off on their own meant one less concern.

"The second match is almost here, but first, an important announcement."

Garland's voice rang out, an ominous growl. Well aware of what this would be, the audience fell quiet, listening.

"For this battle alone, we're clearing the first two rows. That will leave a portion of the audience standing, but this is for your own safety and to ensure our combatants need not worry about collateral damage. We ask your help to ensure they can fight unfettered."

The bulk of the students were way ahead of him. The urge to stay out of this fight's way had arisen without passing through morality or benevolence. No one wanted to ruin the spectacle to come—and few were foolish enough to stick their hand between gears spinning at high velocity.

"Instructor Gilchrist and I will be positioned directly next to the arena. We promise to handle any stray shots, but in the interests of abundant caution, we've strengthened the barriers considerably. This is why the first two rows were vacated. Apologies to anyone forced to stand, but be mindful of the situation and try not to squabble over the remaining seats."

This rebuke made a few scuffles reluctantly die down. Making a scene here would cause the league staff to eject you; for once, everyone was forced to be magnanimous. They could always kill each other later—after this fight, for example. In its most basic form, that was Garland's entire point.

"It's time. Teams, enter."

With the venue prepped, Glenda's voice echoed more solemnly than ever before. That alone made every back straighten. The tension in the air was like that around an altar before a sacred rite—and from east and west, the teams entered.

"Our fighters here need no introduction. Every student at Kimberly knows their skills and their characters. Any embellishments I might make would merely be a digression."

Always one for motormouthed hype, for once Glenda chose brevity. The implication: For this one fight alone, she, too, wanted to remain a spectator. No one there dreamed of chastising her for that.

"But if I can air one personal opinion—I know this to be true. All my time at Kimberly has been for one purpose alone: to see *this fight.*"

Her words sent ripples through the stands, forcing their expectations skyward. Both teams lined up on opposite sides of the stage. In the announcers' booth, Theodore had taken over for the sword arts instructor. When he saw the teams ready, he called out, "First combatant—step forward!"

Each team's leader started up the stairs and soon were face-to-face onstage. One had saved many a student from peril or had put them out of their misery: the student body president. The other had numerous students under his umbrella, controlling the opposition through skill and magnetism. Each had long since lost count of the conflicts between them and, thus, had few words to exchange here.

"You don't change, Godfrey. You are as you have been since the day we met."

"Same to you, Leoncio," Godfrey replied.

Leoncio smiled faintly and shook his head. "No, I *have* changed. And those changes are your fault."

Speaking of a truth only he knew, his tone almost a lament. Dealing with this one man had forced the tides of change upon him, and the years had at last allowed him to accept that fact with resignation. Anger had proven inadequate. That had given way to hatred and finally transformed into affection. That progression was all too clear to him, and thus, he felt no compunctions about where his passions took him.

"The time is ripe. Today I shall drain your cup, my beloved Purgatory."

"Come at me, Golden Lord."

Leoncio and Godfrey addressed each other by epithet alone before their athames leaped to their hands. They could not wait another second. Perceiving that, Theodore said the one thing he could—the one thing anyone wanted to hear.

"Begin!"

The next ten minutes would be carved into Kimberly legend.

"Ignis!"

"Solis lux!"

Incantations rang out. Red and gold flames spurted from their athames, clashing. Neither was inclined to fuss about oppositionals. All attention that might be diverted there was instead poured into speed and power. The clashing infernos swelled up above the stage, swiftly becoming a sun. Each backed off out of that sphere of influence, shifting to the next incantation with minimized lag.

"Solis lux!"

"Ignis!"

Pouring still more flames into the sun, it doubled in size. The dazzling light of it eliminated all shadows in the entire arena.

*   *   *

"Oh—!"

"Urgh…!"

"Gah—!"

The light was too strong, and it left Guy's, Katie's, and Pete's eyes burning. Oliver and Chela acted swiftly, putting up a protective coating to diminish the light's glare. Chela had her eyes locked on the spectacle beyond, and her voice shook.

"…This is just…"

"…'Tis the stuff of myth," Nanao concluded. She spoke not only for the Sword Roses but for every member of the audience here. Mages dueled each other on a daily basis at Kimberly, yet this fight was so removed from those that it entered the realm of the truly fantastical. Like something from ancient times, a critical moment in history, a singularity bubbling up for one brief, blinding moment.

"……"

Selectively eliminating his own coating, Oliver observed the sights with naked eyes.

"Oliver, your eyes—," Chela said, concerned.

"I have to see this, even if it burns them away."

That said, he siphoned a chunk of his consciousness to adjusting his pupils. In the seat behind him, Nanao followed his lead. Her thoughts matched his.

Burned-out eyes were but a small price to pay to witness a match like this.

No quarter, no retreat, not even any variation in element employed. Each fighter merely cast the same spell over and over, the shock waves swiftly carving away the center of the stage.

"Huff!"

"Haaah…!"

Two minutes since the match began, and both men had cast well over twenty spells. At this point, their spell duel was brought to a halt by a force unrelated to the upper hand.

"Ref, the stage is no more. What's next?"

His athame trained on his rival, Godfrey threw a question to the sidelines, where Garland watched. His words were not the least bit exaggerated or figurative. Save for the small fragment of the rim upon which they stood, the vast majority of the stage had been vaporized. No trace of the original structure remained.

Even Garland winced at that one. They'd put extra emphasis on reinforcing the repairs to the damage from the first match, making the most indestructible stage to date. Yet it had not even lasted the opening three minutes.

Admitting they'd failed on that front, he glanced at Gilchrist, then at Theodore. Both nodded, and the league reached a consensus. Garland merely had to voice it.

"...Very well. For this match alone, we'll classify the entire pit surface as 'the ring.' Do you agree, Mr. Echevalria?"

"Naturally."

"Appreciated, Master."

Leoncio nodded, and Godfrey briefly expressed his gratitude. With mutual consent, the inbounds range expanded, which forced their waiting teammates back into their respective entrances. If the entire pit was the ring, then fighters not yet in play couldn't stand within it.

Once the new fight terms were met, they were given the go-ahead to resume the suspended battle. But the same thought crossed both minds; neither Godfrey nor Leoncio moved. A short wait, and they'd hit the three-minute mark. They'd have to regroup anyway; might as well do so once new faces arrived.

"I like that gleam in your eyes, Lesedi. Too much shackled us during the Rivermoore fiasco. Isn't it nice to finally be free to pulverize me?"

Their second participants stepped forward. The first to speak was

Team Leoncio's own Khiirgi Albschuch, an elf with a perpetually sinister smirk. Team Godfrey's Lesedi Ingwe glared back.

"Lemme clear up one misconception, Khiirgi."

"Mm?"

"I *am* mad. But not 'cause you stole my girlfriends."

As she spoke, she removed each boot. Tipped with adamant, they landed on the ground with an audible *thunk*. Now barefoot, she flexed her toes on the turf—and Lesedi's right leg vanished, severed blades of grass fluttering through the air as if that sweeping kick had been a sharpened scythe.

Everyone thought she wore those boots to enhance the force of her kicks. But that was entirely wrong. Those weights were *protective*. They kept Lesedi safe from the sheer strength of her own kicks.

"The reason I can't let this go—is because you made them cry!"

With this bellow, she leaned forward, an ultralow stance derived from the martial arts of another continent entirely.

Her roar made Khiirgi shiver.

"Oh…that's *it*, Lesedi."

The elf nodded, hand to her brow, beside herself. In that moment, she envied Leoncio like never before—if she'd had his equipment, she'd have had it standing prouder than ever before.

"Your fury is a thing of beauty. When you rage against the unpardonable, when your passions fuel your fight against reality itself—you shine brighter than the setting sun."

Her feet stepped forth, unbidden. Like a moth drawn to a flame, aware it would burn but unable to stop herself. She had to see it close, place it in her hands—the same urge that had led her to plunge so many lights into the darkened depths.

"You must know: I have a need to see you like this in perpetuity—and thus, I have repeated the same course of action."

With no trace of guilt, Khiirgi offered up her dark and dire devotion, emotions so twisted the acceptance of them led only to destruction.

This was not the first time she'd displayed this, and Lesedi was long since done being disturbed.

"Two key words have fallen out of your dictionary: repentance and restraint."

"Haaa-ha! I remember those! How oft my parents used to chant them at me."

"I'm gonna carve 'em into you. The last role I'll play here!"

The ground behind Lesedi exploded, and she disappeared. Thirty yards cleared in a single second; her kick descended on Khiirgi's face twisted with delight. When the elf ducked under that, Lesedi Sky Walked into a second kick from the opposite side. When that, too, was narrowly dodged, she fired a spell on her retreat. A rush without a moment to breathe, yet Khiirgi handled it all, sighing: *Ah, how can this be? You've never been this cool.*

"Ms. Ingwe and Ms. Albschuch join the fray! And they're also going at it hard right off the bat!"

"Magnificent. It's been far too long since I saw Ms. Ingwe barefoot."

In the announcers' booth, Theodore was grinning and nodding. Glenda was keeping commentary to a minimum, so he followed suit, saying little. But what he saw got to him. Cutting the amplification spell on his wand, he spoke to himself.

"Ms. Albschuch was pretty far gone when she washed up at Kimberly. She'd already worked out exactly who she was. I felt sure she'd be consumed by the spell within two years. I invited her here on the condition that I handle the fallout when that happened."

Listening to his murmuring, Glenda glanced once his way. Kimberly might draw the best of the best, but it was exceedingly rare for an elf like Khiirgi to enroll. When they did, there was always *someone* involved— and having an instructor arrange her admission was one thing she had in common with Nanao Hibiya. Theodore was among the few mages who'd taken an elf bride, so perhaps that had played a role.

"My concerns came to naught because of who she met here. They are each far too exceptional. Both Mr. Echevalria, for getting her in his pocket, and Ms. Ingwe, for withstanding all the clashes with her. That she found both is well worth calling miraculous."

And that history meant he watched this match with a hint of gratitude in his gaze. He'd fancied it a gamble with diminishing odds. More than likely, it would simply plunge the school into chaos and benefit no one. And that was precisely why this outcome was a credit to the students alone.

"The elves couldn't handle her. But here, she was never alone. And that—that's something to be proud of."

Theodore's voice was a rasp. A bashful look on his profile spoke volumes—sometimes a long shot pays off. And that's why he'd never stop taking those risks.

To no one's surprise, turning the fight into a two-on-two made it all the fiercer.

"Ignis!"

"Solis lux!"

They'd lost count of how many spells this was. The turf had widened, and there was less to obstruct their spell duel; as the big guns clashed, the second fighters traded furious gambits.

"Haaa-ha!"

Laughing, Khiirgi Wall Walked across the wall right below the stands. With the stage burned away, that wall was now inbounds, and Lesedi soon spotted her goal—trying to shoot Khiirgi there would skirt the edge of the crowds. Lesedi might not manage it herself, but Godfrey's spells could well burst through the barrier, and he couldn't afford to aim her way. They had to protect the students—and that was being used as a shield against them.

"Huff—!"

But she'd always known these people were vicious. Lesedi kicked the ground, rocketing right at her opponent regardless. Khiirgi cast spells from on high aimed straight at her opponent. Rather than divert mana to intercept, Lesedi poured it all into her legs, her explosive speed allowing her to duck beneath the spells and run up the wall. At her ascent, Khiirgi made a new wall between them, perpendicular to the ground. Breaking that wall with a spell or going around it—each required a disadvantageous extra move, so Lesedi chose neither.

"Shaaaa!"

As she neared the blockade, Lesedi leaped off the stands, kicking directly up. Her feet didn't just break the wall but turned the shards of it into projectiles aimed at the foe above. Khiirgi gulped and dodged, eyes gleaming. Smashing a wall barefoot was madness, but using that same action to shoot back? Every bit as laughable as Godfrey's power. Lesedi could likely kick a garuda to death without even bothering to cast a spell.

"Haaa-ha!"

Before she got chased any farther up the wall, Khiirgi jumped away, flitting back to the ground below. Lesedi gave chase at once, Sky Walking into a dropkick. Spotting that, Leoncio shifted his position, moving the center point of the clashing spells closer to make Lesedi flinch and buying Khiirgi enough time to recover.

"…Every time!" the Alp cried, voice quivering with delight.

Lesedi's movements left mages' concepts of the term in the dust. Her own body as the axis, furious, merciless, powerful in its simplicity. The way she fought brought the heroes of legend to Khiirgi's mind, made her yearn like an innocent child. And it brought forth a wish— to be the Alp befitting her. A shabby monster would be an insult to her hero.

"Progressio—!"

Thus, she *became* one. Seeds taken from her homeland, selectively bred for several years, embedded all over her body. Ordered to sprout, these swiftly dug roots into her body, melding with her flesh and bones, forcefully expanding her mana flow. This transformation was not merely internal. Vines burst forth from her left arm, spiraling out into a second wand—a tentacle.

"…Ghiiiiii—hee-haw—gurghhh—!"

Ripples ran down her back, burls containing voluminous mana twisting outward. These brought horrific pain and a sense of maddening omnipotence. Nothing left of her fit what anyone pictured when they heard the word *elf*. Her form grotesque, like a wizened tree subjected to a curse. Khiirgi Albschuch had become the creature people imagined dwelling within the darkness of the forest depths.

"Impetus!"

The expanded mana flow allowed her tentacle to function as a second wand, and a massive bloom at the tip fired a tempestuous gale. Leaping over that, Lesedi observed her opponent's transformation and snorted.

It hardly came as a surprise. Fight enough battles alongside the Watch, and you get used to these things.

"Breaking *all* the taboos. Must make your parents weep!"

Off-the-cuff snark on the way to her next attack. As she applied further secrets to her contorted form, Khiirgi made to answer—and the words died on her lips.

Don't stay up late; don't play with fire.
On a moonlit night, you'll earn its ire.

An old song echoed. One that had guided her path.

The spooky Alp is watching. Waiting to take you away.
Your mother won't know it left a changeling here to play.

Wherein lay the origins? Khiirgi had pondered that question countless times.

Stories of Alps snatching children often revolved around the same concept—the changeling. Where the human child had been was a beautiful monster, surrounded by a circle of colorful mushrooms.

On the face of it, elves would never do that—they were obsessed with keeping their bloodlines pure. But lateral thinking led to other ideas. Specifically, were all the threats to racial purity *external*?

Likely not. Their long history had born many a dissident, even without factoring in outsider blood or influence. Like a nightmare made flesh, two parents everyone knew were decent, proper elves might find themselves raising a child whose nature lay in unadulterated evil. Like the monsters in the stories.

Changelings only got worse as they aged. They learned words, spells, the power to flummox and agitate the *good* elves around them. That threat alone could rock a small, closed community like an elven village. Over their long history, they'd likely been forced to deal with several of these internal blights.

And Khiirgi wondered—if she were a proper elf, how would she handle that?

She wouldn't want to leave the monster close at hand. But simply driving it out of the village was impossible. That would allow elf blood into the outside world. Killing the changeling would be simple, but killing your own kind was every bit as taboo as sharing blood. Sparsely populated villages of long-lived races feared internal conflicts more than anything. Those could easily lead to the village collapsing inward, to divisions within the race as a whole.

If anyone was to act—it was preferable that the changeling's parents took action, "voluntarily." Any lingering resentment would remain within the family confines. Other elves could remain benevolent neighbors, third parties who deplored the tragedy, wept for it, and offered consolation—while being quietly relieved. Yet not all parents chose the same course of action. Elves led long lives in return for low reproduction—wedded couples could not hope to bear many progeny. That served to intensify their affection for their flesh and blood.

How could they kill their own child? They wanted her to live, even if they could not keep her close. No matter how sad and twisted that life was.

And when she mapped that dilemma to her own life—Khiirgi dug up a groggy memory.

My eyes fluttered open. I was lying down, my parents on either side of me. They were crying.

Huh, I thought. What did I do wrong this time? Last month, I wondered what the lizard in the doorway tasted like and took a bite. Last week, I wondered what was inside the stomach of the fairy we kept and sliced it open. Two days ago, I borrowed a friend's pretty eyes to make a ring—I don't remember doing anything after that. But I probably did something. When my parents get mad or cry, it's always because of things I did.

My mother whispered an apology, hugging me.

My father murmured his sorrow and brushed my cheek.

I wasn't sure why. I was usually the one saying sorry. Today it was the other way around. Why would my parents need to apologize to their awful daughter?

Their daughter who preferred her mother crying to her delight.

Their daughter who'd rather see her father racked with anguish than smiling.

No matter how much they scolded, how they chastised me, my heart demanded more.

"_____"

I tried to ask why, but my lips wouldn't move.

My body felt sluggish, heavy. My mind hazy. A dull pain below my belly.

Oh, maybe I'm dreaming. That's good. My parents don't need to apologize, then.

Relieved, I closed my eyes. Good night, Mother. Good night, Father. Your Khiirgi will always love you both.

*   *   *

"Haaa-ha—"

So much time had passed since that night, since she left home.

The decadent world outside was so much more *packed* than her tiresome village. She'd taken to it like a fish to water; time that the average elf would register as a passing breeze felt infinitely longer to her.

She'd fled the village before they exiled her, unsure if that helped her parents. To the village, it was a clear blunder. Even if her parents were hesitant, the others should have driven her out far sooner. Call her a changeling if they pleased—but they should have acted before she gobbled up all manner of elf magic, fully intent on taking it away with her.

In hindsight—perhaps there'd been a reason for their failure. Why had they been so careless? If they didn't want her to escape, if they *had* to keep her in the village, then why not merely chain her up in the cellar?

Blood is a prerequisite for most elf magic. She could take that know-how to the outside world, but few of these secrets could be reproduced by humans. Thus, it was the *blood* they protected. That blood escaping, mingling with humans—that was their worst-case scenario, the one thing they truly feared.

So then…then…then what?

What if they had *already* taken drastic measures to prevent that?

"…Ha-ha…"

In the world of humanity, she'd dipped her toes in every type of immorality. Let herself drown in every imaginable pleasure. Treated her first human village like a buffet, mingling with old and young, male or female as the mood struck her. Never once considered using protection—rather, she'd aggressively attempted to scatter her blood. As if that was her sworn duty. A stance that did not waver even after her arrival at Kimberly.

And yet—though elves may be doomed to a low birth rate, after this many attempts, her womb's failure to conceive began to nag. Enough that she cracked jokes about the fortuity.

To know why—she need only cut herself open. Reveal the credible cause.

Why could she still not bring herself to do so?

"Rahhhhhh!"

A steely foot sliced the air. The toes scratched the skin on her cheek, and her eyes followed it sorrowfully.

Ah, dodging is such a waste. How I long for the moment when that blow will shatter my skull and send my brain meats flying. To see you standing in triumph over my battered body—hearing the roars of the crowd. You get that, Lesedi? The stories of champions out to slay the Alp—they always end in victory.

That's why, Lesedi…you are my darling hero, mine alone.

If I may plea—as the monster you defeat, I have but one request.

Before you crush my skull—please, kick me in the guts. *Right here, below the belly button. Pulp my insides so good you cannot tell intestine from anything else. So that when they perform the autopsy, even the best magic doctors cannot find anything but mincemeat and blood no matter how closely they examine me.*

Bury that credible cause forevermore.

"…Haaa-ha—ha-ha-ha—ha-ha-ha-ha-ha-ha-ha-haaaaa!"

At the six-minute mark, Gino Beltrami stepped into the ring, standing alongside Leoncio—who never looked up from his duel with Godfrey. There, Gino found his other teammate, unrecognizable, crying and laughing.

"You're a bit too buzzed, Khiirgi."

"Piss off, Barman! I can't do this shit sober!"

His reproach only earned him a howl. He sighed and elected to accept it. His words still reached her. She might be far gone, but as yet, she was still herself.

"Drunk, but not blackout. So be it. I shall focus on serving mine."

He turned his attention to his own job. Entering from the opposite passage, the Toxic Gasser's elegant drag. As fierce battles raged at either side, the Barman bowed low.

"Welcome. Do come in. What are you having?"

"Red-eye. Overflowing the mug and topped with your blood."

Tim spat vitriol like breathing. Drawing his athame, Gino shrugged.

"I'm afraid that's not the recipe we use here. But don't worry—I have a cocktail just for you."

"That's grand. But you're the one drinking today," Tim replied, pointing the tip of his blade at Gino—who frowned.

"Looking to get me drunk? You're welcome to try, but that's a tall order."

"Nah, you rotten bartender. You're always standing behind that fake counter acting all impeccable and shit—"

Even as he spoke, Tim lunged forward, closing the gap, and stabbed at his foe. Gino effortlessly deflected the attack as Tim kept talking.

"—and I'mma drag you to the ground, watch you puke your guts up!"

"…Ah, always an aspirational moment."

The Barman smiled as their blades crossed. The poisonous sword arts duel was just getting underway.

"Both teams add a third! Mr. Linton and Mr. Beltrami, the Toxic Gasser versus the Barman! A duel between alchemists!" Glenda cried, turning the audience's attention to the third clash.

"Another pair with a sordid history. But not often have we seen them go at it without access to magic tools. Mr. Linton will have to supplement his poison attacks somehow—"

Theodore cut off his amplification spell and watched the match a moment. Then he grinned.

"—doesn't seem like he's overcomplicating things. That boy's here to make his foe eat dirt."

"Phew…"

Between slashes, Gino let out a quiet breath. Laced with a boozy, beguiling perfume and a hint of sweetness, it permeated the air, entangling the Toxic Gasser in an invisible charm.

The rules for the finals eliminated tools—so neither could employ their usual stock of bottled potions. But—they were *both* alchemists. Spells with deceptive effects, production and storage of chemicals within the body, applying that to their own breaths—all in a day's work. Creating a zone of bewilderment for his Lanoff style was a key part of how the Barman had earned his rep as one of the trickiest sword hands on campus.

"Ha, your booze blade again? Some low proof on that. I could inhale it all night and not get tipsy!"

Tim was an old hand at dealing with these tricks. With his resistances, charms didn't do a lot; Gino might as well be spraying air freshener. His faculties fully unhindered, Tim's blade darted at his foe's throat.

"I'm afraid today I have a limited selection."

Deflecting the thrust, the Barman offered a sincere apology. With these rules, he couldn't exactly get anyone plastered instantly. Yet this applied to Tim as well—inevitably, their battle would peak in the later stages, when each side had accumulated a sufficient quantity.

For that reason, his plan had been to lay as many foundations as he could. Gino had begun to serve with that in mind—until he caught a shockingly toxic fume.

"——?!"

"That ain't a problem on my end."

Tim's left hand shot out between the clashing blades. Sensing a legitimate threat, Gino backed off—and his sleeve rotted away. His foe's fingers had barely brushed him. This was a Kimberly uniform, well enchanted by default—and Barman had customized that in accordance with his profession. No ordinary poison could ever damage it.

"...My."

From the tingle on his skin, he could tell it was a strong paralytoxin. Narrowing his eyes, Gino focused on his foe's left hand. There was a faint miasma wreathed around it, and he soon worked out why.

"...Poison Hand? You always were reckless."

"What, is bringing my own bottle against shop rules? Better write that on the sign!"

With a wicked grin, Tim sliced open his own palm, flicking his fingers at his opponent. The highly toxic drops of blood were deflected in two directions by Gino's spatial-magic winds.

Poison Hand had its roots in Azian assassination. Closely monitored toxins, dosed and coated over a long time frame, turned your hand itself into a secretive organ. Like Miligan's enchanted eye, all components were biological, getting it past the restrictions on magic tools. But the technique caused the wielder no small amount of pain and side effects. Most abandoned the attempt early in the process of creation, and those who didn't often found the poison took a lasting toll on their bodies.

Worse—this usually took years. But Tim had rushed the treatment through in less than a month. Functionally, it was sound, but balanced against his health—it was clear he'd never intended to keep it long. This was a gambit designed from the get-go to be *cut loose* the moment he was done here. Since mages regularly regrew severed hands, this was arguably a classic mage move—but the reckless aggression made Gino repress a sigh.

"Indeed, it's not my policy. Especially when the bottle holds *moonshine*."

He forced his voice to remain calm. Like he was placating a bad drunk. Or lecturing a hopeless student. How many times had they discussed this? He knew it all went in one ear and out the other. Yet— he could not quite bring himself to abandon the attempt.

"Alcohol's roots are medicinal. And all medicine turns poisonous at the wrong dosage. When will you learn that, Tim? That is the nature of what you so proudly scatter."

He looked the boy in the eye, querying once more the fundamentals of an alchemist's role.

"......"

Gino expected Tim's typical vulgarities. But not this time. Relentlessly coming after Gino with athame and Poison Hand alike, Tim spoke with unprecedented tranquility.

"Yo, bartender. What happens when you mess up one of your precious cocktails?"

"I throw it out. I regret my failure and polish my skills so that I may never repeat the error."

"Ha-ha, I figured. Still..."

The Toxic Gasser's eyes wavered; he made a face. That alone told Gino what was on his mind. Everything that Tim Linton had gained from meeting Alvin Godfrey. That one saving grace had kept him alive to this very day.

"...he knocked it back without a word."

"Urk—!"

That innocuous phrase sent echoes deep inside Gino. The man himself could not fully parse what emotions these were—but they rushed through him. Dregs of memories that had settled to the bottom of his bottle.

He'd made a perfect drink. Even today, he was convinced of it.

"Oh, Gino. My lovely Gino."

She picked up the glass and drained it in two gulps. He knew that gesture—it meant he'd aced it. If he'd messed up at all, she'd have turned up her nose at it, then played with the glass in her hand, sipping at it, lamenting the flavor, lambasting his errors for hours. Delighting in tormenting him.

"Your drinks are flawless. If there's anything you still lack—"

She put the empty glass down with a sad sort of smile. Gino was shaken. He'd been far too young to take the measure of her mood.

"—you don't yet know how a drunk feels. That's really it."

The next morning, Gino headed to her workshop and found it flooded by a sea of fragrant liquor.

He knew on sight—this was how she'd ended things. It had already been over the night before. He would never be forced to deal with her messy drunk act again.

He'd fallen to his knees in that amber pool, scooped up a handful of her remains, and taken a sip.

It was too much for him. He could not tell if it tasted good or foul. Like a child getting their first taste of anything alcoholic. How should he savor it? What should he make of it? He could not begin to tell.

And so—what he did was sob.

…Master, tell me this.

I've pondered it ever since. Back then—what if I had given you a different drink?

Perhaps one less than perfect?

One that made your eyes pop with how bad it was.

How dare you let this pass your master's lips. Graduation just got a lot further off. I've got a lot more to teach you. I'd have offered no apology, just listened to your red-faced lecture the whole night long.

Then—would you have stayed in this world awhile longer?

*　　*　　*

"Har?"

Tim let out a weird gurgle. His foe's hand was right there—Gino's left hand, fingers locked with Tim's *Poison* Hand.

"Then let me do the same."

With a hiss, his skin festered. The pain dizzying, his whole arm turning numb. He was resisting it as hard as he could, forcing more words out.

"Make me drink. I'll analyze it for you. Tell you where you went wrong, what you could fix to make it better. See if that process turns you into a drink of note."

No mixer whatsoever, just the raw spirits in his glass. Yet Gino believed—he'd served many a drink since losing his master. Faced many a customer, most of whom were not easily pleased. Unable to give them the buzz he desired, he'd pulled out all the stops, yet their tenacity had brought him only frustration.

And that repetition had taught him the thirst perfection cannot slake.

He'd learned that facing someone—sometimes required abandoning one's creed.

And now—yes, that final sip—today, he'd have understood.

"Lay it on me. All of you. I'll drain the glass, no matter how dead-drunk it makes me!"

"Stop, you're making me blush! Where's this romantic twist coming from?!"

Tim's tongue had lost its bite. This, he couldn't deal with. No spite, no sarcasm, just a man trying to *connect*—leaving him with far too few recourses.

As the two alchemists crossed swords, another fight on this field was nearing its climax.

"Gah—ah...!"

A powerful kick snapped Khiirgi's left knee, and she toppled over. Lesedi didn't stop there, Sky Walking into another hit. Khiirgi's tentacle snapped up to shield her, but the blow landed so hard it crumpled the block, the remaining momentum hitting Khiirgi hard in the chest.

"Kahhh—!"

"Huff—!"

Wood shards scattered, Lesedi landed soundlessly, and Khiirgi hit the ground a few yards away, spraying blood from her mouth. Her lungs half collapsed, her left leg bent the wrong way at the knee. No longer able to stand, she backed away—the athame in her right hand still aimed at her rival.

"I— I'm not done yet, Lesedi!" Khiirgi cried. "I need more... It's too much fun!"

It was almost a plea. The roots inside her reconnected her broken leg, stretched anew through the shattered tentacle arm, struggling to get her back on her feet. Coughing up blood, struggling to the final moment against the end bearing down on her. As if that was her sworn duty.

"...The evil elf is right here! Take her down...! Save those precious children! Slay the Alp...like the champions in fables..."

Summoning all the strength she had, Khiirgi unleashed one last bolt. As it bore down on her, Lesedi toppled forward, slamming both hands on thin air into a handspring over the bolt. A full forward flip into a heel kick that struck Khiirgi's athame from her hand, and as Lesedi landed, she pinned the hilt beneath her foot.

"...Evil perishes, peace returns, and the people are safe to live happily ever after?" she said. "No, thanks. Never did care for those stories. Don't you dare cast me in that role."

Even as she gave her answer, Lesedi's off hand balled into a fist. Unable to fight back, her rival stared up at her, her eyes begging—and Lesedi met that gaze.

"I never once considered myself heroic. I don't like you, so I'm here to kick the shit out of you. That ain't ever gonna change. Until you see the error of your ways, I'll be back to do the same."

Her fist lightly bumped her rival's head. Then she drew her in close, forcefully.

"Relax. I've got more ass kickings where this came from. Just not today," Lesedi growled. "Go on, sleep. That much, we all deserve. Rest comes for the good people and the evil elf alike."

"…Haaa-ha…"

With a hint of relief—Khiirgi blacked out. Lesedi fell to her knees beside her. That two-handed Sky Walk handspring had not been a choice for style or flair. It had been her only option. With her protective boots off, kicking as hard as she could—her legs were a mess, her injuries every bit as extensive as Khiirgi's.

When that spell came her way, she'd been unable to jump, much less dodge in either direction. If she'd gone for the oppositional, she'd have lost momentum and stood no chance at winning. She'd used her arms as a last resort, launching herself forward. That had been Lesedi's sole path to victory—and with that achieved, she hit her physical limit.

"…The rest is all yours, dipshits."

Calling out to her teammates, Lesedi closed her eyes. Garland came running in, catching both fighters in each arm and pulling them quickly out of harm's way.

Meanwhile, the stands were in chaos. The vaporized stage had expanded the fight's range and created blind spots. Some students were pushing up to the front rows, trying to get a better look.

"Hey, don't go there!"

"Settle the hell down!"

"The stairs are in the damn way!"

"Let us go! This is worth dying for!"

The staff were pushing back, but the students pushed harder. A group of underclassmen broke through the line, and the students on their heels pushed them farther forward.

"Ugh—"

"Augh?!"

Worse, the constant spell barrage had left a hole in the barrier right before them. The kids were pushed right over the barrier, falling into the arena.

This happened near Tim's fight with Gino, out of the corner of his eye.

"Ah!"

Tim blanched—and a projectile escaped Godfrey and Leoncio's exchange, headed right their way. Their duel was far too close for either to worry about which way they deflected each other's spells. And this happened just as Garland's hands were occupied by Lesedi and Khiirgi—while Gilchrist was positioned on the exact wrong side of Godfrey and Leoncio's fight.

Gino paid it no heed. He was against the Toxic Gasser—how could he possibly focus on anything else? Tim knew full well he *should* do the same. Too much rode on this fight to consider anything but their victory. He couldn't afford to care about students dumb enough to burst into the ring here.

He thought all that—and not long before, Tim would have acted accordingly. He'd have felt no compunctions about that choice. The old Tim had nothing to protect outside of Godfrey and the Watch.

"You're a wonderful person, Mr. Linton."

And yet—

Those dumbass kids, falling in—brought another face to mind.

"Dammit!"

Tim broke away from the duel, into a run. Leaping in front of his panicking juniors, chanting an oppositional against the inbound flames. But this was a stray blast from *their* duel. Tim's output couldn't begin to cancel it. He'd have to use his body as a shield—and steeled himself to do just that. Red and gold flames filled his vision...

"____?"

A moment later, he wasn't burned to a crisp—which was baffling.

And another moment later, he realized this was because the very man he'd been fighting had soaked the burn for him.

"...The hell are you doing?" he murmured.

Gino had stepped in right as the oppositional hit, and when the flames proved undeterred, he'd soaked them on his back. On the brink of death, Gino mustered a feeble reply.

"...Your sudden exit surprised me, patron. I have not made you drunk yet."

Tim tried to argue further, but Gino sealed those words off with his lips.

"____?!"

This proved one straw too many for the Toxic Gasser, and he froze up, unable to think of a way to fend this off. The saliva flowing into his mouth contained a powerful paralytic that swiftly invaded his entire body.

Having narrowly managed to complete his task, Gino pulled his lips away.

"...It seems...I've had a bit too much to drink. How very...unlike me..."

With that self-deprecating whisper, he crumpled—his arms still around Tim. That made Tim's legs give out, too. Studying his rival's unconscious face, inches from his own, Tim swore.

"Well, shit. You even look good blacked out."

He had an urge to punch him for it but no longer had the strength. Even with his resistances, he couldn't stave off the paralysis of direct injection from someone with Gino's skills. He had no feeling in his hands and feet, and his vision was narrowing by the second.

The man he loved was still up there fighting, and he caught one last look, muttering, "Sorry, Prez... I'm...dropping out..."

"With one pair down, Mr. Linton and Mr. Beltrami bow out, too! Problems in the audience played a factor—but...well, that's a twist I sure didn't see coming!"

You could hear the surprise in Glenda's voice. Watching Gilchrist's spells toss students back out of the ring, Theodore smiled. Even if Tim hadn't stepped in, the faculty would have been there in time. Nonetheless, he was disinclined to dismiss his students' choices.

"I saw the signs," Theodore said. "Mr. Linton's a changed man. Enough that an impulse like that no longer feels out of character."

He turned his attention back to the stands, a rare glint of steel in his tone.

"Underclassmen pushing to the front—back off now, before I get mad. Every one of you owes them a debt. Mr. Linton would have done the same no matter who fell in. And I'm sure you're aware by now—at a school like this, a man like him's a rare commodity."

The students stopped pushing, and after a brief stall—they began moving to the back again, surprisingly orderly. Not just because the faculty were glaring at them, either. Quite a few of their eyes were on Tim, as Garland carried him to safety.

Their teammates were going down in pairs. Catching those eliminations out of the corners of their eyes, Godfrey and Leoncio both broke off the spell duel. Neither suggested it, but both their circumstances demanded it. The no-holds-barred barrage had walked a tightrope no other student could have matched, leaving both dizzyingly drained.

Still at range, they glared at each other down the length of their athames. Managing to catch his breath at last, Leoncio threw out a question.

"Tell me, Godfrey. What are your thoughts on perfection?"

Godfrey looked perplexed. But he was born diligent and gave it his best shot.

"Hard to say. Not a notion I've ever been near."

Smirking at how predictable that response was, Leoncio put a hand to his chest.

"I'm closer to it than anyone else here. I was brought into this world expected to embody the concept."

He let out a sigh, eyes drifting to the ceiling. His beautiful smile turned rather sour.

"But these days—I believe there is no curse more absurd."

His fists clenched so tight the bones creaked as he voiced this for the first time ever. His own rejection of the Echevalria mission. The primal fury that drove him.

"What *is* perfection? Where does the standard lie? Who made that up—and when? If someone made that decision before I was born, then were they more perfect than me?"

"I'm considering dropping out."

It had been a year since he'd invited Percival Whalley to join his followers. The boy had arrived looking unusually cornered and opened with those words.

"…I suppose I should ask why?" said Leoncio.

"I can't take it. I've got no talent. I'm sure you're well aware."

Whalley's head was down, his fists clenched, feeling powerless and beaten.

At Kimberly, students were perpetually locked in combat. It was hardly the first or last time a student arrived where he had. Unable to find their own strength, unable to overcome their inadequacies—they found their feet leading them to the door.

Whalley was on the verge of this, and that made Leoncio's eyes narrow.

"Are you testing me? Though you dismiss your own potential?"

"___!"

Whalley bit his lip, saying nothing. Leoncio rose from the couch.

"Who put these thoughts in your head? They're in your year, I'm sure. Name names."

"...I..."

"Don't get ahead of yourself. I'm not offering tawdry retribution. I will be investigating their abilities and then providing you with a strategy to defeat them yourself. To prove your earlier claim wrong."

He took a firm grip on the boy's shoulders as if dragging his heart back into the fight. His lips quivered with anger, the heat audible in his tone.

"You are my successor, Percy. I saw the potential in you and chose you for the role," Leoncio told him. "Why does that not earn your faith? Why succumb to negativity, when you should take pride in that fact?!"

"How dare you *give up*!"

Leoncio's roar shook the arena. He spun around, raking the stunned crowd with his glare, allowing the fury to erupt from him.

"Such arrogance! What do you humdrums know? You have no value?! You've crested the peak, and it's all downhill from here? The prattling of fools! None of you even know what you're worth to begin with, so why do you think you're capable of deciding you have none?!"

This had rankled him. Ever since he was too young to put the anger into words, Leoncio Echevalria had let this fury fester deep within. The words he'd wanted to shout at every soul who left him.

"Know that you know nothing! Trust me, instead! I shall decide if you are worthy! I shall find a place for every one of you, find a way to make the most of your talents! Enough with your misplaced disappointment! Stop with the casual self-harm! You are all just getting started!"

As he roared, a witch's face crossed his mind.

Diana Ashbury. The world's fastest broomrider, the mage who'd sped through life swifter than anyone.

She'd undoubtedly completed her path, and not one student alive doubted her greatness. But—while she still lived, Leoncio had been waiting. Waiting for the day she tried and *failed*. So that when she crumpled, he might take her hand and guide her life in a *new* direction. Show her the life that lay beyond.

If she failed to set a new record, then her life would be a failure. Ashbury may not have said that in so many words, but he could tell that was how she thought, and Leoncio could not abide it. He'd been seething below the surface. It made no sense.

Why do you insist on limiting yourself? Why do you not get that you can be anything? Whether you break the record, even if you abandon the broom altogether—you are a human possessed of infinite fascination.

There is always a next time. If one path closes on you—as long as you live, another will open.

"And if that fails, if you still cannot find meaning in your life?" Leoncio demanded. "Then I shall send you off. In a ball of beautiful golden fire!"

His voice pained, Leoncio raised his burning wand before his eyes. Like a funeral rite. With that one gesture, he lamented all lives lost before him.

"So know this to be true. With time, meaning will come! Your lives or deaths, within me!"

A solemn declaration. The students watching were silenced, beyond words. Aware he spoke not just to those who had died, but to every single one of them.

The old council leader had never before exposed his heart like this. His words spun from the heart within. A side of his rival Godfrey had never seen—and that came as a relief.

"…For the first time," he said, smiling, "I wouldn't mind if you won, Leoncio."

He raised his athame again, back bolt upright, pushing aside his fatigue, rousing himself.

Only then could he face this man. To fight a man this powerful, he had to be his own self.

"So the rest—is just me being stubborn."

What could be better? Leoncio grinned. They forgot about spells, both plunging straight in, blades slammed together, feet locked to the floor as they pushed against each other. No magic, let alone swordplay. A contest akin to a children's squabble—and thus, the resolve was also free of technique.

""Rahhhhhhh!!!""

Overlapping howls. Fingers balled, their left hands swung in, punching each other's cheeks. The impact forced them apart, but they closed the gap in the blink of an eye, once again punching their opponent's face with all the might they had. No trace of thought. Blows faster than meaning, blows so hard they knocked meaning away. This felt unbearably right, and they couldn't get enough of it—dragging their minds back to consciousness again and again.

Teeth broke, blood spurted, cheekbones cracked. Their faces became increasingly wrecked, yet both were flashing identical smiles. As if they'd just now realized this was what they'd always wanted to do. And—rather than apologize for taking so long, they let their fists speak for them.

"____"

"…This isn't exactly…"

Watching, stunned, the Sword Roses knew—this was no longer *myth*. Both men had leaped from those heights, engaging in mortal loggerheads.

And yet, that made sense. These mages existed in mythical realms— which was exactly why they needed this. Leaving all logic and meaning behind, seeking only to be as they were wont to be. That was permitted—perhaps here and only here.

Oliver believed in the unconditional value of this enterprise. And so he watched, not allowing himself the luxury of blinking, searing it all into his eyes. Soaking in the light he would not forget, no matter where his spell took him.

"...Ahhh..."

Before that same sight, Nanao couldn't help but smile. Much the same as the smile she'd worn watching Oliver and Andrews fight. Admiration—and envy.

"That's what I call a brawl...," she whispered.

He'd no clue how many punches Godfrey had thrown. But when this one bounced off his cheek, Leoncio's vision went black.

"Oh..."

The ground vanished; his knees buckled. All his senses floated away.

"Don't go down! Is that all you've got, Leoncio?!"

A voice from the stands. Light came rushing back, and Leoncio's eyes darted toward it: Percival Whalley, standing proud and tall, a far cry from when they'd first met.

"...Of course not, Percy," he said with a chuckle. His legs moved; he caught a thrust on his athame and grabbed Godfrey's collar. Their foreheads collided, eyes locked inches apart.

"...I'm here...to win, Godfrey. You heard him...right? I've got...a fine successor..."

"...Yeah..."

Godfrey's free hand went to the back of Leoncio's head. His palm grabbed tight, holding him still. His eyes, too, were on a junior—his teammate in the passage leading out, surrounded by the students he'd saved, all working to heal him. Something he'd never imagined happening to Tim Linton.

"...True for us both."

That gave Godfrey one last reserve of strength. His opponent pushed, so he worked with that, a one-armed headlock pulling down on his torso. Their blades locked in between—and this led Godfrey's tip to Leoncio's chest, burying it deep.

"Kah..."

A breath escaped Leoncio's lips. His hands went limp, and the athame slipped from his fingers.

"......You bastard..."

Spitting words and blood, he started to crumple—supported only by the hand locked on Godfrey's collar. Fingers shaking, he touched Godfrey's cheek, looking him in the eye.

"Promise...me this. Don't...let anyone best you."

Godfrey didn't hesitate. He just nodded. A dazzling response. Leoncio's eyes wavered and then his lids closed, hiding that look.

"...I never made you mine...my beloved...Purgatory."

With that, the last of his strength left him. He crumpled, but his body never reached the ground. Godfrey dropped his athame and put both arms around Leoncio instead.

That settled things. Everyone knew it was over, concluded.

No matches followed. Any reason to hold them was gone. No one wished to sully this with meaningless fights—all teams but Godfrey's voluntarily dropped out.

And the festivities ended. A sight to remember, carved into the minds of many a student—and curtains descended on the passion and fury of the Kimberly combat league.

CHAPTER 3

Courting

The day after the combat league concluded, the hype not yet died down—the students cast their votes for president. The faculty carefully reviewed the results, which would be announced that very afternoon.

"AHHH-HA-HA-HA-HA! The ultimate high! Watching your inevitable victory come to pass!"

Laughing maniacally, Miligan stood at the center of the Forum, the banquet hall on the school building's fourth floor. Oliver's group was sitting awkwardly at the table with her. Nanao alone was cheerily helping herself to the snacks provided, while the rest were largely occupied with apologizing for Miligan. They were stressing this not just because their class belonged in the Fellowship, but because Whalley's camp was parked nearby.

"...Y-you're certainly in good spirits, Ms. Miligan."

"Chela, you may as well begin addressing me as *President* Miligan now. It's a foregone conclusion. The votes are cast! My election is set in stone!"

Chela had been quietly trying to tone her down, but Miligan was in no state to do anything like that. Katie had her head buried in her hands. Attitude aside, Miligan had every reason to be confident—given the candidates running, she was the logical choice for Godfrey's camp to back. And having dominated two levels of the combat league, his camp's victory was assured.

"You did your best, Mr. Whalley! But the advantage of years is not easily overcome. Had you been a year ahead of me, perhaps this would have been different! A thought that must rankle. But wipe your tears away! Victory is ever a harsh mistress!"

She'd turned on her rival, living it up. Whalley's brow twitched, but he knew he'd lost and wisely said nothing. To the kids stuck between them, that was far more terrifying than if he'd taken the bait. Especially for Oliver, who'd been avidly recruited by Whalley not long ago.

But in actual practice, that was hardly the greatest burden on their minds. Before the election, Godfrey had sent out a directive—and one kept secret from Miligan herself. That was pouring oil on their discomfort.

Unable to handle it any longer, Guy leaned in, whispering, "Katie…"

"…I know. But please. Don't breathe a word."

She knew only too well how he felt but insisted on silence. That left Guy and the others with no choice. They would just have to sit here in this hot pot, until Garland's voice rang out and brought an end to it:

"Silence! Students, the wait is over. We're prepared to announce the election results."

"Say it loud, Master!" Miligan cried. "Today marks the birth of Kimberly's first ever pro-rights student body president!"

Garland didn't bat an eye. Oliver was deeply impressed. If he'd been in the sword master's shoes, he wouldn't have maintained that poker face.

"Before the announcement, let's look over the campaign once more," Garland began. "As I'm sure you're all aware, this was a particularly hard-fought contest. Both sides were forced to review their strengths and weaknesses—and thoroughly reexamine the positions they espoused. Demonstrating the fierceness of this struggle, we see markedly different results from each school year."

Heedless of the eager looks around, the man launched into the necessary preamble. Elections proving overly dramatic was a Kimberly thing, but the announcement of the results need not follow suit. This was a vital moment that would determine the future of Kimberly, and the gravity in his voice served as a pointed reminder of that fact.

"Thus, we can say for certain these results were not merely a reflection of the combat league standings. Bear that in mind as you hear the outcome."

A silence settled over the room. Completely certain her name would follow, Miligan fidgeted, eager to launch into her victory speech. And at last, the word came down.

"The next Kimberly Magic Academy student body president will be the sixth-year student Tim Linton. Step up to the podium."

At least a third of the students present looked aghast, turning to the boy in question. He'd been sitting in sullen silence in the corner, and now he quietly rose to his feet.

"...'Sup."

Still in full drag, Tim cut across the sea of stares, stepping up to the podium at the back of the Forum. Miligan watched him go, blinking furiously, her mind not able to process this at all.

"..................Mm?"

"Steady, Ms. Miligan," Katie said, putting her arms around the witch's shoulders. The rest of the Sword Roses kept their eyes down, like they were attending a wake.

Tim glanced at them, then around the room, then cast an amp spell on his wand. Looking tense.

"...Uh, so yeah. I'm as shocked as you are. Gonna ramble a bit here. Hope that helps us all figure this out."

With that, he paused for several seconds. The audience hung on to his every word.

"Honestly, I didn't think I'd be picked. Ain't really the type for this sorta thing. Plus, I filled the Fellowship with poison once—no way someone like that would end up president. I figured everyone here's heard about that, right?" he asked the crowd. "I ain't making excuses. Where my head was at then, I was ready to murder everyone. Hated the shit outta this place. Students killing or feeding off each other—it was just like where I grew up."

Tim had nothing to hide, so he put it all out there. The students watched, waiting to see where this was going.

"You ever heard of the bug urn? One way they whip up poison out in Chena. Basically, you fill an urn with a bunch of poison bugs, have 'em eat each other, and use the last survivor to make your poison. Real nasty shit. Anyone who knows anything knows that's halfway to a full-on curse." He continued: "I was raised in one of those urns. Harsh truth, but the Lintons did that shit with *people*. Grabbed promising kids up from all over, dosed 'em all with poison, and fed the ones who died to the survivors. I was the one who lived. The poison bug who survived on the flesh of his siblings. That ain't a metaphor: I *literally* survived a bug urn."

That got gasps from everyone. The Toxic Gasser was infamous for his freakish tolerance for his own virulent poisons, but the reasons were even worse than they'd imagined.

"Coming from that, I thought the whole world was shit. Didn't imagine I'd live that long. Coming to Kimberly didn't change much. Same filth I had back home, just watered down a tad. And honestly, it *was* a whole lot shittier than it is today. No safe spaces anywhere on campus. In my eyes, everyone looked like a starving insect."

A bitter smile played on his lips, then he got serious again.

"That's when I ran into Godfrey. When he first came knocking, I thought he was off his rocker. Everything he did and said was batshit. No matter how many times I drove him off, he wasn't dissuaded. He drank my poison, collapsed on the spot, came rolling back in the next day like it was nothing. Then this Watch madness? Gathering comrades, trying to change this place? Insisting it could be done, without a soul backing him?"

To the side of the podium, Godfrey sat with arms folded, arguing with none of this. Tim glanced his way once, then leaned in.

"But when I doused the Fellowship with toxins, ready to bid this world adieu—Godfrey alone waded right into the toxic fumes and dragged me out. Do you get how it feels to have a life you discarded picked up by someone without even asking for it? I threw in the towel. What I did with myself from then on was all in his hands."

Tim's grin grew bashful. Seeing that, Oliver sensed that was the moment this boy's life had truly begun.

"Everything after that felt like the strangest dream. Our ranks swelled, we found one way after another to get shit done, his madness proved practicable. That's when I realized Godfrey'd never been crazy. The other way around—he was the one sane man in this madhouse. And he was there reminding everyone: We ain't poison bugs, we ain't kindling—we're human goddamn beings."

The words were flowing freely now. This was the essence of the Watch's efforts. The unshakable core of his beliefs.

"None of this came easy. Can't recall a single easy second. Nearly got killed by monstrous upperclassmen so many times, had kids our year or younger on our ass on the daily. As our numbers rose, internal conflicts surfaced, and we fought each other. That led to one of my friends getting pushed out. Could I have done more for her? I still lose sleep wondering."

Having been there to the bitter end, Oliver knew exactly who he meant. And how Tim regretted not being there for her.

"But lately I worked something out. I actually kinda like looking after you assholes. When I'm fussing over my juniors, all my regrets fade away, and the world's colors start coming back. I wanna see how far that takes me. I might have had this big old 'president' title slapped on me, but it ain't gonna change what I do. If a kid's in trouble, I'll hear 'em out, step in if need be, and if someone tries to stop me, throw some poison to shut 'em up. Don't give a damn who they are—or what they are."

He finished strong, then breathed out.

"That's about all I got. Dunno if that counts as much of an acceptance speech. But I hope it tells you a bit about just who you placed in charge."

He flashed a grin and was done. Having heard him out, Godfrey took over the podium, facing the students assembled.

"Alvin Godfrey, former president. I'm gonna take the liberty of saying a few words here, but only a few. I put my faith and the future of the Watch in Tim Linton's hands, and I know he'll live up to my expectations. I imagine many of you voted for him because you felt the same—and to add a gentle breeze to your sails, there's one more thing I want you to know."

He paused for a moment before continuing.

"In the senior league finals, problems in the stands resulted in underclassman falling into the ring. Tim ran to help them instead of finishing the match. When I saw that, I decided to back him for the presidency. If he'd ignored the threat to his juniors and moved to ensure our victory, that would have made him *my* ally—not *yours*. But that's not Tim. When push came to shove, he made the right choice. He knew who he should protect, who I've been striving to protect all along."

He turned to face Tim, who'd sat down near the stage. Godfrey shot him a warm smile.

"That tickled me pink. Thrilled me so much I wanted to run out and tell the whole world about it."

Those words hit Tim hard, and he clapped a hand to his face, head down. Godfrey watched him a moment, then turned back to the crowd.

"Unshakable evidence your new president has got what it takes. I'll admit—he's lacking experience. He may cause you some headaches. But I know that where he falls short, you'll step up to help him. If you do that, he'll wind up being a far better president than I ever was," he said. "Consider the torch passed. People—look after my buddy here."

He bowed low, and that ended his speech. Oliver's group started clapping, and that got the rest of the room to do the same. That, more than anything, spoke to their genuine faith in the new leadership.

"…Uhhh…?"

Miligan alone was left at sea, her shoulders visibly drooping. Without a word, Katie and Chela each put their arms around her.

* * *

After all the Sword Roses made their apologies to Miligan, they left Katie in charge of aftercare. At three that same day, the crest of the election behind him—Oliver put his mind to what came next.

"...Haah..."

Seated in a lounge, he allowed himself a sigh. Once his league final ended, he'd rested as much as he could, so it wasn't fatigue blocking his thoughts. The problems before him were all simply too massive to handle in any condition.

First, Katie. They'd come together and talked it over but resolved nothing. For her own safety, they needed to take steps soon.

Then, Chela. She was acting fine, but clashing with her father in public had to hurt. Oliver would have to find a moment to talk about it with her—and help her heal.

Finally, what happened with Nanao after the victory party. They were clearly dragging that around and had barely made eye contact all day. Not only was this in urgent need of resolution, it directly involved Oliver himself.

"...Where do I even begin...?" he whispered, clutching his head.

As he shriveled up, a familiar presence approached from behind.

"Lot on your mind? Yeah, I can imagine."

He turned to find Guy looking down at him. Before Oliver said a word, Guy took a seat next to him. Clearly aware of what was on Oliver's mind, he got right down to brass tacks.

"Not to butt in or anything, but for now—lemme handle Katie. I'm gonna be stuck on Miligan duty with her anyway. I'll keep an eye on her then."

"Guy..."

"I'm also worried about Chela, after that nasty business with her dad. But I'm looking out for her, and she won't fall apart that easy. If there's a problem you gotta handle *now*, it's Nanao."

A simple ranking by priority based on the info he had. At a loss for words, Oliver stared at his hands. His profile alone proved he was unusually far gone. Guy pulled out his wand and cast a soundproofing spell. Digging deeper.

"...Can I ask? What exactly happened?"

"......"

"Okay, hard to talk about. I'm guessing not just your run of the mill fight, then."

Not rushing him, Guy sat back and waited. It took him a long time to work up the nerve to share, but at last Oliver managed it.

"She...came on to me. That...should tell you everything."

Guy's eyes went wide, not having expected the answer to be that unvarnished.

"For real...?" He groaned, rubbing his temples.

"Don't...jump to conclusions. The fault is mine," Oliver stressed. "I wasn't paying enough attention to her state of mind."

Guy put up a hand, stopping him. Whose fault it was, what had led to it—neither mattered to him.

"Let's break this down real simple. If you're not into her..."

That was what really mattered. Oliver was already shaking his head. He looked ready to cry, so Guy kept his voice placid.

"I figured. Then you'd best give it some thought. Are you up for taking that step? In, y'know, a peaceful manner."

He was just stating the obvious, but once he had, his head started spinning. Part of Guy wanted to give his friend a push, but part of him suspected he was being awfully tactless. He scratched his head.

"Or am I rushing this? Nah, that's the thing. If Nanao gets there first, Katie and Pete won't object. I mean, they'll grumble, but..."

"...? Why Pete...?"

That name just brought questions. Oliver had certainly been aware of Katie's straightforward affections, but the bespectacled boy was still out of sight, out of mind. Guy rubbed his brow.

"You didn't notice? Fine, forget I said anything. For now, focus on

Nanao. I don't need the deets, but I'm guessing she wants to make it physical?"

"…That's…half of it…"

"Then leave the other half for later. I got nothin' for that half," said Guy. "…Either way, I bet she just wants to be special to you. All your unique baggage aside…you two have always been tight."

Guy pushed all the other factors out of the way, paring the topic down to its essence. Well aware that was forced, but also convinced it was his role here. His friend always overthought these things, so coming at him from this angle might help him adjust.

"……"

Knowing Guy's simplicity was appropriate, Oliver still couldn't make the next step.

Sensing that step was a huge deal for him, and confident this was violating boundaries, Guy stepped right into it.

"You're hesitating. Is that because of Nanao, or…?"

As he asked, Guy watched Oliver closely. Oliver hung his head and shook it listlessly.

"…Pretty sure the hang-up's on my end," he managed.

Guy nodded. That made the answer obvious.

"Okay, cool. Then tell her that."

"Huh?"

"It's a big freakin' deal, right? If you lay it on her, Nanao'll get it. And that info'll help her figure out how to approach you. If it's, like, a family secret thing? Well…at least tell her how you feel about it."

Don't dwell on it alone, work through it together. No need to share the specifics *here*. Part of Guy was frustrated to be left out, but if he demanded inclusion, then he'd just give Oliver something else to fret about, and he didn't want that. Guy was convinced it was his job to be the easiest Sword Rose to talk to.

And in light of that, he threw a heartfelt arm around Oliver's shoulders.

"Ya feel me? Don't stress over this alone. Talk it out; see what you make of it together. In my mind, that's called trusting your friends."

Oliver nodded, digesting those words. He'd looked inside and found that trust. In which case—he need only find the courage.

Letting that conversation loop through his mind, Oliver made his way down the hall, and as the crowds thinned, a new voice popped up right beside him.

"You're troubled."

Unsurprised, he turned to face her. This girl served as his covert operative.

"…Teresa."

"I am seeking your opinion on our performance in the main round of the combat league. I am not pleased with the outcome, but I wanted to ask again for your evaluation of it."

He'd been expecting a report, but this was clearly a personal question. Unusual. Her team had gotten pretty amped up at the party the other day, so perhaps that was still nagging at her. That thought made him smile.

"Naturally, I thought it was a good match. Can't say you fully realized your team's strengths, but I could tell you were feeling your way through an unfamiliar situation…"

"Appreciated. I take it this means you approve of my performance."

She pushed ahead to the conclusion. This rattled him a bit. Was she *not* here for an evaluation?

"I am aware this is presumptuous, but might I beg for a reward?"

"If it's something I'm capable of, sure."

"Then I request a celebratory kiss."

Teresa looked dead serious about this. The intensity versus the contents of the request perplexed him, but it was a small price to pay. He raised an eyebrow but nonetheless knelt down next to her, amused at the thought of imitating what Chela had once done. Even Oliver was a bit surprised by how little resistance he had to kissing Teresa on the cheek. It seemed entirely natural to him. And fortunately, there was no one looking.

"Not there. *Here*."

That changed everything. Teresa had blocked the kiss to her cheek and was pointing to her lips. Oliver blinked at her, pulling away.

"...Teresa, that—"

"Gives you pause?"

"...It means...very different things."

"Does it? Yet you did this with *her*."

Her words a javelin flung right back at him, sinking into Oliver's chest. Reminding him that those events had been right after the party, and they'd just seen the second-years off to their dorm. Teresa had been making merry with her teammates, so he'd assumed she'd accompanied them—but given her primary role, that was unthinkable. She'd have split off from her friends soon after leaving the building and quickly resumed her real job. Nothing remarkable about it.

"...You saw—?"

"Unfortunately. As my task demands."

Again, she talked over him, looking him right in the eye, her voice tense. Only now did he realize her behavior was rooted in fury. Even as the realization dawned, she spoke again.

"Allow me to formally inquire. Was that act desired on your part?"

"...Well..."

That took his breath away. How should he answer? He wasn't immediately sure. Even if it hadn't been something he'd desired, he didn't want to sound like he was blaming Nanao for it. He was convinced his own carelessness had driven her to that act.

But in this moment, silence was disastrous. Teresa was already acutely aware of her master's character. If he had desired the act, he would have said so. Any other response meant he was carefully picking his words to avoid discrediting Nanao.

Which meant anything other than swift agreement was all the

answer Teresa needed. Namely—her master had been *assaulted*. And that was unpardonable.

"I understand completely. You did not desire it. She forced that act upon you."

"——! Wai—"

He worked out what she was thinking a moment too late and tried to stop her—but at a speed that left all that behind, she threw her arms around his chest.

"I adore you, my lord. Awake or asleep, I have no eyes for anyone else."

The passion in her words shook him deep. As he stood frozen, Teresa pushed through his robe to his shirt, rubbing her cheeks and nose on it. Like she was imprinting her scent on them. Like a vow to let no one else impinge upon him. Or perhaps—a curse.

"And right now…my blood is boiling."

Her ritual done, Teresa turned her mind to a completely new objective. Oliver tried to grab her, but her heat vanished from his embrace. He gaped at his empty arms, eyes wide, and he called out to his surroundings.

"Teresa?! Where are you?!"

But no answer came. He couldn't even detect her retreat, but he knew where her feet carried her. She was making a beeline toward the subject of this vendetta. Driven by anger, she would make no stops along the way.

"——!"

Oliver whipped out three scout golems and shared their vision, racing down the hall. This was the worst possible timing. He and Nanao had kept their distance from each other since the events in question, so he had no clue where she was or what she was doing.

Unaware of her approaching predicament, Nanao was aimlessly wandering the second layer of the labyrinth, the bustling forest.

"…Hrm. Is that the summit?"

She paused, looking up. She'd been climbing the irminsul and found herself nearly at the top. Choosing steep paths, urged by a vague desire for greater heights, she'd pressed on—but hadn't been trying to get here in particular. Her unexpected speed was the result of an absence of obstacles—she hadn't encountered a single beast along the way.

"…Hmm."

With nothing better to do, she absently scanned the whole floor. This brought back memories of the rolling hills back home, and she was rather fond of it. But today she was disinclined to take any trips down memory lane. The indiscretion she'd committed occupied the majority of her mind.

"…I am at a loss. How can I make it up to him? Time passes, yet I find no threads to follow."

Hearing her own words made her wince. Threads or no, after her misdeeds, the desire to wrap this up neatly was itself presumptuous.

And part of her wondered—even if, by some miracle, this state of affairs was resolved, would she be capable of being by Oliver's side afterward?

It had been too much for her. The sight of his duel with Richard Andrews.

How it agonized her to know that no such battle could ever occur between her and him.

Nanao had grasped at every straw to control that urge. Followed every form of meditation, followed all the advice Chela and Katie had given. Made more friends, tried new things, attempted to dilute her passion between them. All these things had done their part. They alone were how she'd gone this long without taking a swing at him.

Yet another part of her knew—those approaches could buy her no more time.

In which case…what should she do next?

"…Urgh…"

She shook off these dark thoughts. This was beyond "*The thoughts of a fool are indistinguishable from a nap."* The more she pondered it, the deeper her heart sank. Conclusions reached in this state would hardly be accurate. At the least, she still knew that.

Nanao took a deep breath, trying to still her heart. Some unsuspecting third-years nearby passed her. One pointed at her back.

"Yo, that's Ms. Hibiya! From the league champion team—"

"Wait, don't bug her."

"Something feels off. Let's just move along."

When he cheerily tried to approach, his friends quickly dragged him away. By their third year, most students developed a sixth sense for these things—and they avoided Nanao for much the same reasons as the beasts on her climb did. They went behind her, keeping their distance. Feeling them fade into the distance, she sighed.

"Of all days for no one to pick a fight… A duel might well free my mind."

Not a thought she'd ordinarily entertain. Half her purpose in roaming here was an absent search for trouble, but ironically, few at Kimberly were foolish enough to throw down with Nanao now. They'd see just how good she was in the combat league, and worse—knew her weaknesses had been compensated for. When they'd had a shot at winning through schemes or compatibility, sure; but with that off the table, no one wanted to mess with her. Perhaps someone from the upper classes—but assaulting a junior delving solo would be an affront to their honor.

Standing here did not seem to be getting her anywhere. Abandoning hope, Nanao turned to head back.

"My head spins in place, moving nowhere. Perhaps I should merely steel my stomach."

She began her descent. No good ideas to be found, her feet like lead. Ordinarily, she would be delighted to head to the Sword Roses' base after exploring, but today each step closer fanned the flames of her fears. Wondering if Oliver would be there. What she should say to him if he was.

"Hrm?"

But not long after she stepped off the branches of the giant tree into the woods below, an unexpected salvation dragged her from the depths of her melancholy.

"...My, my. Hostility like unto the naked blade."

She could feel the prick of it upon her skin, and she let out a soft chuckle. *There.* She could not see them but knew for a fact that in the darkness lurked someone intent on causing her harm. This was no mild aggression. Mirthless retribution, pure bloodlust—like a samurai on the path of vengeance.

"I know not who you may be. Where or what manner of grudge I have incurred—the nature of it eludes me," Nanao said. "But why let that stop us? Why waste time with queries?"

Deeply thankful, she drew her blade, casting a dulling spell at half strength. Nothing but gratitude for the foe who'd come after her now.

She had but one more request— *Do not be easily bested.*

"Ready when you are. *Draw.*"

Katana at her side, Nanao issued a challenge. She could feel them move. In the green-tinged gloom around her, they moved helter-skelter, never letting her pin them down.

"You've no intent of showing yourself? You must be some manner of spy."

Having determined the nature of her foe, Nanao returned her blade to its scabbard. This didn't mean she'd dropped her stance. The scabbard held in her left hand, her right palm resting lightly on the hilt—

"Then make full use of your wiles—and make your way into my range."

Hibiya-style Tachi-Iai Ring Stance. Stealthy opponents attacked from where you least expected, and this was a classic counter—allowing her to issue swift reprisal no matter the direction. But in Nanao's case—

"Gladio!"

—the range of her iai was tenfold.

"......!"

The spell was flung directly at the thicket where Teresa lurked.

Thirty-plus trees in its path, all sturdy trunks, well past the point where "sapling" applied, toppled over before her eyes. Looking down at that from her perch on a tilting branch gave her goose bumps.

That output was broken. Her foe might be a third-year, but even by that standard, this was not what any singlecant severing spell Teresa knew could do. And even more chilling: the cross sections. They weren't just smooth; they gleamed like polished metal. That sharpness must be a factor in the absurd force.

"Gladio—Gladio—Flamma!"

Just three spells. That was all the incantations it took to flatten the forest in a twenty-yard radius around her enemy. The fire spell that followed ignited it all, the output once again uncanny, the raging flames designed to flush an opponent out of hiding.

"...Copifigura...!"

She'd be downed in no time, so Teresa quietly whispered a spell, releasing the result into the darkness. Enchanting her robe with the oppositional, she threw herself into the flames.

Nanao had just unleashed a second fire spell when a figure came darting out of the brush to one side.

"Gladio!"

Her magic blade aimed true, severing the torso—and the figure vanished. As it did, the *real* Teresa fired an electric bolt from atop a fallen, burning tree—from the rear. Aimed right at the end of Nanao's swing, yet the samurai smoothly shifted into an about-face, using her two-handed Flow Cut to catch the spell on her katana and deflect it to the ground behind.

With that handled, Nanao's eyes turned to the flames—but her foe was already gone.

"Splinters, mm? I rather thought I'd seen my fill of those in the last tourney. *Gladio!*"

The technique had seen wide use in the combat league's free-for-all.

Another figure leaped out from behind a fallen tree, and she sent an iai spell after it. She showed no surprise when it swiftly vanished; she'd kept the bulk of her attention on her surroundings. Sheathing her blade once more, Nanao considered the matter. She'd certainly been bedeviled by the two types of splinters in the league, but this was not the same.

"The quality of your splinters is no match for Mr. Mistral's. Rather, the presence of the real body is unnaturally faint. To the point where I cannot distinguish you from your splinters, even in motion."

That was her read on it—the last attack had proven her opponent was swiftly darting about between the flames and fallen timber. Moving at that speed should make it far easier to detect them, yet "should" clearly did not apply here. Save the fleeting moment of an incantation, this foe was always as hazy as the splinters they created.

"You've piqued my interest."

Clearly, they were well trained. But the strength of her foe brought an indomitable grin to Nanao's lips. Feeling her cycle of fretting draining away by the second, Nanao waited for her opponent's next move.

"…She's a monster…," Teresa whispered.

The fight thus far had driven that fact home.

She'd been *seen*. Both her strengths and the strategies they lent themselves to. She knew whatever she did, it would be handled. No amount of splinter subterfuge, no angle of attack—Teresa could not picture any of those attacks breaching her target's defenses.

That alone was one thing. If that was the ceiling, she could accept it. What truly galled Teresa: Her enemy was still not *serious*. She was playing wait and see, responding only when attacked.

Her stance, unmoving and unyielding, demonstrated that fact. And Teresa's mind refused to accept it. She'd been running all over, yet her target had yet to take a single step in any direction.

"…Ha-ha…"

Despite the dire straits, her lips were twitching: *Right. Good.* Be *a monster.*

If a mere human had defiled her master, that would have complicated things. But a monster—that she could kill. Monsters were a detriment to humankind. Left unchecked, they'd bring no end of suffering.

And she wasn't about to stand for that. Refused to let it happen again. So what if the monster was stronger?

"...Copifigura... Copifigura... Copifigura..."

Teresa flitted soundlessly from tree to tree, dropping as many splinters as she could. A glance upward, verifying the position of the second layer's artificial sun. These conditions were her one shot at victory— now she need merely wait for the moment to arrive.

Groundwork laid, Teresa thought: *If you are a monster, then I am a vengeful spirit.*

Clinging to human obsessions, even in death. An evil soul, a curse that will claim your life.

"Hrm?"

Locked in an iai stance, ready for her assailant's next attempt— Nanao noticed the world around her growing dark.

"An eclipse? Or..."

Stance unwavering, her gaze flicked toward the light source. A false sun that kept the second floor bathed in a perpetual glow. Between it and Nanao's position, a colossal leaf on the irminsul. A parasol absent mere moments ago.

A parasite toolplant. Where your standard seeds were sown in soil, this type absorbed nutrients and mana from a host to urge their growth. The use conditions were far harsher than soil-based toolplants, but the giant tree was mana rich and an ideal seedbed. Teresa had tailed Nanao up the irminsul and planted it on the way—choosing to stage her ambush at the location the shadow cast as it grew, and the faux sun moved.

In other words, this one spot was a limited patch of night in a forest that knew no sleep.

"Fascinating. This was what lay up your sleeve?"

Nanao was deeply impressed. She hadn't seen it coming. Shadowy nights were the domain of the stealthy fighter, but to make your own night?

If this was a smoke screen, then she merely needed to move out. But to escape this patch of night, she would have to run a considerable distance. And she'd be moving through forest to do so—there was no avoiding an attack while her vision was diminished.

Naturally, she had the option of creating her own light source. With Nanao's current output, she could easily light up the entire area. But to maintain a light at a distance from her wand required a spell cast with a considerable amount of mana worked into it—in her current predicament, would her foe really allow that?

"Very well. Come at me."

She drew her blade, switching from iai to mid-stance. The hostility prickling her skin told her plain as day her foe was about to go for the kill. She need only meet it at full strength—nothing less would allow her survival.

In darkness lit only by the flames on the fallen trees, she sensed hazy figures bearing down on her. Nanao could not tell which were real and which were splinters. That left her with but one recourse.

"Haaaaaaaaaaaaaaah!"

Cut them *all* down. With that one thought in mind, she sliced at every approaching presence. Swing, move, swing, move, no pausing, turning as each figure crumbled. The wild abandon reminding her of yesteryear. As the tides of war turned against her side, she'd fought many a battle on these terms. Unsure how many she stood against. Counting not the number slain. According to the Hibiya way, the divinities would tell you that number once you yourself perished.

*　　*　　*

"…Ngh!"

Her strategy bore fruit, conditions ripe—yet still Teresa could not find a path forward. How could she finish off this foe? When could she attack without being cut down herself?

No openings existed. Each swing took down a splinter like a windmill made of swords. If that blade came her way, she would not last a moment. Yet if that fear stayed her hand, she would run out of splinters. Her rational mind was screaming at her to finish this first, to make her move within the next five seconds.

At the two-second mark, she lost hope: *This approach cannot defeat this foe.*

At the four-second mark, she asked herself: *Then why are you even here?*

At the five-second mark, she howled: *To put this bitch down!*

"——!!!!!"

A soundless war cry, and Teresa shot through the night. Not shooting from within range when her splinters made an opening, but mingling with the splinters herself, stabbing her foe right in the heart. All risk forgotten. All prospects out of mind. Neither meant squat. This was a goal she *had* to achieve, and that math did her no good here.

Before her eyes, two splinters were cut down. Her target's back was to her; she felt she could stab it home, and so she did. Then she stepped in, utterly silent, her athame extended. Perhaps her foe had sensed her approach, but it was too late to respond in time. She knew that for a fact; her blow's timing was that good.

But her best thrust was batted aside like a waking nightmare.

"Oh—"

A squeak escaped her throat. Her foe did not even turn around. Yet Teresa's blade had gone off course—on the back of a katana swung fully overhead. An absurd technique, found in no schools.

Hibiya-style Oral Creed: Back Stance. With that unbelievable block, her target spun, showing Teresa her loathsome profile. A covert operative tackling this monster head-on meant only death. She wouldn't last a second. Without accomplishing anything. Without making her foe pay for what she'd done.

Without easing his suffering one iota.

"Ah—!"

This *could not be.* Her emotions erupted, and her left hand shot out without conscious thought.

Nanao turned to strike down the assailant behind her—and her cheek was struck from below with the force of an anvil.

"Ohhh…!"

Her foe had put their whole back into that slap. The heel of the palm connected, rattling Nanao's brain and making her vision flash white. Before her eyes focused, she woozily slashed downward, catching only empty air.

She felt her foe melt into the darkness without ever catching a glimpse of their face. Just a vague sense of a tiny figure speeding off into the woods behind the burning timber.

"…That made my skull ring," Nanao muttered, holding her swaying head. She knew her way around a close-quarters slugfest but had not expected a slap at that juncture.

A punch—she'd have gritted her teeth and withstood it. But the open palm had connected with the damnedest force. As it struck her cheek, Nanao had instinctively sensed this was a blow she should *let hit.* No telling what manner of empathetic phenomenon brought that on, but inside, she knew it to be true.

"I know not your face, yet you have my gratitude, stranger. With your help, my path grows clear again."

Nanao bowed her head at the darkness that had swallowed her assailant. The thoughts weighing her down had been utterly banished. She felt as if she'd died and been born anew.

Perhaps that blow had cleared away the part of her mind caught up inventing futile excuses. That thought made her all the more grateful—and she clapped her hands together toward the darkness, as if before a statue of the enlightened one.

Teresa fled headlong through the darkness of her own creation in a full-out run until she escaped its range—then she collapsed like her strings had snapped, toppling into the brush.

"…Hfff, haah… Haah—!"

Her arms folded, her mouth pressed against them, her breathing ragged. No matter how exhausted she might be, making noise exposed her, and she would not let that happen. She'd been raised as a covert operative, and these habits were imprinted deep. They were a biological imperative.

"……Hfff…… Hfff… Hfff… Ngh…… Ngh…"

It took a long time to catch her breath. And doing so made her head cool off. The intoxicating fury ebbed away, and her reason regained control. She was rational again.

Looking down at herself from on high.

What are you even doing? A query delivered by none other than her own self.

"……"

Her earlier thought came back to her. *If you are a monster, then I am a vengeful spirit.* Words to whip herself into action against a superior foe. An internal howl that she might not lose the battle in emotional terms.

But in hindsight—what words those were. The plain, unvarnished truth.

"……!"

Think. Would killing Nanao Hibiya have brought a smile to his face?

Remember. Had he ever once smiled after an act of vengeance? Had he looked upon their demise with satisfaction?

She knew that all along. He had never been a man who took pleasure in the death of another.

"......Urgh..."

What a mess. Why was she even here?

Because she couldn't let it go. That girl had forced her lust upon him and made him suffer, and Teresa couldn't stomach that fact. The more hurt he was, the more he agonized over it, the more certain she'd grown that someone had to pay.

Her act was every bit as ill-considered as the Azian girl's, but now was not the time to dwell on such things.

Was that really...all that drove her to it?

Don't hide. There were uglier thoughts behind that.

Like...that girl was always at his side, while she was always in the shadows.

Or...that girl got a kiss upon the lips, while hers came on the cheek.

"...Rrgh..."

Had that been too much for her to bear? As mad as she'd been about the assault itself, was the difference in their status what broke her?

The urge to eliminate anyone he loved more than her. Could she really say that hadn't been lurking somewhere, deep inside?

"...Ah......"

Why not just admit it? You act like you love him, but you're only thinking of yourself.

You want him stroking your hair. You want his arms around you. You want his lips on yours. Peel back the deception, and that's all you've got on your mind. Your lust is swelling up inside that skull, but split it open, and the brain within is no different from the girl you just slapped.

Every time you show him that, he tries to meet you halfway. The burdens he already bears must be crushing, yet you have the gall to pile your garbage on top. How's he supposed to deal with it? What if this was the last straw, and it brought him to his knees?

Enough rambling. You've got your answer now. Picture your wishes granted—and your master on his knees. Imagine yourself running happily up behind.

You see what you are? A vengeful spirit, personified.

"…Urgh… Augh…!"

The verdict had been passed down. Unable to bear it, a sob escaped the gap between her arms, rustling the brush nearby. Guilt and self-hatred had her kicking herself. Her thoughts were in a downward spiral, ballooning up within her.

Racked with remorse, her entire body quivered. She couldn't move. She couldn't go back to him. A disaster like her didn't even deserve to breathe. She cursed the foul desires pent up in her tiny frame.

Someone, tell me. I live to protect him, to support him, so how did I turn out so hideous? Why can I not be who I was supposed to be?

"…I'm sorry… I'm sorry…!"

Teresa sobbed like a child who had lost her way home. She apologized to the man she loved until her throat was too raw for her voice to emerge, until her lips no longer formed words. On and on and on—

"Nyuuu?"

—when the strangest thing cut in.

"……Huh?"

Something was bobbing through the air, bathed in orange light—right by her face in the brush, inches from her eyes and nose. Forgetting herself, Teresa gaped at it.

"Kipaaa!"

What the—?

This vaguely humanoid thing let out an odd cry, making faces at her. Its nose, eyes, and mouth were spinning freely around, delivering a dizzying whirlwind of bizarre expressions. Eyes red with tears, Teresa could only stare in stunned silence. Then she heard someone else pushing through the brush nearby. Snapping out of her stupor, she leaped to her feet, aiming her athame.

"You're back here, Ufa? I said, don't run off—"

A man appeared, branches braced against his shoulder. His tall

frame was clad in customized ecclesiastical vestments, like an evil priest. By the time she saw him, he was already at a range that could well be fatal. A hiss escaped Teresa's throat.

"Hm? Already occupied?"

The man seemed unruffled by the surprise encounter with a junior. Kimberly's most wanted, the Scavenger himself—Cyrus Rivermoore.

∗

The moment he was certain she wasn't on campus, Oliver turned toward the labyrinth. But the nearest entrance—the one they always used to get to their base—was out of order, and he was forced to make a major detour.

"Is Nanao here?!"

Panic lending wings to his feet, he took the shortest possible route to the base. Chela and Pete met him with shocked looks.

"Wh-what's going on, Oliver? You look like you've seen a ghost."

"Nanao's right over there. She got back and chowed down."

Chela left the sink, concerned. Pete had been checking a dissertation and pointed at the table. True to his word, the Azian girl was stuffing her face with a gigantic sandwich. Oliver let out a huge sigh of relief.

"...Good..."

"Mmph? Something wrong?" Nanao asked.

"That's what I want to know. Nothing happened? Anyone ambush you while you were wandering the labyrinth?"

He was bracing himself for the worst. But Nanao just polished off the last of her sandwich at top speed and shook her head, grinning.

"Nothing of the sort! 'Twas a fine stroll, like upon the moonlit bank of a river!"

Her smile was blinding. Less a lie than simply her authentic take-away from the events that had transpired. She went out for a walk, enjoyed a first-rate duel, straightened her head out, and came back in high spirits. In her mind, that was all that had gone down. No part of that fit the term *ambush*.

"...Oh. Well, good. Maybe I was just overreacting. Just in case, though, make sure you come with me on the way back."

Saying no more, he left it at that. Oliver didn't want to voice his concerns about Teresa unnecessarily, and if he took Nanao at her word, she hadn't actually tried anything. He could talk to his operative later, after getting Nanao safely home—and it would hardly be proper to besmirch her name without real cause. His willingness to let that slide was perhaps a sign Oliver was a bit too fond of Teresa.

"By all means! Say, Oliver—"

Agreeing to his suggestion without question, Nanao rose to her feet. Her eyes bored into his. Oliver had a hunch where this was going.

"—I should like to bend your ear awhile. Do you have the time to spare?"

The gravity in her tone sank deep into the pit of his stomach, and he nodded grimly. Pete and Chela saw this, glanced once at each other, and started packing up.

"We'll give you some space."

"I'll head back to campus. Guy and Katie won't be by until tomorrow. Feel free to talk this through."

With that, they were out the door. In the silence that followed, Oliver and Nanao were left alone with emotions neither of them could adequately measure.

They had the base all to themselves, so they moved to the room they slept in. No real significance to that; it just felt right. Given the gravity of the topic at hand, the living room felt far too open, and that proved daunting.

"...How thoughtful our friends are. It fans the fires of my shame," Nanao said, sighing.

She let that serve as her preamble, turning to face Oliver head-on. She had never been the sort of girl to work her way up to a topic with small talk.

"In which case, let me make it formal. The insults I suffered upon your personage that night, in hindsight, are beyond—"

"Wait, Nanao."

Her words were starting to run away from him, but he cut her short. She blinked, and he met her gaze.

"You're trying to apologize, right?"

"I could think of no other course."

A forlorn smile played about her lips. This cut Oliver to the quick. He had never once intended to be the cause of a smile such as this.

"There's no need. I'd rather you let me say my piece, actually."

In lieu of an answer, Nanao closed her eyes tight, waiting for a tongue lashing. Her stance made it clear she was prepared to accept a strike upon the cheek, even a dagger to the heart. Perhaps what she truly feared lay elsewhere altogether, Oliver thought. In the words he might utter. No other thing could truly deliver a blow like those.

Yet at the same time, he knew—she had come here, ready for that outcome as well.

"I'm afraid I'm not letting you off that easily."

He kept his tone flinty, betraying no emotions. He saw her shoulders flinch. That alone was heartrending, but he told himself this *must* be said. Nanao's guilt was palpable. Forgiveness by itself would leave her dragging that around. Certain that harshness here would prove her salvation in the future, he pressed on.

"____?!"

Wordlessly, he took her shoulders and stole her lips. Or perhaps—stole them *back*. He did this with a roughness that ill-suited him, an unfamiliar forcefulness that left even him shocked—but for the time being, he was sticking to his guns. With the intensity she'd brought that night, he now paid her back in kind.

A long, long kiss. Oliver was far past measuring the passage of time. Thus, he kept it going until shortness of breath intruded upon it. A moment of silence that felt eternal, and at last they breathed again.

"...Oli...ver..."

Nanao's eyes were barely focused. Facing her, he took a deep breath, ready to speak again. For once, no other considerations or concerns serving as filters on his heart.

"...You're not the only one restraining yourself!"

More than a confession, this was a primal cry. The force of it shook her bodily, and he reached out to pull her into a second kiss. Arms around her back, and this time she grabbed him in return. She could not believe this was permitted but knew failure to answer would be even less so.

"Hah! Oliver, one thing..."

The second kiss was a bit shorter than the first. An unfamiliar pressure against her nether regions made Nanao curious and caused her to beg for recess. Both were panting like they'd just run a sprint, their eyes inches apart.

"...What...?"

"...I can sense a...powerful organ pressed against my belly."

Nanao's eyes dipped down below, mincing few words. A beat later, Oliver grew cognizant of his own condition. His cheeks flushed crimson, and hands still on her shoulders, his head sank low.

"I envy your lack thereof. Can you begin to imagine just how mortifying this is?"

"Um, mm. I'm getting the gist. Palpably."

Nanao nodded, but her tone suggested she was out of her element. She did not have one, after all. She might get that he was beside himself with shame but had her doubts on whether she could truly sympathize. Beyond their physical differences, their cringe thresholds were inherently tied to their different cultural backgrounds.

But she was not about to let all the shame rest upon his shoulders. A moment of anguish and deliberation brought her to knowledge of what she must do.

"In the interests of fairness, I shall not let you alone suffer."

Once settled, she moved swiftly. Losing first her cloak, then undoing her buttons and flinging the shirt aside, and last unraveling the sarashi wound around her chest. She remembered him catching a glimpse of these sometime in the past, but it was far more excruciating to show them off herself. Hoping this would even the playing field, Nanao put her hands on her hips and puffed out her chest.

"M-my body is hardly a thing of beauty. There are scars no matter where you look. I had not imagined the opportunity to flaunt it would ever present itself."

"......"

Oliver took a long look at her exposed frame. As he did, the front of his trousers grew taut from the pressure within. Nanao witnessed this transformation and went stiff.

"...Is my mind playing tricks on me, or is that getting...more prodigious?"

"Why did you think it wouldn't? After what you've shown off?"

His voice was almost a growl. Trying to restore his equilibrium, he took several deep breaths, then put his hands on her shoulders once more. The shame was not going anywhere, but communicating this took precedence—eyes unwavering, he looked right at her.

"You should—know this, Nanao. In my eyes, you have always dazzled. From the moment we met to this very moment, how often have I dreamed of touching you?"

His voice was on the verge of choking up. Nanao chewed over each word, then put a hand to her cheek, pinching first left and then right. Oliver was uncertain what to make of it.

"...What's that for?"

"Attempting to wake myself from this dream."

"You think you're dreaming?"

"Mm, nothing else makes sense. These past few moments, all you say and do is far too tailored to my liking."

Nanao freely admitted this did not seem remotely real to her. Why would it? They had burst right through the ceiling of the most remote possibilities she had allowed herself to imagine. That invoked fear before joy. With her heart floating like this, she could hardly survive the drop once she woke.

Oliver got that much. At the least, this was no joke to her, but a serious concern. Thus, he reached out to her to unravel it. Prying her hands from her cheeks and cupping them in his own palms.

"What's so odd about it?" he asked, gently stroking her smooth skin. "I'm just saying I find you immensely appealing."

The warmth of his hands made tears swell up in Nanao's eyes. She could not stop herself. Leaning her full weight on his shoulder, her voice shook.

"If...I wake right now, I will howl like a newborn babe."

"Should that happen, go see me in the real world. I'll do this again."

"Unlikely. The real Oliver hates me now. He scorns me as a wild thing, starved for blood and fleshly pleasures. Such was the extent of my sin. I came here half expecting to be beaten black-and-blue. No better outcome could possibly await—"

Unable to bear her tear-soaked protestations any longer, Oliver sealed her lips with a kiss. Swallowing up all further words before they could take shape. Only when her heart was stilled did he release the cap, whereupon he looked her right in the eye.

"...I'm not letting you put yourself down anymore," he said with fervor.

Cheeks still wet with tears, Nanao smiled and nodded.

"I hear you. In light of that... Pray, let this dream continue."

With that, they clasped hands. And by mutual consent—their bodies were drawn to a nearby bed.

Meanwhile, in a passage leading through the first layer to the school building, Chela spoke to the friend beside her.

"Pete, I do hate to say this—"

"Way ahead of you."

He didn't let her finish. Eyes wide, Chela pulled up short, and Pete turned to face her. The eyes behind his glasses betrayed the depth of his thoughts.

"Their relationship has always been a tightrope act. They're drawn to each other, but the greater their passion, the more likely they are to kill each other. Yet—after all this time spent together, facing death side by side… How can we ask them to keep their distance?" Pete asked. "They've hit their limit. The delicate balance they've maintained is no longer remotely possible. In which case—even if it's still a tightrope act, we've gotta have them switch to a different rope."

That was the best metaphor he could muster. Chela thought it was entirely fitting. Oliver and Nanao might look unwaveringly close, but they had long teetered on the brink of collapse. Their respective efforts had thus far staved that off, but if either let go, it would all come tumbling down. And it might well not be Nanao who set that off.

"Physical intimacy as a proxy for dueling. I have no clue if that logic will prove successful, but at least, it's worth a try. We've got to explore every option we can to stop them from killing each other."

Pete's grim summation. Chela nodded, watching him closely.

"Quite right," she said. "But…it does come as a surprise. I wasn't sure you'd be able to process this with such…detachment."

"You thought I'd fall apart? Please."

"I do apologize. Deeply. But…you're in love with Oliver, yes?"

She chose to spell it out. This deep into the conversation, the topic needed broaching. She saw Pete stiffen up—but not back down.

"Even so. No, *because*—now's not the time to fall apart," he told her. "Not to change the subject, but I've got a terrible relationship with my family. You're perceptive—I'm sure you've picked up on that."

"…Honestly, I had a hunch. What of it?"

Her gaze probed the connection here. Pete leaned back against the passage wall, sighing.

"Nothing, really. Simple truth. That base is the only place I've got to call home."

A bitter sort of smile. Rueful, self-deprecating—and something beyond either. And that made Chela realize—he'd been thinking about the future of the Sword Roses as much—or more—than she had.

"I doubt I'll get another. Don't feel compelled to make my own. I want *this one*. No replacements. The Sword Roses is where I belong—and I'll do anything it takes to keep that safe," Pete avowed. "Are you any different, *Michela McFarlane*?"

"——!"

The dagger abruptly swung her way, and she shuddered. Pete kept the blade of his gaze upon her, not letting her hide, pressing the point.

"Don't you run. We're talking here because I know your fixation on the Sword Roses is even greater than my own. High time you showed your hand. When we were discussing Katie, you alone were not appalled by my suggestion. Rather—you went, *Oh, that's an option.*"

"...Kgh...!"

He'd hit the nail on the head and left her flat-footed. Pete flashed a grin and looked away.

"Kids are great. Why? Because they turn people into family. Put a chain between you that can't be severed easily. The word *friend* is pretty and all, but it's fragile in a way I just can't trust." He then added, "If it's in the cards, I'd like to be more than that with *all* of you."

He voiced a wild notion, sounding deeply sad. Chela tried to say something, but he didn't give her a chance. His gaze rose again, as sharp as before, like that alone could cut her down.

"So I know I'm a lot. But you're just as bad. Groups formed at school are fleeting things. No matter how the chips fall, it won't stay this way forever. Nanao picked our group's name in full knowledge of that... But *we* can't help but hope it stays eternal. Neither one of us can let that go."

Chela hung her head. How could she deny it? This was the lot of anyone who'd ever been truly alone.

The nature of that isolation varied. Everything from being cooped up alone in a darkened room to sitting at the center of a bustling party.

What they had in common was the thirst for anything that could fill that void. For some, that quest might last a lifetime—but once *found*, their hands clasped tightly upon it, they would defend it to the death.

Both knew this to be true. And knew they were alike in it. Suffering the same symptoms. Desirous of any means, no matter how drastic, that could turn this fleeting paradise into an eternal one, caring not what Herculean effort might be needed to make that manifest. They shared that same warped fixation.

"……"

Chela's smile mirrored her friend's. How could it not? They had long shared the same dream, about a rose made of swords that had bloomed that miraculous day.

They'd made the choice to dwell within that dream. To keep it safe. That would never waver, not even if it meant turning these bonds into curses with their own two hands.

Neither would budge on this—no matter what, they would not let this dream come to an end.

"It is what I crave."

Chela's words were almost a lamentation. Pete nodded, stepped closer, and patted her on the shoulder. They knew for certain now. To these two, that was equivalent to a contract signed in blood.

"Sorry for forcing the issue. My point is—the two of us oughtta be honest with each other. We don't want Katie and Guy getting this deep, right? I'd rather they stay happy-go-lucky, the way they've been."

Chela nodded slowly. A concern she'd kept locked up tight since their first year at last escaped her lips.

"We'll…be upperclassmen soon. The time when everyone here draws closer to the spell. We will hardly be exceptions," she said. "My worst projections have Katie consumed first. Nanao not far behind… After that—one of the four of us, myself included."

Just saying it out loud made her shudder. Not because the thought terrified her—but because the foundations for it were all too evident. There was far too little reason to dismiss these concerns.

"Optimism is not an option. I am sure of it—this worst-case scenario is nigh destined to happen."

She minced no words. This threat was bearing down on them, and nothing could be more urgent. Desperate to share that threat, Chela spread her arms, and Pete pulled her into an embrace.

"Let's keep them safe, Pete. All those who we love."

"We will. I swear it on the rose we made."

Their hearts and warmth overlapped. Listening to each other's pulse, they prayed—for a dream without an end.

In bed with Nanao, his skin on hers, their hands on each other, Oliver ran up against the wall he'd seen coming.

"......!"

His heart started racing, his pulse erratic. A virulent rejection rising up his spine that made his teeth clench up—and Nanao was too close to miss the signs.

"Oliver? You've gone pale..."

"...Sorry. I knew momentum was hardly going to get me over this, but..."

Sweating, he swallowed his distress, reluctantly prying himself away. Nanao sat up, and they faced each other at eye level. It took several deep breaths to relax his throat enough to speak the words.

"I have a confession to make, Nanao. I've got some long-standing trauma related to the act itself."

That made her back straighten. She could tell it had been a struggle for him to even admit. That, to this boy, it was like ripping open his chest and offering up his very heart.

"...Meaning..."

"Yes, I've done it before. Just...not in any acceptable way. The events leading up to it were horrible—and the outcome...far worse. No one got a happy ending. All of us were left...with wounds that will never... ever heal."

His voice grew raspy, his words halting. Racked by surging memories, Oliver forced himself to keep talking. Nanao's arms held his shaking body tight. Sending a clear sign she was getting all of this.

"Enough," she said. "Painful memories are not easily shared."

"…Sorry… It was our first, and…"

"Why apologize? I have glimpsed yet another piece that lies within you. That brings me nothing but joy."

Nanao meant every word of this, and her smile was genuine. It lifted the gloom, like a sunflower on a cloudless day.

"And thus, I say this to you—Oliver, you were perhaps moving too fast. Look again—against all odds, you are here with *me*. Not some lady from a storied household or the greatest beauty of the imperial court. There is hardly a need to fall upon the sword of nightly duties. This was never once a matter of success or failure."

With that frank assessment, Nanao slid her fingers under his ribs and tickled him mercilessly. The surprise attack shocked him and made him writhe. He grabbed her shoulders.

"…Ngh! Ha…ha-ha…! S-stop, Nanao…!"

"There you have it. This is but an extension of such frivolity. We merely add licking and petting to the games we've played for some time."

That got through. No need to stress out about it. Here, there was no demand for any outcomes, no terms to meet, just a natural expression of their affection. They need merely play, as children do. Talk all night beneath a blanket. From the moment this began, each knew that it would all be memorable and filled with love.

"Again, you seem convinced you must do something specific with me, yet I have no earthly clue what put that in your head," Nanao said, abandoning her tickle attack and turning to face him again.

Her passionate gaze poured over his honed body. He made no attempt to hide, letting her eyes feast upon the details.

"Even if you lift not a finger, I have more than enough ideas for the two of us. But of course! I swear I shall do nothing you object to."

Realizing her lust was making her a trifle too eager, Nanao back-pedaled, fanning a hand before her face. Oliver took her wrists, parted her hands, and placed his lips on her brow. Striking back.

"...In that case, I'm not about to be outdone," he said, smiling.

Nanao met his eyes and grinned.

"Then it is a contest! Victory to the aggressor!"

"?! H-hey! Don't just grab—"

Her hand had gone straight for his crotch, and Oliver caught her wrist, fending her off. Nanao's assault proved relentless, so he tickled her sides and strengthened the stimulation via an application of healing that made her whole body shiver.

"Hnggg! Th-that's most unfair!"

"It's absolutely fair. You did the same thing!"

He grinned impishly. Nanao struggled to turn the tables, and they wrestled naked for a time—loving each other as an extension of their typical play.

Meanwhile, in the school building—at a lounge on the upper floors, ordinarily off-limits to lowerclassmen, referred to colloquially as the Pub.

"...Zzzz..."

After quite a lot of drunken grumbling, Miligan had toppled over the table, sound asleep. Katie had spent a long time being her earpiece and looked rather relieved.

"She's finally under. Sorry, Guy. I didn't mean to rope you into her bender..."

"It's all good. She's helped me out plenty."

He shrugged, rising from his seat on the far side of the table and gathering up the bottles. He was at least half collateral damage here but had stuck with Katie throughout the ordeal.

Normally, they'd have been turned away at the door, but that line got pretty vague in the third year. Miligan had just said "They're with me," and they'd sailed right in. No one had uttered a word against it. Or perhaps they'd simply been conscious of Miligan's mood.

Helping Guy clean up Miligan's mess, Katie murmured, "The new council's stepping up, at least. They're taking on a solid eighty percent of the debts she ran up and have named her a core member. President Godfrey even came by with a box of cookies."

Remembering how that had gone, Katie clutched a bottle to her chest. It had been just that bad. He'd apologized profusely, while she'd berated him, red-faced, then he'd gotten stuck refilling her glass as fast as she could empty it for the better part of an hour. Godfrey himself had taken it in stride, as the natural result of his own actions, sticking it out to the bitter end. Katie and Guy had made no attempt to intervene. The warm looks from the tables around proved this was his attempt at an apology.

"Well, yeah," Guy said, eyes on Miligan's sleeping face. "She was all fired up about being the first pro-rights president. And…likely wanted to show *you* a glorious victory."

This line gave Katie a swell of emotions, and she put her arms around Miligan's shoulders. She could certainly be a handful. The transplant operation the other day had hardly been the first off-the-cuff outrageous request. Katie had lost track of how many times she'd wanted to bury her head in her hands. And she'd nearly had her brain dissected shortly after they'd met. Katie wasn't about to forget all the experiments she'd done on demis, either.

But she was still a mentor. One who'd recognized Katie's skills, helped guide her, given her the push she needed.

Their thorny past, the trouble she made—all of that included just brought them closer together.

"…Mm…"

Miligan's hands grabbed Katie's arm, pulling it to her chest. She hadn't woken up; this was entirely unconscious. But it still amused Katie, and she spent a while locked in that embrace.

Guy grinned at that for a minute, then glanced at Katie's face, muttering, "You're gonna need a bender of your own."

"Mm? What'd you say?"

"Never mind. Just enjoy the quiet while it lasts."

He waved a wand at the pile of bottles, sending them to a nearby collection bin. As he cleaned up the rest of the mess, he thought, *This hardly counts as trouble. If what I said shakes things up—then I'll really have my work cut out for me tomorrow. And for a while after.*

In the labyrinth's second layer, beneath a gloomy canopy of forest leaves, a small campfire sputtered.

"Well? Feeling any better, tiny meat?" Rivermoore asked.

Teresa was across the fire from him, clutching the tea he'd handed her, arms around her knees. She glared up at him.

"...Second-year Teresa Carste," she said. "I'm not meat, and I'm not that tiny."

"Ufa!"

At its name, the orange thing let out a cry and started spinning. Teresa couldn't tell if it was just a chirp or if it was introducing itself. Rivermoore smiled and sipped his tea.

"If you've got spirit enough to talk back, you're fine. Still, this isn't exactly the place I'd pick to sob my eyes out."

"I was not sobbing. You misheard. You must have ear problems, poor thing."

"Perhaps, but I'm not the one who heard anything. It was all Ufa here. Direct your excuses thataway."

Rivermoore pointed at the bobbing creature. Perhaps it *had* been introducing itself. Teresa gave the mystery creature another look over. It was about the size and approximate shape of a four- or five-year-old child. Entirely a translucent orange, but the eyes alone faded yellow. It was stretching and shrinking, so it was fundamentally of no set shape. There were vague indications suggestive of a nose and a mouth, and these shifted like the rest of its body, making it quite expressive.

"...What is it? It's not a ghost or a fairy. I've never heard of anything like it."

"You wouldn't, no. Right now, it's the only one of its kind. It's an astral life—kind of a long name, and clunky, so I might end up calling it an astra. Basically, think of it as a ghostly human child. That wouldn't be far off."

"Off! Off!"

Rivermoore talking about it made Ufa dance even more—and Teresa connected the dots. She hadn't directly taken part in the assault on the Kingdom of the Dead, but she'd heard reports about this creature from those who had. Not especially interested, she'd let it go in one ear and out the other—having not expected to meet it in person. Or expected it to be this chatty.

She looked it over as one would a rare animal—while he gave her a look of curiosity.

"I was equally unsure what to make of *you*. Even face-to-face, you're awfully insubstantial. I bet your average ghost is easier to handle—they've got less covert training."

"...I was born like this," she said, shifting uncomfortably. Covert operatives spent a lot of time observing, but not much being observed. Rivermoore picked up on her discomfort and looked away, changing the subject.

"So? What made you so sad you had to go cry in the woods?"

"I wasn't crying."

"Oh, right. So what made you so sad you stuck your head in a bush? If that's just your thing, don't let me stop you."

Rivermoore stoked the fire with his wand. Not about to admit the reason out loud, Teresa glared at him, firing back.

"...I should ask what *you're* doing, Mr. Rivermoore."

"Ah, you know me? I didn't think we'd met."

He shot her a look. She'd peeked at him a few times in the labyrinth, but more than that, he'd been on-screen during the combat league, so it was hardly strange for anyone to recognize him. She could have explained it that way—but she'd embarrassed herself enough. Prepared to flee into the brush behind her if she had to, she went for the barbed response.

"A deduction from your description. I doubt anyone else on campus wears such incredibly dated clothes."

"Dated! Dated!" Ufa did a loop in the air.

Rivermoore just sighed.

"Another bizarre word to learn. You're already making as much of a racket as your mother," he said to the small creature. "But oh. I'd had a hunch—these aren't exactly the current vogue, then?"

He looked down at his clothes, despondent. This rather rattled Teresa. She'd been trying to pick a fight and had not expected it to actually cause damage.

Before she recovered, he smiled at her.

"You're the first junior to comment on my appearance to my face. Thanks, tiny meat."

"...No thanks necessary, and neither meat nor that tiny."

Repeating that was the best she could manage. Trying to escape the awkwardness, she picked up the teacup—but Ufa wrapped itself around her arm, tugging on her. Teresa tried to peel it off, but her fingers slipped right through its body. She couldn't even touch it.

"...Ngh... I...c-can't get it off..."

"It really likes you. Odd. Maybe you have a ghostly affinity?"

He looked as puzzled as he was interested. Ufa's curiosity was boundless, and it was always flitting around, but that was hardly the only mystery here. First and foremost, the fact that Ufa had found her sobbing in the bushes in the first place. Rivermoore himself hadn't detected her until their eyes met. This girl's presence was just that intangible; if she hid, just about anyone would look right past her. So why had Ufa alone heard those soft sobs?

"......Hmm."

Maybe that meant something. A vague sort of hunch, but Rivermoore was a mage—he wasn't about to dismiss that. After a moment's thought, he put it to action.

"Well, that works. Spend some time with it. It'll be living up on campus soon enough."

"Huh?"

Ufa had wrapped itself around Teresa so much she looked like a ring puzzle. And she blinked up at him.

He chuckled, adding, "Once I negotiate with the instructors anyway. I've got some demands to handle there—my own standing among them. But they'll likely not refuse. Given this thing's value, it's a pretty fair settlement. Which, I guess, answers your question about what I'm doing here."

He pointed at the oversize backpack beside him.

"Either way, it was high time I reported in. I keep them waiting too long, I'll get outsiders in my workshop again. Got plenty of dissertations ready to submit."

"…That…looks like a lot of work."

Ufa released her, bobbing away, and Teresa looked relieved. She rose to her feet and turned to go.

"Already?" Rivermoore chuckled. "If you're back on your game, I imagine you have this layer handled. I can tell you're skilled enough."

"…I didn't ask for your concern."

"Don't be like that. I'm in my last year here. If I see a lost second-year, and I'm in the mood, I'll look after them a bit."

He waved his wand, dousing the fire. Realizing he was about to move out, too, Teresa made to hurry away. She definitely didn't want to walk all the way back to campus with him.

But it felt wrong to leave without another word. If he hadn't shown up, she might still be crying in that bush. Ufa's goofy faces and Rivermoore's gruff hospitality had helped lift her spirits.

Her stubborn streak prevented her from thanking him. Instead— she spoke without turning around.

"…Let me correct myself."

"Mm?"

"…I dismissed your clothes as dated. That's not true. I actually think they're just a *little bit* cool."

And without a glance over her shoulder, she dove into the thicket, her back soon dissolving into the night. Rivermoore and the astra both gaped after her—and a few moments later, he burst out laughing.

Dawn arrived at the end of the long night. Oliver realized that as he regained consciousness in bed.

As his lids opened and his eyes focused, he saw a girl sleeping next to him, not a stitch on her. This drove home everything they'd done, and unable to fully process how he felt about it, he lay studying her sleeping face.

Steady breathing. Her expression utterly secure. No trace of the fierceness she displayed with a sword in her hand.

A little lower down, their hands were clasped together. They'd drifted off, staring into each other's eyes. And stayed like that as they slumbered. He hadn't let go of her, either.

"……"

He loved her. That was his sole thought.

He was sure of those feelings—so he chose to trust them.

"Nanao. Are you awake, Nanao?"

His heart sorted out, he called her name. Her lids fluttered open.

"…Mmm… Oliver…?"

"It's almost morning. We've still got some time, but best not to push our luck. We should get dressed."

That got her eyes fully open. Both awake, they sat up together.

"…I remember now. Last night, we had the most passionate battle…"

"That sounds metaphorical, but you definitely put me in an armlock once. My elbow still hurts."

"Oh dear. But that is because your fingers rather relentlessly prodded my sensitive regions..."

"Same goes for you. Once you get a grip on it, you are merciless—"

He trailed off, turning bright red and burying his face in his hands. The rational side of his brain had caught up with what they were saying, objectively—and it proved too much for him.

"...Let's move on. I'll get the water heated. You take the first bath."

"Why not together?"

"Nope! I know it would *not* end with that."

He managed to spurn her invitation and get out of bed. Well aware of how this was affecting him, he was growing increasingly nervous. How would they get through the day without anyone noticing?

Each bathed and dressed, then moved to the living room to put up some tea. They'd have a proper breakfast in the Fellowship, so this was more a snack.

When the tea leaves opened, Oliver poured a cup.

"We never did make it to the end," he said.

Nanao smiled across the table at him. "What of it? The lecture that replaced it was highly educational."

He made a strangled noise. He'd definitely gotten sidetracked into a lesson about birth control at one point. Laying out the different types atop the sheets, explaining the usage and effectiveness of each, along with a list of precautions—and yet, they'd wound up not actually making use of any. A huge swing and a miss, and in hindsight probably primarily an effort to restore his own equilibrium.

"Sorry, that...was long. Yet you hung on my every word."

"It was enjoyable! All that we did lying down together—and all the things you said."

Her smile was dreamy. Where she might well grumble, she'd merely enjoyed herself. That made him choke up, so he put the kettle down and turned to her.

"I had fun, too. For the first time, I took pleasure in these things," he told her. "You brought me there. And I thank you for it, Nanao."

He put both hands on his knees, sitting bolt upright, head bowed—adopting Yamatsu mannerisms to express the depth of his gratitude. Nanao gently put her hands on his shoulders, lifted his head, and met his gaze.

"I should be thanking *you*," she said. "It was beyond my expectations. Being touched, rubbed... That such sources of pleasure lay hidden upon my own body."

Her hand was on her bosom as she chewed over her own words. As Oliver watched her eyes up close, they filled with tears.

"Yet you say such sad things. We did not get to 'the end'? Perish the thought," Nanao urged him. "Surely that was merely the *start* of our intimacy?"

She asked this with a tremor in her voice, and Oliver put his arms tightly around her. She was right. Given her view on this, he should have reassured her of that before voicing any such regrets. This had not been a one-night stand and would hardly be their last.

"...True, we *will* do that again."

He put it plainly and followed it with a light kiss. Nanao's face lit up. She kissed him back two, three times, her embrace tightening, and then she whispered in his ear:

"How about tonight?"

"Maybe space it out a *little*..."

"Tomorrow morning?"

"At least wait for cover of darkness."

"Hrm, you sound reluctant. Practice makes perfect! Try every means that avail us, offer sufficient supplications to the divine, and soon—or in due time—we shall manage to get the pole in the hole."

"Uncouth! Nanao, that was uncouth!"

Her turn of phrase was so appalling he began issuing reprimands, yet Nanao simply cackled merrily. And their banter continued without ebb, until it was time to head up to school.

*　　*　　*

They arrived at campus together to find their friends waiting in the Fellowship.

"Oh! Good morning!" cried Katie, the first to spot them. She waved them over to the table, so they headed that way.

"Yeah, good morning, Katie."

"'Tis a good one, indeed."

Making their greetings, they took their seats. Katie's mouth was already running.

"You slept down there? I wish I could have! Ms. Miligan's grumbling was positively endless. But then once I got back to my room, I got all lonely and couldn't fall asleep. I wound up with Milihand in my—"

At that point, she trailed off, having picked up on the tranquil vibe between Oliver and Nanao. The faintest whiff of something *else*.

"...Mm?"

She cocked her head, stood up, and moved closer. The faintest of changes, only noticeable because they'd been close for so long. A sweetness, like a lingering odor. Unable to dismiss it, she eyed them up close.

"......Mmmmmmmm......?"

"Urk—!"

"What ails you, Katie?"

Oliver was freaking out inside, but Nanao was merely confused. Katie soaked up both reactions, then backed off, calmly sitting down.

"...Nothing," she said. "Let's just...enjoy our breakfast."

She began silently working her way through her omelet. Guy, Chela, and Pete all exchanged glances. What Katie spotted was hardly lost on them.

After a very quiet breakfast, Oliver and Nanao headed off to class, and Katie hung back in the corridor, watching them go.

"...I get the feeling everyone *else* knows, too," Katie said.

Everyone braced themselves, and her next words proved that necessary.

"...They've, uh...*done it*, right? Oliver and Nanao—probably last night?"

They'd been standing a bit too close, a subtle shift in proximity that was not lost on Katie. Acutely aware of how this might be affecting her, Chela cleared her throat.

"...I can't exactly rule it out. We did give them some space last night—to talk things out," she began. "Still, Katie. They've always been close—"

"Don't you run from this, Chelaaa," Katie said, glaring up at her. Chela squirmed, avoiding her eyes.

Rummaging through his bag, Pete grunted, "Even if that is true, why kick up a fuss? We're mages. By our age, the inexperienced are the minority."

"...That sounds defensive, Pete. I bet it's hitting you just as hard as it is me."

Feeling her eyes boring into him, Pete stopped rummaging. There was a long silence, none of them saying anything.

"Okay, enough of that. Lashing out at each other ain't cool," Guy said, stepping in.

Katie pursed her lips, turning on him. "Guy..."

"We know how you feel, and you can gripe about it to me all you like later. But—you gotta remember what's going on with them otherwise. Neither one of 'em could afford to keep things undefined. Frankly, I'm kinda glad they hooked up this fast."

Chela and Pete both gulped. That last phrase was clearly designed to earn Katie's ire. This fact was not lost on Katie, who gave him a long, searching look and then forced a smile.

"...All right, Guy," she said. "Back in first year, I'd definitely have slapped you and run off."

"Go ahead. Let it out. You might think you're all grown-up now, but humans ain't that sensible."

He proffered up his cheek. Chela put a hand over her eyes, horrified, and Pete watched as Katie softly cupped Guy's cheeks. She gave her most merciful smile—and then her grip tightened. Caught in her talons, her bones creaking—she let loose a thunderous headbutt.

"Whoa...!"

"I'll take that offer, asshole!"

With that howl, Katie darted off like a startled hare, giving Chela and Pete no chance to speak. Reeling from the shock, Guy turned to his friends.

"...Best to make her blow her top early. I'll handle the fallout; don't you worry."

"...Guy...you leave me at a loss for words."

Fully aware of why he'd made this choice, Chela was as impressed as she was appalled.

Staring off down the hall after Katie, Pete muttered, "How are *you* handling it, Guy?"

"Huh?"

"I'm asking your honest opinion on the new relationships within our group," Pete said, very serious. "Long-term, is this a positive change? For the Sword Roses?"

"I ain't no augur," Guy said, rubbing his cheek. "How would I know? But...right now, it feels like a relief."

"Meaning?"

"...Oliver. He's started to let me shoulder a bit of his burden. Like now, he's willing to dump Katie all on me so he can focus on Nanao. That's a pretty good feeling. My first year, I couldn't do shit, and I relied on him for everything."

His smile looked so satisfied that Pete gasped, feeling his chest tighten up. Guy was the same. No matter what they were doing, who they were dealing with—Oliver was always in the back of their minds.

"So yeah, on some level, we're headed in the right direction. Just—in my eyes, Oliver ain't the only one carrying some heavy shit."

Guy turned his furrowed brow their way. Both flinched, like they'd been hit with cold water.

"Don't bottle it up. Pete, Chela—you're both smart, but don't mistake that for seeing everything clear from your perch up high." Guy's tone was firm. "I've *always* got an eye on you."

"——!"

Feeling very seen, Chela stood stock-still, eyes wide. But even as his friend's fierce glare raked over him, Pete flashed a grin.

"...That's a new one. When'd you get *cool*?" he asked Guy.

"Heh, you finally noticed?"

"Yeah, my bad—I've been blind. Can I make it up to you with a date?"

"...You've been cracking more jokes like that lately."

Guy rolled his eyes, then turned and stalked off after Katie.

It wasn't really a joke, Pete thought, watching him go.

"He certainly made his point," Chela said, folding her arms. "I didn't know Guy was thinking that hard about everyone."

"No, but...did you really hear what he said? That he's happy to look after Katie to help ease Oliver's burden? I feel like he doesn't fully grasp the implications there."

Pete started to laugh. Like he was one to talk. He knew—since enrolling at Kimberly, he was definitely the one who'd gone wrong the hardest.

He regretted none of it. Even if his thoughts were tinged with madness, that was in service of a purpose, an unwavering reason. He was the right kind of crazy. And he knew that was how a *mage* thought.

"This group's a good one," he said. "We've been with each other this long, yet we still haven't fully plumbed each other's depths. Makes me wanna kiss every one of you."

"...Hmm. Looking at you now, it doesn't sound like you're kidding."

Chela looked mildly perturbed, and Pete swung around to face her. A newfound trace of flirtatiousness flitted along his smile.

"That just means I'm growing into this whole reversi mage thing. Meeting the rest of you at your level."

*   *   *

Guy didn't have to walk long to find who he was looking for. She hadn't even hidden in an empty classroom. He found her back hunched over in the corner of the hall, clearly waiting for him to catch up. So he called out in his usual breezy tone.

"Yo, still pissed at me, Katie?"

She turned around and moved wordlessly over to him. Then she reached up and used healing on the bruise she'd left. She'd had enough time to cool down and regret that.

"…Sorry. I'm better now."

"Glad you got back up so fast. That was one hell of a headbutt!"

That was his way of accepting the apology. The pain was long since gone, but he let her heal him until she was satisfied, observing her close at hand.

"…You're taking this in stride. I thought you'd be all over the map for two, three days."

"Maybe once. No…definitely."

Katie sighed. She'd already resigned herself before he caught up.

"But I get it. I'm past the point where I'm allowed to be *jealous*. I threw that right out long ago. I'm at least that self-aware. So I'm not gonna sulk. I'm gonna keep it together."

She forced a smile. The best she could manage in her state of mind. Guy thought it looked ready to crumble at the slightest push, and something snapped inside him.

"…I'll say this as many times as it takes," he growled, stepping closer and dragging her into an embrace. The Sword Roses had been practicing a free hug policy since their second year, but he didn't often play that card with her. She hugged back, mostly on reflex, watching him out of the corner of her eye.

"…Guy?"

"…Don't go getting *sensible* on me…!"

His face contorted in anger, his voice almost a yelp. Sure, he'd told her to consider what was going on with their two friends. But he hadn't asked for *this*. Hadn't asked her to choke down her own feelings, with that distraught look on her face. Hadn't asked to her cast out her emotions, trample over them on her way forward.

"We don't change! However much you think you have, in my eyes, ain't none of you a lick different! You're the same as you were on day one! Katie Aalto is and always will be a selfish, stubborn crybaby!"

Hearing all this at point-blank range made her shoulders jump. The harder she tried to keep it together, the more these words shook her.

"That's whose messes I'm always cleaning up! The half-cocked, reckless, sky's-the-limit idealist who's never given a damn what other people thought about her! You ain't allowed to be jealous? You threw that right out? Since when the hell do you care about that shit? Don't break character and start breathing platitudes at me now!"

He spoke with vehemence, arms tightening around her. Burying her face in his chest, trying to slow her beating heart, Katie whispered, "That hurts, Guy."

"Shut up! This is nothing after that headbutt."

"…There are people watching…"

"Let 'em! It ain't no skin off my nose!"

Guy didn't care how loud he got. He paid no attention to the students milling around them, and that put them out of sight for Katie, too.

The levees broke, and she let the emotions take hold, hugging him as hard as she could, wailing, "…You coddle me like this… How am I supposed to gain any sense…?!"

Her hoarse sobs echoed down the corridor. Guy's mind was made up—until she was done, he wasn't letting go, no matter who said what.

Not long after, two students hustled into the offices of Kimberly's third-largest press club on the labyrinth's first layer.

"Woo, what a sight!"

"Oh-ho-ho-ho! Such passion! Ah, youth!"

"Mm? What the what?"

A woman looked up from the books on her desk, scowling. The editor in chief, Janet Dowling. The two club members jogged over, explaining.

"Oh-ho-ho-ho! See, we saw a pair of third-years in the hall up above, locked in each other's embrace."

"No hanky-panky going on, but that's what made it a sight for sore eyes! Just makes you wanna keep your distance and watch over 'em. Is there a word for that emotion?"

"*Sigh...* Even we can't spin that into an article. You're both slacking on the job."

Even sillier than she'd feared. Janet snorted once and turned her eyes back to her books. Curious, her companions peered over her shoulder.

"...Whatcha reading, boss?"

"You're pouring over all our back issues? Issue 821?! That's too old to call old! That's over forty years back!"

The number on the archival file shocked them. One eye on their reactions, Janet pointed at the pages left open on her desk.

"Here, here, here, here, here...and this one."

""" ? """

"Give 'em a read. Let me know your take."

Puzzled, they did as she prompted. At a glance, these seemed like ordinary old articles, written by their predecessors. But after a few more read throughs, they started getting it. The keen eyes honed by tracking gossip through the halls of Kimberly did not miss the strangeness lurking within.

"...Wow..."

"...Huh...!"

Their smiles drained away, and Janet dumped a pile of docs on the table.

"Then it ain't all in my head. To the extent you can, verify these

articles and report back," she ordered. "The faster, the better. Or...
things could get way worse."

Seeing the look on her face, they snatched the docs and ran off. Janet
got up, asking the ceiling how much time they had to spare.

With Katie's behavior in the back of his mind, Oliver was restless all
through the class he and Nanao shared. Once he split up with her, he
ran through the building, searching.

"...Nowhere, huh?"

He reached that conclusion in thirty minutes and sighed, drawing
to a standstill.

He'd be meeting Teresa later; right now he was looking for a different person. This person tended to attract attention, so if he was
around, someone would have noticed. If Oliver was finding no wit-
nesses, then odds were strong he'd not been on campus at all.

"You're really doing a number on me. Where are you, Yuri?" he
whispered, concern in his heart.

Around the time of the migration, Yuri Leik had abruptly broken off
all contact. Not only with the Sword Roses—Rossi and Fay also said
they hadn't seen him around. He'd always been hard to track down,
but this was by far his longest absence.

Still, Oliver had no leads to work with—and plenty of other things
on his plate. Shaking off that silver-haired boy's smile, Oliver turned—
and plunged into the labyrinth.

"Not like you to arrive exactly *on time*, Noll."

He'd darted through the first layer to his cousins' hidden workshop and found his vassals already assembled, Gwyn looking rather
surprised.

"Sorry, Brother," Oliver said, catching his breath. "I was looking for
someone, ran out the clock. I don't need a rest; let's get this started."

He took a seat at the head of the table. His eyes caught those of his covert operative, and the moment they did, she hid herself in the room next door. That hurt, and he frowned.

"...Teresa..."

"Sorry," Shannon said, wincing next to him. "She's...been like that. A few days...now. She just...needs time."

Aware the cause lay with him, Oliver could hardly say more. He focused on the duty at hand for now and vowed to have a real talk with her later. Gwyn noticed this shift and got things rolling.

"Today's agenda: First, the election outcome. Standings were close throughout, but our work in and out of the shadows paid off, and Godfrey's camp pulled off the victory. We've worked with the new president, Tim Linton, in the past. He's a bit half-baked, but we can cover for that and maintain good relations."

They'd fought long and hard, and yet this was all the time he spent on it. That got a round of grimaces and shaken heads from the room.

"President Linton, huh? Still sounds like a joke."

"Did anyone call him winning this?"

"Don't be stupid. They'd be a prophet."

"I hear Miligan's taking it pretty rough."

"She'll be fine. Godfrey went and sat with her."

"Plus, she'll have her hands full paying off her debts."

Takes flew fast and furious. Oliver sensed the mood was a little less tense than usual. While they might have plenty of concerns about the student council's future, the Watch victory was clearly very good news. Especially since their hard work had played a major role in it.

"Since her name's come up, let me throw an idea out there."

"Mm? What this, Gwyn?"

All eyes converged on him. Staring back, he said, "Would Miligan be worth recruiting? I'm starting to think so."

"____!"

Oliver's heart started racing. He kept it from showing, as Gwyn went on.

"She was always on the civil rights beat, and the way she thinks is in line with us. That's why she's worked well with us and the Watch. Previously, we had concerns about her underhanded side...but this election largely served to assuage that."

With that, he fell silent. Their comrades folded arms, mulling over the idea.

"I get...where you're coming from. Credit to our lord for his work here. Since she started hanging with you and yours, Miligan's been operating in public more—for better or worse."

"Yeah, quite a change from her days skulking around in the shadows."

It was nice to have his efforts recognized, and he appreciated their attempt to highlight that. But he was not about to make a careless answer here. After considering this from several angles, he responded.

"...I agree her character has come to light. But whether we should recruit her is another question. Even if our positions overlap—I'm not sure she'd agree with our methods."

"Fair. And that's not a topic you can broach lightly just to check. Revealing critical intel only for her to refuse—worst-case scenario, we'd have to kill her on the spot."

Gwyn nodded, mincing no words. Theirs was a harsh reality. This was hardly recruiting for an after-school club. Failure was not an option—and letting that failure stand even less so.

"But even in light of those requirements, Miligan's approach to the combat league made an impression. Not her rule-skirting strategies, mind you. I'm referring to her decision to drag Zoe back into public before she was consumed by the spell. I doubt anyone bought the retraction she uttered afterward. Just look at the odds—the risk clearly outweighed the return."

Everyone nodded. Miligan's team had given the impression they'd snatched that victory through cunning strategy, but no one here missed the huge gambles hidden within. In that state, it was hard to believe Zoe had been fully under her control, and even if so, there'd been a strong chance the faculty would call it too risky and stop the match. Ultimately, Garland's keen eye had avoided that outcome, but given the inherent risk factor, it was hard to claim that team had been put together purely in the interests of winning.

"Whether she's aware of it or not, Miligan acted for something greater than the math of it. That's my take anyway. And that resembles one means we've used to increase our ranks. We consider not just their character and views—we've proactively recruited isolated mages nearing their spell. In and out of campus, that's helped us reach our current size. Naturally, the flip side of that is that the cleanup is easier if they turn us down..."

Gwyn was not trying to hide anything under euphemisms here. Just stating the cold, hard facts.

But at this point, another hand shot up. Carmen Agnelli, the necromancer who'd briefly overseen Oliver's team during the Rivermoore incident. She had the gloomy aura that was characteristic of her vocation, but her big round eyes went a long way to countering it.

"If I may? Given the topic at hand, I've got a suggestion of my own."

She'd clearly been waiting for this. Oliver had not learned she was one of their number until after their first meeting. He was their leader, but Gwyn intentionally kept the bulk of their roster secret as a counterespionage measure. Oliver had not been surprised—during their search, he thought she seemed like the type.

"Go ahead, Carmen."

"The third-year, Katie Aalto. I'm sure you know her. One of the lord's friends, close to Miligan, hard-core rights activist since year one. And she *just* screwed up big-time."

Miligan had been bad enough, but this nearly made Oliver's heart stop. Carmen wasn't letting up, either.

"One, if we bring her in first, it'll be easier to recruit Miligan. But before that—she's dangerous as all hell. Reeks of getting consumed by the spell. Might be every bit as bad as Salvadori at that stage," Carmen ventured. "And when she goes, it'll be a doozy. I bet I'm not the only one expecting her to wreak havoc, right?"

That earned a loaded silence. They'd all spent long enough in this hellscape to hone a sense on which students were bad news. And all their senses were going off—she was a ticking time bomb.

"…Whether our instincts pan out or not, if her interests are turning to tír, that's not good. That's a field where the smallest actions can lead to catastrophe. And there's apostles in the mix. The more passion the mage has, the more danger there is."

"No need to tunnel in on tír stuff. Her major's magical biology."

"Curiosity drives all research. How could a place filled with unknown creatures not captivate her imagination? She's hardly the only one who's fallen for that trap. I know there's at least one person in this room who picked up a gnarly forbidden tome and paid the price."

Similar experiences were common in the upper forms, and this concrete example silenced the room. Carmen piled on further weighty words.

"Better we take her under our wing before she takes a wrong turn. I'm well aware that phrasing sounds hypocritical, but I also believe it."

Their comrades' voices heard, Gwyn slowly turned his eyes to his brother.

"Noll, we must know your thoughts."

The grim hand turned his way. Furiously trampling down all panic, he searched for an answer like threading a needle—a response that would justify his wishes.

"…It's clearly worth considering. But making our choice now would be hasty."

After a lengthy pause, he slowly began talking, deeply unsure he'd kept the tremor from his voice. Still, he could hardly remain silent here. Both for his comrades and his friends.

"Remember our priorities. Even if we add Vera Miligan and Katie Aalto to our ranks, it will not be today or tomorrow. While both have great potential, this is a holistic assessment based on their strength of character—and who they may become. Neither one possesses standout combat skills. In other words—they're a far cry from recruiting President Godfrey."

To support his rationale, he put out the best point of comparison. That produced a round of frustrated groans.

"That just makes me wanna take a run at him! We're sure we can't pull him?"

"Absolutely. We settled that debate ages ago. The way he thinks and acts certainly overlaps with us, but deep down, he's a protector. And we're assassins. That's not a trench you just fill in. Same goes for anyone drawn to his leadership."

"So how is Katie Aalto different? That girl came here incapable of killing a *bug*."

"True. But she's in the midst of a metamorphosis. Changes so drastic no one can tell where they might lead her. That's why we'd want to get our hands on her soon—it's dicey phrasing, but we've got a chance to imprint ourselves on her. I'm pretty sure she's the type to sacrifice just about anything for her goals."

This solemn proclamation came from a comrade who sat with his arms folded.

Oliver caught the invective in his throat, clenching his fists as hard as he could, trying to stifle the outburst. He was not permitted to blow his top here. At this table, Oliver Horn must serve as their unshakable lord.

He deeply regretted not wearing his mask here. Instead, he donned an invisible one. Allowing his comrades no glimpse of the stormy emotions within, turning the muscles of his face into an iron mask—and speaking.

"I won't stop you laying the groundwork for an eventual recruitment. That's an extension of default operating policy. But it's not the problem we need to concern ourselves with at this moment." Oliver then said, "Who do we *kill*? That's the topic that truly matters here, Gwyn Sherwood."

He shot his cousin a firm look, and Gwyn dropped his eyes, aware of how Oliver might be taking this.

"…I apologize for the distraction. Right you are, my lord."

This response pained Oliver. He'd known it would come but did not desire it. The mood grew tense, and his comrades turned their focus to the new discussion.

"Our attempts to rattle the faculty—built around red flags waved at Vanessa Aldiss—have been somewhat effective. During the migration incident, the rifts between her and her colleagues were on display. Probably time we threw more fuel on that fire."

"Assuming we keep Vanessa herself seething, four remain. We're still lacking the manpower required to tackle the headmistress or Instructor Gilchrist, and given the cleanup on her curses, we'll want to leave Instructor Baldia for later. Which means…"

The conditions laid out left only one answer. Gwyn spoke for them all.

"The process of elimination leads us to the astronomy instructor, Demitrio Aristides."

Silence fell. Facing this fact required the grimmest of resolves. Carmen got there first, throwing her arms out across the table, head resting on them.

"So we're finally after him! Hoo boy, I'm scared already. Might just piss myself."

"…Can it at least be easier than Enrico?"

"Not likely. His sorcery was pretty high-level, but since it all came from magineering roots, we could break it down a bit. Demitrio's deal ain't that straightforward."

Their target's threat level came up first, and Gwyn nodded, summing it up.

"He polished his skills on the front lines of the Gnostic hunts and developed a unique set of techniques melded with Azian philosophies. Worse, those spells."

The mood shifted from fear to awe. Their sources had given them a measure of the nature there, yet this was still the mystery to end all mysteries. He'd used those spells in plain sight during the migration, which proved invaluable, but that in no way meant Demitrio had exposed himself. He knew full well the sight of them meant nothing. They could not be conquered—and could not be imitated.

Nearly every mage in the world would reach that same conclusion, yet Gwyn voiced direct opposition.

"But we've got a way past that. Our strategy is simplicity itself. Once the battle begins, get Noll into sword range as fast as possible and finish him with a spellblade no one can possibly dodge," he explained. "You're all aware that Demitrio Aristides does not carry an athame. Thus, the spellblade will reign supreme. The moment our lord gets close, Aristides won't be able to do anything."

Recovering somewhat, everyone nodded. That was their greatest card on the path to victory. No one had ever witnessed Demitrio using sword arts; like the anti-athameist Gilchrist, his fighting style leaned toward spell range. And they could use that. Use their ultimate ace in the hole—the fourth spellblade.

"The attack team will be on the same scale as Enrico. That's as many as we can deploy without the faculty suspecting. If that proves impossible, we should delay the attack itself. And...as for *where* we attack, we've got a solid candidate. I'd go so far as to call it our only option."

Everyone nodded in agreement. From that point on, the discussion turned to specifics, plotting how to get Oliver in range to take down the warlock.

Everything that needed to be said had been, and their comrades left the workshop. Only then did he let the mask fall away, turning immediately to the man beside him.

"Brother!"

Gwyn looked up from the documents he was collecting. A gruff sort of smile, but one filled with love.

"What's wrong, Noll?"

"I—I hated doing that. Sorry."

He finally let out the apology. His voice sounding far younger, putting the lie to his performance as their lord. The trembling lips spoke volumes to his inner strife.

"Using you as an excuse to change the subject..."

His voice rasped. He'd been cornered and made that choice consciously, his decision trampling on his cousin's good will.

"I know why you suggested it—a lot of our members will graduate next year, and you don't want me feeling left behind. That was your thinking? If Miligan becomes one of us, that'll be someone else I can rely on. You put more stock in that than her contributions."

Remorse was making him positively dizzy. How often had his cousin's kindness saved him? It was saving him even now. He couldn't put that into words—but neither could he bring himself to accept that proposal.

"I'm grateful for that, but...also scared. Maintaining clear divisions between my outer and inner circles has allowed me to get through this. Miligan and Katie are both on *that* side. If I pull them over to *this* one..."

Just the thought sent a shiver down his spine. The nature of that fear went beyond the impulse to keep his friends out of this. The Sword Roses and his other public friends were what kept him going. With their help, Oliver could stand up to the burdens weighing on him. He was terrified to even consider the consequences of losing any part of that.

"And adding Katie Aalto's name only fanned that fear. Am I right?" Gwyn said, striking at the heart of the matter.

Oliver nodded listlessly. Gwyn put his hands on the boy's shoulders.

"Keep your head up, Noll."

That got Oliver's eyes up, but gingerly. Anxiety and self-reproach glistened therein, plain for Gwyn to see. Oliver momentarily looked every bit as young as he had been when they first met—and so Gwyn gave the boy a hug. Cursing his inability to do anything to ease the turmoil within, any more than he had back then.

"If I'll serve as an excuse, use me as one. Force anything on me you need to. There's absolutely no need to fret about it or even think twice. The opportunity to ease your burden helps me. The burden is one I forced on you in the first place."

"No, Brother, you never—"

He cut off Oliver's protestations by burying the boy's head in his chest. Convinced he could not bear to hear any words that followed. Instead, he spoke himself, trying to cover up his younger brother's thoughts.

"Shannon and I are staying at Kimberly, studying souls and working as curse cleanup and consolation consultants. We won't leave you on your own in this hellscape. But we won't be students—and that adds distance. We may be forced to act differently around you in public, on campus. When that happens, the more people you've got to help you through it, the better. That's all I was thinking. Flipping what Carmen said, I also know it'll help if we need to pull Katie Aalto in later." Gwyn went on to say, "But you've got a point. At this stage, all speculation about our future is optimistic. If we can't take Demitrio Aristides down, we have no next year."

That had been a mistake. Talking about the future just made things harder for his young cousin. They shouldn't be dwelling on that now. They need spare no thoughts for anything but the enemy at hand. So that's what Gwyn did. Well aware that would only increase his own suffering.

"After the Enrico fight, our comrades have a lot of faith in your skills. Thus, our plan this time leans heavily on them. It's going to be very hard on you."

Oliver felt drops falling on his shoulders. When he realized they fell from his brother's eyes, all he could do was return the embrace. Shannon joined them, putting her arms around both, rubbing against her brother's wet cheek.

"Gwyn's…at peak pain…right now."

As they held each other, Teresa watched through the slit of the door. "……!"

She wanted to join them. Desperately. Run right over and throw her arms into the huddle. Make this not a one-sided yearning but a connection where pain and suffering could be shared.

But she could no longer tell if this stemmed from consideration—or from her own desires. That kept her from taking a step. Teresa bit her sleeve so hard her teeth creaked, searing into her eyes a sight she could not be a part of, crouching alone in the darkness.

After the meeting, Oliver returned to campus. As he drew near his dorm room, he spotted something tucked under the door.

"…Mm?"

He carefully picked up the little envelope, examining it. Mindful of magical traps—but the moment he recognized the handwriting of the name, that caution dissipated.

"Yuri?!"

He tore open the envelope and read the letter within. As he did, Pete must have heard the noise; he opened the door, looking sleepy.

"…What's up, Oliver? Did you just get back?"

"Sorry, I'm heading right back out. You go on to bed!"

The letter's contents made Oliver ditch the dorm. They specified the garden next to the school building, so he ran past the fountains and, once on-site, scanned the area for any sign of the boy.

"I'm here, but where is—?"

"Yo! Oliver!"

Startled, he looked up toward the voice. Yuri's face was peering over the edge of the roof far above.

"Wha…?! What are you doing up there, Yuri?!"

"Best place to see! Come on up!"

But he didn't have a broom with him, so he couldn't exactly just fly

up there. He considered going through the school and out a window
but felt like Yuri would vanish again if he took that long. Abandoning
the idea, Oliver merely ran up the wall itself. The shortest route to the
roof, where he scowled at his friend.

"Dammit, man! Where have you been all this time? I've been worried sick!"

"Sorry! But hey, have a look up there! You can yell at me after."

"Up there? In the—?"

His gaze went up—and words failed him. The darkness was pocked
by infinite stars.

"……"

"See? More than you'd think." Yuri grinned, seated on the roof's
peak.

Sighing, Oliver settled down next to him, eyes on the view above.

"…You called me here to show me this?"

"Yep. Well, more like I wanted to see it with you. It's an unusually
clear night."

"…True. Kimberly doesn't get this clear often. All the magic particles in the air tend to pollute it."

"Labyrinth activity's at a low ebb, which might be why. I'm glad I
found a clear night. I'm not sure when the next chance'll be."

That sounded ominous, and Oliver turned to look at him.

"I think," Yuri began, eyes on the sky above, "I might not be back for
a while."

"…Something stopping you?"

"Yeah. But I can't say what. It's a big mess, and trying to explain any
of it would likely make things worse. Sorry, but I'm gonna have to stay
vague."

Yuri met Oliver's eyes with a sad smile. And that was enough to
stop Oliver from asking questions. All mages had secrets. Ones you
couldn't even share with friends. Oliver told himself he was no different and fought down the urge to put Yuri in an armlock to keep him
there. He looked up at the stars instead.

"You've always been a broad-strokes guy. But…let me worry, at least. You see a way to sort this out?"

"Honestly, can't say… But I know what I'm gonna do. That much I'm sure of."

Yuri looked back up, reaching a hand toward the stars above.

"I'm walking my own path. Like you are. I've made my choice."

"……"

Oliver just nodded. Neither spoke another word, just lay there stargazing. A comfortable silence settled over them.

And eventually, Yuri sat up. "Got a hunch I should get going. You hurry back to the dorm. You should still make it in time."

"…You're gonna vanish again?" Oliver asked, looking lonely.

At the edge of the roof, Yuri glanced back once.

"Sorry," he said. "But I promise I'll invite you to see the stars again."

And with that, Yuri disappeared. Oliver sat still, staring after him until he could no longer hear his friend's footsteps.

That same night, after Shannon and Teresa retired to bed, Gwyn was up late working on strategies when he heard someone running to him.

"Gwyn, you here?"

A comrade burst in the door, and he rose to meet her. A bundle of files in her hands, the editor of the third-largest school paper—Janet Dowling—was badly out of breath.

"What's wrong, Janet? Is it that urgent?"

"Dire. Look at this."

She hunched over the table and started spreading out a number of papers. All clippings from ancient newspaper articles. Following the parts underlined in red, Gwyn furrowed his brow.

"……!"

"You see it? Yeah. For the past forty years, students who act just like Yuri Leik have been popping up on campus—and in the labyrinth," said Janet. "Different names, different faces, but everyone who meets them gets the same impression—uncannily friendly, to the point of ignorance. Later on, if they tried to figure who these strangers were, they found out no such student existed."

That was the common point in each of these articles. Janet's demeanor and tone unrelenting, she dug deeper.

"Once upon a time, a student died on campus—boy, I wish it was that cute. But this horror story's been repeating on the regular since that first incident. Naturally, Yuri Leik's a bit different in that he's actually enrolled—that whole transfer student thing. But...given what's going on in Kimberly, it makes sense they'd shore up his identity."

She had the data and the analysis. It was time she voiced the conclusion.

"He's been at Kimberly the whole forty years. That's my read on it. And what do you make of that number?"

Gwyn put his hand to his chin, considering this deduction. It didn't take him long to get there, and his eyes widened.

"...Demitrio Aristides started teaching—"

"At exactly the same time."

The same answer Janet had reached. Gwyn's fists tightened up, and Janet added, "Honestly, I don't have a clue *what* Yuri Leik is. I can guess he might be some sort of customizable spy, a type of familiar— but the conceptual framework underlying that is so out-there it likely doesn't tie into anything I know about. So we're better off ignoring that aspect. Focus only on what we do know."

With limited information, speculation only got you so far. So Janet narrowed it down. What was their biggest concern right now? And how should they deal with it?

"He's gotten close to our lord. You know that. If that's because the one who sent him wants him there—then he's already got Oliver Horn listed as a prime suspect."

Gwyn nodded, panic roiling within. Janet leaned in close.

"We've gotta kill them *soon*. Yuri Leik *and* Demitrio Aristides. Or none of us will live for long."

*   *   *

Unaware of their conclusion, the boy at the heart of the issue was in the forest on the labyrinth's second layer.

"Hmm, looks like I made it back," Yuri muttered, eyes darting all around. Shortly after the combat league ended, he'd been possessed by a vague fear of any teachers finding him and had spent the bulk of his time lurking down here to avoid them. His trip up to see Oliver had been his first time on campus in a while, and getting back here had required a lot of sneaking.

"What now? What do I do? I can't run from the faculty forever, so maybe I should ditch this place entirely—but then I couldn't see Oliver, or—"

But even as he spoke, a wave of dizziness sent him to his knees, clutching his head. Like a pressure so strong it bent his very thoughts. Once, he'd been unable to perceive this happening, but now he gritted his teeth, struggling against it.

"Rrgh! This again! Anytime I consider leaving Kimberly…"

That thought always brought on revulsion, an impulse to put it out of mind. Once he started fighting it, it was clear how weird that was. The moment he realized this was *implanted* with no regard for his own free will, Yuri got a hazy idea of just what he was.

"…That's not my *role*. Someone's very insistent on that," he said. "But too bad. I know better. I've made up my mind to go my own way!"

He forced aside the alien thing inside him. The urges were stronger than ever, but the more times he felt them, and the more he analyzed them, the better he gotta at enduring—and stifling them. Keeping his breath even, Yuri focused on self-control.

"I'm afraid your way leads to a dead end."

Before his efforts panned out, a man took shape before him, out of nowhere.

"…Instructor Demitrio…"

The astronomy instructor wore an old-fashioned robe. Clutching his head, Yuri struggled to his feet. Demitrio let out a soft sigh.

"Quite a run you gave me. But it was always a matter of time. You are *me*. You cannot flee yourself."

That calm proclamation proved Yuri's theory correct.

"...I knew it! I'm *something* under your control."

"I've done the same on eighteen previous occasions, but you're the first to become aware of it."

"Is 'familiar' close enough? Or am I more of a splinter?"

Yuri's irrepressible curiosity led to these questions, but he was backing away, trying to find a chance to run. Demitrio knew that but didn't budge, slowly drawing his wand.

"No point in considering it. You'll know once you return to me."

"Fragor!"

Yelling over him, Yuri laid down a smoke screen and dove for the thicket yonder. Getting caught was bad news, but the second layer offered no shortage of hiding spots. Once out of eyesight, he was upbeat about his chances of escape—

"■ ■ ■ ■ ■" Swell.

He'd taken a few steps before a massive wall rose from the ground ahead, blocking his path. Yuri blinked in surprise. He'd heard the man say *something* but seen no spell hit that ground. What logic generated this wall? He couldn't begin to imagine.

"Like I said, no point."

Demitrio's left hand reached out and clutched his skull. A moment later, a spell echoed.

"Altum somnum."

"Augh—"

His mind cut out, and Yuri's limbs went limp, his body dangling. Holding him upright in one hand, Demitrio cast again.

"Conflandum."

And then he absorbed him. Soul, ether, provisional flesh, everything that composed the Yuri Leik persona within that provisional flesh.

With the insides gone, it fell to the ground, and the man aimed his wand at it.

"*Ignis.*"

The flames consumed Yuri's body in seconds. A few to reduce him to ash and a few more for that to crumble to nothing. Flecks of ash scattered on the breeze, and then he used another spell to clean the scorch marks off the ground, leaving no trace behind, no evidence that a boy named Yuri had ever been there.

"...You've gathered quite a lot of information. An entirely different person than you started out as. Such a change in less than two years..."

Analyzing the soul he'd absorbed, Demitrio was both bemused and impressed. What he read here was the detective's final report. After reviewing it for a while, he had to admit it came up short.

"Nothing definitive. After his last report, I implanted the urge to focus on Oliver Horn, but he ignored that, going everywhere else instead."

Gathering that it would be futile, he checked all interactions thoroughly. Mostly trifles. He reached the end of the memories, and his analysis concluded.

"...Stargazing, hmm?"

That last image lingered. For an instant, Demitrio was drawn to it... but then he pulled his eyes away, vanishing into the forest. A gust of wind caused the leaves to stir—and then there was nothing left but trees that held their tongues.

CHAPTER 4

Aristides, the Philosopher of Ignorance

Mount a broom and you could fly anywhere you liked. Ordinaries often envied mages that luxury.

But that notion had a flip side—there were plenty of places even mages could not lightly tread.

Even close at hand, there were natural hills and forests. A dense veil of leaves hid the terrain below, obscuring what threats might lie within. Burning that away was an option, but that would incinerate nature's bounty, too. Thus, the standard village mage was expected to have at most a practical grasp on the local ecosystems, keep the local threats from harming the ordinaries—but otherwise, live and let live.

"Haah, haah, haah…!"

Badly out of breath, young Demitrio was running through these hills. Ordinarily, he would have been enthusiastic about the life teeming in these forests, but today he merely cursed the trees for limiting his vision. Something could be lurking in the shadows behind any one of those. Wild things—or the girl he sought.

"…Maya! Where are you, Maya?!"

An hour earlier:

Demitrio had arrived at the little schoolhouse, armed with supplies to teach the village children.

"Good morning, boys and girls! Mm? No Maya? Not like her to oversleep."

She was always in the front row. The other children exchanged glances.

"…She's not here."

"Yeah…"

That sounded ominous, so he gave them a look.

"…What happened? Let me hear it."

The children fidgeted and began talking.

"…I saw her this morning! She said a shooting star fell nearby."

"She saw it from her window at sunrise. It landed in the forest over there."

A boy pointed through the window. Then he looked at the boy seated next to him.

"But Flett said she was making it up. They had a fight, and Maya got mad and ran away."

The other boy shifted awkwardly. That was enough for Demitrio to connect the dots.

"You think…she went into the hills?"

There was a grim silence. Demitrio dropped his things on the podium and ran out.

"Free study today! Don't leave the room till I get back!"

He let the village grown-ups know and plunged straight into the forest. He'd been searching for his student for the better part of an hour now. He'd raced all around this section of forest but found no signs of Maya anywhere, and his panic was starting to reach a fever pitch. The late autumn leaves hid her tracks, and the spores released by mushrooms during this time of year dulled his familiars' noses.

"…Stay calm… Deep breath…! Don't search blind! What would she do?"

He forced himself to imagine her choices.

Maya was diligent, always listened. She knew how scary the hills could be and wouldn't leave the path without good reason. If he still couldn't find her, some accident must have knocked her off the path. Maybe she fled an animal attack. Or something distracted her, and she slipped off a cliff.

"......! Wait—"

With that thought in mind, Demitrio reexamined his surroundings and found a patch of brush that showed signs of something living pushing through. He peered through the gap, saw a steep slope just beyond—and plunged right in.

"...This way—!"

He followed the marks down. If she'd taken a tumble, she might not last long. Odds were high that her injuries immobilized her, and there were plenty of magical beasts here that would prey upon that.

And that conjecture proved accurate; at the bottom of the slope, he found Maya leaning against a sturdy tree root, surrounded by three wild wargs.

"T-Teach..."

"Maya!"

His wand snapped up. The wargs bared their teeth, growling, and he roared back:

"Get away from her! **Tonitrus!**"

The bolt hit the ground and spooked the wargs; they fled. Demitrio swiftly turned to Maya. She had a broken ankle and a tree branch impaling her chest. Likely from the momentum of the fall. Given the sheer quantity of blood, he had to act fast, or she would not be long for this world.

"Lemme see that wound, Maya. You're safe now, I'll heal you—"

"...I'm fine..."

He'd raised his wand to chant a spell, but Maya smiled up at him. He froze to the spot.

"...What...?"

"This thing made it all better. It doesn't hurt anymore."

Something half Maya's size stepped out from behind the tree.

"Quuuuu..."

Tufts of blue fur, three scared purple eyes, all staring up at Demitrio.

No scroll he'd read had mentioned the like, but there it stood, alive and kicking.

Urgent treatment complete, Maya pleaded with Demitrio to take the creature back to the village with them. He wrestled with the idea but ultimately agreed. The villagers were relieved to see the girl safe, but they soon became curious about the unknown life-form.

"Whoa, what is that thing?"

"It's a giant furball!"

"You ever seen the like, Granddad?"

"...Not in all my years. It sure don't hail from these parts."

The elder shook his head, peering at the creature in the cage. Demitrio had been examining Maya's condition in a room nearby, but he emerged to chastise them.

"Please, keep your distance from it. I put up a barrier, but I'm not sure it's safe."

"It's not bad!" Maya yelled, running out after him. She darted over to the cage. "Teach, let it outta the cage! It kept me safe! If it hadn't helped, the wound on my chest—!"

"I know! I hear you, Maya."

Demitrio knelt down, patting her head. He looked her right in the eye.

"But listen to me. I've got to be careful. There's a lot of danger out there, and I have to protect the village. That's my *job*."

The girl couldn't argue with that. He nudged her back inside and then turned to the villagers.

"While Maya recovers, I'll be observing this creature and studying it. Making sure to keep it separated. If that's okay with the mayor."

"Of course. We'll trust you with this."

The elder nodded, smiling, and glanced at the thing in the cage.

"But that is the damnedest creature. I've seen my share of magic beasts, but nothing remotely like this. Is this a visitor from the stars?"

"That's one possibility I'll be investigating. I'll need a little time."

Demitrio forced his tone to stay calm. But in truth, curiosity made his heart leap—worse than any other villager here.

The creature had been in a weakened condition even as he brought it back, so Demitrio began by searching for a viable food source. He tried everything close at hand, and the creature eagerly ate fresh apples and grapes.

It prefers fruits, then? Neither its diet nor its physical composition betray any immediate signs of aggression.

Watching it feed, Demitrio pondered the matter. On a whim, he spoke to it, and it broke off its meal, coming over to him. He gave it a few more grapes, digging further into that thought.

It's fairly intelligent. But not enough to converse with us or guide our thoughts. At this stage, I'm assuming a chance migration. The lack of similar creatures in the vicinity supports that notion...

He knew a decent amount about tír. Given the current celestial positions, this thing likely hailed from Ayrioneptu, the Rotting Sea's Shoals—one stop closer than Vanato, the Chthonic Retreat. But beyond that, he was in the dark. Few scrolls contained detailed accounts of creatures from that tír.

But the way it healed Maya—that seems a bit too pat for an ordinary migration.

He was hung up on that point. He hadn't told the girl, but her chest wound should have been fatal. If the creature hadn't patched her up, she'd never have held out long enough for Demitrio to get there. This creature had prevented the worst—but it hadn't actually *healed* her. The wound remained—but the tree branch impaling her had *fused with her flesh*, staunching the bleeding. The border between the plant fibers and her human flesh barely remained.

He'd surgically removed a section of that for further study, but he couldn't begin to predict what influence it might have on Maya in the future.

Keep a close watch on her progress. I should have time to assess the risks afterward.

Despite his concerns, Maya's recovery progressed steadily. Just in case, he kept her resting for a solid month, but as her condition improved, that made her grumble. Demitrio was forced to allow her to go back to normal.

"Just don't start out running all over the place. Nothing feels wrong?"

"Nope! I'm fine! Nothing wrong with me!"

She hopped up and down to demonstrate, giggling.

"Have it your way," he said, grimacing but nodding. "Okay, you're cleared to go back to normal life. But promise me no more children running into the hills alone."

That made Maya go very still.

"I promise," she said, looking serious. "But what's going on with that creature? Can I see it?"

"It's doing fine. And it's not in the cage anymore; don't worry. I'm still studying it, so I can't let you see it right away..."

He trailed off there.

"...Did it come from another world?" Maya asked.

"...I can't say for sure, but I think so."

Demitrio picked his words carefully.

"It's super nice!" Maya said, grinning as if trying to wash away his concerns. "Just like you said it would be!"

That same night, her words looped through Demitrio's mind as he watched the creature sleep, sprawled out on the floor of his room.

Maya's too optimistic. But...

He was trapped between caution and hope. He couldn't quite put the desire to believe her out of his mind.

It's a tír creature with the power to heal, friendly toward humans, docile... If all of that is true, it's a major discovery. It'll shake the foundations of what we know about tír.

Could he let that possibility get away? The tragedies of the past had left the magic world with extremely negative views on tír. Only solid evidence to the contrary would turn that around. Bringing him one step closer to his dream of one day visiting a tír.

I know I should just incinerate it. Or at least report this to the Gnostic Hunters. Either way, the outcome would be the same. Regardless of whether it poses a real threat, this creature would perish.

And imagining that left him mussing up his hair.

I can't just...let that happen. I've got a shot at making my dream come true here!

His hand reached for the sleeping creature, stroking its warm, soft fur. He bit his lip.

"If you hadn't saved her, Maya would have died... That's a fact."

After a long struggle between what was right for a mage and what he *wanted* to be true, he gingerly turned the rudder toward the latter.

"Oh, Fluffball's out!"

"Is it allowed out now?!"

"I'm gonna let it get used to things slowly. As a start, I'm giving it short walks around the village. You'd best keep your distance for now."

The sight of Demitrio and the creature delighted the children. The villagers had long since given it a name befitting its appearance, and seeing it out and about failed to raise any hackles. If he hadn't been stopping them, they'd have run right in and started petting it. Demitrio was well aware of the implications, but he kept on walking.

"...Worried about the kids? Don't worry; no one here will hurt you."

Fluffball kept stopping to look back at the children—but its attention was soon drawn elsewhere: to the red orbs growing in the fields.

"Oh, the tomatoes are ripe. Curious?"

On impulse, he got permission from the farmer, plucked a tomato, and gave it to Fluffball. It gobbled up the fruit, and the children watching got even more excited.

"Whoa, it's eating a tomato!"

"It really likes it!"

"It eats its veggies!"

"Unlike you, Flett!"

"Hey! I eat my veggies! If they're cut up small!"

Demitrio couldn't repress a smile. They'd likely make friends fast, he thought, relieved.

They repeated these walks awhile—and then Fluffball did something unprecedented.

"Mm? What's up? You want to go over there?"

Demitrio followed after it. It headed to a just-sprouted field, where a villager was taking a breather, drink in hand.

"Oh, what's this, Teach? Got Fluffball with you?"

"It wanted to come this way. Not exactly tomato season, though…"

Baffled, Demitrio cocked his head. Fluffball was tugging on a bag of compost, trying to drag it off the field.

"…You don't approve of that fertilizer?"

Catching its drift, Demitrio removed the bag from the field, and Fluffball stopped moving, like its work there was done.

Then the farmer's wife came rushing out of the house, yelling, "You grabbed the wrong one again! That's for millet!"

That shocked both men. They turned and looked at Fluffball.

"…Well, I never. It knows which fertilizer to use?"

"News to me. I had no clue…"

Demitrio had seen no evidence to suggest this. Meanwhile, the villager rubbed his hands together.

"Let's give this a shot! Show it the whole stock!"

They took Fluffball to the shed. When it saw the bags of fertilizer, it burst into action, almost sliding across the floor. Tentacles extended from inside the fur, leaving marks on every bag it could reach.

"Those are all bad, huh? Mm? What's it doing now?"

As Demitro watched, Fluffball started sketching a simple picture in the dirt on the floor. Long, tall stalks—reminiscent of the millet the villagers often grew. Realizing why it would draw this before these bags, the villager looked impressed.

"Use this on millet, not tomatoes? If it can distinguish different crops, that impressive."

Demitrio agreed. Shaking its fur—happy it had made its point—Fluffball moved to a different bag and drew another picture.

"Mix those two and use them on the melons? You can figure that out, too?"

"I'm curious, now. I got extra field space; let's give it a shot."

All excited, the villager got to work. A little hesitant, Demitrio let him go. The creature wasn't touching the crops itself—just changing how the existing fertilizers were used. He didn't see how that would pose a problem.

And a few months later, the dramatic outcome stood before Demitrio.

"See, Teach? Look at this bounty!"

The villager was standing behind plants laden with tomatoes. At Fluffball's side, Demitrio just gaped—and the villager grabbed a tomato, taking a bite.

"Huge—and lots of them! Taste great, too! All fields where we followed Fluffball's advice. The bringer of the harvest!"

Word was spreading, and villagers were gathering, huddling around Demitrio and Fluffball.

"Bring it to my fields!"

"What about cabbage? Does it do wheat?"

"Not fair! I want it first!"

"Actually, I was thinking about growing sugarcane…"

Ultimately, Fluffball paid a visit to every field. The results were dramatic—and the whole village doted on the bringer of the harvest. Some even began praying to it—but this, Demitrio strictly forbade, not wanting to arouse unwarranted suspicions in outsiders.

Naturally, Demitrio *was* being careful. The more it contributed to the village, the more it proved just how much influence it had on humans. After gaining trust with better harvests, would it start agitating the villagers? He was watching for that. But years passed with no evidence of anything untoward. It never objected to living with Demitrio, never tried to leave the house on its own—Fluffball seemed entirely content.

"…You tell them how to get more crops and then feast on them, huh?"

Fluffball was considerably larger than when it had first arrived. It was munching away at a bunch of grapes, and that sight made it easy to believe all his fears were in vain.

"You're a simple creature. I guess I really did make the right choice…"

Creatures like this lived on tír, too. Demitrio didn't think that was at all strange. Just as their world had all manner of creatures, tír ecosystems were highly varied. It made no sense that all of them would be harmful to humans. It was possible to coexist with some, and others might well bring bounty. The creature before him had basically proven that—and he was extremely grateful for it.

"…Um…Teach?"

"Can we…play with Fluffball?"

He looked up and found a group of children peering through the open door. Demitrio smiled and stood up.

"Sure. But don't wear it out. It just ate a lot."

"Yes!"

"C'mere! Let's go to the creek!"

The children led Fluffball out. Demitrio walked along behind them, thinking—recording all this and telling the world? That was his duty in life.

A long time spent in close proximity had told him much about Fluffball's life cycle. But the next step baffled him. The contents of his research were revolutionary, but he had nowhere to publish them.

"…I've got a pile of papers written. But who to show them to?"

Arms folded, he looked up at the shelf filled with scrolls—and a panicked cry came from the door.

"Teach! It's Flett—he's…!"

Right away, he knew this was bad news. He switched from researcher to village-mage mode, grabbed his wand, and ran out the door.

He arrived to find a mudslide just outside of town. He dove right in, trying to extract the student trapped within.

"Supernatet!"

Working carefully, Demitrio made rocks, which ordinaries could never lift, float away. With people buried inside, he could not use a doublecant to yank it all away at once; a further collapse could cause a secondary disaster. Fighting off his panic, he maintained precision and finally got the boy's body out of the dirt.

"Flett! Wake up, Flett!"

"Can you heal him? You can, right, Teach?!"

His student was no longer breathing, but Demitrio did everything he could. Spells to force the heart and lungs into action, closing up visible wounds with healing. But ten minutes later—the outcome was all too clear.

"……I'm sorry……," Demitrio whispered, his wand hanging limp.

The nearby villagers turned pale.

"…No… *No!*"

"He's all healed up! His chest is rising and falling! He'll wake up any second!"

Demitrio shook his head. That was just his spell at work. There was no life left for him to save.

"…It took too long to get him out. Even with his wounds healed, his brain……"

That was everything. If the heart and lungs ceased to function, the brain died first. Anyone who'd studied healing knew that ironclad rule. Mages were no exception, much less the far more fragile ordinaries. Once a certain length of time passed, the odds of resuscitation dropped like a stone. Demitrio had done everything he could but had not been in time.

"Even if his body lives, his mind is not here… Right?" the elder said, stepping out in front. He'd lived longer than anyone else here and had seen the like before.

Demitrio nodded, and the boy's parents collapsed in sobs.

"Very well." The elder closed his eyes. "Then let him go. If you do not, the soul will be trapped here."

It took him a long moment before he accepted that request. He raised his wand to his chest, seared the dead face of the boy he'd taught since early childhood into his mind—and cast the spell.

"…**Impediendum.**"

The false pulse stopped, as did his breathing. Before his eyes, a student went still forever.

"…Flett…!"

The parents clung to their child's body as it went cold. Demitrio had been helpless to stop this, and he could only stand and stare.

He treated the other wounded and carried the body back to the village, where the funeral took place. A village this small, nearly everyone was in attendance. Demitrio, too, joined the throngs in black in the town's largest building—one used for just about everything. The boy had often played with Fluffball, so he brought it along.

"Don't take it so hard. You did what could be done. We all know that."

In the crowd of mourners, Demitrio was sitting hunched over, and the elder patted his shoulders. He knew no one blamed him. But that didn't stop him from blaming himself. He could imagine countless ways the boy might have lived, ways he could have stopped this from happening.

"...I'm...gonna step outside."

Having villagers comfort him was making it worse, so he fled the funeral. With no one to stop him, he pounded a fist into a rock wall.

"...If I'd been watching the kids instead of writing papers...at least kept a familiar on the headstrong ones...!"

His mind was so full of regret, he never realized—Fluffball was no longer at his feet.

"...Ah..."

"...Fluffball..."

The children grieving by the coffin saw Fluffball join them. Their eyes turned its way, reaching for its fur as if seeking salvation—and tentacles extended from within, carrying little scraps of flesh coiled in their tips to the children's mouths. In their sadness, the scent proved invitingly familiar to the children.

"...What is it?"

"...You want us to eat these?"

It seemed odd, but they loved Fluffball and didn't refuse. One after another swallowed the flesh, and only Maya sensed anything wrong. She jumped to her feet.

"Wait, don't—"

But several had already swallowed. The soft texture and smell, like fermented beans, made their faces scrunch up.

"…Ugh, that's nasty…"

"But also…"

They frowned, unsure how to put it into words. Their friend's coffin lay in front of them, a symbol of their grief…but it no longer seemed like something to be sad about.

"…Huh? Flett…?"

"Are you…there…?"

Finally noticing Fluffball's absence, Demitrio came rushing back to the funeral, alarmed. It was worse than he'd feared. At a glance, he knew it was all over.

"No…"

The adults stood stunned before a fragrant mound of dirt. The children were buried within, only their faces sticking out, melting into the soil. The coffin lid had opened, and the boy inside was among them. His face was drained of blood, yet otherwise terrifyingly lifelike. His eyes turned toward Demitrio.

"Oh—Teach—"

He smiled. As if following his lead, the other children all smiled, too. Innocently.

"Wow, Fluffball—"

"Flett—came back to us—"

"Why—didn't we realize? If we rot—we're all the same! There are no boundaries between us—"

A shudder ran up Demitrio's spine. Instinctively, he knew this was not a sight that belonged in this world—and that this *was* Fluffball. There were hairs in that mud, three purple eyes placed about it.

"Come on—join us—"

"We'll be together!"

"All one—inside Fluffball—"

The children were calling out, and drawn to that, the adults rose to their feet, approaching the pile of mud. Snapping out of it, Demitrio grabbed one after another, trying to stop them.

"Wait, if you go—"

"…But…"

"…The children are calling…"

Not one lent him an ear. He could tell they'd already taken leave of their senses. The corruption of their minds had progressed too far. And that had not started here. The charm on this mud heap was not nearly strong enough. Even an ordinary could fight it off. Unless they'd been exposed to a fatal dose of something else, over a long period of time.

"…I'm sorry, Teach…"

An apology from the dirt heap. His student's face twisted with tears, there with the other children.

"…Maya…"

"…I did…a bad thing. I buried…pieces of Fluffball…in the fields. It said we could get lots of crops that way…so I did what it said. At night…over and over…"

That explained everything—and took Demitrio's breath away. The cause of this calamity was all too clear.

How had he not noticed? That abundance was too dramatic to be the result of adjusted fertilizers. He should have suspected direct interference.

Demitrio had kept his eyes on Fluffball itself, not giving it a chance to act. But—Maya was taking care of the fields for it. She'd been the first to fall under its influence, unconsciously in its thrall. It would not have been hard for it to pass pieces of itself along. All it had to do was drop them while out for a walk or when the children came over to play. It could communicate directly with Maya, so she was free to pick them up and bury them at her leisure. And the village's entire food supply subjected the villagers to tír influence. It had likely picked this evening's funeral to finish things because the shared grief made it easier to assimilate everyone. All right under Demitrio's eyes.

It was too late now. It no longer mattered, but one fact floated into his mind—this was how Ayrioneptu's god invaded. Rot as a vessel for universal unification.

"...I wanted to believe, Teach. That Fluffball wasn't bad...that your dream wasn't wrong...!"

His student's cry shot Demitrio through the heart. Like Maya, hope had clouded his vision. A tír creature, friendly to humans. That had blinded him, and he'd drowned in it, completely missing the true threat. Though this was an all-too-classic path to the birth of a gnosis, one repeated countless times throughout human history.

"...Come..."

"Join us...!"

The adults behind grabbed hold of him. Not a shred of hostility anywhere, just trying to pull him into the alien rules governing them. His hand shaking, Demitrio reached for his wand. He knew now. The error he'd made and the outcome it led to.

"AahhhhHHHHHHHHHHHHHH!"

With a heartrending scream, he drew his wand. And began massacring the village he'd loved.

The next morning, the first Gnostic Hunters arrived, responding to the missive his familiar had delivered.

"Ugh, that's a bad one."

"What happened? You the village mage?"

Houses and fields alike reduced to ash, one man standing at the center of that scorched earth. Gazing at the results of his own actions, Demitrio spoke without a trace of emotion.

"...They're all dead. I killed every last one of them."

A single tear rolled down his cheek. He could see the sights of yesterday overlaid upon those ashes. The peaceful village lives. The children's smiles. Everything he'd ruined. Everything he'd failed to protect.

"...And it's all...my fault..."

*   *   *

A month after he was taken to the Gnostic Hunters' base for questioning, Demitrio was released. Harboring a tír creature was hardly forgivable, but since he'd taken care of it himself, they'd let it slide. That was largely how Gnostic Hunter verdicts came down—he'd certainly received several stiff penalties but was sent back home.

"You're back, Demitrio!"

"We heard all about it. How awful… But at least you're safe."

His parents greeted him warmly. The repercussions of his error hurt them, too, but neither one said a word about it. As grateful as he was for that, warmth was hardly what he sought now. He told his side of the story and apologized for it.

"Father, Mother…," he said, his voice like ice. "May I see the results of your research?"

An unforeseen request, and they looked perplexed. The moment he'd left for a country village, their research no longer had any bearings on his life. Clueless as to the reason for his sudden interest, they began to pry.

"…Magic techniques based on eastern philosophies?"

"But your sister already—"

"I'll work under her. If need be, I'll subject myself to her experiments. No—I'll volunteer for it."

He bowed his head. Sensing grim resolve, his parents' eyes went wide.

"Slow down, Demitrio. There's no need to rush—"

"I'm going to be a Gnostic Hunter."

That took his parents' breath away. The one path they'd thought this son would never take. But Demitrio—was no longer the boy they'd known. The boy who'd gazed at stars and talked of dreams no longer existed. Before them stood a mage, cursed with a *duty*.

"I'm too old to start conventional training. I know that much. So I need a weapon. Something all my own, that no one else has."

*   *   *

The labyrinth's fourth layer, the Library of the Depths, was Kimberly's largest reserve of writings, protected by reapers—and all upperclassmen knew the layer itself extended far beyond the library's confines. That proximity meant many students wanted workshops there, but competition was fierce, and only a few managed to get their hands on one.

"Everyone here?"

In one of those premium spaces, Oliver and his vassals had gathered for a common cause. Gwyn surveyed the comrades present, and the seventh-year necromancer Carmen Agnelli answered.

"We are, but we're not quite ready. The stealth squad is resupplying."

"Understood. Make it snappy."

With that, Gwyn fell silent. Next to him, Oliver was marshalling his emotions—but then a girl came over to them.

"Gwyn, can I get a moment?"

"Mm?"

"Just behind that column. It won't take long."

Gwyn considered the request, glanced once at Oliver and Shannon, and then followed her behind the column. Seeing no reason to stop him, Oliver let him go but was vaguely puzzled by his cousin's demeanor.

"……?"

"Your bro's a popular dude," Janet said, leaning in from behind.

Oliver blinked, then his eyes went wide.

"…Huh? Oh—that's what this is?"

"What, you didn't even notice? You're lagging behind, my liege. Not that I'm complaining."

She dug her elbow into his shoulder. This flummoxed him a bit, but Janet's smile faded as she gazed at the column.

"Just…let it be. No telling how many of us are coming back today, and a surreptitious smooch in the shadows might just provide the morale they need."

"I…wasn't planning on saying anything. Just…genuinely surprised. It's a side of him I didn't know."

"Oh, really? Then I guess I win this one."

Janet flashed a grin. That phrasing nagged at him, but Gwyn finished his momentary tryst and emerged. He said one last thing to the girl before rejoining their comrades.

"…Done."

"We've wrapped up, too," Carmen said, raising a hand.

The time was nigh. She moved past Oliver to the workshop door and spun around theatrically, proclaiming, "Then let's go murder my mentor!"

As previously mentioned, the fourth layer had vast reserves of space beyond the library itself. And the bulk of that "exterior" space was dominated not by students, nor by their workshops…

But by a field. The sort of grassy expanse where you'd let sheep graze, stretching as far as the eye could see. A sharp contrast to the views afforded elsewhere in the labyrinth, no beasts dwelled here; aside from the false sun on the ceiling above, there was not a single magical artifice of any sort. Like a section of the continent had been cut away and dumped here without further ado—that was the impression it gave.

To most mages, this area held no meaning whatsoever, but one man made a habit of meditating there daily. Today again, he sat at the center of this flattened field. In the lotus position, freeing himself of thought—the astronomy instructor, Demitrio Aristides.

"……Hmm."

Sensing their approach, his lids fluttered open. Then his eyes darted sideways, observing the students in uniforms scrubbed of anything identifying their years.

"…They're here. It must be my turn," Demitrio muttered. He'd seen this coming.

*   *   *

At the head of his comrades, Oliver spoke:

"…In 1525—"

"Chloe Halford's people?"

Demitrio spoke over him. That alone was all the answer required. Oliver's brow furrowed.

"You're not surprised. I suppose the finest mind of this day and age *would* have a good memory."

"If I'm next on your list after Darius and Enrico, what else would this be? Even if I were the densest mind, I'd surmise that much," Demitrio replied. "Still…only thirty-two of you?"

The number he named sent a chill down Oliver's spine.

He *knew*. That number included those who'd yet to show themselves. Demitrio had nailed their exact number—a fact that made Oliver gulp.

"If you took out the others with this few, I'm impressed. You must have had a very good plan—or an ace beyond compare—or perhaps both?"

Demitrio's probing gaze swept the crowd. Then his eyes closed again.

"Begin whenever you please. As you've predicted, there are no magical alterations here. To you, this is an untouched canvas."

He did not even rise from his seat. But Oliver and his comrades spread out, ready for anything. Surrounding their target at a distance.

"We'll do just that. **Tonitrus!**"

*""""""***Tonitrus!***""""""*

A full-strength spell volley to start things off. Dozens of bolts converged, but Demitrio was unperturbed.

"■ ■ ■" *Rise.*

The ground beneath him rose, lifting Demitrio up on the crest of a small hill. Their electric spells burst at the base. Their magic doing naught but scorching grass, a result that made Oliver mutter:

"…Figured."

They'd predicted this. Seeing no surprise, Demitrio spoke again.

"So you do have *some* prior knowledge. Yet you came after me anyway—a fact that boggles the mind. If you had simply been ill-prepared, that would be correctable.

"You conspire against Kimberly and have slain two instructors, yet you are still *students*. Thus—I speak now as a *teacher*. Lecturing on the nature of knowledge that you have yet to comprehend."

"...Let's hear it."

Their target acted as if he stood behind the podium, which raised his brows, yet Oliver chose to play along. Any extra time before the battle truly began worked in their favor. While he talked, they could form ranks to match the shift in terrain—and set up barriers.

With no regard for the disadvantage that gave him or the bloodlust in the air, Demitrio began to speak.

"There are two primary types of knowledge. That which you gain yourself and that which you are given. The first, you are familiar with. Truths gained inductively through the senses and experiences—or comprehension of individual events brought about by the application of those truths. Mages strive for greatness via the accumulation of this knowledge. For the purposes of categorization, I refer to this as *active knowledge*."

The start of his speech was a bit of a letdown, Oliver thought. Whatever his larger point, he clearly intended to start at the *very* beginning. While maintaining a listening pose, Oliver continued to adjust his comrades' formation via the mana frequency.

"But in its primal state, that is not how knowledge originally existed. For the majority of this world's history, god was in control, and all knowledge was bestowed at god's discretion. God possessed all knowledge about all things in this world and granted portions of that knowledge to the creatures under its control as it deemed necessary. The opposite of active knowledge—passive knowledge."

Now he'd taken it back to the age of the divine. Yet this had begun to tug at Oliver's interest. Facts he knew, shared from a very different perspective—that was the impression he gained.

"The progenitor race was accustomed to this arrangement. Knowledge was granted by god, and god was the owner of it. As the recipients of it, they did not store that knowledge within themselves. That very simplicity earned them god's affection," the philosopher explained. "But as racial divisions arose, things changed. Elves, dwarves, centaurs, and humans came into existence and were not satisfied with passive knowledge alone. They analyzed and solved problems from a perspective all their own, seeking ownership of the answers gained."

Oliver nodded to himself. Demitrio spoke of nothing but the dawn of humankind's karma.

"From that point on, we can see the rift beginning. God was displeased with man's intelligence. It believed all knowledge belonged with it and considered attempts at self-teaching to be inherently disrespectful. As the races learned more and grew smarter, god began to loathe their nature. If you'll forgive the informality, it thought we were *gross*."

Even as Demitrio spoke, Oliver's comrades were edging closer. Interrupting his speech with an attack was an option, but the order died on his lips. His spellblade was their ace; gaining all ground he could at this stage was preferable.

"The ensuing rebellion against god—you're all aware of *that*. Let us turn back to the nature of knowledge itself. Even after god's demise, those vast reserves of knowledge were left behind. Known as the Grand Records, they persist and operate independently of god—rather like the sun and moon. The Library of the Depths is but a portion of them. As the reapers on guard suggest, this facility was originally a reluctant concession by god to humankind's pleas. During the rebellion, god itself burned the bulk of books dating from the age of the divine—thus it is now primarily a depository of forbidden texts." He went on: "Yet even before the fire, it was but a fraction of god's total knowledge. By their nature, the reserves of the Grand Records could only be given to people as passive knowledge."

The man's explanation matched Oliver's knowledge of the subject. In other words—at least from the fourth layer down, this labyrinth was a relic from the age of divinity. That was why the reapers patrolled it.

"There are two primary conditions for receiving that knowledge. First, selflessness. The progenitor race had no concept of self—or an extremely weak one. They were but an extension of god, a part of the world itself—and that mindset opened the door to the Grand Records. They did not resent the gift, merely accepted it with reverence."

This sent ripples through Oliver. Had that been the end of it, perhaps this world would still be a peaceful one. That notion crossed his mind—but he soon shook it off.

"But the races that came afterward were not the same. Some were worse than others, but all had a strong individual will—and as they advanced, that only got stronger. Distancing them from that passive knowledge. That tendency is all the more pronounced now that we have freed ourselves from god's dominion," Demitrio said. "Yet the appetites of mages know no bounds. Some began to seek a way to tap once more into the reserves our own races had once abandoned."

His focus shifted back to the deeds of mages in more modern times.

"If appropriate conditions are met, perhaps there is still a way to access the Grand Records. Over the years, a number of attempts have been made to prove that hypothesis. Attempts to revive progenitor bloodlines are but one. They were born without much self, and it was believed that was a factor connecting them to the nature of the world.

"But ultimately—that approach likely failed. Attempts to resurrect the progenitors through adjustments to bloodlines and prompting atavism were not successful. Similar methods for other extinct species—succubi, for example—have achieved some partial success, but far too much time has passed, and the progenitor aspect has likely faded out completely. Not just in our blood, but at the level of our souls."

He spoke with resignation, of something known to exist but now lost to us forever.

"But the attempts demonstrated a fundamental flaw, primarily in the educational environment and practicality departments. Even if they had succeeded in reverse engineering a progenitor or bringing something similar into the modern world—could anything brought up in our information-rich modern times be pure enough to be granted access to the Grand Records? Or was that only possible because of the sheer lack of impurities existing under god?

"Even if they somehow overcame *that* hurdle—how would those who contact the vastness of the Grand Records communicate that knowledge to us? They could only reach that place by knowing nothing. Naturally, we could not expect them to parse and translate anything complex. It's like taking a child too young to read and write and setting them loose in the library."

Here, Oliver realized the irony of knowledge only obtainable by those who knew nothing. And simultaneously—that this was exactly the sort of problem mages lived to solve.

"With those concerns in mind, we can reverse engineer an alternative approach. Specifically—if impurities prevent success, we need only extract the purest portions. Use that as a key and perhaps we can enter as *ourselves*."

"Your soul's…fractured, I think," the etheric doctor examining him said.

The man had run through every conceivable possibility before coming to see her, yet he was still floored by the diagnosis.

Ever since taking Gnostic Hunter orders, he'd found himself prone to sleepwalking. With no regard for time or circumstance, his mind would cut out—and some time later, he'd find himself in a completely different place. As if someone else had been moving his body—and his memories of the interlude would be hazy at best.

"…A problem beyond the ether, in my soul?"

"And that means I can't be sure. We've got no means to directly observe the soul. Still—a mage with your self-control, prowling like a sleepwalker? We can eliminate most other causes."

This witch was well over a hundred but looked more like a child.

The basis for her diagnosis suggested the problem ran deeper than he'd imagined. Demitrio put a hand to his chin, mulling it over.

"I've poured over similar cases in the course of my research," the witch said. "There were patients like that among mages and ordinaries alike—but what they all had in common was an oppressive environment. Not allowed to do as they pleased, forced to do something they loathed—if you catch my drift."

She gave his face a searching look. He had to admit she'd hit the nail on the head. The peaceful joys he'd felt as a village mage were no longer with him. All he had left was inexhaustible panic and a sense of purpose that felt ready to incinerate him from within.

"Naturally, not everyone in those environments develops these symptoms. Far more people simply crumble under the pressure. Thus, I consider it less a disease than a defense mechanism. A soul placed where it does not belong divides itself in an attempt to preserve its true nature. Perhaps your soul simply possessed the capacity to do so."

This was an unexpected take on his condition, and Demitrio raised a brow. Interesting—perhaps it could be seen as an *ability*. That would change how he handled it.

"...Then within my body, I've got a soul fractured in two?"

"Might not be two. Could be three—or far more. Where life leads you, that number could go up and down. There's so much we don't know about the soul."

The etheric doctor shrugged. Demitrio did not resent that—he was grateful for all her help.

"I believe I understand," he said, rising. "I appreciate your feedback immensely."

"What's the plan? As I doctor, I'm supposed to recommend rest. Somewhere quiet?"

Classic medical advice, and it certainly never hurt. But Demitrio had no intention of trying it. He could not afford such luxuries. When the call came, he needed to race to the scene, and when the situation settled down, he'd monitor the ordinaries involved while dedicating himself to his own training—that was how he lived now. He still worked temporary positions in towns and for mages, observing and teaching how to prevent gnoses from happening. But his eyes no longer turned to the sky he'd once so admired.

"From what you've said, the split itself is less of a problem than multiple fragments existing in a single body. I intend to give it a body of its own. If it works out, I'm considering making it a familiar."

"Oh-ho! Fascinating. A splinter made from a split soul. Let me know how it works out."

Her curiosity piqued, she encouraged him—but as he turned to go, she issued a final warning.

"But remember this—even if you give it a whole new body, fundamentally it is still *you*. Don't imagine the new body will rid you of the problem, and the idea that you'll be fully in control of it is optimistic. If it was that easy, your soul would never have fractured in the first place."

Ancient memories flitted across his mind. In the distant present, Demitrio talked on, speaking of the results achieved by experimenting on himself.

"The impetus was pure accident. Or...perhaps inevitable. Drawn to the unknown and defeated by it, I grew foolish enough to desire omniscience."

A hint of self-mockery. Given what he'd said, Oliver quietly voiced the question that he'd had all along.

"Then let me ask—where is Yuri Leik?"

He half expected the answer. Demitrio's off hand rose to his chest.

"He's in here. Or perhaps—nowhere. He was a sliver of my soul, temporarily parted from me. Now that he has melded back inside, that name no longer holds any meaning."

He chose that icy phrasing to inform Oliver of his friend's death.

The boy desperately stifled the waves rocking him within. Not mindful of his response, Demitrio resumed his lecture.

"As the progenitor species was, humankind, too, is fundamentally linked to the world itself. Possess no strong will; accumulate no excessive knowledge. Remain in that unspoiled state, and the world will tell you all you wish to know. That is part of the Grand Records' function.

"Thus, *ignorance*. Like selflessness before it, ignorance is the secondary condition for accessing passive knowledge. Maintaining a baseline degree of each is what allowed the supernatural instincts Yuri demonstrated. If there was a cliff before him, he was told to turn back. If he was hungry, he was told there were apples growing yonder. This is not *knowing*. It is information gleaned directly from the world without an intermediary."

Oliver had managed to get his emotions in line enough to glean the point of all this. By their very nature, ignorance and selflessness degraded as the host absorbed information. Thus, Demitrio had regularly absorbed memories, making adjustments to keep his soul splinter operating. That was why Yuri regularly forgot things.

"The progenitors were much like him in the age of the divine. But situations far more complex than injuries or starvation demand a high degree of intelligence. In those cases, they held rituals. The purest of the progenitors was selected as an oracle and sent into the Grand Records. Using every means possible to remain in god's good graces, they carried out these missions repeatedly."

Oliver knew this history well and thus understood despite himself. Demitrio was capable of carrying out these rituals *all by himself.*

Examining time spent with his friend, Oliver thought—Yuri's selflessness had never been all that complete. That was why his passive knowledge was never more than basic instinctual responses, and as his ego strengthened, he'd escaped his role as a familiar. But that did not apply to the real Demitrio. This man had raised it to the level of an operation of the heart, a mental technique.

"Curiously, in Azia they have written much about the lack of self.

Abandoning what is you, eliminating your boundaries, becoming one with the world. A way of thought the antithesis of a mage's, but thus, an ideal means by which to pick up what we lost so long ago."

These words underwrote Oliver's ideas, and he grew even more certain of them. By obtaining both ignorance and selflessness, Demitrio had earned the right to access the Grand Records. No—he had achieved that in the distant past, and was *already inside*.

"Spells are sounds of power, originally a part of god's authority. Those we use have been downgraded by the process of communicating them, their strength grown limited—but the primal power is far greater. Words that could alter the world, once taught only to the chosen few among the progenitors, their usage allowed only when strictly necessary. Only usable by those connected to the world itself, impossible for modern man to pronounce or even hear—yet those mystic prototypes really *do* exist."

This was the greatest result he'd achieved there. Sensing the end to this lengthy lecture, their own adjustments complete, Oliver eyed his comrades, feeling a terrible unease rising within. He knew now just why their foe had spoken at such length.

"You are about to catch a glimpse of them. Let me warn you—this battle will not be win or lose. Given what I've explained, all that will be asked of you is the speed at which you comprehend."

The lecture's design—to demonstrate the futility of this endeavor. They dwelled in different planes, and he had spoken only to impress that point upon them. To urge the students before him to make the wiser choice.

"We are in an ordinary field. One I carried here myself from a remote region of Azia, untouched in any other way. A place predating the dirt from the boots of mages—one far closer to the age of the divine." He then asked, "Are you with me yet? Where you are now is, from the start, tantamount to my own Aria."

Demitrio held his wand before his eyes. His students braced themselves.

"Let me offer you the conclusion. You have *no* chance at anything resembling victory."

He spoke with utter conviction. And that proved the starting signal— all comrades sprang into action.

««««««««“Tonitrus!*”»»»»»»»»*

Spells converged on Demitrio. Last time, their shots had been level, but now they'd adjusted the angles into a three-dimensional cross-fire. Spells from the front, behind, left, right, and above—altering the terrain alone could not protect him. And seated as he was, he could hardly dodge in time.

"■ ■ ■ ■ ■" *Swirl.*

Sitting still, he countered with a primal incantation. The air around him began to spin, sweeping all spells up and diverting them. Even as they shifted to their next attack, he spoke again.

"■ ■ ■ ■" *Wave.*

The ground undulated. Waves ran down the hill he sat on, becoming a twenty-foot-tall land tsunami that forced them back. All comrades responded quickly. Half of them used doublecants to guard, while the other half took to their brooms. But this, too, was only the start.

"■ ■ ■ ■ ■. ■ ■ ■ ■ ■" *Spike. Burst.*

Before the waves even died, conical shapes thrust up from beneath them. As the students took evasive actions, these detonated right before their very eyes. Several failed to defend in time and were peppered with fragments, but those who'd blocked moved swiftly to counterattack. They raced toward their foe atop the hill—or cast spells as their brooms swooped in.

"■ ■ ■ ■ ■ ■ ■" *Push back.*

A force spread out in all directions, shoving them mercilessly away. Like a massive hand slapping his comrades back. Righting themselves, regaining their balance in the air, and landing—only to find Demitrio much farther away. Not only losing all distance they'd gained but pushed back beyond their start line. A brutal truth.

"…Ha—ha-ha…"

"…What a nightmare…"

Hollow laughs echoed. In much the same state of mind, Oliver tightened his grip on his athame.

They were badly outclassed. The length of the target's incantations was equivalent to a singlecast, but the effect was easily what your average mage would need a triplecast to achieve. Even more absurd—he didn't seem to need a *charge* between incantations. He was casting terrain-altering spells with all the ease with which his students might manipulate wind and fire.

This was primal power. The sheer scale of it might be a match for Godfrey, but where he relied upon his innate reserves of mana and impressive output, the mechanism here was entirely different. Demitrio's spells encouraged the world to change itself. The mana employed was not his but an innate part of the world's resources; they could not even hope for him to *run out*. Fundamentally—as long as he still lived and spoke, Oliver's side would be assailed by these unreasonable spells. But even as Oliver shuddered, a necromancer's voice rang out.

"Damn impressive, Instructor Demitrio!" Carmen called. "But it ain't like there's no cracks in your armor."

He followed her gaze—and spotted a black mist surrounding Demitrio's perch. Left behind by the familiars she'd placed around him and allowed to perish in the path of the primal spellcraft. The strength of that curse growing over time.

"The age of divinity *had* no curses. So how do you handle them?"

Carmen grinned malevolently, watching the cursed mist attach itself to the philosopher. She was every bit as skilled with curses as she was with necromancy. When she learned Demitrio's power was based on the old world order, this idea came naturally to her. After all— every expert knew curses came into being with the end of the divine age. Thus, no matter how powerful those primal spells might be, they contained no means of handling *this*.

"I don't need to, Ms. Agnelli."

As he spoke, all the mist around him dissipated, vanishing entirely.

Like a drop of ink falling into the ocean, immediately consumed by the blue. Carmen looked shocked, and the man offered an explanation.

"You intended to curse me as an individual. But linked to the world as I am now, I am one with the space around me. Before you question my handling, your curse itself lacks sufficient energy. If you insist on trying, bring a maelstrom."

"Ha-ha… Not likely," Carmen said, grimacing.

By no means a practical suggestion. Even if she pumped in every cursed object she'd brought for the occasion, and everything she harbored within her own body—she would never reach that level.

"Still, you try?" Demitrio sneered. "Though as yet you cannot even make me stand?"

The comrades gnashed their teeth, and Oliver's voice rang out.

"Don't let him get to you. Half this attitude is a bluff! It's not that we can't make him move—the man himself does not *want* to move."

That made sense to everyone. Maintaining enough selflessness to connect to the world required incredible focus. The lotus position likely aided with that; mental resources ordinarily used to move around were poured into maintaining his trance. Which meant getting him up would hasten an end to it.

"Damn straight. Don't let him freak you out," a girl said, stepping forward.

Janet Dowling, editor of Kimberly's third-largest newspaper and no stranger to picking fights with authority.

"Don't take his words at face value. Always overstate the facts— that's the first law of tabloid writing. It ain't the exclusive domain of our esteemed philosopher here."

Her sarcasm went a long way to putting the fight back in her comrades. Grateful for the push, Oliver turned his wand back to his target.

"■ ■ ■ ■" *Blow.*

A blizzard roared. The chill of the rapid temperature drop pricked their skins, but that itself was not a threat. The focus here was their line of sight and their footing—thus Oliver's comrades darted rapidly forward. An application of Lake Walking ensured their feet were not caught by the snow, and with Shannon's zone following their foe's position, they need not fear losing track of him.

"*ɷɷɷɷɷɷɷ*Frigus!*⁗⁗⁗⁗⁗⁗*"

"■ ■ ■ ■" *Burn.*

They tried mingling ice spells with the storm, but Demitrio ignited everything around him. The snow melted from the heat, turning into a deluge that rushed down the slopes. Soil already loosened from the ground tsunami liquified—

"■ ■ ■ ■ ■" *Swirl.*

And the next spell turned that flow into a whirl. Mud and rock mingled, the scale of it like an avalanche—only circular. Lake Walking alone would not suffice; the comrades took to their brooms before it swallowed them, or were forced to retreat beyond the whirlpool's reach.

"…Ngh…!"

Desperately fending off these disaster-level attacks, Oliver told himself: *Don't panic. This is fine. Your target's skills aren't as removed from your own as they seem to be. His performance makes them appear that way, but he is hardly omnipotent.*

This wasn't just wishful thinking—he had a solid basis for it. First and foremost: the Grand Records behind this foe's mystic arts. Demitrio had accessed those and made contact with the vast reserves of knowledge within—that much was likely true. But had he gleaned *everything* stored there? Absolutely not. If he had, every textbook they used would have been rewritten to bear this man's name.

"■ ■ ■ ■" *Shoot.*

The sides of the hill Demitrio sat upon swelled rapidly, ejecting rocks with all the force of a volcano. Working together, the comrades cast spells, pinpoint dropping only what projectiles were strictly necessary. Doing his part, Oliver reminded himself of his brother's summation of the Grand Records' nature—following a lengthy debate among their ranks:

"Picture the data stored there as a single book. One too thick to hold,
even in both hands. And even worse—it contains no index. *You have*
no clue which page to open to search for what it is you wish to know.
And the quantity of information contained within surpasses the limit of
human perception.

"As it should. This book was never meant for humans. It is a store of
knowledge belonging to a god, a being whose mental makeup matches
not our own. No matter how great a mind Demitrio Aristides truly has,
he cannot make up that difference."

"…Hmmm," Demitrio growled from atop the hill.

He was demonstrating an overwhelming power differential, yet the
students did not flag. This was not merely courage—he was forced to
admit it was based on accurate comprehension of the phenomenon
before them.

"You're on to me, then. Your analysis is correct. I struggled for quite
some time to locate any of the primal spellcraft, and relaying that to
anyone else would be borderline impossible. Doing so at all would
require they be connected to the world, their perceptions and ideas
aligned with it."

"Ha-ha, even my brain can figure out that much. Typical mage shit,"
Janet said, laughing at his admission.

Demitrio glanced once at her, then turned to Oliver.

"In that sense, you are right. I am no god; I remain but a mage. Yet—
that changes nothing. Neither the gulf between me and god nor the
gulf between me and *you.*"

Oliver merely shook his head. The distance it would take to cross the
gulf didn't matter. From the get-go, they'd never had a shot in a battle
of comparative knowledge. But this—was a fight to the *death.*

However disadvantaged they were, they were not merely enduring
it. They might be no match for the Grand Records, but fighting and
observing added to their reserves of intel. Primal spells that seemed
insurmountable at first were beginning to demonstrate patterns.

For instance—he could not chain cast them without *limit.* Presumably, he could use at most three powerful incantations in succession, and the subsequent spells appeared diminished in strength compared to the first. He assumed this was not a matter of Demitrio's mana but a limitation to the world's motions. He could only force so many cataclysmic shifts at once before the world he commanded ran out of breath.

"…The conditions are right. Brother, Sister—begin."

Thus, Oliver's side saw their chance to take back this fight. The Sherwoods went straight for it, none of the hesitation they'd shown versus Enrico. *This* had been part of their approach from the planning stages.

"…Duaedetroni… Misce… Misce…!"

Shannon's spell poured gold into Oliver. His entire skeleton transformed, his manaflow expanded, capillaries burst, tears of blood streamed down his face. A soul merge with his mother, and the boy threw himself astride a broom, taking to the sky—and it took Demitrio but a glance to glean the outlandishness of *that*.

"Hmm. ■ ■ ■ ■" *Roar.*

Oliver plunged into a gale laced with thunder. Maneuvering through lightning bolts that could fell a wyvern, he shot toward the enemy perched upon that hill. Watching this, Demitrio narrowed his eyes.

"You move like Chloe? I had not imagined that imitable—"

"Gladio!"

An iron-cleaving severing spell cast from on high. That glimpse of Chloe's shadow meant the man could not block with an ordinary shield. Primal spells raised a wall thick enough to block it—but the added protection there unavoidably diminished his defenses in other directions, a fact not lost upon the comrades.

"""""""""Tonitrus!"""""""""

"■ ■ ■ ■!" *Flow!*

Primal spells swept aside the volley of incoming spells. Deflecting them, but moments after blocking that severing spell, the output was weakened, and his assailants' spells got closer than ever before. Given the limitations to how the world would move, they were improving their attacks' efficiency—yet Demitrio's eyes never once left Oliver.

"No…that is no imitation. You're *linked* to her? ■ ■ ■ ■!" *Gust!*

Violent wind racked the skies above him. Before attempting to shoot his assailant out of the sky, he'd tried to curtail those outlandish maneuvers. Yet this foe rode upon even tornado-strength winds.

"Even then," Demitrio muttered. "It's counterfeit. Not even worth comparing."

"GAAAAAAAAAAAAAAAAAAA!"

"""""""""""**Flamma!**"""""""""""

Oliver dropped through the gales to the air below. As Demitrio intercepted with a primal spell, all comrades fired a volley from his far side. A second primal blocked that, the shock wave preventing their follow-up.

Yet Demitrio furrowed his brow, conscious of an irritation within. Caused by Oliver but not something he could have predicted—the very similarities made the sight of him hard to bear.

"…Which means I, too, was once captivated by her blade."

A barb directed inward—then Demitrio put it out of mind. Given his opponents' strength, anything that might disturb the upkeep of his self-lessness was undesirable. Best to eliminate that first and foremost—he turned his sights on the boy in the air.

"■ ■◇ ■!" *Ro◇r!*

The primal's timing was impeccable—but as he spoke words unde-tectable by human ears, something blocked their utterance.

"——?!"

"GAAAAAAAAAAAAAAAAAAAAAAA!"

Oliver's descent transitioned to attack. Too close, no room to use a spell—a snap decision got Demitrio on his feet, standing right into a leap out of his foe's range. His first step since the fight began—at last they'd forced him to budge.

"…Was that…"

Certain Oliver had gone back into an ascent, Demitrio's eyes glanced the other way, toward a student on the ground. And the viola in his hands. The cause of the interference in his primal spell.

"...spelljamming? Indeed, it is possible. As these *are* spells."

Demitrio nodded to himself. Conscious that the performer must be Gwyn Sherwood, he focused on the entirety of the space his mind was linked to—and the other zone overlaid upon it.

"And there is another—not quite selfless, but with a personal space shaped much like my own. The cause of his preternatural evasion? Impressive. Primal effects tend to make everything one-sided, but you've turned that around."

These words raised Gwyn's hackles.

Their foe had noticed Shannon, whose support was critical in keeping them all in play in a battle of this scale. It was only a matter of time before Demitrio tracked down Shannon herself.

"So far, you've got three aces beyond compare. All of which carry a strong whiff of the progenitors. At last, I see how you bested Darius and Enrico."

Swiftly updating his evaluation of their forces, Demitrio turned his wand their way. Everyone braced themselves. The battle had shifted—and the main act had begun.

"You've gotten me up and taken a major step—diminishing my focus. Show me what you've got next."

"«««««««"Tonitrus."»»»»»»»"

Their incantations rang out over his last phrase, and he responded swiftly.

"■■■■. ■■■■" *Swirl. Swell.*

The first primal deflected the bolts, and the second caused a cylindrical rock to shoot up underfoot, lifting him into the air above. All eyes followed him.

"Way up there...!"

"After him!"

Half mounted brooms to pursue, while the others took aim at the pillar's base, working to demolish it. Looking down from on high at those in flight, Demitrio calmly swung his wand.

"A quick pursuit. A lineup of skilled riders."

"""""**Fragor!**"""""
"""""**Impetus!**"""""

Two types of spell cast from broomback. Arced explosion spells aimed at the pillar top, and swirling wind blades placed a bit higher up. An attack no ordinary movements could have dodged, but Demitrio bounded away, stepping repeatedly on air to do just that. He easily took five steps on nothing, each adjusting his trajectory—a sight that made every comrade goggle.

"Wha—?"

"How many *was* that?!"

"I am linked to this space. Sky Walking is like breathing. ■ ■ ■ ■" *Gust.*

The primal spell created a downdraft, pushing the students lower. But they'd expected that—and more students appeared from the far side of the pillar.

"Skirting it? ■ ■ ■◇ ■ ■" *Fre◇ze.*

Demitrio spun to cast a primal at these new arrivals, but interference killed the spell on his lips. The cause was clear—Gwyn, riding a broom *and* playing the viola.

"""""""**Tonitrus!**"""""""

"■ ■ ■ ■!" *Gust!*

Forced back by these winds, all comrades fired spells. Arched shots covered the pillar's top in lightning. Again, Demitrio Sky Walked to safety...

"Hmph!"

...but as the winds died, and he touched down, someone else landed with him.

Oliver was here. He'd leaped from his broom as his comrades' spells went off, landing in range too close for a spell to stop him.

"Finish it, Noll!" Gwyn yelled.

"AAAAAAAAAAAAA!"

Oliver lunged forward, an absolute blade that could not be fought screaming his enemy's end.

"___"

Demitrio merely turned to face him, wand lightly gripped. A mage of his caliber could dispatch most foes even without an athame—but that supposed his opponent lacked a spellblade. Their positions said it all, and Oliver was certain beyond all doubt that he had already won.

And yet—as he took that last step to victory, a shudder ran down his spine like fire.

"...Kh...?!"

He'd felt this before. But he had no time to identify it. The threads lay before him. He plucked a future from one. Limbs forced by the pressures of fate, driven to a single outcome.

And events transpired as per that intent.

As he himself had chosen, Oliver's chest was struck by the tip of Demitrio's wand.

"Kah—"

The impact of the thrust killed his breath, but his feet dug into the ground. The tip of the wand and his body separated just enough that the bolt did not course through him, but it burst, scorching the air.

"Oh-ho..."

Demitrio looked impressed. Attacks with a bladeless white wand generally involved injecting magic directly into an opponent's body from the point of contact. But Demitrio's finisher had arrived an instant too late, to his surprise.

"...So that's the fourth? A blunder on my end. My first time seeing fate itself."

He spoke almost to himself. Oliver backed off, his mind catching up, that shudder running down his spin again. Barely maintaining his stance, his lips parted.

"...You've...got one, too...?"

The results before him led inevitably to that conclusion. Oliver had used a spellblade. An ultimate technique, the use of which spelled certain death—and he'd been in range.

And yet, the battle had *not* ended. In which case—there could only be one cause.

"...The fifth spellblade. Papiliosomnia, the butterfly's dream of death...!"

The butterfly's dream of death. With the exception of the yet-unnamed seventh, this was the sole spellblade thought up by an Azian mage.

The titular concept derives from a Chenese fable. A wise man has a dream in which he is a butterfly, fluttering about. When he wakes, he finds himself questioning whether he dreams of being the butterfly or whether he was actually a butterfly—and if what he now perceives is merely part of the butterfly's dream.

Not just a simple prompt to urge skepticism, this fable demonstrates the inherently primitive nature of perception itself. Namely—while actively dreaming, the distinction between one's self and the butterfly is not nearly as distinct as those words imply. The knife of reason divides them upon awakening, but arguably these are categories applied afterward based on human biases. In actual practice, neither the self nor the butterfly exist, and the two are intermingled within the sea of consciousness.

To change the metaphor, imagine the perspective of a newborn babe. They've yet to develop a self, so possess no knife with which to divide the world from themselves. Thus, their experience affords no distinction between themselves and others. They are in a natural state of selflessness, and all subsequent actions stem from that. When they hungrily search for nipples, when they cry to alert us to a wet diaper, they do not direct this toward a father or mother—or even distinguish their parents from themselves. Their actions are projected to the world as a whole, themselves included in it.

And this is not exclusive to babies. Even full-grown adults may find their perceptions in a similar state. Like the earlier fable, when dreaming—but perhaps closer at hand, the state of hyperfocus both mages and ordinaries enter when engaged with their primary subject of interest.

For instance, let us examine an accomplished dancer. They do not consciously think about moving their limbs at specific points in the music. Where amateurs may move in response to what they hear, the more they train, the more that distinction fades; they move without consciously listening to the accompaniment. This is the result of removing the line between themselves and the sounds—and in Azian philosophy, they say the objective and the subjective become unified, and we reach a realm that precedes divisions. A limited form of selflessness.

Similar phenomena are observed in the world of sword arts, too. Where one false move will lead to death, both parties swing blades in a state of extreme focus. Neither the motions of their bodies nor their thoughts are able to function as they do in daily life. Everything unnecessary is trimmed away. For a fleeting moment, perception is compressed and their worldview optimized.

Sword arts duels mean battling within each other's personal space. In the extreme, neither sight nor hearing are necessary. As blades clash, they perceive each other directly, without the intermediary of sensory organs, burying themselves in gambits and predictions. Actions taken within those overlapping personal spaces are a mutual operation in the form of a fight—almost like a single thought performed with two heads.

Demitrio's spellblade hacked into that extreme state of mind. It invited an occupant of his personal space into the depths of the zone preceding the divisions between the objective and the subjective, forcibly removing their ability to perceive the distinction between themselves and their opponent, between stabbing and being stabbed. Then he took advantage of his own acclimatization to the state of selflessness to guide the exchange to an outcome where only his foe was stabbed. No resistance occurred in the process. Why? Because his opponent *agreed* to the outcome.

That was the fifth spellblade, Papiliosomnia, the butterfly's dream of death. In a state like and yet distinct from delusion and delirium, an undefeatable trick to turn the very nature of perception against them. Even the greatest master could not fight against it. The extraordinary concentration developed over a lifetime of training only worked against them, ensuring their doom.

Thus, this was their final dream. A dream from which they would not wake, a dream of a butterfly's death.

"Why so surprised? As we stepped in range, you instinctively *knew* we both had one."

Demitrio spoke flatly, his stance never wavering. But then his eyes dropped to the white wand in hand. No blade, not even a scrap of metal anywhere.

"Oh, this? I'm no Gilchrist—and I do not preach anti-athameism. Yet there is a reason why I do not carry one," he began. "First, metal is simply a poor fit for selflessness. There was no metal in the early age of the divine. The dwarves were the first to create it, and god had a low opinion of that act. Metal is a symbol of our division from the world. It's not just the athame; having any metal anywhere on my person causes some small interference in my state of selflessness."

That certainly explained it and came as a bitter blow. How foolish it had been for them to assume he did not have a spellblade based on such flimsy evidence.

"The other reason might make more immediate sense. Camouflage— this way, few suspect I have a spellblade. But that does not mean much against a foe who has one of their own," said Demitrio. "I'm sure you've heard the term: Grand Arts Synchronicity."

Naturally, Oliver knew of it. It was a popular rumor among mages, a prophetic instinct that took hold when two spellblade masters faced each other in earnest. Namely—without the benefit of actually *using* their spellblades, each would know the other had one.

In hindsight, Oliver recognized the sensation. The shudder he'd felt when he'd faced Nanao shortly after enrolling—part of that had been *this*. That had not been a trick of his mind—he now had confirmation. Even in this instant, that same sensation was making his skin crawl.

"Let's examine this exchange: I lured you into a state preceding divisions, making ambiguous the distinction between you and me and between stabbing yourself and stabbing me. I attempted to lead you to the former. Meanwhile, you employed an augury's future observation and the uncertainty principle, attempting to select from innumerable potentials the extremely rare outcome in which I would be slain."

Oliver bit his lip. The uncanny sensation of that moment, the blow to his chest that immediately followed—both memories were horrifyingly vivid.

"The upshot is both attempts failed, but the scale of the failure differs. My spellblade's failure is merely an error on my part. With no previous experience perceiving the fourth in action, once my subjectivity unified with yours, I was forced to act swiftly and was not able to pick the correct outcome on the fly. A minor miscalculation caused by inexperience—nothing more than that."

With that conclusion established, Demitrio's eyes pierced Oliver.

"But what about you? Once the fifth caught you, you were helpless. You did not resist the lure, did not even realize your perception no longer distinguished the subjective and the objective."

"………!"

"And in that state, suspecting nothing, you used your spellblade. The art itself succeeded, and you chose a future—but one I picked, that ended with a blow to *your* heart."

Oliver could not argue that. He was left flat-footed, his heart sinking. Adding insult to injury, Demitrio summed up the exchange.

"You understand me, boy. My spellblade *consumed* yours. My failure can be corrected next time. Yours—is a fundamental, fatal flaw."

As they reached that conclusion, the platform beneath their feet swayed. The comrades below saw the duel undecided and resumed the destruction of the pillar—they'd left it at a precarious balance on purpose. Gwyn's squad swooped in again, surrounding them, but Demitrio's tone betrayed no concern.

"That was the last ace up your sleeves. In which case, you have no path to victory." He then cast a spell: "■ ■ ■ ■" *Sink*.

The ground beneath their feet dropped, and Demitrio and Oliver were swallowed up inside the pillar. Gwyn's squad jumped off their brooms, chasing after them into the depression. With the base shattered, the pillar slowly started to topple. As Oliver desperately searched for an option, Demitrio lightly jumped down.

"Foolish. ■ ■ ■ ■" *Stop*.

His back to his assailants, he chanted. Gwyn's jamming required him to see Demitrio's mouth move—so the full force of it hit them. Gwyn included, five comrades ceased to move. Frozen statue-like, in mid-motion—which took the rest of their breaths away.

"Gwyn…!"

"Petrification?!"

"No! They've stopped in midair—"

Demitrio swung around, forcing them to back off, leaving their stopped comrades behind. As the man moved past Gwyn, he raked him with his wand, and everything below the right elbow fell to the ground. An absent-minded nail in the coffin on a foe already out of commission. His spelljamming was a threat even Demitrio could not ignore.

"So far, I have only used primal spellcraft on the environment, indirect attacks. But at this range, the spells will affect you directly. ■ ■ ■ ■, ■ ■ ■ ■, ■ ■ ■ ■" *Stop, stop, stop*.

A series of spells locking down more and more students. They tried to evade, but in this depression they had few options—especially since the pillar itself was busy toppling over. If they had simply fled, perhaps escape would have been possible—but that was not an option. They were duty bound to save their lord over themselves.

"■■■■, ■■■■, ■■■■" *Stop, stop, stop.* "Cancellations and evasions are not possible. No more than I can stop your spells creating fire or electricity. You generated those elements as a means to attack, but I am using no intermediary—this spell's sole affect is to rob you of motion."

Even as he spoke, his assault continued. The toppling pillar had turned walls into floors, but he handled that effortlessly. He was linked to this space, and no matter how it changed, it posed no threat to him.

"Spelljamming was your sole means of resistance. But you cannot replace the source of that. ■■■■" *Stop.*

Oliver excepted, the last of his comrades were caught. At the exact same moment—the toppling pillar hit the ground below, lying prone.

"Noll—!"

The impact sent up a huge dust cloud. Racing in with their comrades, Shannon searched for her cousin—and a gust of wind cleared the debris, revealing all: Demitrio in a spotless robe, standing there alone.

"…Ngh…!"

"That's you, Shannon Sherwood. I can sense the progenitor vibe about you. A successful throwback? If so, an unexpected windfall."

He was walking right toward her—and something lunged out of the rubble behind him. Oliver, who'd blunted the blow of the impact with a last-second spell.

"Get away from my sister!" he yelled—as covered in wounds and dirt as his opponent was spotless.

Sensing the bloodlust at his back, Demitrio sighed softly.

"A futile effort. ■■■ ■■■■" *Get heavy.*

He pointed his wand up, chanting a heartless primal spell. The comrades attempting to back Oliver's attack all fell to their knees. The pressure from above affecting everyone in the area alike.

"…Gah…!"

"M-my arm…!"

"I can't lift it…!"

"■ ■ ■ ■" *Stop.*

And as they slowed, the next attack came without mercy. The first round of the fight, he'd been keeping them at bay—and now that they'd closed in, he merely used that against them. The nature of the primal threat adjusted to the battle's range. And this close-up—they could not afford to let him chant at all.

"■ ■ ■ ■. ■ ■ ■ ■. ■ ■ ■ ■. ■ ■ ■ ■… ■ ■ ■ ■" *Stop. Stop. Stop. Stop… Stop.*

Light footwork dodging what spells were cast against them, Demitrio locked up one remaining student after another. Twenty of them rendered helpless in rapid succession. Shannon attempted to help her cousin escape but was caught herself toward the end. Right before Oliver's eyes. A tragedy unfolding in less than a minute flat.

"… Tonitru—"

"■ ■ ■ ■" *Stop.*

Oliver's spell had been a shriek—but Demitrio's incantation did not even allow him to finish. Silenced and helpless, Oliver was rendered immobile, like his comrades before him.

No more resistance remained. The silence this man brought was more thorough than death. Fatal blows might well leave curse energy behind. But *stopping* them—that afforded no such concerns.

The man surveyed his surroundings, certain nothing left still moved.

"That's all of you? You held out longer than I anticipated."

With that appraisal, he moved toward Oliver, reached up—and peeled his mask away. Revealing the face of a third-year boy.

"So it *was* you, Oliver Horn. I had suspicions, but for a mere third-year to be at the center of all this? No wonder our response lagged behind."

Demitrio shook his head, then aimed his wand at the boy's head.

"But it ends here. I'll uncover your motives, your purpose, your scale, and who backs you… **Somni ludere**."

His invasion began. Deep into Oliver Horn he went, to dig up all that lay within.

The next thing Oliver knew—he was in the first-layer hidden workshop, seated across the table from his cousins.

"Mm?"

He blinked. There was a plate of piping hot pancakes in front of him. Something felt wrong here, but he could find no basis for that impression.

"What's…wrong, Noll? Your pancakes…are getting cold."

On his right, Shannon sounded baffled. When Oliver found no words, Gwyn looked concerned.

"Not hungry? Should we go with something easier to get down? A sorbet?"

"You're pale, my lord," Teresa said, leaning in from his left.

Feeling guilty for worrying them all, Oliver shook his head, still reeling.

"N-no, it's not that. It's…"

He tried to speak, but not one satisfactory phrase came to mind. Across the table, Gwyn sighed.

"The fatigue's catching up with you. That's it! Today, you rest."

"Come. To bed, Noll," Shannon said, getting up and tapping his shoulders.

Teresa stood up, too, tugging his sleeve. "I'll accompany you."

"Heh-heh. That's nice… Gwyn?" Shannon asked as Oliver rose.

Gwyn hesitated, then smiled. "Sure… It'll be a nice change of pace."

The four of them headed for the bedroom. Leading him, they pulled off his robe and laid him down on the bed. The others went to lie down on either side of Oliver.

"It's been...so long." Shannon giggled. "It's just like...we used to do."

"The bed is a bit small. Teresa, scoot closer to Noll."

"Don't mind if I do."

Teresa buried her face in Oliver's chest. Even as her warmth flustered him, Shannon whispered, "Should I tell you a story...until you drift off? The three clever ball mice...and their adventure...or the long journey...of the bent broom...searching for a friend?"

Two fairy tales she'd often relayed to him. That took him back, her kindness wrapping around him, easing the confusion within—and drowsiness rose up inside.

"...The bent broom," Oliver whispered.

"Mm, okay. A long...long time ago. There was a broom with a very curvy shaft..."

His sister softly began to regale. Letting her voice wash over him, Oliver drifted off to sleep.

Again, he snapped out of it. Seated at a table in the Fellowship, his friends chattering away.

"The nest's temperature is just right, and I've added soundproofing. Like this article said, I've taken leaves out of its diet..."

Katie was muttering away, scribbling in her notes. Oliver watched closely, and she clutched her head, yelling.

"Arghhh! It's not working! Nothing I do will make the digwing warm their eggs!"

"Don't let it get to you," Guy said, refilling her cup. "Have some tea and sit on it for a while."

This was an everyday sight, and Oliver watched in silence. Then Nanao leaned in from his right, examining his face.

"You seem not quite here, Oliver. Does something ail you?"

"...Nanao..."

"You have a habit of taking on too many worries," Chela said, smiling across the table at him. "Katie will be fine! Leave her be for a few days, and she'll come up with something brilliant. She always does."

A board game was thrust onto the table from Oliver's left.

"Exactly! That's why you should play Magic Chess with me!"

Yuri Leik, with an innocent smile. When Oliver saw that, he felt a surge of emotions he could not put a name to. Fighting off tears he knew not the cause of, he managed an answer.

"…Yeah, Yuri. That might hit the spot."

Yuri gleefully began laying out the pieces. Oliver joined in, keeping himself in the moment.

Watching the same dream from on high, Demitrio was carefully observing Oliver.

"His guard's gone down. Time to pry into his memories."

He began taking stock. As Oliver adjusted to the dream, more memories grew available, and Demitrio carefully checked these over. One image after another of times Oliver Horn had lived through. A deadly battle not far in the past among them.

"So this is who took down Enrico. The Sherwoods, Karlie Buckle, and Robert Dufourcq… Aha, she was a force, and he knew his curses. Good choices to tackle a Deus Ex Machina."

The fight against the machine god was a furious one. Demitrio ran through it thoroughly and then dug deeper into the past—finding his first victim.

"And here's Darius. A pure one-on-one? Using his arrogance against him, but still…luck was not with you, Darius. The shock of a first-year with a spellblade—but if you had spent just a little more time on your sword arts or been just a bit less talented as an alchemist—you could have obtained a spellblade of your own."

A whisper of regret. This man knew full well why Darius had not followed that path.

"I've seen their primary members on-site. Let's go back to before he arrived here, explore his background…"

But when he tried to go further, he ran into a wall. Like a miner stymied by hard rock, he could not dig further into the past.

"…A powerful barrier. Less caution than unvarnished trauma. These years must have been very unpleasant."

Considering the cause, Demitrio swiftly changed tactics. There were several ways to get past a memory block—one of which was changing the angle of approach. Sealed memories were like blood vessels with a valve that partially blocked the flow. He might not be able to go directly there from the present, but looping before them and moving chronologically often made it possible.

"A slight detour, but I'll take the long way around. Let's head back to when you were happy. No need to rush. Just dream away as we follow the time line."

He adjusted the dream, and the sights Oliver saw followed.

"Nice, nice! Just a bit more! You're almost there!"

Encouraged by her voice, he pushed his little hands on the floor, getting up. His gait was too unsteady to really call a walk, but still he moved forward. The moment of his first step.

The boy reached his limit and toppled into his mother's arms.

"Goooooooood boy! So, so, so, so good! You did it, Noll! Not just standing up! You took two and a half steps! Did you see, Ed? He'll be tap dancing by this time next year!"

"Let's not get ahead of ourselves. But good work, Noll. Impressive effort."

His father reached past the blond witch, rubbing the boy's head. A wiry body clad in a plain, solid-color sweater and slacks, eyes framed by square glasses. His movements tidy in a way that suggested "teacher." An awfully drab-looking man to be the legendary Two-Blade's husband.

Watching this scene play out, Demitrio recognized his face and nodded.

"…Her boy with Edgar? Gave birth while holed up in that forest, did she? Hard to believe she kept it hidden. She was called up by the Gnostic Hunters several times while raising him."

A few years later, the baby was now a toddler. Sitting on his mother's knees, Oliver was examining the alchemy materials before him.

"This one's winding weed. And that's a chuckleshroom. And… stained lantern."

"Good job! So what's this one?"

"An onion. Is that for dinner?" The boy laughed at the vegetable in his mother's hands.

Next to them, Edgar folded his arms, thinking.

"He remembered all these just watching us brew? He learns like I did. Makes a father proud…"

"What other reaction could there be? You're brilliant! So smart! My son is the best in the world!"

Tickled pink, Chloe picked up Oliver, swinging him around. Edgar quickly put a stop to that, helping the dizzy boy into a chair. It was his job to stop her from overdoing things. Just as it had been before they married.

Observing this same scene, Demitrio muttered, "He isn't doting like Chloe… Must have realized the boy took after *him*."

More time passed. Oliver was on Chloe's knees in a darkened living room, his eyes on a man in a projection crystal.

"I'm home. Sorry, I ran a bit late—"

""Ah-ha-ha-ha-ha!""

Edgar came in, greeted by peals of laughter. He came over, then put his bag down, shaking his head.

"Watching Mr. Bridge's magic comedy again? I'm glad you're enjoying yourselves, but it's not really meant for a five-year-old."

"Ha-ha-ha-ha-ha...! It's a bit late for that. He was hooked from the first one! The hand of destiny at work!" Chloe insisted.

Young Oliver pointed at the image, insisting, "I wanna use spells, too!"

"Oh, do you? Well, we'll just have to practice!"

"Ch-Chloe! Not so fast! We've agreed to gauge the moment carefully!"

"Yeah, the moment he got interested! C'mon, Ed, bring it over!"

Swept up in her enthusiasm, Edgar moved to a shelf in back and took down a wooden box. He held it out to Oliver, who looked surprised.

"...What's that?"

"Open it. There's something nice inside!"

Oliver did as he was told, lifting the lid. Inside was a wand, the smooth surface gleaming.

"Isn't that a pretty wand? Ed and I picked the materials and carved it ourselves. This is *your* wand, Noll."

"......"

His hand was drawn to it. Oliver picked it up, held it aloft—and stopped moving. Forgetting to blink at all.

"Déjà vu!" Chloe said, hands on her hips. "Everyone acts the same when they get their first wand. It makes you feel so powerful, your body just starts shaking. What is that about?"

"I've heard it described as...filling in the missing piece. To a mage, a wand is like a part of their own body."

Many a mage would agree with Edgar's sentiment. He knelt down before his son, eyes at the boy's level. The boy noticed, turning his gaze to his father.

"Listen, Noll. You've just gained a lot of power. And because that power is so big...it can also be scary."

"...Okay."

"There's a lot of things you can do with it. You can make fire and lightning—and hurt someone you're mad at. Or even burn down this house."

"?! I don't wanna do that!"

"Exactly. That's why you always have to think before you act. You're going to learn a lot of magic. And I want you to always think about what'll happen if you use a spell.

"Magic can make things…and it can break things. But it's much harder to make than to break. And most of the time—if you break something, you can't fix it. Do you see why that's scary? Think it through and imagine why."

Oliver frowned, thinking hard.

"It's important that you do," his father said. "All mages have to handle their own spells. That's our *responsibility*."

"…Responsi…bility……"

"That's right. Since you're still little, Mom and Dad will help. But as you grow older, you'll have to take care of things yourself. When you can do that, you'll finally be a proper mage. Don't forget what I said here."

He rubbed the boy's head. Chloe knelt down next to them, smiling. Her eyes filled with trust—as long as his father was here, she need not worry.

A warm family moment. Watching it, Demitrio muttered, "…Standard-issue upbringing. Like it's not *Chloe*'s boy at all. It's like watching some village mages raise a kid."

He almost smiled. What he was watching now told him exactly why they'd told no one about their child.

"…That's exactly what they wanted."

"Flamma! Impetus! Tonitrus!"

Older again, Oliver was now a young boy. Practicing spells in the garden under Chloe's and Edgar's watchful eyes.

"Good, good, your element switches are getting smooth. You're improving, Noll!"

"Haah, haah…!"

Out of breath, Oliver stopped chanting. A beagle came up, rubbing against him.

"Doug…you're encouraging me, too? Okay! I'll hang in there!"

Motivated, he went back to practicing.

"…No real variation by spell type," Edgar murmured. "He uses all elements equally well. And before improving his strengths, he tries to correct his weaknesses—that studious personality is like me, too."

"Mm-hmm. So what?" Chloe asked, eyes on Oliver.

Edgar folded his arms, pulling a face. Neither of them realized that Oliver was watching this. And listening to what they said.

"He's very much *my* son. But…he's also yours. And yet…so tame. No spikes in his talent. I can't put that thought out of my mind."

"Does that disappoint you?"

She kept her tone light, but Edgar wheeled around to face her, angry.

"*Non!* How could it? Quite the opposite—I love him all the more!" he insisted. "Just—I know he'll struggle with it later. Everyone will see him as Chloe Halford's son, and at some point he'll start to be conscious of that himself. I worry about whether…he'll find a way to be proud of himself."

Edgar trailed off. Chloe kissed him on the cheek.

"Good. If you'd nodded, I'd have punched ya."

Their son came running up to them. A pall had hung over their conversation, and even at his age, he knew he was the reason why. That's why he chose to smile.

"Mommy, Daddy, watch this!"

"Mm?"

"What is it, Noll?"

"I'm not Noll. I'm an angry dahlia! Always mad about something."

He scowled. Was this some sort of game? Edgar looked baffled.

"But on a day like today, the sun feels too good… **Lanarusal!**"

Raising his wand, Oliver cast a spell. Somewhat misshapen petals appeared all around his face, like a sunflower in bloom.

"Shit, I accidentally bloomed," Oliver swore, still scowling.

This was famous gag by a popular magic comedian. Edgar clapped a hand over his face, and Chloe broke up laughing.

"Ah-ha-ha-ha-ha! What is that?! When did you practice this?!"

"Eh-heh-heh! When you weren't looking!"

"I never saw it coming! C'mere!"

Overflowing with love, Chloe hugged her son tight, kissing him on the lips. His arms and legs started flailing, and Edgar had to call out, "Ch-Chloe! Noll can't breathe!"

"…Bwah! You're next!"

"——?!"

No sooner had her lips left Oliver than she tackled Edgar. With both males down, she stood triumphant.

"Husband! Son! You've made me far too happy, and a mere kiss will not suffice! How can you be so lovable?! It's not even fair! No matter how hard I love you, it's never enough!"

She flung her arms open wide, wrapping them around Oliver. Rubbing his cheek against her chest, he whispered, "I love you, too."

"Ugh, you're going for the kill! Ed! Whaddaya mean, no spikes?! Your son's a born gigolo! And a future comedian!"

"…Apparently. I retract that statement." Edgar nodded, bemused, gazing happily at Oliver, as if savoring the joys of a son this wonderful.

"There!"

With a *clang*, an athame flew from his hand and landed on the turf. Older again, Oliver toppled over backward on the grass.

"…You're so strong, Mommy…!"

"Ha-ha-ha-ha! Of course! I'm the strongest in the world! Catch your breath and let's go another round!"

Chloe brandished her athame enthusiastically, but Edgar cut in.

"*Non*, that's enough," he said sternly. "Noll, come review the fundamentals with Dad. Mom's...definitely strong but pretty out-there. Not really worth copying."

"Why not?! You're leaving me out again?! Fine, be that way! I'll just go play with Doug!"

Sulking, Chloe led the dog out. Making a face at her, Edgar started teaching his son basic forms. Oliver studiously practiced them.

"...Sorry, Noll," Edgar said. "My lessons are boring, aren't they?"

"? No they're not!"

"That's good to hear. It's a different path than your mother took, but this is how I got strong. Lots of practice, lots of study, lots of thinking...and bit by bit, I got there."

This was basically an admission that he'd had no talent. His son took after him in this, and Edgar felt a twinge of guilt about that.

"Working hard like this is tough, even for grown-ups. But—the harder you work, the more your strength feels like it belongs to you. Like a building erected on solid foundations, no matter how hard the wind blows, you won't fall," Edgar explained. "That's how Lanoff-style works. You're tenacious, so it's a good fit for you."

As a father, he was sure of that much. Practicing alongside Edgar, Oliver said, "I like Lanoff, too."

"You do?"

"Mm. It's, um, very precise. There's lots to remember, but there's always a reason for everything, and the more you think about it, the more it makes sense. Whoever invented it must've taken a very long time, thinking about how to teach it. And how to make it so people learning it didn't get confused or mess up..."

That was his best explanation. He already had the imagination to pick up on that. As his father had hoped he would.

"And that's a lot like you, Daddy. That's why I like this style."

"——!"

Edgar dropped his wooden sword and pulled his son into a hug. The sudden embrace surprised the boy.

"...Daddy?" he asked. "We can't practice if we're hugging..."

"Ahhhh! No fair, Ed! You can't cuddle Noll without me!"

Chloe came racing in, Doug on her heels, and joined in. A big family hug—and Oliver looked thoroughly fulfilled.

Naturally, not every day was a happy one. Everyone has painful experiences as they grow, no matter how great their parents' love is.

"...All animals grow cold in death. Isn't that sad, Noll?"

Chloe's voice weighed heavily. Oliver was crying, clutching Doug's body as the warmth faded from it, his efforts to save the dog in vain. He'd made a mistake, and the price had been this life. A loss he could never make right.

He'd been given a wand, learned spells, begun to study alchemy. So many more things he could do—and that's exactly where it starts to go to a mage's head. When the dog got sick, his parents had examined Doug's symptoms and decided to wait for it to get better on its own. Nonemergency treatment for nonmagical creatures, ordinaries or animals, was best done without the aid of magic.

But Oliver hadn't waited. Wanting to relieve his friend's suffering right away, and knowing that mages could do that, he'd made a potion himself—with his limited knowledge. There'd only been a trace of poison in the ingredients. He'd taken a dose himself, trying to verify the safety of it. But—this dog had not even been a magical beast. It was far more fragile than Oliver had realized.

"...I'll study...harder...! Never use the wrong herb or mushroom... again!"

"Good idea. Let's study all that together." Edgar nodded, sitting next to the sobbing boy. Both he and Chloe behind him had made no contact with Oliver. As much as they wanted to hug the boy, they knew this was an experience their warmth would only sully.

"Remember how cold he feels. Carve it into your heart and never let it go. That is the last gift Doug will give you. The most important lesson your first friend left behind."

A great loss impressed a mage's responsibilities upon the growing boy.

"Whew, I worked up a sweat! We've gotta wash up, Noll!"

"M-mm…"

They'd been practicing sword arts in the summer sun, but Chloe dragged him right into the shower. He was old enough now to be embarrassed about these things, and so he kept his back turned, refusing to look upon his mother's naked form.

"What, are you all ashamed now? Too old for this? Don't wanna shower with Mommy?"

"…No, I just…," Oliver squeaked.

Water gushed from the showerhead above, hosing Chloe down.

"Whoa, that's cold! The elementals are working overtime! Keep at it! Ten degrees lower!"

The deluge was quickly cooling down her overheated body. The whole time, Oliver was stuck in the corner, eyes down. Less shame or embarrassment than *awe*. The more of a mage he became, the more his instincts told him he should not lightly gaze upon a body as flawless and filled with mysteries as Chloe Halford's.

She chuckled. Perhaps she got that on some level—she turned to her son, spreading her arms to show herself off. "Go ahead. Admire it, Noll. Now is the time."

That made him hesitantly look up, his gaze drawn to her form. Already the Platonic ideal of a mage, yet this petite witch's power was growing even now. Every inch of her skin, every muscle in her was aesthetically unrivaled. It took his breath away.

"…You're beautiful, Mommy," he said, the words slipping out.

"Whoa! Straight shooting!"

Chloe blushed and took his hands, pulling him into the shower.

Playing in the water with him until Edgar came in with a towel for each.

One night, Oliver was nodding off on the couch, having trained all day and studied all evening.

"How'd the meeting go?"

"Uh...honestly, not great."

His eyes barely open, he heard his parents talking. Chloe had just arrived home.

"I never expected it to be easy to persuade them. But I feel like their attitudes toward me have shifted. Like no matter what I say, they'll take it like I'm speaking for the civil rights movement. I ain't never made any claims to be that..."

"Your ability to inspire people is working against you, then." Edgar sighed. "But...that's hardly a surprise, isn't it? Between your influence with the rights movement and your proven prowess as a Gnostic Hunter, you could easily upend the magical world if you wanted. The conservatives are gonna fret over how to deal with you."

Oliver often saw them looking this downbeat. Even half asleep, it made him anxious.

"And we've put an awful lot on Emmy's back, making her lead negotiations. That alone makes this impasse painful. Think it's about time we told her about Oliver?"

"I wish we could... But given how she feels, I think we should wait. She's neck-deep in tricky negotiations as is. Don't wanna yank the rug out from under her. Or...see her struggle to give her blessings."

Chloe wasn't often this reluctant. It was a side of her Oliver hadn't seen. He didn't know who they were talking about, but they were clearly worried—and that scared him.

"...I know it's a lot to ask, but I don't want Emmy turning on Noll. I want her to love him. And I want Noll to look up to her, like she's his big sister."

"…If only."

"Yeah, not that easy. But—you know I'm greedy, Ed. I want it *all*."

With a sad smile, she put her arms around Edgar.

"You being a man wasn't why I chose you. I'm sure of it," she said. "But—now that we've had Noll, she won't see it that way. I could talk myself blue in the face, and she'd stay dead certain her gender was why I didn't go with her. And I just know—Emmy will take that as an unequivocal rejection."

Oliver was too young to fully grasp just how thorny this problem was.

When Edgar said nothing, Chloe added, "So when we do tell her, I want it to be full of positivity. Before they meet, I wanna fill Oliver's head with everything great about her. So he comes in, eyes gleaming." She then said, "'This amazing boy we made has nothing but respect for you, without even meeting you. He loves you like he would his real sister.' I think that's the bare minimum for a happy ending. That's how Noll and Emmy should meet."

Chloe was almost pleading, and Edgar smiled softly.

"I get that… But we're putting a lot on Oliver. I mean, first we've gotta make sure he turns out amazing."

"*Oh?* Was that in doubt? Is he not *already* amazing? Have you grown too blind to see his sleepy face? Do I have to slap your vision back into whack?"

"*Non, non!* I misspoke. Don't bring back the Fisticuffs Champion!"

"Ha, I never hung up my belt. Just you watch: One day I'm gonna land a punch right on Instructor Gilchrist's sour kisser. How do you like *that* anti-athameism, ya old kook?!"

Chloe did a little shadowboxing as Edgar backed away. *Ah*, Oliver thought. *They're themselves again*—and with that, sleep won out.

"Ed! Grab Oliver and run! *Now!*"

Chloe nearly kicked in the door upon her entrance, already yelling.

Edgar had been teaching their son how to look after his wand; he bolted to his feet.

"What's wrong, Chloe? Did the negotiations fall apart?"

"Those are still going nowhere! But my neck's tingling! I dunno who or when, but they're coming right after *me*. We can't be here! I told Emmy to hide herself, too."

The clear urgency in her tone made Edgar nod and turn around. He picked up their confused boy and held him tight.

"Got it. I'll take Noll to your folks. What's your plan?"

"Greet our guests. If I run, they'll just catch up."

Chloe was already prepping for the fight. Her athame never left her side. Oliver glanced at that, instinctively realizing how bad this was. His mother was about to *fight*. That much was unmistakable.

"...Mommy...!"

Seeing the look on his face, Chloe stepped toward him and gave him a hug.

"Don't worry, Noll. Like I said, your mother's the strongest in the world. The Gnostic Hunters could send a whole-ass squad after me, and I'd brush them off like so much dirt," she assured him. "You might find my family a little stifling, but it won't be for too long. Once I'm back, we'll make pancakes. Lots of syrup and butter. So much that Ed'll scold us for it."

She looked him right in the eye, trying to assuage his concerns. Oliver hugged her back.

"...I'll be waiting, Mommy."

"Thank you. I love you, Noll."

She kissed him on the cheek—and watching this play out, Demitrio realized the truth.

"...Oh. *This* night."

Leaving his mother behind, Edgar fled through the night with his son in his arms. Their journey was long, and Oliver could tell he was picking his route with great care. Sometimes they even employed disguises or transformation spells. It was almost noon the next day before they reached Chloe's family home—the Sherwood estate. A manor so big Oliver's little eyes could not see end to end.

"Well met, both of you! It must have been awful. Come on in!"

They let the gate guard know of their arrival, and the door soon opened, a cheery-looking elderly couple emerging to greet them. The moment they stepped onto the grounds, Oliver sensed an ominous oppression in the very air, and that only made him even more frightened. His father looked equally grim. They were led into the largest building, likely the main residence.

"Oliver will probably want someone his own age around. Gwyn, Shannon, your cousin's come to visit. Play with him, would you?"

A row of servants met them inside, along with an earnest-looking boy and a gentle-looking girl. Oliver knew at a glance that they were his relatives.

"...I'm Gwyn. Nice to meet you, Oliver."

"I'm...Shannon. Let's...have fun."

"Yes. The p-pleasure is all mine."

Not quite hiding how nervous he was, he bowed his head.

The old lady tittered. "My, my, what a well-mannered boy! Can't believe he's *hers*."

"You must have taught him well, Edgar. Go get some rest in back. You smoke a pipe?"

"No, not anymore—I appreciate the thought."

Edgar politely declined the offer. Each move his father made told Oliver loud and clear: This was not a place where you let down your guard.

Given the gravity of the situation and their lengthy escape, the reception was kept short and simple. They were soon deposited in a guest room. His father told Oliver to get some rest, but even if the mood here had been less oppressive, Oliver wouldn't have been inclined to lie down.

"…She's still not back?"

He was plastered against the window, eyes on the night view. Unable to sleep, he'd been like this since the sun was still high in the sky.

Edgar couldn't bear to watch. "Don't worry about Mommy," he said. "Come here, Noll."

Oliver left the window, and his father wrapped his arms tight around him. Oliver hugged him back. He was scared—but his father had to keep him safe and must have been even more frightened. Even at this age, his thoughts were on how others felt.

"Ah—"

He sensed it, then.

"…? What is it, Noll?" Edgar frowned.

Oliver pulled out of his father's arms, running to the window.

"Mom's *here*."

His eyes were fixed on something outside—and then Edgar found it, gasping.

Chloe. Half a woman's figure, pale and transparent, liable to disperse when next the wind blew.

"No…"

Edgar's voice shook. Before them, the etheric body let out a voiceless cry.

"Ah—ah—"

As Oliver stood stock-still, Chloe's ether drifted his way. Her wispy arms wrapped around her son, and she smiled. Relieved to have made it home.

"—Ed—Noll……"

With that, she faded away completely. Like the last remnant of a dream.

Neither Oliver nor Edgar dared speak a word. After a long silence, footsteps came down the hall.

"Are you up, Edgar? Shannon felt an etheric body enter your room! Is someone with you?!"

The old man's voice, accompanied by a thundering knock at the door. Both sounds passed in one ear and out the other.

"...She's gone..."

His mother's arms had been around him a moment before. The memory of that lingered. Oliver turned around, looking up at his father. Still not comprehending what that all meant.

"...Daddy...what happened to Mommy...?"

Once Edgar recovered enough to relay what had happened, the mood in the Sherwood manor changed completely. They'd been on high alert, feeling out the situation—but now they were preparing for battle.

"We don't hear from her for years, and then she comes back as a ghost. How like her! To the bitter end."

The grown-ups assembled in the living room. Oliver watching from the corner, with Gwyn and Shannon on either side. They were using a lot of words he didn't understand, but he was doing his level best to follow along.

"How much do you know about what led to this, Edgar? Wayward she may have been, but my granddaughter was a once-in-a-millennia virtuoso. No matter who came after her, she would not have been beaten easily."

"...I know bits and pieces, but...not who carried it out. Only that it must have been someone opposed to her."

"She didn't say a word? Not even her spirit?"

"...From the glimpse I got, her ether was in tatters. It held a form for mere seconds. The fact that it reached us at all...was nigh miraculous."

Edgar's voice shook. Wanting to break up the volley of questions, Gwyn spoke up.

"Grandfather, that's enough for one day. Edgar's grieving."

"I know! But we can't do anything until we know our enemy. There's a limit to what we can achieve with this information, though. What else can we do?"

The old man paused, chin in hand. Then his eyes turned to his great-granddaughter.

"…Her soul's still with the boy, Shannon?"

"…Yes. Holding him tight…not letting go…like an embrace."

Mindful of Oliver's response, Shannon answered. The old man was far less hesitant.

"You can ask the soul yourself. Set the scene."

"——! But that means—"

"Wait, Grandfather!" Gwyn cried. Arguing like this was not a luxury he was afforded often, but he had to. "Yes, Shannon can make that happen. But let's consider the implications. Chloe's soul is tied inexorably to Oliver's. If she connects to the ether to glean information from it—all of that will be relayed to the boy."

That made Edgar gasp. But the old man just gave Gwyn a puzzled look.

"I fail to see the problem. Or are you saying this child should go through life not even knowing who slew his mother?"

Snapping out of it, Edgar got up and took a knee, pleading.

"Please, sir, not that. Noll's too young! He's not ready to handle what happened to her."

There was a silence. The old man folded his arms.

"A father's love. Yes…I can sympathize with that."

He put his hand on Edgar's shoulder, his smile filled with mercy.

"But, Edgar, you're forgetting something: My granddaughter's death is a *crisis*. One that affects the very survival of the Sherwood clan."

With that, his expression changed—to that of a mage ready to trample the hearts of man to achieve his purpose. Edgar let out a squeak.

"In light of that, I ask you this," the old man growled. "Do you insist? Though you are but an *in-law*?"

"——!"

The words slammed down from on high, silencing any and all protests. The cruelty in that was evident, but Edgar had no position from which to argue. He was the one mage here who did not carry

Sherwood blood, and with Chloe's death, his status has fallen to the depths of this man's estimations. In fact—given that his granddaughter had brought in outside blood without permission, he had likely never once rated any consideration at all.

"…I'll…be fine."

Oliver's voice made everyone turn, surprised. Part of this was certainly because he couldn't stand to see the old man browbeat his father. But—far more than that, Oliver simply had to *know*. If there was a way to get answers to all these questions, he was ready to jump at the chance.

"I don't understand…the hard parts of this. But Shannon has a way to talk to Mommy, right?"

He'd gotten that much from the conversation. He turned to the cousin he'd just met.

"Then—I want to hear that, too. What happened to her? What went on while I wasn't there? I…want to know the truth."

Shannon gulped, and the old man grinned. He gave Edgar a frosty glare.

"You've got a good son, Edgar. He knows what's going on better than you."

"——! Don't, Noll! You can't let—"

"Altum somnum."

As Edgar tried to argue, the old mage planted a spell on his chest—and he fell over, unconscious. Oliver gasped and ran over to him.

"Daddy!"

"Don't worry; he's just asleep. I'll wake him up once this is over."

"Then let's get things ready!"

Without another glance at Edgar's prone form, everyone started moving. Cowed by the intensity, Oliver found the old man's hand on his shoulder, eyes locked on his.

"You're a fine young man, Oliver. This may be rough on a child. But—can you hold fast?"

Oliver knew this was a question that could only be answered in the affirmative.

*   *   *

He was first required to thoroughly cleanse himself in the bath. Once that was complete, he was ordered to drain a glass of green fluid, so astringent the first sip nearly made him splutter. A rather potent herbal liqueur.

"The boy's body is cleansed, so let's get started. Come, Shannon."

"...Ugh..."

Oliver was led to another room and sat upon a chair at the center. The old woman waved Shannon to a chair nearby—but she froze up.

"Hesitant? You have a kind heart. Those with a strong progenitor aspect always do. My brother was like that till the very end."

The woman looked touched—but then her hand clamped down on Shannon's shoulder.

"But you can't refuse. Nor could my brother. This is your *duty*."

The intensity made Shannon shiver. Unable to watch, Oliver spoke up.

"Shannon...I'll be fine."

What were they doing to him? What was going on here? Those questions were scary, but nothing compared to his need to know what happened to his mother. And Shannon no longer had a reason to stand her ground. She hesitated a long moment and then drew her wand, tapped it to Oliver's chest, and said the spell.

"*Animae nexum.*"

His vision cut out, replaced with an avalanche of new memories rushing in from his mother's soul.

"I'm impressed you survived. But we both know struggling is useless."

Oliver now witnessed the desperate peril Chloe faced in her last moments of life. In a dark forest, the ground around her boiling, molten. And the warlocks swooping in to attack.

"Ahhh, how cruel you are to cut me off! I'm lonely, so lonely! Let me be one with you!"

Giant claws shot out of the darkness. A cursed mist, a voice like a sheep with a crushed windpipe.

"So you're the lightbearer, huh? Must be a real honor, you old hag."

"……"

A full, false moon in the sky above. The silhouette of a towering golem bathed in that pale light. A maniacal laugh.

"Feel free to try me! Kya-ha-ha-ha-ha-ha-ha!"

"■ ■ ■ ■" *Stop.*

An incantation she could not hear hit her hard. The straits were dire, but his mother's spirits uncowed.

"This way!"

A sole light in this darkness—and Chloe darted toward it. Relief and joy welling up. Never once doubting that this girl would be here to save her.

"Emmy…?"

She never saw the betrayal coming. A blow from behind, piercing her chest. A voice in her ear.

"I'm sorry… This was my only option…"

Why? Chloe thought, doubts swirling. Yet her true nightmare was only just beginning.

"Stabbed her in the back? Nice trick if you can make it."

Looking up from below, she could see them standing over her, deep in a cave. The wound to her heart had been fatal, so they'd done the bare minimum to extend her life, leaving her prostrate for them. Unable to talk back, unable to move at all.

"Kya-ha-ha-ha-ha! Even Chloe didn't see that one coming!"

"Yes, she's always, *always* treasured you."

Baldia's sarcasm slithered under the old man's laughter.

"The rest…as per the agreement?" a flat voice said.

Chloe's betrayer nodded quietly and vanished into the depths.

The philosopher nodded and drew his wand.

"Then let's begin. I've no taste for this task, but who shall go first?"

"Allow me."

One man stepped forward, an arrogant heft to his chest, a dangerous gleam in his eyes. He glared down at Chloe.

"A pathetic sight, Chloe. In all your confidence, you never once entertained the thought that one day you'd wind up sprawled at my feet."

With a twisted smile, he waved a wand.

"Dolor!"

Violent pain racked Chloe's body from within.

Had Shannon not been adjusting the sensory feedback, Oliver would have screamed aloud, and the rest of this would have been lost. But his cousin's kindness helped him hold out. Allowed him to endure.

"You were a blight!" Darius roared. "I've always, always, always loathed you! Dolor!"

Another pain spell tormented her. All the while, Darius's rant echoed.

"That bitchy sneer! Those snide remarks! That unparalleled blade! Constantly, constantly, constantly burning themselves into my eyes! I loathed you, yet I couldn't look away! Dolor!"

"Get it now? Do you understand anything? Existing in the same universe as you is nothing but agony! Whether you glare or smile, whether you swear or issue compliments! Every time that lifted my spirits, it made me hate myself all the more! I've dreamed about killing you! Dreamed about torturing the hell out of you! Dolor!"

"Don't compare me to Luther! Especially not in his favor! I-I'm—I'm not like that sword-brained fool! I was born to lead the imbeciles to their betterment beneath my wand! I knew my duty and could not afford to spend more time on savage dustups! Ah, why would you not listen?! He has no talent and could remain a fool! Don't ask me to do the same! Don't make me *want* to! Don't stand around shining like a beacon before me! Dolor!"

An endless stream of curses—the warlock lost himself in his torture. The others watched and laughed.

"Kya-ha-ha-ha-ha! So young! Such pure, unvarnished love!"

"Heh-heh-heh, I'm sure she was just doting on both Lu and Darry. She never noticed what it did to them. It was a blessing for Lu but a curse upon Darry."

When his invective started going in circles, the man's torture came to an end. Not due to lack of motivation—more the sheer anger had left him out of breath.

"…Haah, haah…! Haah…!"

"Okay, enough. This shit ain't just your party."

A mean-looking woman pushed the man aside, stepping in herself.

"'Sup. I ain't as fixated as that guy, don't worry. We went at it a few times as students, but you helped me some, too. It all evens out. Ain't got no pent-up grudges. Still…"

The last trace of warmth left her face, and she waved a wand.

"Knowing there's someone stronger than me around just rubs me the wrong way. Dolor."

Thirty pain spells at regular intervals. When her torture ended, she stepped back, and the girl-shaped mass of curses took her place.

"My turn, now! Heh-heh-heh… Is your mind still in there? Do you remember me? It's Baldia! Baldia Muwezicamili!" the figure said with a cackle. "You came to talk to me several times at Kimberly. A cursed little rag of a girl, but you just acted like I was any other underclassman. When Vana and I picked a fight with you, you didn't hesitate to punch me bare-handed. I've never been so surprised!"

Baldia sat down next to Chloe, leaning close.

"You didn't discriminate! Just looked down on *everyone*. And I've aaaaaaaalways hated that. People like us belong in the darkness and the murk, and I loathed how you just marched on in, shining your light around. So right now? I'm absolutely delighted! I mean, now? At long last? I can finally drag you down into the gloom. Heh-heh… I just have to welcome you! Dolor!"

A very nagging sort of torture. Unlike the first man, she never rushed, delightedly savoring the piled-on agony. After thirty-two spells, her torture ended, and a tiny old man stepped in.

"I'm next! How are you faring, Chloe? I'm ever so sad it came to this! You were a total nightmare to have in class, and every time you crushed a golem, I found new ways to improve it! I lived for that! Do you know how that feels? I'm crushing the very thing I lived for under my feet!"

At that, all emotions drained from his face. Like he was carved from white rock.

"Frustrating though it is, this is the way of sorcery. Dolor."

Enrico's torture ended after twenty impassive spells.

"You go next, Gilchrist," Vanessa growled. "I don't recommend going last. Lest we start doubting your stance."

"……"

Under her baleful glare, the elderly witch straightened up and stepped forward. Her eyes snapped down to Chloe.

"Can you still see, Ms. Halford? I make no apologies. Curse me all you please."

With that, she placed the tip of her wand on her target's chest.

"I will say this. You were vulgar, crude, and impudent. You could not have been further from the ideal mage I teach. Even your spells were so slapdash it made me cover my eyes—"

With that, her lips pursed. And she failed to stop herself from saying more.

"—but your blade alone I could not bring myself to despise. Dolor."

Three spells, as if duty bound. Her turn complete, the philosopher stepped in.

"You're the last act, Aristides. Bring the curtains down."

"…Quite."

The unpleasant-looking woman urged him forward, and he drew his wand.

"Not much to say at this juncture. Just—none of us were capable of joining your cause. And I genuinely do feel that's a pity," he said. "Dolor."

Twenty spells delivered mechanically, and then all six were done. Demitrio watched this all, two layers deep in memory.

"…That was the devil's work, if by my own hand."

He rebuked his past self. As the cave fell silent, all eyes turned to the darkness in back.

"We're done! Come on out, Esmeralda. You're this party's hostess."

The witch drifted back out of the gloom. The one who'd betrayed Chloe, stabbed her in the back.

"You betrayed her. We tormented her. All as was planned. Now—"

"I know."

She knelt down, cradling Chloe's body. Her gaze turned to the ceiling, her lips parted—revealing *fangs*. Four teeth, too long for any human—sank into Chloe's throat.

"Oh—"

"Whew."

Her throat quivered, swallowing. Obviously drinking Chloe's blood. Yet instinctively, all knew she was draining something *else* along with it. The last light in Chloe's eyes faded, and her heart stopped. The woman's arms clasped around her so tight the corpse's bones creaked.

"That was a display!" Vanessa sneered. "How'd it taste? The soul of the woman you loved?!"

The woman turned. This was now *his own* memory. The face Demitrio knew all too well, the witch who would become the pinnacle of the magical world.

"None of you will *ever know*."

"Ah—"

The lengthy recollection was followed by a deep slumber—and Oliver woke up in bed. Edgar was by the side of it, holding his son's hand.

"Noll!" he cried, throwing his arms around the sobbing boy. "You're back with us? Oh, Noll… Noll!"

Shannon was with him, eyes red with tears. "Sorry," she said. "That was…so awful. I'm sorry…for showing you that…"

Oliver was not allowed to listen to this long. Word reached old man Sherwood, and he paid a visit.

"You're up, Oliver? You've been asleep for three days. Even I got worried!"

He pushed Edgar aside, taking a seat by the bed.

"So," he began. "Did you see the faces of your mother's killers?"

A chilly gaze locked on his great-grandson's eyes. Oliver didn't need to search for words.

"I did. And I won't forget them."

His tone alone made his feelings clear. The old man grinned.

"…They took half her soul away. Right, Shannon?"

"…Mm. Like…what I do but…very, very different…"

Shannon sounded very sure. The old man looked grim.

"…Esmeralda Catena Draclugh. Assumed she was my granddaughter's remora, left her alone—clearly an error. Her middle name means *fetters*, a sign she inherits a tainted bloodline, but I had not imagined she'd resurrected the vampires' powers within."

The old man rose, moving from the bed to the window.

"A small salvation, but they know little about us. That is no way to treat a soul; her soul absorb will not serve as interrogation. Personalities and memories are fragile, delicate things; an absorption like that will have shredded them."

He spoke with his back turned. Oliver didn't follow all of this, but he listened intently.

"Regrettably—she may have stolen things far more fundamental. The fixed qualities a soul possesses. What we call soul skills—the very things that lent her the Two-Blade name."

Edgar hung his head. This was forcing him to directly confront what he had lost—what had been taken from him.

"Unlike Shannon, the progenitor blood was not strong with her. Thus, she will not have gained our biggest secret—the soul merge. Even if she had—I do not imagine it reproducible by any race as corrupt as the vampires," the old man intoned. "Either way, our course is clear. She must die. All who betrayed and tormented my granddaughter—and fundamentally, we cannot allow the vampire race to survive. The very existence of that mutation is an insult to the progenitors. The jewel at the heart of a man, treated like that? It is intolerable."

He turned away from the window. His lips contorted with festering fury, the lines around his eyes and nose empowering that diabolical grin.

"Above all—they believe this outrage has put a stop to the mission my wayward descendant dedicated herself to. And that shall not stand."

He may have paid lip service to the family connection, but it was clear to Oliver that *this* was what really mattered to the old man—and thus, to all Sherwoods.

"Yet our enemies are towering. Putting aside the vampire, the other six faces are no less a threat. While the Sherwoods' sorcery is hardly combat-oriented. Our first priority must be the acquisition of might."

With this shift in subject, the old man's eyes turned to Oliver again.

"That's where *you* come in, Oliver."

"W-wait! How does Noll—?" Edgar stepped in between them.

"Does it really elude you?" The old man shrugged, exasperated. "Her soul was rent asunder, but commendably, half of it returned to her son's side. As you yourself said—this is nothing short of miraculous. How can we let that feat go to waste?"

Not a moment of consideration for the father's feelings. His own rationale was all that mattered.

"The principle is simplicity itself. They've gained power through vile means—so we shall take every measure to gain it legitimately. As head of this family, Oliver, I order you to attempt a soul merge."

A solemn preamble to a dire command. Edgar reeled.

"You mean...," Oliver said.

"Figured it out, have you? Exactly. Make the power in Chloe's soul your own. Don't tell me you don't want to. Your beloved mother's soul, blending with your own—what more could a boy want? My grand-daughter came back to you as a ghost—and only this will let her rest."

Edgar could only be mindful of his place for so long. His anger erupted.

"*Non!* D-do you even grasp what you're saying here?! You yourself called the soul a jewel at the heart of man! How can you directly meddle with a child's and hope to alter it to your convenience? The very idea is intolerable! Even if it is his mother's soul, I cannot—"

"Prohibere."

The spell halted Edgar's movements. As he went stiff, the old man glared down at him.

"Hold your tongue, stud horse. I am speaking directly to my great-grandson who, unlike you, bears my blood."

The old man's eyes snapped back to Oliver. Not daring to look away, the boy did his best to answer.

"…If I do that, it'll make me…stronger?"

"That it will. You'll inherit your mother's soul and be strong like she was."

"And if I'm strong like her…I can beat those people?"

"Undoubtedly. Do you know why they had to form a *team* to kill Chloe? Because they feared her strength more than anything."

A flawless answer. And having seen it all himself—Oliver never had a choice.

"I'll do it. Please…let me do this."

His words echoed, reaching Edgar's ears even as the spell wore off.

He gasped for air. "N-Noll…don't! If you chose that path…!"

"How cruel, Edgar. Look at your boy's hands."

The old man yanked the covers away, revealing the arms hidden beneath.

"——!"

Edgar's jaw dropped. His son's hands, clenched on his knees, so tight the bones had snapped, and the skin turned purple and swollen.

"Ha-ha, yet still his grip tightens! That's what I call *fury*."

The old man's laugh was a merry one.

"…Sorry, Daddy," Oliver whispered, his head down. "But if…"

He looked up, meeting his father's eyes. Voice shaking with tremendous emotion not yet taking shape as either grief or rage, just pouring out of him.

"If I do nothing, I'll explode."

This boy *could not be stopped*. That realization made Edgar's face crumple. The old man moved behind him, patting his shoulders with a tenderness that bordered on spite.

"The boy himself consents," he told his grandson-in-law. "Don't even think about taking him and running. You know full well I'll not stand for that."

This last threat silenced Edgar completely. He was aware. He was already in the lion's den. With Chloe herself out of the picture, he and his son had no escape left.

"If we're raising him for strength, that must go side by side with training. I could find a tutor somewhere in this family… But on that point alone, I'm inclined to extend some generosity to your familial affection."

An order wearing mercy's name. This was not a choice. As a father, Edgar could do nothing else. His voice clenched, he spoke the words prescribed unto him.

"…Please…let me handle that."

"So be it."

The old man nodded, as if this was generous. And offered one final threat.

"But do not coddle him. The instant I see the slightest hint of that, you will never see your son again."

Demitrio watched the training that followed, eyes narrowed.

"…Brutal. I've put myself through my fair share of reckless punishment, but even then…"

Training that left his body racked with pain, followed by risking his life on a soul merge. And worse, more training to make his body adapt to the soul. This was pure madness. No teacher in any school would agree with the principle here.

"Words like *training* and *practice* hardly apply. This is mere torture, a long-suffering suicide. That he still lives is mere happenstance. Though considering the original nature of his soul, perhaps he is still dying, even now."

Every day was the same. Their daily basement work left Oliver covered in countless wounds, and Edgar's lifeless voice signaled an end.

"That's enough for today. Ask Shannon for treatment. Rest early and prepare for tomorrow."

"…Dad…"

"Call me Master. Only that is allowed here."

His father turned to go, but Oliver managed a whisper.

"…Sorry I'm so weak. I'll…do better…tomorrow…"

"Ngh—!"

Digging his fingers into his quivering shoulders, Edgar dragged himself bodily out of the training room. Shannon and Gwyn took his place, running to their cousin where his father could not.

"Good work, Noll… Another…hard one, yes?"

"…Sister…"

Oliver barely had the energy to meet her eye. Gwyn put his arms around the boy's tiny body.

"No need to move. I'll carry you to your room."

"…Thank you, Brother."

"Don't thank me. Please."

As they spoke, they carried Oliver to bed.

Demitrio frowned. "Their positions don't seem to line up with the Sherwoods'. I'd like to know more, there. Let's change perspectives."

He stepped out of Oliver's dream. After a moment's consideration, he turned his wand toward Gwyn, invading his memories. Not long after, he'd found his perspective on that period of time.

"…You'll be okay. Rest up, and the wounds and fatigue will be better by tomorrow."

"…Mm. Sleep…tight."

Oliver's treatment complete, they laid him in bed. Gwyn and Shannon left the room. They moved down the hall, out of their cousin's earshot.

Only then did Gwyn speak, his voice quivering. "How is this okay?"

His fist hit the wall. A rare display of emotion from her taciturn brother, and Shannon flinched visibly.

"Every single day spent utterly demolishing him, body and mind. He finally pulls through that, and then a soul merge almost kills him. And then more, more, and more training to make his body adjust to the results! This is no way to treat a human being. Especially a grieving child who's just lost his mother!"

Everything he'd been storing up came pouring out. Shannon put a hand on his shoulder, soothing him.

"I…feel the same way. But don't…lose your head, Gwyn. If Grandfather hears you…"

"He's the one who needs to hear it! Why? Why is he doing this to Noll?! Does he seriously think calling torture training will actually make Noll stronger?! It won't! It's just tearing him to pieces! Breaking him down, shattering what's left, ruining him for good! Until he stops getting back up permanently!"

His voice was almost a shriek.

Shannon hesitated a long time, then said, "Grandfather…doesn't think it'll work."

"What?"

Gwyn swung around to face her.

Head down, Shannon elaborated. "He doesn't…think that…will

make Noll stronger. He just…wants to try. To see how much…a soul merge…can change someone. To see…how far they can…be pushed. Before they collapse. He's using Noll to find out."

Gwyn's heart skipped a beat. The last shred of faith he had in the old man ripped apart.

"Did he *say* that?"

"No, but I can tell. I…feel these things."

His sister's word was beyond refute. Gwyn staggered, feeling dizzy, and put his back against the wall.

"Why…? What has he got against Noll? He's his own flesh and blood! His great-grandson! Even allowing for the bad blood between him and Chloe, even if there was no family bond—he still carries Sherwood blood. Does he not even warrant that deference?"

This doubt, too, Shannon eventually answered.

"Grandfather…is convinced Noll…does not have much. Neither Sherwood blood nor Chloe's. No…prominent talents…anywhere. A thoroughly mediocre boy."

Her voice shook. Gwyn knew why. He knew repeating their great-grandfather's cruelty aloud, conveying these thoughts to her brother—both were as painful for her as the twist of a knife.

"If he's not…going to be anything significant. Then…there's no harm…in using him up…here. That's…how Grandfather sees it."

The last words were delivered through a sob. Gwyn's eyes became grim, and he turned to rush off. Shannon grabbed his shoulders, stopping him.

"Don't, Gwyn!"

"Let me go! I'm telling him off!"

"No use! Our voices won't reach him. You know…they never have. You remember what he made us do!"

"…Rrgh—"

A reminder of their shared history made his feet freeze to the floor. That alone told him how futile a protest would be, and his anger turned once more to his own helplessness.

"…Why couldn't *I* handle the soul merge? Why?!"

"This is how it works. Souls…are compatible…or they aren't. Noll and Chloe work…because they loved each other…very, very much. They barely resist…the fusion."

"Barely? *That's* barely?!"

"It'd be *far* worse with you, Gwyn! Or with me! Chloe never…even *met* us while she lived. Her soul…is too removed from us. We could never…fuse with it."

Shannon wept. Gwyn's wave of anger left, leaving only emptiness behind.

"…Nothing we can do but watch?" he whispered, staring at the ceiling. "Watch as it crushes him?"

Shannon shook her head, clutching her brother's hand.

"Gwyn…let's go back to his room."

"How can we…?"

"Just act…normally. No need to…overthink it. Just…be with him," she urged. "Noll's…very, very alone. While he's training, the anger and pain fill him up, help him…forget. But—at night, it hurts so much it almost makes him…like a candle in the wind. He bites his pillow… trying to bear it…"

And that made Gwyn realize how often Shannon had seen Oliver do this after training. How obvious the signs of her cousin's suffering had been to her.

"What we *can* do now…is ease that loneliness. That's all. But without that…I don't think…he'll last long. He might…break down tomorrow…or even tonight…!"

The sorrow in her voice shook him. Gwyn let out a long breath and straightened up.

"Gwyn."

"Sorry for losing it. Do I look more like a brother now?"

Shannon wiped her tears, smiling. He might've been forcing it a bit, but this was the brother she knew and loved.

"...Mm, you're being...cool again."

"Then let's go. I don't want to leave Noll alone."

They nodded and went back to their cousin's room. After knocking on the door, they stepped in when Oliver answered.

"We're back, Noll. Sorry...to keep you waiting."

Shannon ran over to the bed. Seeing the tall boy behind her, Oliver smiled like a bud unfurling.

"...Oh, you're here too, Brother?"

"Not bearing gifts, I'm afraid. But I figured I'd join you."

He waved a wand, pulling two chairs over to the bedside. They sat down, and Oliver's lips flapped a few times before speaking.

"...Um, you can say no, but..."

"What?"

Hesitant, Oliver looked up at him.

"...could you play for me?"

Gwyn stood up and left the room. Less than a minute later, he was back, laden with instruments.

"Which one? Viola, contrabass, violin? Anything else, you name it. I can play anything with strings."

"Wow...that's amazing! Um... Wh-which should I pick? I wanna hear them all!"

"Then I'll play them all. Violin's easy to like. How about...?"

"I know... The dance. The ocean of stars," Shannon suggested.

"Absolutely. Then here goes."

He began to play. Oliver and Shannon listened with rapt attention— and watching this unfold, Demitrio nodded to himself.

"The love of his cousins did the trick...? I see—this is the last thread keeping him together."

He slipped out of Gwyn's memories, invading Oliver's dream once more.

"But if the old man's plans panned out, he wouldn't have wound up like this. What else happened?"

✳   ✳   ✳

Time flowed on. Oliver grew yet was still facing his father in the basement.

"Gah…!"

"Again, Noll."

Cutting down his son, his father barked an order. Oliver scrambled to his feet, but a few swings later, he was cut down again.

"……!"

"Again!"

Over and over. The gap in their skills was far too obvious. Oliver could go at him a hundred times and never win—and that's *why* they kept trying. Until he obtained the one means of overturning this cycle of defeat.

"I know I'm asking the impossible, but please. You need it.

"I cannot teach you how. But it already lies within you."

In answer to this plea, Oliver picked himself up, an undaunted will in his eyes.

"…I *will* make it mine. You can be sure of that, Master."

"…You're hurt…worse than usual."

After training, in his room, in bed, Shannon was healing his wounds.

"I need it. Sword arts and spells alike, we've done all we can to shore up my techniques. From this point on, it's a slow extension of what I know now. If there's any other way to make a huge leap forward—it's the spellblade my mother used."

Oliver's fists clenched, frustrated by his own limitations.

"Dad's desperately searching for a way to make it mine, to keep me alive. I know that, but I can't pull it off—and that's agonizing. The more my skills improve, the more I know just how much better Mom was."

"…You're trying so hard, Noll. You can't work any harder."

Shannon's eyes filled with tears, and Oliver hastily turned to face her.

"Don't cry, Sister. I'm getting more time to rest now than before. You talked Grandfather into that, right? With my father and brother?"

"We did a bit. But the only reason he listened…is because you've done so much more…than Grandfather ever expected."

Finishing the healing, Shannon took his hand. Oliver smiled gently.

"Then good. I *will* get stronger. Strong enough that your great-grandfather will have to acknowledge it. And then—it'll be my turn to protect the two of you."

A hint of steel in his tone. Love swelled up within Shannon, and she threw her arms around him.

"…Noll… Noll…!"

"S-Sis…"

He loved her, but having her arms around him was still embarrassing. Then—he froze up completely, the color draining from his face.

"…Sorry. Can you let go?"

"Huh…?"

"Let go! Please…!"

Hands on her shoulders, he pushed her away, turning his back. But not before she caught a glimpse—of the tent in the thin cloth of his underwear.

"…Oh…"

That was why. She didn't know what to say. Oliver curled up, muttering.

"Sorry… It didn't used…to get like this…"

His voice was a squeak.

This wasn't just sexual maturation. His harsh training had made his body aware of its mortality; the reproductive urge was in overdrive, an aspect of the survival instinct at work. He'd adapted to his new way of life, but the constant threat was in no way diminished.

"I-it'll go away soon!" Oliver insisted, tears in his eyes. "It's not real, just a mistake! I swear it isn't me! I've never looked at you like that!"

He didn't dare face her, but he turned his head as far as he could.

"I'll fix this! Just…Sister, don't hate me for it."

The moment she saw those tears, all doubt left Shannon's mind. She'd been kneeling on the side of the bed, but now she went to lie down, embracing him from behind.

"Noll. It's fine, Noll."

"…Ah—w-wait! It's not yet…!"

Oliver tried to curl into a ball, but she stopped him, turning him to face her. The cause of the tent in his underwear was still at attention and pressed against her belly, but she no longer minded. None of that mattered.

"Who cares…if it's hard? There's…nothing wrong with that."

And she put her emotions into words. Knowing he could not *feel* them like she did.

"No matter what…happens to you, I will *always* love you, Noll."

Her voice filled his heart with warmth. Clear drops fell from his eyes, landing on her shoulders. Wanting to stop them, he tried to hug her tighter—but ironically, that increased the stimulation down below.

"…Hee-hee. It *does* make it difficult to cuddle."

"…I'm so sorry…"

"Don't say that. It'll just make me hug you tighter."

Her embrace was every bit as tight as his, and they lay together, waiting for him to settle down. Eventually, Shannon realized—he got how she felt, but that was demanding a lot from him.

"…Um, Noll…," she said. Not really thinking, mostly on impulse. "It's tough for you…isn't it? Wouldn't it…be better to…take care of it…?"

His shoulders bucked. Head down, unable to look up, he rasped, "Don't…say that. I don't want…to make you do *that*."

Behind his words, she could tell. His love for her was so deep—he didn't want to sully it with anything carnal. Accepting those feelings, she hugged him again.

"That's fair. Sorry," she said. "You're so kind, Noll. That's what I love about you."

"Ho-ho! How you've grown, Oliver. I barely recognized you!"

Oliver was in the parlor, summoned by his great-grandfather. Old man Sherwood was accompanied by several relatives, his father with them—saying not a word. Meeting most for the first time, he greeted each in turn and then faced his great-grandfather.

"…Can I ask what this is about, sir?"

"Let's not get ahead of ourselves. We old-timers do love our small talk!"

He waved Oliver to the chair across from him. Oliver took a seat, but his eyes never left the old man.

"Too old to relax that easy?" The old man chuckled. "How fast the young do grow. Very well. We'll do it your way—to the point."

Oliver braced himself for anything, and his great-grandfather got down to business.

"You certainly are stiff as a board, but don't be. I'm not asking for anything difficult. Simply your help with something that anyone with Sherwood blood will know the importance of."

"…Help…?" Oliver frowned.

"Our mission is as I've said before," the old man explained. "But accompanying that—is a duty to preserve the progenitor bloodline. Accidents are unacceptable. Even if, in the distant future, our sorcery bears no fruit—we must still bear heirs to their blood *here*. Ensure that it is not lost to the world."

He spoke with solemn gravity. Oliver nodded carefully. He might not share this goal, but he could comprehend it.

"But to this task—we have several *limitations*. First, we cannot allow the blood to get *out*. The progenitor blood is sacred—and sanctified. We must not allow it to flow into the secular world. Second," he added, "to preserve the purity of that blood, we must minimize the introduction of outside blood. This is hardly an unusual practice in mage households, despite Chloe's flagrant violation of the principle."

The old man's words were contemptuous, yet his tone was amused. Oliver knew his mother had been at odds with the old man—but perhaps they had not entirely hated each other. While he speculated, the speech continued.

"In light of that, Sherwood heirs are frequently the product of two close relatives. This applies to my wife and me, Gwyn and Shannon, and Chloe, too."

"......!"

Oliver's cheeks tightened. He knew enough about the workings of this house to predict that, but having it spelled out still came as a shock. Seeing that, the old man sighed.

"I gather you weren't informed? Honestly, to not even tell her son? That girl never did grasp what being a Sherwood *meant*." He then said, "Be that as it may—this is where we want your help, Oliver."

"...You want me to father a child?"

"You're way ahead of me! Don't tell me you'll refuse. I'm providing you and your father safe haven. A little seed is hardly too much to ask in return. A simple favor."

He made it sound trivial. Oliver did his best to disguise his revulsion.

"Oh, don't overthink the matter," the old man said breezily. "It's nothing life-changing. We simply have reason to go for quantity: This focus on bloodline preservation has left us struggling to conceive. Mages have all manner of means to compensate for infertility... But in our case, the issue remains dire. And the more pronounced the progenitor aspect is, the graver that issue presents itself."

He spoke with deep sadness. Even for mages, preserving specific aspects of a bloodline over the ages was a challenge.

"Simply put, mating with one or two will likely not produce any children. Even if they get lucky, they miscarry, or the baby doesn't grow up right. We struggle to produce any viable heirs. We must drop as much seed as possible into these delicate wombs, attempting to bear as many babies as we can."

The old man went quiet, and Oliver's head spun. His heart rejected the idea, but his mind knew he could not easily refuse. He chose the next best option—verifying how much leeway he had before this task was demanded of him.

"...When are we talking about?"

"When? Bwa-ha-ha-ha! When! You ask that?!"

The old man slapped his knee. Oliver was baffled, unsure what this meant.

"As if there is time to spare! *Now.* I'm demanding your seed today. What part of this sounded like the distant future to you?" his great-grandfather asked. "Do not tell me you cannot produce. You cannot hide this from me. You've spilled your first seed already."

"Ngh—!"

A chill ran down Oliver's spine. He had underestimated this opponent *again.* He tried to stand up, but his great-grandmother's hands reached in from behind, holding him still.

"Wha—?"

"Don't, boy. Other matters we might let slide, but when it comes to heirs, the head of the household's word is law."

Her arms were thin, but the strength within held him fast. Oliver fought to free himself, yelling, "N-no! Let go! Let go of me!"

"Ho-ho, what a lively boy. He's grown up well! Let's hope this mettle proves fertile. Gwyn's attempt was dispiriting."

That name made Oliver go still, his eyes like daggers.

"...You made *him* do this?"

"Of course! Like I said, it's the duty of anyone with Sherwood blood," the old man replied. "You, I cannot fathom. Why the resistance? I could see not wanting to bear a stranger's child, but the demand on the male is simplicity itself. You need merely buck your hips and *let fly.* And you can't tell me you dislike the girl."

He spoke as if he was dealing with a temperamental toddler.

"You knew when you heard Gwyn's name, right? Think! Who have you met here who has the strongest progenitor aspect? Fill in the gaps. You know who I want you pairing with. And let me add, she's already agreed to it. Now you need merely do your part."

This was not worth a response. Oliver clammed up like steel, putting his rejection into action—but the old man spotted it.

"Mm— **Impediendum!**"

His drawn wand hit Oliver with a paralysis spell. Going limp, his mouth fell open, revealing the bloody tongue within.

"That was close! The boy tried to bite off his tongue. He knew perfectly well that wouldn't kill him; he was just trying to diminish his condition so that he could not perform. Ha-ha—you can't give this one an inch!"

The old man seemed richly amused. His eyes turned to Edgar—who had not said a word.

"Big balls for his age, yes? The result of your education, Edgar?"

"…!!!"

This spite was met only with silence, like oozing blood. Unable to bear the sight, two relatives Oliver had just met spoke up.

"…If I may, sir, perhaps the time is not yet ripe."

"I agree. Oliver's emotional response aside, the girl is still too young a receptacle. Whether she can conceive or not, the physical burden on her would be—"

Their hesitant protests were silenced by a single glance.

"With Chloe dead and our enemies clear? Mind your words, youths of the branch clan. If you are too foolish to understand where our priorities lie, we may have to rethink what seats you take."

As he spoke, Oliver recovered from the paralysis and began to struggle again. His great-grandmother had a gag in his mouth so he could no longer bite off his tongue. Still he fought. His eyes glaring at his great-grandfather with complete rejection.

"——! ——!"

"Blimey, if we send him in like this, he's liable to rip off his own pecker. Fine! Bring the drugs."

A servant came back with a potion and some needles on a tray. The old lady took them and made ready, injecting the potion into Oliver's neck with practiced ease. Feeling foreign material entering his system made him fight even harder.

"_____! _____!!!"

"One dose won't cut it. Go to five—no, ten. Nigh-fatal dosage will inflame his lusts and overwhelm his reason. Leave no capacity for thought left in his brain. Reduce him to a wild thing, incapable of all else until the deed is done."

"_____! _____!!!"

"How long must you maintain this futile resistance? It's nothing to be frightened of! Once it's over, you'll see how little it meant. Gwyn balked at first but ceased arguing after the third time. Though, now he seems far more devoted to you than he is me. If I had not sent him packing before this began, he might well have attempted to intervene."

"_____!!!! _____!!!!!!"

The boy's struggles lasted awhile. One dose of this drug would rob most of their faculties, but ten were injected into his neck, and still he fought. By then, he could only move the tips of his fingers, but those clawed at the floor, tearing off his nails, attempting to use that pain to keep his wits about him. The sheer violence of his resistance made the old man realized he'd come ill-prepared, but injecting more medicine would kill him before he went mad. His only choice was to cast mind-control spells on top of the drug's effects. Even *then*, Oliver fought.

The gathered relatives gulped, and the fight raged on for another twenty minutes—and at last, the boy's resistance ceased. Or rather—he was now half unconscious. The drug he'd been dosed with stimulated half his mind and numbed the other—with too much injected, this was the natural outcome.

"Quiet at last! My, my, what a display. Can't believe he held out this long with all that in his system."

The old man was as impressed as he was appalled. With all portions of the mind capable of human thought and reason thoroughly numbed, the boy was like an animal, moving purely on instincts—and those placed in a state of *excitement*. It was no longer possible to converse or communicate. His personality had been thoroughly exorcised.

"…Okay, throw him in the room," the old man ordered. "It'll be a rather rough coupling, but Shannon can handle it. I've left her a wand for such eventualities… And if she loses an arm or two, we can always stick it back on."

The great-grandmother nodded and carried the mindless boy to the nearest bedroom. As he was shoved in the door, his witless eyes saw *her*. His sister, seated awkwardly on the side of the bed in the gloom.

"…Noll…?"

Oliver's body moved. Regardless of his will, it staggered toward her.

"What's wrong, Noll? Please…look up. I'm right here— Mm?!"

He stole her lips like he was devouring them, forcing her down onto the bed. Realizing his condition, Shannon's shoulders trembled with fear. Her wand was by the bed, but her hand did not reach for it. It did not even occur to her to turn that on her brother.

"Ah—w-wait, Noll, don't……!"

Nailless fingers dug into her arms, and she screamed from the pain of it.

"O-oww…! That hurts, Noll! Don't…grab my arm…that tight…!"

But her pleas went unheard. The Oliver she knew was nowhere to be found. The drugs had locked his personality away in the jail of his mind, his body driven on animal instinct alone.

"P-please…listen…! Do what your sister says!"

Screams echoed through the darkened bedchamber. Still Shannon called out to him. To the brother she'd sworn to love no matter what happened. Trusting she would get through to him.

"…Noll…!"

*   *   *

"_____.........?"

The next thing he knew, Oliver was flat out on an unmade bed in an unfamiliar room.

".........Ow...... What the...?"

The pain turned his attention to his hands. All his fingernails had been peeled off. With a sinking feeling, he looked around.

And beheld the truth. In bed with him, with not a stitch on—his sister's limp body.

".........Noll...," she gasped, her voice emerging from torn lips. Her frame covered in innumerable bruises, dried blood, bite marks everywhere—

Oliver's throat wheezed. "Sis...ter—"

Shannon met his eyes and smiled. She was beyond recognition, yet the gentle look in her eyes remained unchanged.

".........Good. Nice Noll...is finally...back."

As she spoke, Oliver realized—blood wasn't the only bodily fluid spattered across her. It was still dripping between her legs, mingled with blood.

"......Ah...... AH......"

That reeled his memories back in. The drugs may have taken control away, but his eyes had seen everything—and remembered. It all came flooding back, what he'd done, what violence he'd committed on his beloved sister, with his own two hands.

"......aughhhhhHHHHHHHHHHHHHHHHHHHHHHHH.........!"

His howl echoed through the darkened room. His throat tearing, blood in his voice. But none of that altered the facts that lay before him.

"Bwa-ha-ha-ha-ha! My word! You really did it!"

A few weeks later. The old man received word from his wife and summoned their great-grandson to the living room.

"You're a fine boy, Oliver! A winner! Your seed knocked Shannon up! I had a hunch you might be compatible, but I didn't think you'd plant one in her on your first go! Hat's off to you!"

Dark eyes gazed listlessly up at him. Standing by his side, Gwyn was shaking. So busy suppressing his anger, his jaw clenched so hard his molars broke.

From that day forth, Oliver's frayed nerves and self-harm had left him noticeably thinner. He could not get water down, much less food; he was reliant on IVs and prone to cutting himself furiously at the drop of a hat. Gwyn and Edgar were on watch day and night, never letting him out of sight. This had forced the old man to grant him some respite.

But now only delight was on the man's mind. Fueled by that emotion, he beamed at the broken boy before him.

"Don't take it so hard, great-grandson! You should be proud of this result! How can you not be? Gwyn could not manage it! Bringing the great progenitor blood to the next generation—you've provided us with a ray of hope!"

Only now did Oliver's dulled mind begin to think. The words flowed in one ear and out the other, and he wondered just why this man was so pleased. He'd been told of his sister's conception earlier. He'd tried to shove his fingers in his eyes, but Gwyn had caught his hands in time.

"*Ahem.* Perhaps I'm getting ahead of myself. Certainly, we can't deny these pregnancies often don't end well. In fact, that outcome is far more likely. It's too early to assume we've got another candidate for succession on our hands," the old man said. "But regardless of the outcome, one fact is clear. Your seed *did* make Shannon pregnant. If you weren't compatible, that would never have happened. Flip that, and it tells us that as long as we try with you, we have solid odds of success. Even if the first try fails, do not lose spirit. Twice, three times, five, six! We need merely do the same thing again!"

The patriarch's voice soared. The boy's heart had been cold as ice to begin with, but now the very core of him froze.

What did he just say? Do that again?! Multiple times? Use my seed on—?

While Oliver struggled to absorb the meaning, the man's hands clamped down on his shoulders.

"Oliver, my great-grandson. Allow me to apologize for how we've treated you," he offered. "I'll admit I underestimated you. You look so much like the man my fool of a granddaughter picked without consultation that I assumed your value would be little more than his. I now regret that assumption. I was wrong! Deep down, you are of *my* blood."

Oliver could not even figure out what he was apologizing for. What this man had thought of him, what the reason was—none of that mattered now. Who was he even apologizing to? It was his sister who'd been hurt. The only thing here was the beast that had hurt her.

"And this change of heart is not brought on just because you impregnated Shannon. What turned my head more than anything is the fact that you've remained alive. One in ten survive a soul merge, yet you pulled through countless times, growing into the rock-solid spirit we see before us. Even I cannot deny that moxie! I have no choice but to recognize your accomplishments."

None of this meant anything to Oliver. The one thing he understood was that this man's praise was genuine. This confused and perplexed him so much—it struck him as funny. What was this? How long had he been here, in this madhouse?

"Hear me, Oliver. You represent two values, both irreplaceable. First, you are a rare instance of a mage surviving long-term soul merges. Second, you're a good stud for Shannon. Neither of those things are likely to waver as long as you yet live. Thus—in accordance with those accomplishments, know that your position in this household is set in stone. You are no longer a guest granted shelter, no longer an expendable test subject. You are now unmistakably a *Sherwood*."

Far too heady a word storm, and it left Oliver clinging to fragments of comprehension. He was now one of them. As a reward for defiling and hurting and impregnating his sister, he was now honored to be part of the family. Oh, that made sense. The way every vein in his body felt so choked with bile he could barely keep the vomit down explained it all. He hadn't realized this old man was just the same.

"And not just that. I like the way you tick. You know I outrank you, but you've got the nerve to stand your ground against me. Your love for your mother made you volatile and gave you the endurance to forebear in the face of endless agony—all of those are qualities our family currently lacks. Gwyn and Shannon are skilled but so well-behaved! It's honestly a bit dull. But then you arrived and confounded my expectations—ha-ha! That hits hard. I feel like I did when Chloe was still here."

As the old man babbled with delight, Oliver managed a faint smile imbued with every dark emotion. This was taken as good will, and the elderly man's tone grew even brighter.

"So! Your treatment will be drastically improved. As will Edgar's. You'll be moved to a first-rate room, given all manner of freedoms. Naturally, you may go see Shannon whenever you like. The child in her is yours. If the father never visits, that would just be sad."

What an amusing jape. In lieu of clutching his guts and doubling over laughing, Oliver broadened his smile. The man grabbed his shoulders, his pitch rising.

"I say all this, but by now you've begun to see, yes? Let us work hand in hand! Until Chloe's death is avenged and the Sherwood mission is a success. My beloved great-grandson, surely you will not refuse!"

"Eh-heh-heh-heh." At the table behind him, his great-grandmother chuckled. "At last the two of you see eye to eye. You and your darling great-grandson."

Her smile proved she thought this was a fine thing. She was slicing a celebratory cake with the same hands that had locked him down and pumped him full of drugs. His stomach had forgotten how to hunger, but perhaps he could actually eat this, Oliver thought. It was exactly the sort of pig slop he deserved.

"Noll—do you mind if I call you that?"

Oliver nodded. *Why not? You're free to call a beast by whatever name you please.*

"By all means," he answered. "I'm looking forward to it, Great-Grandfather, Great-Grandmother."

A perfect answer, with a flawless smile. On his brother's sunken cheeks, fashioned by the abyss within—it sent a quiver through Gwyn's shoulders.

Three days passed. Food turned to sand in his mouth, but he'd remembered how to shovel it down. He had a mage's body; it was soon back to normal. His complexion and behavior were just as they'd been before. He could walk from his room without assistance, and he told Gwyn and Edgar they no longer needed to watch over him. He didn't want to tie their hands like that.

Then he started fretting over what mattered most. He did not dare to go see her, but he could not put her out of his mind. What was she up to, how was she doing, was it taking its toll on her? The more his head spun, the more the panic mounted, and in time it moved his limbs for him.

"……"

Holding his breath, he paced back and forth outside her door. He knew she was inside, but he couldn't find the courage to knock. He'd rather she sent him packing. Imagining her eyes if she let him in turned his spine to ice. The moment he knew that kindness would never return to them—he knew he'd turn to ash on the spot, never to live again.

"Noll? Are you out there?"

Her voice, though the door. His heart leaped; his feet turned to flee.

"Don't go. Come in... Let me see your face."

If that was what she wanted, Oliver had no right to refuse. He took a deep breath and opened the door like he was stepping off a cliff. Slowly opening eyes he'd had twisted tightly shut.

His sister's smile hadn't changed at all. Her eyes gazing at him, as gentle as before. Gwyn was on the chair next to her. A wave of boundless relief welled up, but then his rational side kicked in, and he looked away. Even if she hadn't changed—he was no longer allowed to bask in the saving grace of that warmth.

"Don't...look away. Please. Come here. Come closer."

But she kept asking. Feeling trapped in an emotional grater, he took one trembling step at a time closer to her. Three steps out, his feet refused to budge. As if the floor ended there for him. Shannon's face crumpled.

"...Noll..."

"...I don't...have the right to touch you," Oliver said, staring at his feet.

At that, Gwyn clasped his hands around his own throat.

"Oh? Then I have no right to breathe."

His grip tightened. As he shut off the flow of both air and blood, his face swiftly turned purple from the hemorrhage.

"...Kh..."

"Wait, Gwyn—"

"Brother?!"

A moment later, Oliver and Shannon went pale. She moved first, leaning across the bed, reaching for Oliver.

"T-touch me, Noll! Or Gwyn really will die...!"

"Ah—ah... Ah...!"

Panic overwhelmed his hesitation. Fingers shaking, he clasped hers. The moment Oliver felt her warmth on his hands, Gwyn released his neck and resumed breathing. The flow of blood resumed, and his color soon went back to normal—though he was slightly out of breath.

"...Close one. Thanks for saving me, Noll."

"Wh-why would you...why would you do that?!"

Oliver's voice shook, lost. His brother leaned back in the chair, eyes on the ceiling.

"Simple, really. If you must be punished for this—well, I should be punished for it first. I'll never forget the fact that I forced this onto you. I was left helpless and ashamed, and a violent death can hardly begin to pay for my sin."

This speech left Oliver stunned, Shannon's hands on his. Gwyn stood up and faced his brother.

"I'd like to touch you. Do I have the right, Noll?"

"...Yes, of course..."

"Then let me."

With permission granted, he stepped forward and put his arms around the boy.

"If you want anything from me, say the word. If you want my death, ask for it. But if possible, I'd rather you say not yet. I do not wish to die while you're still *here*."

A tear ran down Gwyn's cheek. The warmth of this made him choke up, and Oliver hugged him back.

"...Live, Brother."

"Okay. As long as you wish me to, I shall," Gwyn promised, nodding.

Shannon got up off the bed and hugged them both.

"I don't know...about *rights*. Even if you won't touch me, Noll...I will hug you myself."

A sob escaped his throat. Not a howl or a shriek. But for the first time since he'd been forced into an act he abhorred, he allowed himself to cry like a child should.

Knowing someone shared his sin proved Oliver's salvation. His eyes gradually began to turn forward. In which case—there was but one thing he had to do, above all else. He kept at his brutal training unabated—but the rest of his time was devoted to *this*.

"Ah, that feels good. Thank you, Noll."

Shannon let out a blissful sigh. She was undressed, her back bare, and Oliver was gingerly fixing the disruptions in her magic flow.

"R-really? It doesn't hurt? I-it doesn't feel…gross?"

"Why…would you think that? It all feels…wonderful. Everywhere…you touch me."

Shannon was quite firm on that point. Oliver was relieved, but his heart was still unsteady. He focused on the task at hand.

"I'm…pretty good at healing," he said. "It always made Mom… happy. I wanted to get better, so I always had Dad help me practice. B-but when I got overconfident…it was bad. His whole back turned red."

"Mm-hmm…"

Shannon nodded.

Mage pregnancies were far shorter than those of ordinaries, and their bellies swelled up much faster. Visible evidence of the life growing within had hastened Oliver's acceptance of his role. Boyhood came to an end, and he had to leap right from teenager to father. Whether he had the right or not, this was his only option.

"…You're sure it's fine? I'm scared the baby doesn't like it…"

"I think the baby…knows. That someone very nice…is taking care of us."

Shannon's voice was soothing, and Oliver wiped a tear from his eye, letting himself believe.

"I hope…that's true," he said. "Not much longer now."

"Mm. If you're tired, sleep here with us. Blame me for it—and sleep in tomorrow."

Everything she said was filled with warmth. Oliver fought off the urge to cling to that, focusing on the baby instead. How could he make this child's life a happy one? With helpless, corrupted hands? What could he do to earn the right to hold this child?

"…Sister."

"Mm?"

Thinking wasn't getting him anywhere, so he asked. Knowing that doing so was clingy—but unable to stop himself.

"...Do you think...I can do it? Be this baby's father...?"

Shannon turned to the boy, putting her face next to his.

"Lend me your ear, Noll."

"Mm?"

"Let me...tell you a secret."

Puzzled, Oliver turned his ear toward her. Shannon cupped both hands around it.

"I actually know...two things," she whispered. "First...the baby's a girl. Second—she loves you, Noll."

Oliver's eyes went wide. It never occurred to him to doubt his sister's word. But even then—he found it hard to believe.

"...She's not even born yet, though..."

"But I can tell. Even without giving birth. This much...is guaranteed."

Shannon seemed very firm on this. There might be no other basis... but maybe she was right, Oliver thought.

Shannon sat back, looking down at her own belly.

"So once she's born...let's cuddle her together. Give her so many hugs...rub her head, cover her in kisses."

She rubbed her belly, the cradle in which their daughter slept. Oliver watched intently, and so she smiled at him.

"Then we'll tell her...together," she said. "Thank her...for being born."

Oliver nodded. And for the first time—he put his hands on the belly harboring that life, of his own accord. Swearing a silent vow—*I may not be much of a father, but I promise I'll keep you safe.*

Logically, both knew: That hope was all too fleeting. Those with the progenitor aspect did not go through childbirth without incident—the history of the Sherwood family showed those odds were dismally low.

But hope was their only choice. The sole path this cruel world provided to redemption, to extract something of value from everything that had happened between them. The first and last chance at a future in which Oliver would ever forgive himself.

Perhaps their prayer would have been granted—if there was a god.

Thus—the futility of it may well have been set in stone long, long ago.

"Sister!"

Informed of the crisis before dawn, Oliver and Gwyn came running to the treatment room. They'd been told the night before the birth would not be easy; until an hour ago, he'd been holding his sister's hand, staying with her through it—but when push came to shove, even that had been disallowed, and he'd been driven out of the room.

"…Ah…"

And once he was allowed back, only the outcome awaited. A haggard Shannon, clutching a tiny body. Eyes devoid of emotion, staring down at the unbreathing baby.

"Shame. We did everything we could. It was alive inside her not long ago, but…"

Their great-grandmother sighed, placing her wand on the instrument tray. Her words never even reached Oliver's ears. Shannon, the baby in her arms—and how powerless he was. Those three things were all he was able to perceive. Nothing else held any meaning.

"…Noll…"

Shannon's eyes turned toward him. The verdict on this sin was passed down. Her fingers brushed the cheek of their stillborn daughter.

"…I'm sorry," she said. "I couldn't…manage the birth…"

An apology. That cast an eternal curse upon one boy's life.

Time passed in silence. No tears were shed. He no longer even fretted.

By this point—in his mind, it was already settled. Everything was.

"…You're sure about this, Noll? It's only been two days," Edgar asked in the basement training room.

Oliver merely nodded. "I said I'm ready, Master."

This silenced Edgar. He could tell nothing he said would make a difference.

"Fine. If this is what you need…I've nothing more to say."

He raised his athame. Oliver lunged at him. Blades clashed, and sparks flew.

Exchange after exchange, with no hope of victory. And all the while, the boy asked his heart:

Tell me, Oliver. Do you remember? What you've done here?

You sought strength. To slay those who tortured your mother to death.

You sought strength. To protect your brother and sister.

You sought strength. To be a father to your unborn child.

"……Ha……ha……"

And what did you achieve? What was the outcome of your efforts?

You raped and impregnated your sister. You let your daughter die before her birth.

What else? Nothing. That is all. You've accomplished nothing else.

"……Ha-ha……ha……"

What a farce. How was it even possible to fuck things up this bad?

Was it a waste to even think about? Struggle all you might, you cannot fix it. It's already too late. You're a beast shaped like a man, unfit to call yourself one.

So what now? Search for a means of atonement where none exist? Take time? *Eat, sleep, wake, think, and worry like any average man, like you have the* right to an average life?

No. That's not right. That's all wrong. No part of that is permitted.

You must suffer. Before you eat, before you sleep or wake, before you even breathe, suffer.

And in that suffering, search. At the end of that suffering, make it yours. Carve that principle into your mind.

Oh—do you still *not get it? How ill-suited you are for what you're doing now?*

"…Ha-ha-ha-ha-ha…!"

A loud, hollow laugh. Directed at himself, derisive, escaping his throat uncontrollably.

That's right. Exactly. All too true.

A move that guarantees victory in one step, one spell range? A spellblade that finds that one chance of victory in a million?

Don't make me laugh. Your hands are not worthy.

That is your mother's light. You cannot hope to imitate it. Your filthy, tainted hands can grasp no part of that.

You have naught but darkness. A murk well suited to your nature. That's what you must reach for. Not that one-in-a-million shot at victory, but a one-in-a-million carefully selected suffering.

You must live, that you may suffer.

You must defeat your foes, that you may live.

The result is the same. That is the nature of your spellblade. The same as the nature of your life to come.

Go on: Choose. Of the infinite possible futures, pick the one that will make you suffer most.

Make it yours—so that no one else will ever suffer like that again!

"AaaaaahhhhhhhHHHHHHHHHH!"

He saw the threads and made his choice. The form decided, his blade rushing toward the outcome.

A wrist, sliced. An athame, fallen from loosened grasp. His own, still held.

He knew the deed was done.

"……Wha—?"

Edgar gaped down at his empty sword hand, at the deep gash in his wrist, still oozing blood. A long, stunned silence, then he lifted his eyes—

"Noll, was that…?" he asked.

There stood his son. Exposed to the strain of fate, every inch of the

boy's body bled. Far more gravely injured than the opponent he'd beaten. He'd seen corpses in better condition.

"…I did it, Dad," the boy declared.

One thing snatched from the jaws of all that had been lost forever.

No trace of the original form left. Twisted and snarled into a knot that could never again be undone—but no less a *spellblade*.

Only his father witnessed this firsthand—they told no one else of the success. Edgar said that Oliver's standing was strong enough that he need not reveal it. He had the favor of the head of the house without needing to use his spellblade as a bargaining chip.

Oliver merely nodded. This decision jelled with his plans.

"Ohhh, Noll! You show yourself again. How I worried!"

That same evening, Oliver went to see the old man. Not in the usual living room—for once, he was in his private quarters. The man looked tickled pink to see his great-grandson for the first time in two days.

"This one was a shame, but not to worry. Similar cases have shown the first delivery rarely succeeds. Our house always needs multiple attempts to produce an heir. You can't let a single setback get you down."

"Exactly!" his great-grandmother said, preparing tea nearby. "As long as she gets to the birth, we'll take as many out of her as we have to."

Oliver acknowledged this with a glance and faced forward. Across the table, the old man pulled a chess set off the shelf, placing it between them.

"Since you're here, let's not waste time dwelling on the dismal. How's chess for a change of tune? I've heard you and Edgar used to play rather often."

"I'd be glad to. I appreciate the honor," Oliver said.

Lining pieces on the board, the old man cheerily prattled on.

"Most things, we purchase the magical-world version, but for chess alone I prefer boards made by ordinaries. That Magic Chess thing simply will not do. Garishness over class or beauty. The innumerable gambits and stratagems on a limited field—is that not the epitome of a board game's pleasures?"

"I entirely agree."

Oliver meant that wholeheartedly, no lip service involved. For the first time in any interaction with his great-grandfather. A strange feeling—but as he savored it, the board was set. Playing white, Oliver took the first turn. As the game reached the midpoint, the old man crossed his arms.

"You certainly do play an unruly game. You'll have to give me a moment—this bears some thinking."

He put a hand to his chin, pondering. His wife placed some tea by the board, and Oliver absently took a sip. And the full fragrance hit his nostrils, surprising him. He was certain the leaves were perfectly ordinary—the batch had simply been well brewed. From the temperature of the water, to the warmth of the cup, to the preservation of the tea leaves, all mindful of the recipient.

"Okay, that should do it... Heh-heh, a brilliant move, if I do say so myself. You'll not easily catch my intent."

"Indeed not. I'll have to think about that one. Give me a little time."

A moment of silence passed. The only sound the ticking of a clock on the wall. At long last, he made a move.

"My mother...," the old man began.

"___?"

"Your great-great-grandmother, that is. She was a die-hard chess fan. So much so she taught the game to everyone who passed through this house. Young or old, even the servants. Fundamentals to advanced strategies. When I was young, I often played against her."

His move complete, Oliver looked up from the board. This was almost the first time he'd heard the old man speak of his childhood.

"She'd demand you play day or night, no consideration for your time. My siblings were all deeply frustrated by it. But—I always rather liked those moments. When my mother was seated across the board from me, for that brief time—she only focused on me. And that was nice—back then, I wasn't exactly the most promising child and didn't get much of her attention otherwise."

He managed a forlorn smile, quietly moving a piece.

"Perhaps one reason I took a liking to you was…you remind me of how I acted right after my mother passed. In hindsight, I had a very long spell where I just had to grin and bear it. I worked my way to the top of the family—naturally, because I spent considerable time and effort finding where my talents lay and polishing them accordingly. But—also because I made it through those hard times. These days, I believe perseverance is virtue that trumps all other talents."

Moving his own piece, Oliver listened intently. Last time, he'd been unable to understand a word the man said. But this time, the man's words felt like genuine praise.

Really—he *had* done one thing here beyond hurting his sister and letting his daughter die. He'd *endured*. Kept his knees from buckling under the agony and suffering each day piled on his shoulders. That may have meant little in the long run, but he had persevered. Doing so was the only way to stay alive in a house like this.

And for that reason, it made sense—when this man had been his age, he might well have gone through much the same.

"I hope you follow in my footsteps. This is more an ambition than a prediction—perhaps little more than wishful thinking. Ha-ha, the sleepy musings of an old man. A slip of the tongue, best forgotten."

Oliver shook his head, smiling. "…No, I'm sure I'll remember it for quite some time."

And made a bold move that demanded a response. The old man groaned, frowning.

"Here I think you'd been endearing, for once—and your move is downright vicious. What a great-grandson! I'll need time, here."

"Go ahead. I'll think things through myself."

As the wheels in the old man's head spun, Oliver watched his face, thinking— *Right now, he's just a great-grandfather. Doting on his great-grandson, pleased to find a common enthusiasm, his lips loosened into sharing old memories. As if that heartless mage was all an act.*

Oliver wondered which was real and concluded they both were. If he had two faces, that just meant he'd needed them both. There were times when he had to be a cruel, arrogant mage—and times when he was just a simple man. That was normal enough. Just as Oliver himself was acting like a good boy here and saying what he really felt when he was with his cousins.

Then—had his great-grandfather once acted the part of a good son with his own mother? When a house that put preservation of the progenitor blood above all else demanded he also be a good mage? If they had not demanded that of him—he might have escaped this fate. Never developed a cruel, arrogant streak, never learned to trample on the hearts of others. He'd have just been another nice old man.

"…If things had just been a little different…"

"Hmmmm… Mm? Did you say something?"

The man looked up at Oliver's whisper, so he shook his head. The old man looked back at the board, grinning.

"…I've got it! Eighteen to check! Here. Well? Ready to resign?"

He made his move and looked at his great-grandson, eyes gleaming. Oliver examined the board, realized he had no path to victory, and nodded.

"My loss," he said. "You are far better at this. I held on as best I could, but your experience won out."

The old man puffed out his chest proudly, then began moving the pieces back a few moves. Clearly moving on to the postmortem. Oliver pursed his lips and quietly rose from his chair.

"That was fun. Probably the most I've enjoyed myself since arriving here."

He meant that. His hand went to the hilt of his athame. The old man was busy getting the pieces set up, not on guard at all. He only looked up when all the pieces were in place again.

"Good-bye, Great-Grandfather."

Thanks for asking me to play with you. Genuine gratitude, even as his blade slashed sideways.

The old man didn't so much as budge. The athame cut through bone without resistance. His head rolled away, falling to the floor. And with that dull *thud*, his body went limp, making the chair creak.

Oliver almost laughed. All the work he'd put in, and he hadn't even *needed* a spellblade.

"Huh?"

Hearing the sound, his great-grandmother looked up from the plate of treats she'd been readying. Tiny little financier cakes, ones she knew her great-grandson loved. Oliver smiled at her. And walked her way. In his hand—an athame stained with his great-grandfather's blood.

"Wait, Noll, why?"

Only then did her hand reach for her wand. Far too late. Oliver stepped in, stopped that hand with his left, and buried the tip of his athame in her heart. The magic he poured in destroying her source of life.

She passed before his very eyes. To the end, no emotions overtook the confusion on her face.

"…I wish you could have understood *why*," he whispered, knowing she could no longer hear. He withdrew the blade and laid her body down on the floor at his feet, only then realizing how small her stature truly was.

"……"

Looking over their deaths, Oliver thought: *They were* mages. *They lived far longer than me, were far craftier, and their true strength dwarfed my own.*

But they were also human. And they were his great-grandparents.

Oliver's familiar called them to the old man's chambers. Gwyn, Shannon, and Edgar came in—to find it was all over.

"Oh…my."

Speechless, they gaped at the boy—and the pair of corpses. Leaving the evidence of his actions on full display, Oliver spoke from the corner.

"It was the only choice I had, so I went ahead with it. I didn't want to wait another day—so I took care of it tonight."

He knew that was all the explanation anyone here required. He turned to face them.

"This is good-bye, Brother, Sister. Sorry to end things by tramping on all the blessings you've given me," he intoned. "But I can say this: You no longer need to protect me."

He managed a lonely smile that took their breath away. Edgar stepped forward, facing his son.

"…You've made up your mind, Noll?"

"Yes. Sorry, Dad. Will you come with me?"

"What's your plan?"

"Avenge Mom. Achieve her goals." Oliver shrugged, admitting, "Anything else—I don't really know."

An honest answer. Edgar nodded and drew his athame.

"Very well—then be *bolder.*"

He knelt down by the old man's corpse, lining up the severed head with the body. Healing the wound, though that would not restore his life. With the body intact once more, he cut off the head again himself.

"——?! Dad, why—?!"

"Shush. Just watch."

Edgar stood up and moved to the old woman's body. Once again, he healed the wound and thrust his own athame into the exact same spot. When he withdrew it, he left it in his hand, his back to the children.

"That should do it. I killed them both. Anyone who sees this will know that to be true."

All three gaped at him. Edgar was a cautious, thoughtful man—not given to anything this rash.

"They were in charge of the Sherwood clan, the heads of this household. If they go down together, there'll be a power struggle. And I know who'll step in to try to seize control—people who've long deplored the state of this house, who feel very much as we do."

That made Gwyn gasp—and Oliver remember. On the day he'd been forced to do the unspeakable, only two relatives had voiced objections.

"Travis and Rose?"

"Exactly. I've spent the last few years speaking to them in secret. Conspiring, biding our moment to revolt. Didn't imagine my son would beat me to it."

"I—"

"Surprised? I was hardly going to stand by doing *nothing*. Not that that excuses anything."

Edgar turned back, smiling ruefully. Oliver caught that gleam of self-reproach in his eyes. Like father, like son—he knew just how much these years had hurt him.

"But this script is not yet complete. The perpetrator still stands. Only if you dispatch me with your own hand—Noll, only then will your place in the new Sherwood house be secured." ⋅

"——! No, Da—"

"Prohibere!"

Realizing where this was going, Oliver took a step—and Edgar's spell prevented it.

"Don't worry; I won't make you do it. You need merely handle the cleanup. Like I just did, doctor the wounds and weapon. If your cousins help, it should be simple."

"——!"

Gwyn and Shannon both reached for their wands, but Edgar held out his hand, stopping them.

"Don't stop me, Gwyn. Shannon. You know full well this is the best way to keep Noll safe. Anything else will lead to consequences. Especially if you're on the run without a plan. Given the enormity of who he has to face, I can't leave any of you in such a precarious position."

"Guh—"

"......!"

He was right—and it left them flat-footed. They'd each sworn long ago to never leave their cousin on his own. But there was a wrong way to do that. Like Edgar said, abandoning their home would be the worst option. They might manage to find a place to hide and survive, but to assassinate seven of the world's best mages would require a *lot* of help. And those on the run could not negotiate for it.

Once he'd impressed that fact on them, Edgar turned to his son.

"Noll, when they forced you into that act against your will, I'm sorry I couldn't save you. I heard every one of your screams. I could feel your eyes begging me to step in. But—but I couldn't lift a finger," he said. "I'm not like Chloe. Drawing my wand and throwing myself into that fray—that would not have accomplished anything. At best, I'd have suffered a pathetic death. But with me gone, your position here would have been even worse. That thought—gave me pause."

His voice shook. He gritted his teeth, eyes downcast, the regret overwhelming.

"But perhaps I *should* have acted then. Even if I achieved nothing but my own death, at least you'd have remembered me as a father who was there for you when it mattered. Perhaps you'd have lived the rest of your life proud of me for it. A far better image of me than what I'm reduced to here."

Oliver wanted to refute this, but his lips would not move. Edgar looked up, wiped his tears with the back of his hand, and forced a smile.

"But, Noll... I long ago lost the right to say this, but let me end with it anyway: More than anything in the world, more than anything else at all, more than I ever imagined possible—"

He put his athame to his throat. Speaking words that would never waver.

"—I've always, always loved you and your mother."

With these heartfelt last words, Edgar cut off his own head. One slice through flesh and bone so that death could not elude him. The two pieces of his father's body fell to the floor, spraying blood—and the spell binding Oliver wore off.

"Daaaad—"

He made to run over, but Gwyn and Shannon each grabbed a shoulder.

"Don't touch him, Noll. Any disturbances will make doctoring the body harder. Someone might notice something out of place."

"Th-the body? No, that's—that's my dad! I've always loved him; he always put me first—"

Oliver was hardly thinking straight. As he stared at his father's body—he saw the chessboard. The game he'd been playing with his great-grandfather. Memories of their old lives rolled off his tongue.

"We used to play chess together all the time."

A tear fell from his eye. Gwyn's grip tightened.

"And you're going to keep his final wish. Please, Noll. Please."

He was pleading, shaking. Bracketed by his cousins, Oliver looked long and hard, eyes blurred by tears—but in time, they focused.

"…I just figured it out…," he whispered.

His cousins peered in.

"…What my father asked. What I'll do after I avenge my mother—and achieve her ambitions. What do I want to do next?"

As he spoke, he felt his very core shaking. Now he got it, he knew. The sight before him was hardly unusual. It overlapped with his mother's memories of her brutal death, and that told him everything.

The world outside was full of this. Lives stolen, dignity torn away, hearts trampled—the world mages made had far too many reasons to do so. And so they did. The *morally correct* pursuit of sorcery allowed it. And it ground their hearts away. The view before him was but one of countless such tragedies.

So he would not stop once Chloe was avenged. Nor would achieving his mother's goals be enough. Not if he wanted to prevent anyone from ending up like this again.

"…I'll make the world *nicer*. Maybe it won't be a big change. Just…a little bit better than it is now. So that things this sad no longer happen anywhere..."

He knew what he should do. In his heart, a spell he'd once believed in. A destination to dedicate his life to, a distant hazy ideal—that he *spoke aloud for the first time.*

"So the nice things...can stay nice...!"

When he reached this moment, Demitrio cut short the progression of the memory dream.

"...I've grasped the history. I know enough," he muttered, sounding extra sour. A flower of vengeance, a twisted growth sown by his own hand, nurtured out of sight. This man's heart was ostensibly inured to the tragic, except for the first time in years, he found himself perturbed. "Chloe's brutal death came at our hands. Yet—this was *not* the goal. None of us intended to plunge anyone into this crucible of grief."

He knew such defenses were meaningless, but he made them anyway. With what he'd seen, Demitrio was convinced—there was no salvation in Oliver Horn's life. An indirect consequence of Demitrio's own actions, the boy was now pursuing an unattainable ideal, punishing himself with the infinite suffering that pursuit entailed—this was a life tantamount to a hell on earth. It could lead to nothing but lamentations and despair.

The boy himself bore no sin. At the very least, Demitrio had found not one thing in the boy's memories that a child his age could possibly be held responsible for. Yet he had shouldered that blame. The adults around him had helped, but the boy had made the choice to do so. Thus—however malformed the shape of it, Demitrio was in no position to argue the point.

In which case, he thought, he needed to merely act as an enemy should.

"Let me put an end to this. Whether you defeat me or not, your life will soon burn out," the philosopher said. "At the very least, I can provide you a tranquil death. Your time here has been naught but suffering; let it end with the warmth and peace you've long since lost."

With that, he changed the dream. All too aware this was but an empty gesture.

The boy found himself sitting in their old house in the woods.

"Huh—?"

"What's wrong, Noll? You look like someone threw a stone at a basilisk."

That voice took him back. His mother had her chin in her hand, elbow on the table, and was looking right at him.

"...Mom..."

"Yep, it's your mom. I'm always here with you. Why wouldn't I be?" she said. "Ah-ha! You were nodding off, right? Did you dream I was gone?"

Chloe laughed like he had nothing to worry about. A chessboard slid into view from his other side. Oliver turned to find his father smiling at him.

"Bad dreams, Noll? Then join me. Play some elegant chess with Dad and forget all your woes."

"This again! Better humor him, Noll. He just lost Magic Chess eight times running and is in a funk."

"I am *not*! Your tactics merely destroyed my will to live."

Oliver watched his parents bicker, stunned—and then realized Gwyn and Shannon were seated across from them. Eyes full of warmth, gazing at their cousin.

"I'd like...to watch you play...chess, Noll."

"Don't hover, though. That'll rattle his concentration."

"...Brother, Sister..."

Urged on by all, Oliver began playing chess. But a few moves in, his hands stopped. An irrefutable wave of panic roiled in his heart, preventing him from focusing on the game.

"What's wrong, Noll? It's your turn."

"Oh? Not in the mood? Then let's try something else."

Chloe snapped her fingers, and cheery voices echoed through the window.

"Look, out in the garden. Your friends are here to play."

A lineup of familiar faces came into view. Chloe pushed him toward the entrance, and he drifted out the door.

"...Hey..."

"Oh! Oliver! We have arrived!" Nanao cried.

"We're borrowing your yard for a tea party," Chela explained. "Would you care to join us?"

They waved him over. On the far side of the table, Katie and Guy were deep in an argument.

"Argh, Guy! That's your third financier! There's only two for each of us!"

"Aw, quit it. There's more where this came from! That stone oven's already making some."

Guy pointed, and Oliver turned to look. The oven was pumping out more cakes into a basket in front of it. He gaped at that a moment, and Pete looked up from his book.

"...Despite the racket, this is a nice place to read. Just the right amount of light makes it through the leaves."

"Great for tag, hide-and-seek, or naps!" Yuri said between mouthfuls of cake. "You've got a lovely place here, Oliver!"

Oliver's eyes snapped to him.

"...Yuri..."

"Mm? You're coming to me? That's nice! You've got so many people to choose from."

Beckoned by his smile, Oliver took a seat next to him, glancing around. His family members were inside, but all his friends were here outside.

"The best life you could ever ask for," Yuri said, taking the words out of his mouth. "That's the impression I get anyway."

"…Sounds about right. Nothing here but happiness. Everywhere I look, I see only *nice* things."

Oliver nodded, unable to argue. Yuri swallowed another bite of cake.

"Then why not accept it? If you're happy here, why go out in search of suffering? Just stay warm, at ease, and fulfilled. Or do you have something against those things, Oliver?"

Yuri's eyes bored into him. Oliver smiled in lieu of an answer—and shook his head.

"They're all fine. Just—not for me."

"Who says? Not your parents or friends. Who else is there? Pretty sure this world's got no god."

"No one said anything. I made up my own mind. I don't have the right to be happy. No matter what, no matter when, no matter who around me is happy—my path should always lead to suffering."

This was the life he'd settled on. Yuri folded his arms, thinking this over.

"That doesn't make much sense. I get wanting to make someone *else* happy. But what good does your suffering do? It's not creating anything; it's not leading you anywhere. It's utterly meaningless. All it does is make you one miserable dude, Oliver."

Demitrio was controlling Yuri, attempting persuasion—and kicking himself for it. He knew he had no grounds to argue this from, but he could not let this warped state stand. A side of him he'd acquired working as a village mage; he couldn't watch a child mess things up without attempting to make them see the light.

"There *is* meaning. At least, for me," Oliver said.

Gazing upon the joy around him as one would a distant star.

"A whole lot of awful things have happened to me. Too many to count. And quite a few of them I instigated. No, I'm not crazy enough to think they're all my fault. For most of them, I was simply helpless to stop it." He paused. "But now—that's no longer the case."

Oliver looked down at his hands. Stained with the blood of the battles he'd been through, yet still possessed of the ambition to grasp for more.

"...I want to gather what I can. As many fragments of what was shattered as I can find. This act will bring nothing back. But if I don't act—they'll all just be *left there*. Sad things happened, so many people wept and suffered, and it'll fade into the past with no one left to remember. And I just can't bring myself to accept that... So I'm gonna shoulder that burden. Until the day I think I've made up for everything that happened. And then all the pain and suffering, all the guilt and regrets..."

At last, Demitrio understood these were not things that could be separated from the boy. Memories without emotions were merely a record. They would not leave behind what he most held dear. The hearts of the people who had lived—and were now gone. And their feelings that he still carried with him.

Oliver looked right at him. Demitrio gulped, feeling seen.

"You should know that now, Yuri. It doesn't matter how hard it is. It doesn't even really matter if there's joy in my future. What matters is the pride of walking the path you chose," said Oliver. "In that final battle, you found a path of your own."

At this, Yuri went very still. His eyes wavered a long moment, and then he raised a trembling hand to his chest.

"...Yeah, I did. Why...? How did I forget that?" he wondered aloud. "I'm just like you. Or I *was*."

He was whispering, as if woken from a dream. Seeing realization dawn, Oliver nodded and got to his feet.

"I'm glad you see the light," he said. "It's time I got going."

"...Yeah. Same."

Yuri followed him. Headed out, away from the clamor of the garden. Their friends noticed and leaped to their feet.

"Wha—?! Come back, Oliver! Mr. Leik!"

"Where are you guys going?!"

"Why are you leaving us?! Was Guy's joke that bad?!"

"Hey, speak for yourself! You've stuck your foot in your mouth way more than I have!"

"No need to be hasty, gentlemen. We have cakes aplenty!"

Oliver *was* tempted, and he winced at that. Impressed by the precision. Hardening his heart, he maintained his pace—and his family burst out the door.

"Noll…!"

"Wait, Noll!"

"Don't go, Noll! You know better! Only suffering awaits!"

Shannon, Gwyn, and Edgar all tried to stop him. Then Chloe pushed past them, calling out to her son.

"Noll, stay here. Stay with Mom and Dad, your brother and sister, and all your friends. Here you can be happy—and at peace," she implored him. "That's all we need. That's all people ever truly crave."

This was the first tear in the fabric. Oliver turned around, facing the thing shaped like his mother.

"What you're saying is true enough. However—my mom would *never* say that. Chloe Halford was *always* chasing paths yet undiscovered. Even if she clashed with others on the way—she never denied the pursuit."

Chloe fell silent, mouth closing. Oliver glanced at each face in turn, smiling.

"Thank you, one and all. You might be fakes, but I felt your warmth. It was a very happy dream," he told them. "But—it's time to wake up. This place is far too *nice* for me."

With that, his vision began going dark. His house vanished into the gloom, then so did the yard, then his family and friends. Feeling no need to move farther out, Oliver put a hand to his chest.

"Sorry for the delay," he said. "I won't abandon you. I shall carry each one of these fragments inside me. Even if the weight of my sins makes my knees buckle and cave, and I have to drag myself forward on broken arms—"

His direction alone, he'd never lose sight of. Even if his destination retreated faster than he could advance, he would not stop moving forward. As long as he still lived, he would head toward that distant, hazy light. Likely till his last breath. Since that fateful day, this had been Oliver Horn's path as a mage.

He drew his athame. Aimed at his own chest. He took a breath and stabbed himself in the heart, an incantation on his lips. A vow to force himself out of the peaceful dream and back to the suffering of the real.

"Dolor!"

A vivid pain racked his chest. His mind had already left the dream, and now it surfaced fast.

"■ ■ ■ ■!" *Move!*

No sooner had the word left Demitrio's lips than the boy swung his hand.

"AaaaaaAAAAAAAAHHHH!"

His blade shot in, and Demitrio leaped backward on pure reflex, unable to comprehend what had happened. How long had it been since he'd been too confused to *think*?

"————? ————? ————?!"

Panic spurred his mind into motion. His brain was catching up with the facts. He himself had released the primal binds on the boy—no one else here was capable of doing so. He had not desired that act—and yet *he* had.

"...You're not yet melded? You're still there, inside me...?!"

He spoke to the soul splinter, long since absorbed. A part of himself, deprived of flesh, yet acting to save a friend.

That old pain and strife in every inch of his half-broken body, a sign he'd *awoken*. Oliver Horn knew no clearer sign of what was real, and that brought him back home to suffering itself.

And so he fought. Throwing himself back into the suspended duel without further ado. Not a bit off his stride. This was his life. His purpose was ever distant, ever clouded, his goals always a queue stretching out in front of him. The history replayed in that passing dream brought the outline of it all into sharp relief.

A row of corpses stretching across the horizon of his memory. And in their midst, the smallest of them—the body of an infant. On that distant day, cradled in his sister's arms, silenced forever. The greatest of the sins that drove him to his purpose. Branded onto his back, driving him ever onward.

The agony he'd wished upon himself. A veritable hell, befitting his position. His mad lamentations to the inferno raging within his heart.

Oh, daughter of mine. Stillborn babe, conceived in the vortex of vile misfortune, taken before you could even raise your birthing cry.

If you'll forgive my one request, do not be born again to a father like this. If there is a next time, choose not a devil.

For a time, I had the gall to try to be a father—and I thought up many a name for you. Dreamed of all the things I'd like to do for you. Imagined myself walking hand in hand with you as you grew up strong and healthy. Wondered how you'd smile. How your eyes would see me. How I'd feel as I looked back at you.

None of that was to be. You slipped through my fingers before a single one came to pass. Thus—it is all stuck here. All those bountiful emotions your sad excuse for a father would have lavished upon you. All as they were when I waited for your birth, afire with nerves and apprehension. They've become a bonfire, burning on within me.

I promise you this. Until my dying breath, they'll be with me. My heart will always be with you; I shall ever seek to atone, your curse shall ever be upon me. I don't imagine that will make amends. And yet—if my desperate struggles prove some small solace to you, that will be my salvation.

…And sometime, someday…in the distant future, that may or may not ever be.

Perhaps our souls will come back around, as soulology suggests they might.

I'll fight for that day. So that when you're granted life again, it may be under a better father. So that you may smile for him, the smile I never got to see.

And in the hopes that the world you find yourself in is just a little nicer than this one!

Much like with ordinary magic, the range of primal spells varied with the incantation used. Since releasing people required less work than applying stasis, the range affected covered quite a broad area around Demitrio himself.

"Shannon, go!" Gwyn yelled the instant he was free again.

He went to resume his spelljamming, but the last fight had left his viola buried in rubble. He pulled his spare violin out of his pocket and raised his arm—except there was nothing left below the elbow.

"...Tch...!"

That was no reason to give up. He called over a comrade, had them use healing to generate just enough flesh for the arm to function, and then jammed his spare bow in—directly fusing his wand to his arm.

"...Gah...!"

"Gwyn—!"

Her brother's gnarly treatment made Shannon cringe, but he just cast a spell to tighten the flesh around it, barking orders.

"Don't look at me! Keep Noll safe! Back him up!"

That one thought on every mind. Shannon tore her eyes off him, using her sensory zone to grasp the situation, then focused on her spells. Oliver's healing was always her top priority. He was still in the midst of a soul merge. The progenitor blood gave her expansive personal space, and the healing she did within that zone was all that kept his flesh from falling apart.

"...Sanavulnera...!"

Her spell echoed.

Seeing the siblings back in the fight, Janet grinned. "That's more like it. *That's* how you should be, Gwyn."

With that, she dashed past them toward their target. To play her part in all of this.

"Impetus! Flamma! Tonitrus!"

Demitrio had completely shut them down once, but the new status quo was drastically different. First—he wasn't using primal spells. Everything he cast was the standard magic they all knew—and though he *was* a Kimberly teacher, this was still a drastic reduction in output. A number of tactics that had previously been useless came back into play.

"...Gah—!"

Naturally, Demitrio wasn't *choosing* not to use his primal spells. He *couldn't*. Ever since Oliver escaped the dream, something *else* was preventing him from achieving selflessness. Needless to say, this was the splinter he'd not fully absorbed. When not selfless, he couldn't connect to the Grand Record, and in that state neither his perceptions nor his worldview enabled the use of any primal magic. As Oliver had said early in the fight—now he was but an ordinary mage.

"Frigus! Ngh—?!"

Demitrio was fending off their assault with ordinary spells when a sudden pain ran up his leg. Teresa Carste—the covert operative's sneak attack, from his blind spot down low. A shallow gash to the flesh, and she quickly shifted to prepping her next attack.

"Go, little one!"

"We're your wall!"

Comrades skilled in sword arts stepped up, giving her tiny frame coverage. She slipped behind them, always moving. No one hesitated. All were ready to give their lives for this fight. Dying to shield a comrade was part of the bargain, and at worst, merely a matter of *order*.

"———!!!!"

With an unvoiced roar, Teresa ran. All the white noise that had filled her head was gone completely. There was nothing here to think about. Forget the distinction between concern and desire; here she need only worry about keeping him safe and killing their target. All thoughts and acts devoted to those two things; nothing else required.

Thus, she felt it. In that moment, she knew she loved him. Forget the ugliness within her heart—the feelings beating there were *true*.

"A stealth fighter?! At this stage— **Tonitrus!**"

While Teresa had him distracted, a spell barrage bore down on him. Demitrio dodged and countered his way through. His eyes honed on the Gnostic fronts, swiftly taking the measure of his opposition. Who to take out first, where to aim, his mind *solving* the fight—and finding a male student whose position was a tad removed.

"**Flamma!**"

He cast a spell too close to dodge. Given the output discrepancy, he couldn't hope to counter it with an oppositional. Demitrio was sure he'd downed one—but was forced to revise that opinion. His target threw out both arms, soaking the spell head-on.

"———?!"

The flames burned the male student to a crisp. Mere seconds before he expired—*her* grin emerged from the flames.

"Finally tricked ya, Instructor."

Carmen Agnelli—she'd been *disguised* as a male student. And her murder created a channel between them. A horrible pathway that allowed her to send all the curse energy she had stored into Demitrio's body.

"...Ha-ha..."

Just before her mind cut out, she found herself thanking River-moore. She owed him this one. Because he'd completed his research and advanced necromancy to the next stage, she'd been free to throw her life on the pyre here. The future of her craft in his hands, she need only curse the shit out of their quarry.

There was a hint of envy mingled in. But she didn't mind. A mage's final thoughts were all too human. Thus—Carmen Agnelli was consumed by the fire, looking utterly satisfied.

"…Ngh…!"

Demitrio's body grew substantially heavier. The curse energy Carmen left behind clung to him. While still selfless, he could have dispersed this through the vicinity, but now he had no means of dealing with the threat. His only option was to fight on through it.

"——! Frigus! Flamma! Tonit■ ■s! Impetus!"

Each second was sapping away at his aplomb. But that did not dull his thoughts—he was not called a philosopher for his health. The first two spells kept students at bay. While their minds were on defense, he chain cast two more spells, knowing the first would be jammed.

"——!"

And his aim—the man most certain a third spell would not arrive. An arched wind spell bound for the spelljammer himself, Gwyn. The aim of Demitrio's wand was far off his target, delaying his response—Shannon too preoccupied with Oliver's healing to intercept. The wind blade bore down, too late to dodge—

"Prohibere!"

And Janet threw herself into the path. Her oppositional diminished it, but not completely—as she'd expected. The rest she soaked *bodily*. No attempt to evade. The blade cut into her—and through, slicing her chest in half.

"Janet!"

Behind her, she heard Gwyn yell. The top half of her fell to the ground, head up, and she glared at the man behind her.

"Not me, you fool! Your little brother's over there!"

Squeezing what little life she had left, she spat one more rebuke. Mercilessly forcing Gwyn back to his senses.

"I'm…sorry," he said.

If he stopped to heal her, she could be saved. He knew that—but he left her there, advancing on their foe. He'd been too focused on jamming, too removed from their comrades—and that had caused his predicament. He *had* to close in. Leaving the girl who'd saved his life to die.

Watching him go, Janet sighed.

"...Tch. Annoying as ever..."

She went limp. Much as she wanted to cast a spell with less than half a body and shock her foe, she'd used up that reserve of energy. Naturally, she regretted nothing. She'd been pleased he called her name. And glad he left her here.

"...I nursed that crush a looong time... Ha-ha, so sad."

Wouldn't even make a decent tabloid piece. A final thought that was very her—and Janet Dowling, editor of Kimberly's third-largest newspaper, breathed her last.

"What say we talk about our futures. What do you want to be when you grow up?"

Demitrio was at the podium, all his students present. Their hands started shooting up.

"I wanna open a restaurant in town!"

"I want to work at the library! Full of books, like your study!"

"Farmer! With lots of fields!"

Each voiced their hopes. Flett listened at the center of the room—then snorted.

"Such puny dreams. I ain't like you. I'm gonna be a broomrider, slay a dragon!"

"Ew, no way."

"You gotta be a mage to ride a broom."

"I might become one! I'm waving a wand every day!"

He looked indignant. Seeing the argument about to heat up, Demitrio raised both hands.

"Okay, okay, no squabbles. Class is in session. Maya, what about you?"

He turned to the girl in the front row. She smiled.

"I said already. I wanna study lots—and help you!"

Her answer never changed, and it made Demitrio choke up a bit. With some difficulty, he overcame that and turned to his charges.

"...Thank you. It's lovely that you've all got such different dreams. I can't promise they'll all come true, but if you're serious about them, I'm happy to help how I can. That's what a village mage does."

He thumped his chest. Educate the local children, broadening their options. A basic village mage duty—and one he was very conscious of. It was his job to help make many of these dreams possible.

"You shared a lot of goals here. Some will take a lot of work, and some may take a lot of luck. But none of them are as unlikely as my dream of visiting another world. Some of you will likely find your paths blocked and get discouraged. But remember this—the experience *does* mean something. Success *and* failure will both benefit you, as long as you still live."

That was Demitrio's lesson. Reality could be harsh, and these children would discover that for themselves. And so he tried to give them the tools they'd need to handle that. Teach them how to pick themselves up as they fell, wipe their tears, and keep moving forward. Life was all about that cycle. And that was true for mages and ordinaries alike.

"Don't lose your nerve! Always try. I promise, I'll be there for you as best I can."

A promise he had not kept.

He'd lived a long time since, yet that fact still drove him.

"Shhh—"

A foe came swinging in, and their wands clashed; he grabbed their athame tip with his off hand. Shifting the grapple from the wrist to the elbow to the shoulder, then putting his weight on it, dropping them. His foe tried to dislocate their shoulder and escape, but he got the tip of his wand at the base of their neck, forced his magic in, and ended their life.

"——!"

All that in the blink of an eye; it took Oliver's breath away. That was *not* sword arts. This was *wand* arts. Ancient self-defense techniques dating from before the spread of athame culture. Records of it still existed, but no one chose to study them. A dated, outmoded way of fighting only known by mages in ancient history.

"…You carry a burden you can never set down," Demitrio growled, stepping on the student's body. Everyone here was ready to throw their life away, yet his ferocity was so intense it still slowed their assault. "Do not tell me…you believed you were the *only* one."

His eyes bored into Oliver. His voice quivered.

"That would be arrogance, boy. I bear my own!" he screamed. "For *five hundred and sixty-seven years*, I have carried this!!!!!"

A roar that left a mark. Scores of memories erupted across the back of Demitrio's mind.

He knew full well—no one else even remembered. Not that little mountain village, not the simple lives of the people there. The world moved on, and no one looked back.

But *he* remembered. Maya, Flett, Mishka, Famle, Luca…the faces and names of all the students who'd looked up to him, each and every dream they'd confided in him. He alone would remember that forever. Along with his vain promise to be there for them—and the betrayal that left him snatching away their futures with his own hands.

He still wondered. Had he not cut their lives short, how would they have grown up? Some would have achieved their dreams; some would not have. Some from each group would've had children of their own. And those children would have had dreams of their own. As would their kids, and those kids' kids, on and on—but his grievous error had erased all such possibilities.

Their potential had been infinite—and thus, so was the sin of taking that away from them. There was no way to atone. How could there be? Thus, his atonement would never end. His only choice was to devote every fiber of his being to protecting the world, as some small measure of amends. A penance that would continue until his life gave out.

"…Yeah, Instructor. I know," Oliver whispered.

The nature of this enemy was all too familiar. He understood it as he did his own. He'd seen it himself—while the philosopher was peering at Oliver's memories, Yuri had shared some of Demitrio's with Oliver.

Each bore the burden of sin. Demitrio had tried to protect the world. Oliver was trying to change it.

That was the sole difference. Nothing more, nothing less.

"So I will shoulder *yours* as well."

With that promise, Oliver lunged at him. Demitrio braced for the clash. No longer selfless, no longer tapping into the Grand Record, yet neither prevented him reaching that state that precedes the division between the subjective and objective. What came next was written in stone. Spellblade versus spellblade, the ultimate collision.

Oliver had no clear path to victory. Merely a premonition. He'd been

reminded of the true shape of his spellblade, and what it whispered to him would be vital to reaching this foe. Trusting that sensation, he stepped in. As they reached one-step, one-spell range—each activated their spellblade.

Over here, Oliver.

The sign he'd believed in. Oliver set his eyes on it and pounced. Not looking back, forging dead ahead. Down the one future that would make him suffer most.

The fifth spellblade. Papiliosomnia, the butterfly's dream of death.

Divisions melded. Unavoidable, imperceptible, an enlightened act that brought defeat within a primal dream to all with a conscious mind. This man had spent his life polishing his ability to dive into the depths of the mind, and now that craft bared its fangs.

The fourth spellblade. Angustavia, the abyss-crossing thread.

A thread plucked. Unbeatable, inescapable, a fatal act that reeled in the one true path buried in a sea of infinite defeats. The boy had sacrificed his own life to make the absurdity of fate his, and now that craft roared.

Wand and athame crossed, each bearing the crown of supremacy.

"_____"

"........."

Their backs to each other, neither spoke. Like nothing had happened. As if they'd never dueled, never tried to kill each other.

Then the silence was broken by the faintest of sounds—something dripping.

"........."

The ground at Demitrio's feet was slowly turning red. Blood, oozing from the gash on his chest. Dripping from a gouge running from his side all the way to his heart—the crimson shade of life itself.

"…The part of me I could not cast off…proved my undoing."

A whisper, like a sigh. The man's body crumpled to the ground.

The dust had settled. Certain all comrades who still breathed were getting the treatment they needed, Oliver turned to his fallen foe.

"......"

His feet stopped near where Demitrio lay, looking wordlessly down at him. Eventually, the man's lips parted.

"...Very clever. In the heat of the moment...aiming for *him*, inside of me."

"...Yuri called out to me. Had he not...I'd have been the one lying here."

This was how he'd won. At that fatal moment, he'd aimed not for Demitrio—but for Yuri. The one off-note in that selfless song.

The fifth spellblade had robbed him of all distinctions—but Yuri alone, he'd kept in sight. That was directly linked to the true character of his own spellblade. A future in which he slew a friend by his own hand—that was the choice that made Oliver suffer most, and the future that had stood out from all else.

He stood by his fallen foe, unmoving. Unable to move.

"...What now?" Demitrio asked. "No plans to torture me as you did Darius?"

"You know better!" Oliver barked. His eyes were swimming with emotions in conflict. "It's not fair...! *You're* not fair! This is such bullshit!" he spat. "Yuri... He's still there, inside you! My friend's in there! How many times did he come to my rescue? How...how...how can I hurt him more? How can I turn to torture, after...?!"

A sob cut him off.

"Ah...," Demitrio said, eyes on the air above. "That's on me. I did not intend to use him as a shield."

Not a defense that meant anything, really. Oliver wiped his tears, looking down at him.

"I can't torture you. But I'll not let you flee the interrogation," Oliver said resolutely. "Answer me this, Demitrio Aristides. Explain what you did to her. What lay in your mind? What drove you to such acts?"

The fundamental question. Demitrio's eyes turned to Oliver's face.

"......How'd the others answer?"

"…Darius never managed a coherent word. Enrico insisted it was symbolic. The shared experience of trampling upon her soul proved you were each complicit. To him, that was the purpose."

Demitrio sighed, closing his eyes.

"…That was an aspect of it. However—my views on it were a little different."

"……"

"I acted to shore up my resolve. To force myself to never again cling to my memories of Chloe. To never let myself hope for the future she spoke of. By ending our relationship in the worst imaginable light— with that dark suggestion, I sealed away Chloe Halford's light. I knew I'd need it, if I was to continue down this path afterward. To avoid my footsteps faltering."

Choking back the bile, Oliver clenched his fists.

"…Was it never an option? To just…follow her?"

"I can't say I never considered it. But—I didn't make that choice. It just seemed like a reckless gamble. Her idea of the future placed too much hope in *people*. I weighed the damages in the event of a betrayal against the price of maintaining the status quo. Protecting the darkness of the present over chasing a blinding dream…"

His voice faded out. After a long silence, Demitrio spoke again.

"If you call me a coward, I'll not argue. I'm sure you're right. But when you live as long as I have, you start to realize just how dangerous it is to alter your course toward a new bright light without due consideration. You learn to fear giving yourself—and the world—over to the hopes and fervors those lights offer.

"Not to repeat myself, but the Gnostic hunts were always like that. Similar tragedies everywhere you looked. The Gnostics' hearts may be stolen by a tír god, but they are not flinging themselves into darkness by choice. They're all tumbling into that pit, reaching for the light they think they see there. The greater their hopes, the worse the outcomes. I felt certain Chloe's attempt could become one of the worst instances ever. For that reason, I simply could not join her in her endeavors."

Oliver said nothing. This answer did not seem like it was glossing over anything. Yuri had helped their hearts connect—and for that reason, he knew this was all genuine.

"That's about all I can say on a personal level. But I doubt that's what you really wish to know."

"......"

Oliver's silence signaled his agreement.

"Why did Esmeralda betray Chloe?" Demitrio said. "I don't have a complete answer for you, there. She never once spoke her thoughts, and we did not attempt to pry them from her. Her actions were proof enough she was one of us." He continued. "From that night on, she's protected the world, more like a mage than anyone else around. Strong, harsh, and firm to myself and others. Like that duty is a curse she's placed upon herself. Her heart may be hidden, but when you cross death's line together, you come to know these things. And thus, I placed my faith in her."

"......"

"I know not what goes on in her head. But there are a few assumptions I can make from the events that transpired: First—that torture was, more than anything, something Esmeralda herself *required*. I'm not talking about *motives*, here. Regardless of what she wanted, she needed that. Perhaps a need so urgent it forced a hand that wanted nothing to do with it. The most likely cause..."

"...Prepping for the soul absorb."

Oliver had reached the same conclusion.

"That is my assumption, yes." Demitrio nodded. "The destruction of the self is likely a prerequisite for absorbing anyone's soul. The soul merge you practice is predicated on an innate compatibility between the souls in question, yes? Esmeralda's is not. She can absorb anyone. No matter the soul, she makes it hers. Which implies there must be a process, one forcing compatibility upon them."

A reasonable assumption, Oliver thought. Much about the soul remained a mystery, but there were rules. A vampire's powers meddled with the soul via a very different process than the progenitor aspect, but those rules applied in equal measure.

"I believe that was the reason for the torture. And the fact that she kept out of it, yielding it to us—that fits. For the same reasons you cannot bring yourself to torture me now. She could not have managed it if she had not ceded that part to us. Could not have thoroughly demolished all that Chloe was, trampling on it, rendering her soul vulnerable and exposed. Could not make the soul ready for absorption by her own hand."

Oliver gritted his teeth. This made the rest make even less sense. If she had to foist the task off, why do it at all? Or why be with his mother all that time in the first place? If she'd chosen to protect the status quo for reasons like Demitrio's, that was inconsistent with all the time she'd spent shoulder to shoulder with Chloe Halford. And nothing like this could be caused by a fickle change of heart.

"After that—it's covered in darkness. Why did she want Chloe's soul so badly? Why choose the agony of protecting the world with that power? I have no answers to any of that. Thus, this is all I can provide."

Demitrio looked right at Oliver.

"What I will say next is a warning. Not as your enemy but as your teacher. If you don't wanna hear it, fine. Finish me off now."

Oliver considered this, then let him speak. Not that he had a choice. Stabbing the friend inside this man a second time? In a situation that did not demand it, that option was off the table.

"The soul absorb that night let Esmeralda take power from Chloe's soul. You're already aware of that. But—that was not the end. In the years that followed, she's done the same thing over and over. Do you know how many mage's souls she's taken in?"

Oliver shook his head. And Demitrio laid out the cold, hard truth.

"Over a *hundred*. And that's just the ones I know about. Enemies encountered on a Gnostic hunt, colleagues who stood up to her approach, political enemies who dared come after her. The outcome was always the same. Esmeralda put them all down—and those whose souls she deemed worthy became a part of her. Can you imagine it? All those souls are inside her, serving as the source of her power."

"……!"

"This is the cause of her chronic headaches. They're *writhing* inside her. The grudges of so many souls absorbed against their will, crying out this very instant for their freedom. No ordinary mentality could bear it. Madness would be a natural outcome. But she remains the same. Stockpiling the strength of countless stolen souls inside her, swallowing the accompanying curses, but her character has not changed at all since that fateful night. That terrifies me. More than the power she's absorbed—the fact that it *has not changed her* leaves me with a gnawing fear in the pit of my stomach."

Demitrio's voice shook. That same emotion threatened Oliver, but he forced it aside.

"That's the enemy you've made," the philosopher continued. "I know you yourself have gone through unimaginable pain to acquire the strength you have. I've seen your memories—I *know*. But even then— what you have gained is Chloe's strength alone. And only a small portion of it." He then asked Oliver: "How can you fight her? What can you do with that little power? Against that vampire—how can you begin to compete?"

Faced with that question, Oliver let a silence hang before he spoke. He knew the question urged pessimism. Thus—he did not overcomplicate it.

"…We have no chance of victory? You said the exact same thing before we fought. Darius and Enrico likely thought the same."

He would not say they'd overcome those odds. The losses on his side had been too great to take pride in them. Instead…

"We will prevail. Again and again. I can say nothing else."

His words rang out. Less a proclamation than a promise. A vow sworn on the bodies of all the comrades they'd lost.

Demitrio looked at the athame in Oliver's hand.

"…You're banking on that spellblade. As well you might."

As he spoke, a memory flitted across his mind. One from a past he'd long put out of mind, a voice he'd sealed away deep within.

"I don't hold with assholes who talk in absolutes. That's why I go around stomping 'em. You get me, old-timer? That shit's the whole damn point of this spellblade!"

He could see her all too clearly. His old student, grinning up at him. A real thorn in his side, always acting out in class—but always with that open grin.

"…The seal's…loosened up," he muttered.

He didn't see the point in putting it back. He'd already lost and no longer had a reason to insist.

"That's all I have to say. Genuinely—nothing else remains. By way of amends for depriving you of torture… Well, there's not much time left, but for the rest of it, you may speak to *him.*"

With that, Demitrio closed his eyes. A few seconds later, they opened again—but with a cheery light Oliver's philosopher nemesis had never once betrayed.

"Oh, Oliver!"

Spotting a friend, he called out.

"…Yuri?" Oliver gasped.

"Huh? Oh, sorry, mind moving closer? Seems like my hearing's going faster than my eyesight. I can't make out a word!"

Oliver dropped to his knees, inching nearer. An apology escaped him before anything else.

"Sorry, Yuri. I just—"

"You cut me down, yeah? Good. It worked! I was outta ideas, otherwise."

Yuri's voice was infinitely upbeat. Not a hint of a shadow anywhere on his smile, and that hit Oliver harder than a thousand insults.

"…Why…why are you like this, Yuri…? Rebuke me! At least spare me a little spite; I'm begging you! You saved me till the bitter end! And—all I did was cut you down…!"

He couldn't stop the tears rolling. Yuri's brow furrowed, at a loss.

"Uh-oh, he's crying again. Aw man. I'd rather see your smile…"

"…At a time like this?!"

Oliver couldn't repress the sobs. Yuri watched for a moment, thinking, then he had an idea and turned his eyes elsewhere.

"Okay! Take a look, Oliver. Up! Above us!"

"Huh…?"

He did as he was told, turning to the sky above. The false sky had been a pale blue with streaks of clouds, but it was now rapidly shifting to night.

"…Ah…"

And then the stars came out. Oliver gaped up at them, and Yuri grinned.

"Rad, right? He said there were no magical alterations, but that's not true for the sky. Otherwise, it'd always be dark in here! There's no natural day/night cycle in the labyrinth. So I just gave it a push and brought night on early."

Yuri stuck out his tongue. His eyes never left the stars.

"Looking at me makes you sad, right? Then don't. Look at the stars instead. Like we did the other day, lying side by side."

Oliver wiped away his tears, nodding. He laid down next to Yuri, gazing at the stars above.

"…They sure are pretty."

"Mm. I think so, too," Yuri whispered, the yearning within unadulterated. "That's why he always looked up at them. Always wanted to go there. He gave up and looked away, but deep down, that never changed. And that's why…I stayed inside him."

He voiced the philosopher's innermost desires. Oliver said nothing. Yuri's eyes turned to a specific star, his tone brightening considerably.

"That's Vanato! You've heard of it, right? It's full of really lonely creatures. Imagine their faces if the two of us went there!"

"...They'd be pretty startled. Maybe not by me, but you tend to be boisterous."

"Ah-ha-ha! They'd run away from me. We'd have to give chase!"

"That would make it worse." Oliver winced. "It'd be better not to rush things—just sit down, let them come to us. They'd probably get curious and approach, little by little, getting closer..."

Yuri had gone quiet, looking at his friend.

"...You didn't run from me," Yuri said.

Oliver looked away. A bit late to hide his blushing face.

"...You were so shady I forgot to. Honestly—you scared me at first."

"What about now? Do I still scare you?"

"No. And I've given up on settling you down... It's like I'm not even sitting in the dark. With you around, it's always a party."

He trailed off. Scared his voice would break if he said more.

"My bad. I'm a boisterous one, " Yuri said. "Are you crying again?"

"...No..."

Oliver shook his head, forcing back the tears, turning his eyes back to the stars.

Yuri squinted. "I can't see 'em anymore. Oliver...can I borrow your eyes for a sec?"

Oliver nodded and took Yuri's hand. Visual sharing was ordinarily done with wands, but their hearts were already linked and did not need them. The stars Oliver saw—and how he felt about them—flowed into Yuri's mind.

"Wow... They're just as pretty with your eyes."

He sounded happy. His breathing grew shallow, faint.

"...Tell me...Oliver... Are you...smiling...?"

"I am," Oliver insisted. "I can't cry here! The view's too amazing."

He was sure this was true. Maybe a few tears escaped, but he was sure he was smiling. As was the boy beside him.

"...Good... Just......like me......"

He sounded relieved. And with that—Yuri spoke no more.

Thirty-two entered combat on the fourth layer.
Combat goal achieved. Demitrio Aristides slain.
Twelve comrades lost in battle.

Note: There was an unexpected casualty.

One friend.

END

Afterword

Greetings. This is Bokuto Uno. At long last, the third year draws to an end.

They gazed upward together, sharing in that beauty. And thus, their bond came to a close.

With a third pillar fallen, Kimberly will be in turmoil. Meanwhile, students finishing their third year are ready to join the upper forms. The time before the new term is ripe for traveling, and many seize the chance to return home—or further their research aboard. The Sword Roses are no exception.

Leaving Kimberly behind for a while, they'll expand their horizons. After the trials and tribulations of that hellscape, what new shades will the outside bring them?

Take care on the path you follow. For Kimberly is not the only place the spell awaits.